The Red Zeppelin
by
Jack Treby

Chapter One

Monarchy is the bedrock of a civilised society. Even a congenital idiot on the throne provides stability, allowing the politicians to happily knife each other in the back without any fear that they may be undermining the fabric of society. That being said, I must confess a certain admiration for the sombre young republican with the Charlie Chaplin moustache who was waiting patiently, cap in hand, outside the polling station on the opposite side of the street. There he was, standing determinedly in line, all set to cast his vote and give the Dago establishment a well deserved kick in the teeth.

The Spanish nation had recently ridded itself of a particularly loathsome dictator and it was no surprise that the lower orders had now developed an appetite for change. Peering down at the assembled mass of unwashed voters from the comfort of my hotel room on the Pagés del Corro, however, it seemed unlikely to me that they would want to take that extra step and vote in a republican government. Throwing out a dictator was one thing, getting rid of the monarchy quite another.

The man with the cap pulled out a rolled up copy of *El Socialista* from his jacket pocket and began to read it, in full view of the police. I could not help but admire his nerve. Just the sight of a group of Spaniards queuing politely was a novelty. The buildings on the opposite side of the street were plastered with election posters and the two policemen were eyeing the crowd suspiciously; but even they could not misread the cheerful enthusiasm of the voters. The republican was engrossed in his paper but the rest of the crowd were chatting happily among themselves in that infuriatingly over-exuberant Mediterranean way. It was their first opportunity to vote in almost eight years and they were intending to make the most of it.

A few women were passing the time of day among the men, their light but rapid-fire voices floating easily up to the window on the third floor. They were not allowed to vote in

1

this election, much to my annoyance, though they were permitted to stand for public office. It was a small step forward, I supposed. As a woman myself, I have always understood the value of a universal franchise. I may have spent the better part of my life masquerading as a man, but I am not a hypocrite. Whenever possible, I have tried to champion the rights of my sex. Women may be as susceptible to popular sentiment as the male of the species, but a truly democratic election cannot take place without them.

I stepped back from the window and pulled the wallet from my trouser pocket. The telegram was folded neatly in one corner and I pulled it out to take another look. The printed message was virtual gibberish, apart from a handful of numbers and the word 'STOP' in plain text at the end. I had annotated the other characters with a pencil back in Gibraltar using the agreed book code. It had taken me almost half an hour. I have never been much good with ciphers. The encryption key was a paragraph from chapter thirteen of *Bleak House*. Someone back in London had a peculiarly warped sense of humour. The message, when I had finally deciphered it, was barely more than an address:

"HOTEL LA CAVA PAGES DEL CORRO SEVILLE SUNDAY 12 1230"

A more direct summons it would be hard to imagine.

And so here I was, ensconced with my man Maurice in a drab hotel room in the centre of Seville, waiting to discover just what it was all about.

The valet was brushing down my jacket and preparing to hang it up on the outside of a bare cupboard. A hastily packed suitcase was resting on the bed behind me. I was in my shirt sleeves now. It had been a long journey from Gibraltar and a change of clothes was in order before I thought about doing anything else. Maurice was a tall, thickset Frenchman in his mid fifties with a grim, weather-beaten face and a permanently pained expression. He had been my valet for almost a year now and in all that time his expression had never changed. His clothing was immaculately turned out but his manner bordered on the surly.

'Did you find a place to park the car?' I asked him.

'Yes, Monsieur,' he responded, without elaborating. He was a man of few words and, no matter how many times I told him, he refused to address me as 'Sir.' He moved around the bed and began unfastening the front of my shirt. He did not bat an eyelid at the bandages wound around my chest as they came into view. He had seen far more than that of me without passing comment.

Having a Frenchman as a valet was not ideal, but I'd had little choice in the matter. He had been recommended to me by another Frog of my acquaintance whose judgement, for various reasons, I had good cause to trust. This man, I had been assured, was the absolute soul of discretion and as, at this point in my life, discretion was more important than nationality, I had reluctantly taken him on. It was either that or buying a frock and hiring a ladies maid. Maurice was a taciturn fellow, meticulous but inscrutable. I never had the faintest idea what was going on in his head. In the four or five years he worked for me, I rarely heard anything more from him than 'Yes, Monsieur' or 'No, Monsieur'. His previous employer had been something of an eccentric, I gathered, so he had not been at all perturbed by my peculiar lifestyle. He also knew how to keep his mouth shut, which was the most important thing. I never did understand why he insisted on addressing me as 'Monsieur'. It was probably a matter of Gallic pride (the average Frog is stubborn to the point of immobility) but it was a source of irritation nonetheless. I was used to asserting my authority with servants. Thankfully, in his case, I had found the perfect weapon with which to retaliate.

'So tell me, *Morris*,' I asked, as my trousers dropped to the floor and I stepped out onto the threadbare carpet. 'Have you given any more thought to the Americas?'

His face wrinkled up as I wriggled my toes. 'No, Monsieur.'

I gave him a sour look. 'Time's ticking, Morris,' I said, mispronouncing his name a second time. I had been offered a

3

new position at the beginning of May, on the other side of the Atlantic. I needed to know if the Frenchman was willing to accompany me there. 'I'll have to book the tickets by the end of the –'

A loud rap at the door interrupted my words. I tensed instinctively but Maurice did not blink. He bent down to pick up my trousers and laid them out neatly on the bed; then he gestured across to the bathroom. I nodded. It might provoke all kinds of awkward questions if a porter caught sight of me in a state of undress. I made my way quickly across to the bathroom and locked the door behind me. I had had my fair share of close shaves over the years but I had never got used to the experience. I do have a fairly masculine aspect – broad shoulders, square jaw, deep voice – but even with the bandages to flatten down my chest I could not pass myself off as a man in nothing but my undergarments. It was lucky for me that the room had facilities en suite. I perched for a moment on the edge of the wash basin and closed my eyes.

It had not been my decision to live my life this way; at least, not at first. It was all my father's fault. He hated women. When my mother had died giving birth to me, Sir Frederick Manningham-Butler had been mortified. He had wanted a son to take on the family name and a son he was determined to have, whatever the biology asserted to the contrary. My father was long dead now and I had abandoned my inheritance when I had fled England at the tail end of 1929. But now, a couple of weeks shy of my forty second birthday, with no reason whatever to continue the charade, I found I was too settled in my ways to contemplate a change.

I listened as Maurice moved towards the door. He exchanged a few words with some idiot out in the corridor and then closed it up. A moment later he tapped lightly on the bathroom. I opened the door and peered out at him. The pained expression on his face told me nothing, but I didn't really need to ask. 'A message, Monsieur,' he said.

I grabbed the piece of paper from his hand and moved back into the bedroom. I glanced at the far door, to make sure it was properly secured, and then looked down at the message.

4

This time, there was no code. "Gran Café, Plaza de Andalucía, 13:00." It was signed "CL". I recognised the initials. I had thought it would probably be him.

'I'd better finish dressing,' I told Maurice. 'It looks like I have an appointment to keep.'

Charles Lazenby was seated comfortably at a small metal table in front of the Gran Café. He was a handsome fellow in his mid thirties, with a smooth, rounded face and a tasteful pencil moustache hovering just above his lip. He had been attacking a folded up newspaper with the stubby remnants of an HB pencil. He looked up as I arrived. I was red-faced, bedraggled and at least five minutes late. Lazenby set aside his newspaper and rose smoothly to his feet. 'Afternoon, Bland,' he said, with an outstretched hand. 'Good to see you again.'

Reginald Bland. I was still getting used to the name, even after all these months. It was not a title I would have chosen for myself; another demonstration of the adolescent sense of humour of my superiors back in London. My real name was Hilary Manningham-Butler, a far more imposing and respectable moniker. *Sir* Hilary, no less. I had inherited the baronetcy from my father when he had passed away and that had placed me just a whisker short of full-blooded aristocracy. Strictly speaking, of course, such a title cannot be passed to a daughter; but my father's bloody-mindedness, which I had been forced to collude in, had served to ensure the title had not fallen into disuse. And "Sir Hilary" had an authoritative ring to it that had always appealed to me. Now, though, much to my dismay, I had become plain old Reginald Bland. I scowled every time I saw the name emblazoned on the front of my passport.

It had taken me some time to walk to the café from the hotel. The receptionist had marked out the route on a map and assured me it would only take fifteen minutes. But his idea of fifteen minutes was markedly different from my own. If I had known it would take closer to half an hour I would have hopped on one of the box shaped trams that rattled across the Puente de Triana; or got Maurice to break out the car. As it was, I had to make my way on foot across the bridge and along the river front, in the blazing midday sun, picking my way through the sweating multitudes in the direction of the Plaza de Andalucía. Even on a Sunday afternoon, with all the shops shut up, the streets were chock full of people. The happy faces of the working poor were everywhere, fresh from church or the polling booths, and their presence, cluttering up the pavements, only added to my sense of irritation. It was with some relief that I had arrived at the plaza, though the bells of the cathedral had long since chimed one o'clock.

'Thank you for coming,' Lazenby said, as I took his hand. He had a solid grip and a clipped, efficient manner; friendly but formal. We had met a couple of times before in Gibraltar but I didn't really know him. He resumed his seat and gestured to another chair on the opposite side of a small cast iron table. A large mushroom shaped sunshade afforded us both some protection from the glare of the afternoon.

I collapsed into the seat and gesticulated at a waiter to bring me something cold. The young Spaniard regarded me with some amusement. I couldn't really blame him. The people who know about such things claim a white linen suit keeps you cool in a hot climate but I had discovered otherwise. Sweat was pouring down my face.

'I'm sorry to call you here at such short notice,' Lazenby apologised, taking note of my poor shape. 'I only got the train down here myself last night.'

The waiter returned with an ice cold glass and a bottle of *Cruzcampo*. I waited impatiently as he poured out the beer and then downed half the glass in one. I am not much of a beer drinker as a rule – I have always preferred spirits – but even I am prepared to make concessions to the Mediterranean climate. The waiter raised an eyebrow but departed without comment.

Lazenby seemed to be coping much better with the heat than I was. He was dressed in a rigid blue blazer and had a wide brimmed hat on his head. He had been based in Madrid for some years now and his skin had darkened to the point where a turban would not have looked out of place. But his accent, like his clothes, came straight from the playing fields of

6

Eton.

'So what's this all about?' I asked.

He reached into his jacket pocket and pulled out a couple of small photographs, which he handed across to me.

I peered at the first of the fuzzy black and white images. It was a portrait of a man in early middle age. He was balding, with dark, narrow eyes and a heavy beard. I had never seen him before. I looked up and shrugged. I was none the wiser.

'Gerhard Schulz. An Austrian journalist. On his way to Seville this afternoon.'

The name meant nothing to me. 'That's nice for him,' I said. I peered at the second photograph. This fellow was in his mid fifties, a plump face and rounded spectacles peering out from beneath a large felt hat. I looked up again. The waiter had returned with some tapas and was peering speculatively at the photographs. I pressed the pictures to my chest and glared up at him. The man placed the snacks down on the table between us and made a hasty retreat.

'Walter Kendall,' Lazenby informed me, as I resumed my examination of the second image. 'Another journalist. An American this one.'

'On his way into Seville?'

'Already here, so I understand. Flew in this morning. He's booked a room at the Hotel Alfonso XIII.' Lazenby gestured across the plaza to a rather grand looking building on the far side of the fountain. Two pedestrian doorways flanked a short driveway which led up to the entrance and, sure the enough, the words "Hotel Alfonso XIII" were carved out respectfully at the front. Alfonso, of course, was the current King of Spain. Lazenby glanced at his wristwatch. 'Kendall hasn't checked in yet. He must be running a bit late. But once he's booked in at the Alfonso, he'll head off to meet up with the other chap.'

'The Austrian?'

'That's right. Unfortunately we have no idea where the two of them are planning to meet. That's where you come in.'

'You want me to follow the American and see where he goes?' The thought of traipsing through the streets of Seville a second time that afternoon was not a pleasant one. It had to be ninety five degrees in the shade and I knew from experience that it would get steadily hotter as the afternoon progressed. Perhaps this time I could find a taxi.

'Actually, no. I'm going to keep an eye on Kendall. Your job is to meet the first chap. Gerhard Schulz.' Lazenby frowned for a moment. 'I would have preferred to keep tabs on that one myself. Bit of a tricky customer.'

'What's so important about him?'

'It's not him. It's what he's carrying with him.'

Now we were getting to the meat of it. 'And what is that?'

Lazenby grimaced. It was clear he didn't want to tell me too much. That's the trouble with spies. They are never prepared to pass on any useful information. 'We believe he is carrying some documents of an extremely sensitive nature.'

'What kind of documents?'

'I'm afraid I can't go into details. The fewer people who know about this the better. I have only been given the broadest outline myself.'

'But information the government doesn't want made public?'

Lazenby nodded seriously. 'That's about the size of it. It's vital we recover these papers before Schulz has a chance to pass them on.'

'And you say he's some kind of journalist?

'That's right. We believe he's intending to sell the documents to this American, Walter Kendall.'

My eyes widened in surprise. 'What, you mean for publication? In a *newspaper*?'

'Yes.' Lazenby gave out a short sigh. 'We have to prevent that at all costs.'

I was intrigued. 'But why would an Austrian journalist want to sell state secrets to the American press?'

'For money. What else? That seems to be the chap's main motivation. And he'll get a lot more from the Americans than from anyone back home.'

'But if these documents are as important as you say,

surely he wouldn't be selling them to the newspapers. He'd be on the first train to Moscow. The Russians would pay a fortune for military secrets or anything of that sort.'

Lazenby pursed his lips. 'It's not that kind of information.'

'Well, what then?'

'I'm afraid I'm not at liberty to say.'

I growled quietly. I hated working in the dark like this, but I was getting used to it by now. It was the nature of the job, sadly. Officers on the ground were rarely given anything more than the most basic information. 'But he's offering to sell this American fellow a cache of documents purloined from the British government?' It was as well to get that point clear at least.

Lazenby shook his head. 'Not the originals. A photographic copy. The original file is back in London.'

'Photographic? But...'

He waved a hand. 'It's not important. All you need to know is that Schulz is in possession of a copy.'

'Right.' I sat back in my chair. 'But if it's nothing military, then why all the fuss?' What kind of information would interest a US newsman and get the British establishment in such a lather? Lazenby wasn't about to tell me but that didn't stop me trying to work it out for myself. 'What is it? Evidence of corruption?' That might get the attention of the media. 'Double dealing at the highest levels?'

Lazenby regarded me sourly. 'I don't think it's helpful for you to speculate. The important thing...'

'Or some august personage caught with their pants down?' That would be more like it, I thought. The American media had a reputation for prurience and there was nothing they enjoyed more than seeing some revered aristocrat brought low by their own stupidity. 'It's not the Prince of Wales, is it?' I asked. '*Again*?' I chuckled at the idea. The heir to the throne was notorious for his bed-hopping. But no, the British government would not go to all this trouble to recover a few dirty pictures. 'Or something to do with the Prime Minister perhaps?'

9

Lazenby gritted his teeth. I had a feeling I was getting close to the truth but my companion was not about to confirm anything. 'All I can tell you is that it is a matter of national security. It is vital that these documents are recovered before they fall into the wrong hands. To be frank, I would rather have brought my own men in to deal with this.' The necessity of relying on an outsider clearly irked him. 'But we couldn't spare anyone else just now. Not with all this going on.' He gestured vaguely to the posters plastered across the square. Men in republican colours were waving banners not ten feet away from us. I nodded. It was understandable that London would want to keep a close eye on events in Madrid, on this of all days. 'I was reluctant to come here myself, if I'm brutally honest,' Lazenby confessed. 'But our lords and masters insisted. That's the importance they are placing on this.'

I nodded. 'So what time is this…Schmidt arriving?'

'Schulz. Gerhard Schulz.' Lazenby glanced at his watch. 'I'm not altogether sure. But some time in the next couple of hours. I would rather have followed him myself, but there's a chance he might recognise me. We do know he left Friedrichshafen yesterday evening.'

Friedrichshafen. That was in Germany somewhere. 'Is he coming by train?'

'Not exactly.' Lazenby smiled. He was holding something back and he didn't care if I knew it. 'Shall I order us a spot of tea? There might be a bit of a wait, I'm afraid.'

People always imagine spies lead glamorous lives but the reality is often quite dull. I had spent most of the past eighteen months kicking my heels on the Rock of Gibraltar, doing a bit of low grade surveillance work for MI5. The old firm had been thinking of establishing a regular outpost on the Med and, since I was in the area and in need of work, I had been enlisted as their guinea pig. The task was a simple one: turn up, test the water, see what useful intelligence you can uncover. The answer, as it turned out, was not very much. And now, after fourteen months of hobnobbing with various admirals and spending far too much time observing the comings and goings of merchant ships, I was rapidly losing the will to live. I had never much warmed to the notion of paid employment and, after a decade of fine living, being back in the saddle had proved something of a shock to the system. I had a budget, of kinds, but barely enough to keep me in whisky, let alone to satisfy my creditors. Not that I had any right to complain – I had left England under a bit of a cloud – but when the telegram arrived from London, asking me to assist our colleagues in the senior service with a rather delicate matter, I had been more than happy to oblige. A nice jaunt across Andalucía in a rented motor car with my new man was just what the doctor ordered. Now I was beginning to have second thoughts. The prospect of following some bald idiot around Seville in the heat of the afternoon did not fill my heart with joy. I had already spent over an hour sat at the café waiting for the elusive Mr Kendall, who was still refusing to put in an appearance. It was not my idea of an agreeable afternoon. At least on the Rock they knew how to brew a decent cup of tea.

Lazenby was doing his best to distract me but the conversation was proving as tepid as the refreshment. 'How are things going in Gibraltar?' he asked, as if to prove the point. He had told me precisely nothing of his own work. According to my contacts, he had been with the SIS – the Secret Intelligence Service – for three or four years, and Special Branch before that, but everything else was a blank to me and Lazenby did not seem inclined to fill in the details. I had to admire his nerve, though, sitting out on the street in full view of the hotel entrance, wearing a blue blazer and a panama hat and doing the Times crossword. He couldn't have looked more English if he had tried. In fact, he was so conspicuous, I doubted anyone would pay him any attention whatsoever.

'The whole thing's winding down now,' I admitted, in reply to his question. 'Budget cuts, you understand.' Everyone was tightening their belts in the aftermath of the Wall Street Crash. And, despite my best efforts, Gibraltar had been a complete wash out. There was not enough useful intelligence to be gathered there to justify the expense of a permanent post and there was nothing to be gained from prolonging the operation. 'As a matter of fact, I've been offered a new position. Across the pond, as they say. Not with Five. With your lot. The foreign service in America.'

'Sounds interesting,' Lazenby said.

'I'm not so sure about that. Passport Control Officer in some banana republic, apparently. At least, that's the cover story. Same sort of thing as you do, I would imagine.'

'A bit of a step up,' Lazenby observed, without rancour. 'C doesn't usually take on anyone sight unseen. You must have made a good impression back home.'

'The Colonel's a good friend of mine.' Sir Vincent Kelly, the head of MI5, had taken something of a personal interest in my career. I had worked for him briefly before the war and we had always got on. He had offered me the post in Gibraltar – more as a favour than anything else – and now that it was being wound up it was considerate of him to recommend me to the head of the foreign division.

'Have you accepted the job?' Lazenby asked.

I nodded. 'Been trying to persuade my man to come with me. But he's dragging his heels a bit. Not altogether keen on boats. I think I might have managed to persuade him, if it hadn't been for that ridiculous business with HMS Glorious the other week.'

Lazenby suppressed a smile. 'Yes, I read about that.'

'Damn fool of a captain,' I muttered. The accident had taken place at the beginning of April, about sixty miles off the coast of Gibraltar. I had compiled a report on the matter for London. It had made grim reading. 'I appreciate it's difficult to navigate in fog, but hitting a passenger liner. The man ought to be shot.'

'They rescued most of the passengers, didn't they?' Lazenby asked. He must have read about it in the Times.

'Yes,' I grunted. 'But hardly a good advertisement for the Royal Navy is it? And it does rather put one off the whole idea of sea travel. I was going to book our passage from Lisbon later this month but Maurice is refusing to commit himself.'

'Maurice?'

'My valet. I have to call him Maurice. His surname's unpronounceable. Useful fellow but a bit surly. French, you understand. Hasn't been with me long.'

Lazenby was intrigued. 'Yes, I'd heard you had a valet. Bit odd, in our line of work.'

'Surprisingly useful, though. A good distraction, if nothing else. He has been fully vetted by London. Not sure I'll get him on a boat, though. Have you finished with that paper?'

Lazenby smiled indulgently. 'It's all yours. Last Thursday's, I'm afraid.'

'I usually get the weekly one.'

'It's not always available in Madrid. I like to have a go at the crosswords.' He glanced down at the paper as he handed it over. 'Just one I couldn't get today. Six across. *"One of three, and often one more"*.'

I shook my head and opened the paper. 'Haven't the foggiest.' The crossword craze had largely passed me by, though it had been going for some time when I had left England. It was rather a shock when the Times had succumbed to the craze the previous year. What next? I wondered. News on the front page?

A cab was pulling up on the far side of the square, just outside the entrance to the Hotel Alfonso XIII. A short, serious looking man in spectacles and a felt hat was bending down at the window to pay the driver. I flipped over the Times and pointed a finger. I couldn't tell from this distance, but it might well have been one of the men in the photographs. 'Do you think that's your man?'

'Don't point at him, you fool!' Lazenby hissed. He peered across the plaza as the fellow made his way up the steps and into the lobby of the hotel. 'Yes, that's him.' He lifted his wrist and glanced at his watch. 'Later than I expected. The plane landed at eleven thirty. So, let's say…half an hour to check in and change, perhaps. Then off to the meeting.'

'Assuming Mr Schulz is on his way. You didn't say where I'm supposed to meet *him*, when he does turn up.' Lazenby had been annoyingly vague on the details so far. 'Or how we're expected to know he's on his way.' There had

13

certainly been no telephone call at the café, nor any messages passed along while we had been waiting.

'No I didn't. But he'll be here any time…'

Lazenby stopped himself and his head whipped around to the opposite side of the square. Motor cars were grinding to a halt in the middle of the street on the far side of the fountain. Pedestrians had stopped walking and were looking back the way they had come. Jaws were falling open. Fingers were being pointed. And all at once I noticed a strange buzzing noise in the air. It sounded like the propeller of an aeroplane. Several aeroplanes, in fact. I followed the upward gaze of the crowd and my eyes fixed on a bizarre object, floating above the Hotel Alfonso. A huge silver whale was hanging calmly in the sky at the far end of the street.

'Good lord!' I exclaimed. I couldn't think of anything else to say.

An enormously inflated balloon had rumbled into view, a monstrous behemoth all but blocking out the sun. I had never clapped eyes on an airship before; not outside of newsreel footage, anyway. The thing looked unreal, like a giant cigar suspended in mid toss. It seemed scarcely credible that there could be people on board. But there the damned thing was, hanging improbably in the sky; a Zeppelin airship – the D-LZ128, no less, according to the serial number on the side. I watched, my mind numb, as the huge metal dirigible glided serenely over the town hall towards Seville Cathedral. The onlookers in the street were beginning to clap and cheer. Motorists were honking their horns. A little girl with her mother, not four feet away from me, was crying out in amazement and delight.

'"*Cheer*",' I announced abruptly, to no one in particular.

Lazenby could not take his eyes from the Zeppelin. 'What's that?' he asked, his face lit up like an enthusiastic schoolboy.

'Six across,' I muttered absently. '"*One of three, and often one more*". It's "*Cheer*".'

Lazenby tore his eyes away from the ship for a brief moment. 'Never mind that!' he exclaimed. 'I think our Mr

Schulz is about to arrive!'

Chapter Two

Dozens of men rushed forward across the grass as the mooring lines were dropped down from on high. I wasn't close enough to see if the men were wearing gloves, but it was clear that grabbing hold of those ropes was no easy endeavour. The Zeppelin had dipped lower and appeared to be hovering now some two hundred feet above the ground. A number of small propellers on either side of the craft were whizzing around like dervishes. That was what caused the buzzing noise. The head of a man was sticking out of the engine casing in front of each propeller. And in the control gondola, towards the front of the ship, I could just make out the captain and his crew, overseeing the descent as the craft was manoeuvred into port.

On the ground, the mooring lines had been pulled taut and the great balloon juddered in the air as the ground crew struggled to bring it under control. The back of the great beast remained free, however, and while the front end was pulled lower to the ground, the rear hung up, creating something of a slope. The tail end, with its heavy fins, was still swaying in the breeze and I saw one man on the ground lose his footing. For all the great majesty of the beast and all the engineering prowess involved in its construction, I couldn't help but think that the airship looked fragile. The skin of it was little more than cloth woven around an aluminium frame and the buffeting even of a gentle afternoon breeze caused the whole thing to rock back and forth, like a giant whale caught in a net, struggling to break free. But the groundsmen had got a firm hold of it now and were preparing to lead the enormous vessel across to the metal mooring post where the craft would be tethered for the night.

The landing strip was barely more than a field to the north east of the city. Hundreds of grubby looking locals in cloth caps had gathered to witness the arrival of the Zeppelin. Some were taking photographs, others were laughing and joking. A few enterprising individuals had set up food and drink stalls. Automobiles and motor bicycles were scattered across the periphery of the field. There were horses too, mostly for the tourists, with open-topped carriages attached. Loosely shirted drivers stood back from the throng, chatting idly among themselves. Only the area directly beneath the Zeppelin was kept clear. The groundsmen had now pulled the back half of the ship down and were attaching it to a wheeled platform while others were grabbing hold of the gondola towards the front.

The airstrip had not been an easy place to find. Charles Lazenby had only given the briefest of directions. The Zeppelin had circled for some minutes over the centre of the city – I had the curious notion that the captain was giving his passengers the opportunity to take photographs – and that at least had afforded me the time to summon Maurice with the motorcar. I wasn't sure how easily the two of us would be able to follow the great airship, in our rented Hispano Suiza, but as luck would have it half of Seville seemed to be headed in the same direction, towards the fields marked on the map as "Hernan Cebolla". It was a peculiar landing site. The place looked more like a farm than an airport.

'*Cebolla* means "onion" doesn't it?' I asked Maurice, who was sitting in the driving seat of the automobile. His grasp of Spanish was better than mine.

'Yes, Monsieur.'

'So the pride of the German fleet is come in to land on Mr Hernan's onion field?'

The valet shook his head. 'Not exactly, Monsieur.'

I shrugged. Whatever the truth, Mr Hernan would not be growing any onions here any time soon. The field was being trampled to death by sight-seers.

I focused my binoculars on the middle section of the airship. The heads of some of the passengers were visible now through a row of windows embedded into the lower side of the balloon. They were waving enthusiastically at the crowds, who were responding with equal vigour.

I dropped the binoculars and pulled out the photograph from my inside pocket to take another look at it. I hadn't recognised Gerhard Schulz among the passengers, even with the binoculars, but it wouldn't be long before he disembarked with the rest of them. Quite why an Austrian journalist had chosen to travel to Seville by airship was beyond me. The tickets were not cheap and a train journey would only have taken a couple of days. But perhaps he had a private income of some kind.

I envied him that, if he did. I had forfeited most of my estate when I left England, apart from a couple of small annuities which I had managed to keep quiet about. I certainly could not have afforded to take rooms at the Hotel Alfonso, which is where most of the passengers would be staying the night.

A courtesy bus had been sent out to collect them. The vehicle had a rather grand crest stencilled on the side. Gerhard Schulz, however, was booked into another hotel on the far side of the cathedral.

Lazenby had given me clear instructions with regard to the Austrian. 'Follow him to the hotel and then anywhere else he goes. Don't try to intercept him. Let him hand over the goods and leave me to deal with the American.' Lazenby had been insistent on that last point. How exactly he proposed to acquire the documents from Walter Kendall he was not prepared to say, but I had a nasty suspicion he would not be picking any pockets. I had seen the Webley revolver tucked away inside his jacket. There was an edge of steel to Mr Lazenby beneath that amiable façade.

My legs were beginning to get cramp in the passenger seat of the car so I opened the door and pulled myself out onto the parched, sunburnt grass. I needed to get closer to the Zeppelin in any case. I couldn't risk losing sight of Schulz once he had stepped off the airship. There was no guarantee he would join the others on the courtesy bus and the crowd was thickening as the passengers prepared to disembark.

I stuck my head briefly back into the car. 'Wait here, Morris. We may need to leave in a hurry.'

'Yes, Monsieur.'

As I strode forward into the crowd, I noticed a cameraman with a tripod filming the arrival of the ship. I veered right and pulled down my hat. In my line of work, it doesn't do to be documented, especially on celluloid. The fellow was clearly more interested in the crew, however, as the camera was aimed tightly at the control gondola. It was not the first time a Zeppelin had visited Seville but it was still something of a novelty. If the elections had created a party atmosphere here, the arrival of the D-LZ128 had provoked a full blown carnival.

I gazed up at the craft in bewilderment. I couldn't for the life of me see what all the fuss was about. It was just a machine, a way of getting people from A to B. I could admire the engineering involved – the scale of the Zeppelin was certainly impressive – but when all was said and done it was just a giant balloon; a children's toy writ large. And considerably less safe, as a means of transport, than an ocean liner or even an aeroplane.

I confess, the fact that it was German built was also of some concern to me. I did not need or want a reminder of the Kraut's aerial prowess or their industrial efficiency. I hadn't witnessed the bombing raids over London during the war – I had spent most of the conflict in the United States – but I had heard accounts of the devastation and part of me still associated Zeppelins with death in the sky. The fact that this particular airship had been christened the "Richthofen" was hardly reassuring. Manfred Von Richthofen was a war hero and, by all accounts, a man of some integrity; but he was still a German. The so-called "Red Baron" had been the scourge of the Royal Flying Corps during the Great War and had brought down dozens of British planes. Hardly an appropriate poster boy for a civilian aircraft. The gutter press in America had already started referring to the ship as "The Red Zeppelin" in his honour, much to the annoyance of the Germans. Nowadays, the word "red" had more sinister connotations in Europe.

I heard the click of a camera to my right. A tall, sprightly fellow in a casual suit was capturing the moment for posterity. He dropped the camera – a Leica if I wasn't much mistaken – and quickly wound on the film. The man was clean shaven and had an elegant bearing, a cut above the local rabble. Quite a handsome fellow, I thought, with hazel eyes and short cropped hair. Perhaps he was a journalist too. There seemed to be a lot of them about.

The man caught my eye and raised a hand amiably. 'Quite impressive, don't you think?' He nodded his head towards the airship.

I disagreed politely. 'You wouldn't catch me up in one of those things. They're absolutely lethal.' I pulled out a cigarette and fumbled for my lighter.

'Probably best not to light that just now,' the man observed.

I stared back at him in surprise. Who the devil did he think he was, telling me what to do? But then I caught his meaning and the colour drained from my face. I dropped the cigarette to the ground and pocketed the lighter without another word.

We were both standing a short distance away from several million cubic feet of hydrogen.

'It probably wouldn't do any harm,' the fellow reassured me, 'but it's as well to be careful.' He extended a hand. 'Thomas McGilton.'

'Reginald Bland.' I shook his hand firmly, keen not to dwell on the proximity of the hydrogen. 'You're…Irish, are you?' There was the hint of an accent, but it was well disguised. If this Mr McGilton *was* an Irishman, he was a well educated one.

'Belfast, yes. I guessed you were English. The hat gave it away.' He grinned good naturedly. The man was being altogether too familiar for my liking but, as we had now been formally introduced, I decided not to take offence.

'So you know a bit about these airships do you?' I enquired.

He nodded happily. 'I saw her sister ship, the Graf Zeppelin, fly over southern England last year. I thought to myself then, I'd like to have a go in one of those.'

'Rather you than me. These things are a death trap.'

'Not if they're handled right.'

I snorted. 'Tell that to the crew of the R101.' The British airship had crashed in northern France the previous October with the loss of forty-eight lives. The Court of Enquiry had only just reported back. 'It wasn't the crash that killed them, you know. It was the ignition of the hydrogen. The poor fellows were burnt alive.'

McGilton nodded sadly. 'They overloaded it, that was the problem. No disrespect to the English, but the Germans have been building airships since the turn of the century. They've had time to perfect the technology. They know what they're doing.'

'If you say so.'

We looked back up at the Zeppelin, which was now being fastened to the mooring post. My indifference towards the craft had turned in the space of a few minutes to apprehension.

'I hope so, anyway,' McGilton said. 'Since my ticket carries me all the way to New Haven.'

'Good lord!' I stared at the Irishman. 'You're going on board that thing?' I regarded him in astonishment.

'I am indeed! Leaving first thing tomorrow morning. But I wanted to come out here today and watch it land.'

My mouth opened and closed but I couldn't think of anything to say. The fellow was mad. There could be no other explanation.

'They're going to move onto helium with the next ship, the LZ129. Much safer than hydrogen. But in the meantime, they'll take every precaution.'

'I wish I shared your confidence.'

McGilton laughed. 'What's life without a little risk?'

'A pleasant experience?'

He shook his head. 'Planes crash every day, Mr Bland. Trains are derailed...'

'Yes, but...'

He waved his hands enthusiastically. 'And just the elegance of the thing. An ocean liner of the sky. How could you resist?'

I had the answer to that. 'Very easily, I assure you. Well, I...I wish you the best of luck, Mr McGilton.' It didn't seem right to harp on about the dangers, if this man really was

21

planning to travel on board the airship.

'Luck has nothing to do with it,' he insisted. 'It looks like the passengers are preparing to disembark. I might wander over and say hello. Good day to you, Mr Bland.'

And with that he took his leave. I stared after him as he moved forward through the crowd. He was either a very brave man or a complete idiot. Probably both, in point of fact.

I had more important things to concern myself with. The passengers were indeed making their way down a short set of metal steps and onto the waiting platform. I didn't know how many people the Richthofen was equipped to carry, but there seemed to be less than a dozen passengers emerging from the ship. That couldn't be a full load. Not everybody, it seemed, was as brave – or foolhardy – as Mr McGilton. For all the enthusiasm of the crowd, the destruction of the R101 had given everybody pause for thought.

A couple of female passengers were disembarking alongside the men. The last person to emerge, however, was Gerhard Schulz. He was thinner and shorter than his photograph suggested but the beard and the pinched expression left me in no doubt as to his identity. I hung back in the crowd to make sure he didn't see me.

The travellers were lining up to be filmed by the man from the newsreel company but, after a few moments of waving and enthusiastic shouts, they moved along the platform, down the steps and onto the sun bleached grass. The courtesy vehicle was waiting to drive them away. I watched as Schulz had a quick conversation with the driver. I was too far away to hear what was being said, but I guessed the gist of it: Schulz wasn't going to the Alfonso, but the driver had offered to give him a lift anyway. Schulz declined the offer. He had a large brown suitcase clutched tightly to his chest. That was the cargo we were after, I supposed. The driver indicated another vehicle. A couple of taxis were on hand, ready to ferry the airship's senior crew into town, once they had completed mooring operations, and Schulz hurried across to purloin one of the vehicles.

Mr McGilton, I saw with some distaste, had already

struck up a conversation with one of the two women preparing to board the courtesy coach. The younger of the two, in fact. 'He doesn't waste much time,' I muttered, as I turned and hurried back to Maurice.

Gerhard Schulz was making his way rapidly through the entrance to an unprepossessing stone tower. I had already followed him from the airstrip to his hotel, the Doña Sofia. Once he had checked in there he had been straight out again and – for reasons best known to himself – was paying his respects to Our Lord in the cathedral on the opposite side of the square. It *was* a Sunday, I supposed, but he didn't stay long and neither did he meet up with anybody inside.

Afterwards, he made his way on foot towards the river.

Now he had arrived at the Torre del Oro – a lonely phallic construction, seventy feet tall, squatting in splendid isolation on the river front. Despite the name, the tower was not made of gold, but it did have a formidable spiral staircase running through the centre of it. I stopped just short of the entrance and peered up the length of the building. There was no sign of Charles Lazenby or Walter Kendall anywhere near the top, but perhaps they were out of view. There were certainly several people milling about on the battlements up there. Rather them than me, I thought. I had never had much of a head for heights.

When I was a girl, I had once been forced to climb to the top of a lighthouse. It had been a cold day in late June, a few months after the death of Queen Victoria. My father had been trying to instil a few manly virtues in his only begotten "son", but when I reached the top and gazed nervously through the windows at the muddy brown sea, I decided that the quality of the view was not sufficient to merit the energy expended in getting there. My father had given me a sound thrashing for my insolence.

But I had similar feelings now.

If Maurice had been with me, I would have ordered him up in my stead. But the valet had sensibly remained with the car on the other side of the cathedral. He didn't like to get too involved in my secret service work. I growled and stepped reluctantly across the threshold of the Torre del Oro.

Why the place was even open to the public on a Sunday, I had no idea. The Sabbath was meant to be a day of rest. Some people had no respect.

Having expended so much energy following the Austrian across town in the heat of the afternoon, I felt every step inside that tower as if it were a blow to my stomach. After half a minute of huffing and puffing up the stairs my heart felt like it was about to explode. I was finding it increasingly difficult to breathe. I had to keep my mouth wide open just to draw in enough oxygen to keep my brain from overheating.

An attractive young woman was descending the staircase in the opposite direction and I flattened myself against the wall to let her pass. She smiled at me, mistaking my pause for gallantry, and then disappeared around a curve in the wall. I took another huge gulp of air and steeled myself for the final ascent. This must be how Mallory felt, I reflected, when he began his final, ill-fated assault on the summit of Mount Everest.

I had not seen Mr Schulz since I had entered the building and, as I emerged into the sunlight, stepping onto the cobbled stones, I could not see him now. I did a quick circuit of the battlements to ascertain if he was hiding somewhere, but there was no sign of him. He was not at the top of the tower. I had come all the way up here for nothing. I cursed the man under my breath, causing a hefty Spanish matron to regard me with some alarm as I passed her by.

I approached the edge of the battlements and peered tentatively over the sides. My stomach lurched at the sight of the ground, such a long way below me, but I struggled manfully to maintain my composure. My hands gripped tightly to the top of the crenellated wall.

The streets below, along the water front, were typically busy and it was several minutes before Gerhard Schulz emerged from the bottom steps of the tower. He had removed his hat briefly, to use as a fan, and I could see his bald head and the rather thick beard beneath it. How could I have missed him?

There was a room encircling the staircase halfway up the tower. Maybe he had stepped in there, while I had been climbing up, and then doubled back a few minutes later.

Now, he was crossing the road, moving away from me. He avoided a passing tram and disappeared into a side street, heading back in the direction of the cathedral and his hotel.

I stepped back from the battlements in dismay. I had the horrible feeling the Austrian had met somebody halfway up the Torre del Oro and passed on his secrets. But I had not been there to see it.

'We've both been led a merry dance,' Charles Lazenby admitted ruefully. It was eight o'clock in the evening and we had reunited at the Gran Café on the Plaza de Andalucía. The square was throbbing with activity around the elaborate central fountain, the excitement and euphoria of the day overwhelming any sense of decorum. It was hard to believe it was a Sunday evening. In England, on the Sabbath, everything is shut up and it was usually the same in Spain. But nothing today was going to dampen the mood of celebration. Rumours were flying that the republicans had performed much better than expected in the elections. Some were claiming they might even be heading for victory and the *cerveza* was flowing like water.

I, for one, did not feel like celebrating. 'So Kendall gave you the slip as well, did he?' I enquired. Lazenby had been nowhere near the Torre del Oro and, so far as I knew, neither had Walter Kendall.

'That's the queer thing,' the Englishman replied. 'I never lost sight of him. He left the hotel at four o'clock and headed straight for the park. The Maria Luisa. Spent an hour and a half wandering around the gardens like a tourist. He even took a short boat trip on the canal around the Plaza de España. Then he headed back to his hotel and, so far as I'm aware, he hasn't budged since.' Lazenby took a sip of wine and sighed.

'So they were both behaving like tourists,' I observed. Between the two of us we had been given the grand tour of the city. 'It makes no sense.' I stared down at the plate in front of me. It was some disgusting fish and pasta concoction, which did not look fit for a dog, but I had had such a long and tiring day that I was prepared to shovel pretty much anything down my gullet. I swallowed a mouthful of the lukewarm sludge and looked across at Lazenby. 'So you don't think the exchange has been made?'

'It must have been. I can only think Kendall sent somebody else in his stead. He must have got wind someone was following him. Are you sure you didn't see anyone acting suspiciously at the Torre? Or in the cathedral?'

I shook my head. 'No one at all.' A waiter was hovering to our left, waiting for the right moment to interrupt us. 'What is it?' I snapped.

'*Señor, discúlpeme.*' The Spaniard addressed my companion. '*Teléfono.*'

Lazenby nodded. He pushed back his plate, rose to his feet and followed the waiter into the crowded café.

I took another mouthful of fish and reflected mournfully on what I could have been eating had I ignored that damned telegram and remained in Gibraltar. The restaurants on the Rock were a mixed bunch and there weren't that many of them, but on a Sunday afternoon, for all that, you would never be more than a hundred yards away from a plate of roast beef and Yorkshire pudding. Such were the benefits of Empire.

Five or six minutes passed before Lazenby returned to his seat. He leaned forward confidentially. 'That was the receptionist at the Doña Sofia. Schulz has just been enquiring about train times to Madrid. He's asked the receptionist to book him a ticket for tomorrow morning. Paid cash up front. American dollars.'

'So that confirms it,' I said. Walter Kendall had run rings around London's finest, had sent an accomplice to pay the Austrian and collect the file, and was now in possession of whatever scandalous documents Gerhard Schulz had passed along to him. 'What are we going to do?'

Lazenby sat back in his chair. 'I'll get a couple of men in Madrid to meet the train tomorrow, just to be on the safe side. But you're right. We must assume that Kendall now has a copy of our file. A complete photographic record. And the worst of it is, he's booked a ticket on that airship tomorrow morning.'

My eyes widened. 'He's going on the Richthofen?'

'Back to America.' Lazenby nodded. 'Booked his place a couple of days ago, as a matter of fact. I checked the passenger list.'

'You never told me that.'

He shrugged. 'Didn't think it was relevant. I had hoped we'd have the photographs in our possession by now.'

Damn the man. Why did he have to keep things back all the time? 'So somehow or other we have to get hold of them tonight.' I thought for a minute. 'He'll be down for supper by now. We could always break into his hotel room and have a look around.'

Lazenby considered that for a moment. 'It's an idea, certainly. But I don't think Kendall's daft enough to leave the negatives unattended in his bedroom.' Lazenby was of the opinion that the photographs had not yet been developed; and a roll of film could be hidden anywhere. 'And we can't burst into the dining hall, all guns blazing.'

'What other option do we have?' I growled, trying to think of an alternative. 'I suppose we could intercept him tomorrow morning, on the way to the airstrip.'

Lazenby shook his head. 'He'll be in the courtesy vehicle with all the other passengers.'

'But surely one of us could bump into him somewhere. Pick his pocket or something.'

'He'll be on his guard against that. Probably bury the film in the bottom of his luggage. No, it pains me to admit it, but I don't think we're going to be able to touch him before he boards that airship.'

'You can't give up, man!' I exclaimed. 'You said this was a matter of national security.'

'It is.' Lazenby leaned forward across the table. 'There is one other option, of course.' There was a half smile on his lips that I didn't much care for.

27

'What option?'

'Well,' he said. 'We could always slip a man on board the Richthofen ourselves.'

Chapter Three

A smiling steward in a white jacket greeted me at the base of the metal stairs. He was young and smartly turned out. 'Good morning, sir. May I see your passport and ticket?' He spoke with a thick German accent, but his words were clear and precise. I reached into my jacket pocket and produced the documents. My hands were shaking as I handed them across. Most of the other passengers had already boarded the airship. It was only the new arrivals who required special treatment. The steward checked through the documents briefly. Maurice had already handed the suitcases to another fellow, who had whisked them away before we had known what was happening. 'Are you carrying any matches or lighters?' the steward asked us. I hesitated for a moment, unsure whether he was trying to cadge a cigarette off me. But no, it was just another security procedure. I handed him my lighter. 'Thank you, Mr Bland. There is a smoking room on board, but we ask that you do not try to smoke anywhere else on the aircraft.'

I nodded tightly and tried to keep my bladder under control. I could not believe I had agreed to do this.

'You're out of your mind!' I had exclaimed to Charles Lazenby the previous evening, when he had first suggested the idea. 'You're not getting me up on one of those things. It's a disaster waiting to happen.'

Lazenby stared back across the dinner table. 'Look, old chap. If there was any other option…'

I pushed back my plate. I had half a mind to walk out of the café and abandon the fellow to his delusions. 'There must be something else we can do.' I had no intention of boarding the Richthofen. The damn thing was a death trap. 'Can't you wire the office in New York? Get someone to meet Mr Kendall when he gets off at the other end?'

Lazenby shook his head. 'The Richthofen isn't *going* to New York. Not directly. Its first port of call is Rio de Janeiro.'

'Well get someone to meet him there then,' I snapped, grabbing the tumbler in front of me and draining the last of my whisky. 'The Prince of Wales is in Brazil at the moment, isn't he? Some kind of trade mission?' The Times was proving ever useful.

Lazenby frowned. 'Yes, I believe so.'

'He must have a few Secret Service bods with him. You could give them the nod and they could pick Mr Kendall up when he arrives in Rio.'

Lazenby scratched his moustache. 'I don't want to rely on Special Branch. In any case, the Prince will be on his way home tomorrow.' He seemed to know more about that than I did. 'And keeping tabs on anyone in Rio is tricky at the best of times. No, I'm sorry, but it would be far safer to slip someone on board the Richthofen.'

I slammed down my tumbler in disgust. 'All right, then why don't you do it yourself?' I exclaimed, glaring at a passing waiter. 'Then you can make sure the job is done properly. Or you could send one of your many underlings.'

Lazenby poured himself another glass of wine. My anger had not ruffled him in the slightest. 'None of my men can be spared. Not if the republicans really have won these elections.' He placed the bottle back down on the table and calmly lifted the glass. 'They'll be needed to keep an eye on things in the capital over the next few days. In any case, there wouldn't be time to get them here.'

'I see. So you and your men refuse to get involved but you're happy to drag an MI5 operative all the way from Gibraltar to fill in for you. It won't inconvenience him at all!'

'Well, you *were* planning to cross the Atlantic anyway, for this new job of yours,' Lazenby pointed out, tartly.

'Not by airship!' I cried, waving my hand for emphasis and nearly knocking my dinner plate off the table. 'And not until the end of the month. I'm not even entirely sure I want to go.' The events of the last few hours had rather put me off the idea, if this was what it was like working for the SIS. 'I wasn't planning to book the tickets until next week.' *Tickets.* I gazed down at the remnants of fish and pasta in front of me and felt a sudden glimmer of a hope. You couldn't hop on an ocean liner at a moment's notice and I doubted you could hop on a

Zeppelin either. 'There won't be time to book me a ticket,' I declared smugly, pushing my knife and fork together on the plate. 'Not at this stage. If they even have a ticket office in Seville, it won't be open on a Sunday evening.'

Lazenby was unconcerned. 'That's already been taken care of.' He reached into his jacket and pulled out a paper wallet, which he handed nonchalantly across. 'And since you crossed the border from Gibraltar this morning, I presume you already have your passport with you?'

I glared at the fellow angrily, grabbing the wallet. 'You planned this,' I breathed. 'You planned this all along.' How else could he have arranged a ticket for me like this? He had spent half the day following Walter Kendall around and the rest of it talking to me outside the Gran Café. There had been no time for him to go shopping.

Lazenby did not deny it. 'It always pays to have a contingency plan,' he said, taking another sip of wine. 'I'd heard from London that you were heading off to the Americas and I knew there was a chance I might have to put someone on board that Zeppelin.'

'So you thought you'd press gang me into doing it? Well, thank you very much indeed. I'm flattered you have such confidence in me, Mr Lazenby. But I can tell you right now that I have no intention...' I stopped, looking down at the open wallet in my hand. There were two tickets tucked inside. The second was made out in the name of my valet, Maurice Sauveterre. I glanced up, perplexed. 'Why have you bought two tickets?'

The other man raised an eyebrow. 'I thought you would probably want your valet to go with you.' I blinked. So he had known about Maurice from the start as well. 'As you say, it makes a good cover.'

'But do they *have* steerage on an airship?'

'No. It's all first class accommodation.' He placed his glass back down on the table. 'You'll be sharing a cabin, of course.'

'A cabin? With my valet? Have you taken leave of your senses?' The man was insane. 'He hasn't even agreed to go

31

with me. And as to the cost…' The price of each ticket was written out on the front: three hundred and seventy five American dollars. That worked out at about seventy five pounds each, in real money. It was an absolute fortune. 'That's more than I pay Maurice in a whole year.'

'The bureau will cover the cost. And having your man there will make you much less conspicuous. It was either that or sharing a cabin with some Irish chap.'

I grimaced as the image of Mr McGilton flashed up in my mind. I could certainly never share a cabin with him, not without giving the fellow one hell of a shock come bedtime. Lazenby could not know it, but my valet was the only man I *could* share a room with. I slumped back into my chair. 'You've got it all worked out, Mr Lazenby.' I glowered at him. 'You know, there's a word for people like you. And it's not a very nice word.'

Lazenby sighed. 'Look, Bland, I know this is putting a lot on you,' he said, in a conciliatory tone. 'I'm sorry if I haven't been entirely straight. But I thought you were more likely to agree if you were here *in situ*, so to speak, rather than in Gibraltar.'

'In other words, the less time I had to think about it, the more likely I was to agree?'

'Something like that.' Lazenby glanced down at my empty glass. 'Would you like another whisky?'

'I should say.' I needed something to counteract the taste of the fish. He clicked his fingers and gestured for the waiter to bring me a refill. 'But an airship…good grief.' I shuddered. It didn't bear thinking about. 'I went up in an aeroplane once, just after the war. A Sopwith Gnu.' The memory of it brought me out in a cold sweat even now. It had been one of the worst experiences of my life. 'Most of my lunch ended up on the pilot. And after what happened to the R101…'

'I'm not going to pretend there's not an element of risk,' my companion acknowledged. 'And not just with regard to the airship. But look, accidents happen every day. With every form of transport. There was that derailment in Leighton Buzzard just before Easter. Six people killed. But did that stop me hopping on a train to Seville yesterday evening? Of course not. And did you think twice about renting a motorcar because of all the accidents on the road?'

The motor car. 'That's another thing!' I exclaimed, angrily. 'What about the car I rented? I put down a ten pound deposit. I can't afford to lose that. And who's going to drive it back to Gibraltar?' That wasn't the only consideration. 'What about all my clothes? I only brought a couple of suits with me.' The more I thought about it, the more complications there seemed to be. 'And all my possessions back at the flat.' I had already paid the rent for my apartment until the end of April. 'I can't leave everything behind.' Admittedly, there were a few shady characters I would happily see the back of – I owed one Italian gentleman quite a hefty sum after a particularly disastrous game of poker the previous weekend – but that was beside the point.

'I'll find someone to take care of your motorcar,' Lazenby assured me. 'And I'm sure we can get someone else to pack up your things for you. Man alive, its not as if you've been living in Gibraltar that long. And ten pounds will more than cover the shipping costs for any luggage. We can send all that on to you in a week or two. I'm sure you'll be able to manage until then.'

The waiter arrived with my whisky and soda. He placed the glass down on the table and removed the empty tumbler.

'How long is this voyage anyway, if I did go? How long would we be up in the air?'

Lazenby sat back in his chair. 'It depends on the weather, but as I understand it, three days to Brazil and three and a half to New Haven.'

'I won't get a wink of sleep,' I grumbled. I had never yet managed to fall asleep on a train, let alone an aircraft.

'I'll lend you some sleeping pills. And, in any case, you'll be in New York in less than a week.'

'Three weeks earlier than I need to be.'

'Yes, but having proved your mettle to the senior service.' He met my eye then. 'So you'll do it?'

I wasn't committing to anything. I lifted my glass and

33

took a large gulp. The drink was not helping to soften the blow. There was far too much soda in it. 'If I *were* to go, how would I go about grabbing these negatives of yours?'

'That shouldn't prove too difficult. Kendall will be off his guard once you've left Seville. He may leave them in his room or in his luggage. If he keeps them with him, you might have to try picking his pockets. But you'll have plenty of time to devise a strategy.'

'But what if he's suspicious of me? A last minute booking, bound to attract attention. And what if Gerhard Schulz told him he was being followed around by some middle aged Englishman? You said they spoke on the telephone.'

'Well, according to the concierge. But I'm sure you were very careful. I doubt Schulz will have noticed. And now he has his money, he'll have no further interest in Mr Kendall. Besides, no secret service organisation would pay for a valet to accompany his master on an expensive Zeppelin flight. Not in these times of austerity. He's unlikely to give you a second glance.'

'It does sound improbable,' I admitted. 'Seventy five pounds a ticket! Good grief. Has London agreed to that?'

Lazenby smiled thinly. 'Let me worry about the expenses. All I can do is stress the importance of this mission. It's vital that these documents are destroyed before Kendall gets to New York.'

'But you're not going to tell me what's in them?'

'I can't. I'm sorry.'

I laughed bitterly. 'But it's so important that you'd happily send a washed up MI5 officer rather than one of your own men?'

Lazenby shook his head. 'It's important enough for me to send someone who was personally recommended by the head of the Security Service. There's no one else who can do this, Bland. It's for King and Country. It's what you signed up for.'

I downed the last of the whisky and abandoned the empty glass. He had me. I couldn't very well accept a job with the senior service one day and then refuse to help them the next. And with my limited finances, having the cost of the transatlantic journey covered by Whitehall – in advance – was a positive boon.

'I suppose I don't have to look out of the windows,' I muttered.

'Of course not. And they serve very good food on board, so I hear. All included in the price.'

I glanced down at the remnants of the fish, which the waiter had not yet cleared away. Anything had to be better than that slop. I let out a deep sigh. The things one does for one's country. I folded up the wallet and inserted it into my jacket pocket. 'Very well.'

'You'll do it?'

'I'll do it. But I'll have to speak to Maurice first.'

It was always possible that my valet would refuse to go and that would put the kibosh on the whole idea. But sadly, when I approached him later that evening, Maurice seemed perfectly happy with the arrangements. Anything was preferable to an ocean liner, in his book. He even volunteered to telephone an acquaintance he knew in Gibraltar, to make sure our luggage was properly packed up.

So that was that. I was going on the Richthofen and my man Maurice was coming with me.

I spoke to Lazenby one last time on Monday morning, concluding a couple of bits of business and handing over the keys to the Hispano Suiza. Then, after a stiff drink over breakfast to steady my nerves, I hailed a taxi and Maurice and I trundled out to Hernan Cebolla for our second encounter with the LZ128.

The drive took longer than I had expected. The streets were jam packed with Spaniards. Nothing official had been announced as yet, but everyone knew the republicans had scored a decisive victory in the elections. The taxi drivers were blowing their horns gleefully and, for a brief few minutes, I even indulged in the fantasy of us getting caught in traffic and arriving too late for the flight. But our driver had a republican poster slapped on the side of his automobile and the crowds parted amiably in front of him, so my hope was quickly dashed.

I had expected the Zeppelin to be forgotten, amid the euphoria, but the airstrip was just as crammed with people this morning as it had been the previous afternoon. The man from the newsreel company was still here, covering the impromptu carnival. I wondered if he had even gone home. Actually, I wondered if anyone in Seville had gone home. Most of the city seemed to be standing out in the field, many of them carrying republican banners and wearing their button hole ribbons with pride. The food stalls were doing a roaring trade.

The courtesy bus from the Hotel Alfonso had arrived a few minutes ahead of us, but we were not the last in line to board the airship. Thomas McGilton, the Irishman, regarded me with some amusement. 'I didn't think I'd be seeing *you* here,' he teased, handing his passport to the waiting steward.

His surprise was understandable, given the conversation we had had the previous day. I had stated categorically that I would never travel on a German airship and now here I was, about to do that very thing. 'I didn't expect to be here myself,' I admitted gruffly. It was galling, having to explain myself to a smirking middle class Irishman, but I couldn't afford to arouse any suspicions. I didn't want him blabbing about me to the other passengers, especially not to Mr Kendall. 'In point of fact, I booked the tickets a while back,' I lied. 'But I had second thoughts when I saw the damned thing floating above the cathedral yesterday afternoon. Oh, excuse me, miss,' I said, noticing the young woman standing behind Mr McGilton. She had also handed her passport and ticket to the steward. She did not seem offended by my language.

'I understand completely,' the Irishman said. 'There's no shame in a few last minute nerves.' My eyes were still fixed on the woman. She was dressed in a smart spring dress with a short navy coat and high waisted belt. Her face was angular and heavily rouged, not pretty but arresting. She looked to be in her mid twenties and had lively, intelligent eyes peering out from the shadow of a wide brimmed bonnet. McGilton took note of my interest. 'Oh. May I present Miss Lucy Tanner?' He gestured fondly to the dark haired woman. 'My intended.'

'Good lord!'

'Lucy, this is Mr…Bland was it?'

'Reginald Bland.'

Miss Tanner extended a hand. 'Pleased to make your acquaintance, Mr Bland.'

'Is there something wrong?' McGilton enquired, as I continued to stare at his fiancée.

'I believe Mr Bland is in a state of shock,' Miss Tanner observed, in the same mocking tone as her fiancé.

'You're travelling together?' I enquired. That was rather daring of them, I thought. An unmarried couple crossing the Atlantic without a chaperone.

'Indeed we are,' McGilton replied.

'But I assure you, there will be no impropriety.' Miss Tanner beamed. 'We will not be sharing a cabin.'

'No, of course not. Forgive me. I didn't mean to cast any aspersions on your character.'

Her eyes gleamed mischievously beneath the bonnet. 'Well, that's all right then.'

In truth, it was not the impropriety that had caused me to stare. There was something strangely familiar about this girl. I was sure I had seen her somewhere before. 'And are you to be married in America?' I asked politely.

It was McGilton who replied. 'No, we're not getting married until July. We're travelling to America first so I can meet Lucy's mother and father.'

'How delightful for you.' I didn't envy him that one little bit. The first meeting of one's in-laws is a hideous ritual that most people have to endure at some point in their lives.

'I'm looking forward to it,' the Irishman declared, with a creditable stab at enthusiasm.

'We both are,' Miss Tanner agreed, clutching her fiancé's arm.

I was still struggling to place the woman's face. 'I believe we may have bumped into each other somewhere before,' I said, with a frown. And then, all at once, it came to me. This Miss Tanner was the girl I had seen descending the stairs of the Torre del Oro. 'At that tower thing on the river front.'

Her face lit up. 'Yes, that's right. I was doing a bit of sight-seeing.' But without her fiancé for some reason. 'Were you up there too?'

'Struggling with the stairs, I'm afraid.'

'Yes, there were an awful lot of them. But what a super view at the top! It was too exciting!'

'Well, quite.' Although the young woman had seemed in rather a hurry to descend, as I recalled.

'If you'd like to come this way, ladies and gentlemen.' The steward had completed the formalities with the passports and now gestured towards the gangway leading up into the aircraft.

I swallowed hard. This was it. The point of no return. 'Into the belly of the beast,' I muttered, gesturing the Irishman and his intended forward. I had to make a mental effort not to cross myself as I moved towards the metal steps.

McGilton leaned in towards me. 'Who's the other fellow?' He jerked a thumb back towards Maurice, who was bringing up the rear of the queue.

'That's my valet, Morris. He's travelling with me.'

McGilton stifled a laugh. 'A *valet*? On an airship? Now there's a novelty!'

The steward pulled back the sliding door and gestured inside a rather cramped cabin. 'It has no windows!' I exclaimed, moving inside. The room was illuminated by a small electric light. It had the same bare coloured walls as the corridor outside. The floor was carpeted in a garish orange and there were two narrow beds, one above the other, a sturdy metal ladder connecting the two. The place had all the charm of a second class carriage on the London to Glasgow Express. 'You can have the top bunk, Morris,' I said. I had done enough climbing already on this trip.

'Yes, Monsieur.' Maurice was hovering outside in the corridor. There wasn't space in the cabin for three of us.

'The beds are very comfortable,' the steward informed me, pressing down on the orange blanket of the lower bunk.

'And there is hot running water, if you wish to freshen yourself up.' He pulled down a compartment in the wall on his right and sure enough there was a basin concealed within, with two taps for hot and cold water. 'There is also a closet here for your clothes.' Our suitcases had been deposited by the far wall. 'I will leave you both to settle in.' He moved through the door and back out into the corridor. 'We will be taking off in approximately five minutes. There is a promenade on both sides of the deck which provide excellent views, if you wish to view our ascent.'

'Not likely,' I said, with a shudder. 'Do I have to strap myself in?'

The steward smiled warmly. 'You will barely even notice we are moving.'

'That's what it says in the guide book, is it?'

'You will see for yourself, sir. Most of the passengers will be assembling in the lounge. If you need anything else, there is a bell push by the side of the bed and I will be happy to assist you.' He smiled once more. His accent grated a little, but I couldn't fault his English.

'What was your name again?'

'Heinrich, sir.' He was a handsome fellow. Perhaps nineteen or twenty years old.

'Heinrich,' I repeated, fixing it in my head. I have never been much good at remembering names, especially those of servants. I fumbled in my pocket for a couple of coins but the steward raised a hand.

'There is no need for that, sir. Gratuities are included in the price of your ticket.'

'Oh, right.' I removed my hand from my pocket. I wasn't about to offer a second time. 'Well that's handy.'

Heinrich nodded and moved away.

My valet was still hovering in the corridor. 'Well don't just stand there, Morris!' I snapped. 'Those bags are not going to unpack themselves.'

The starboard corridor was filled with passengers. Most of

39

them were simply passing the time of day but a few, like us, were settling in for the first time. The walls of the cabin were paper thin and, as I gave my face a quick wash in the basin, I heard Mr McGilton in the room next door introducing himself to his room mate. I pitied the poor devil who had been lumbered with him.

The prospect of spending the better part of a week shacked up in a cubicle with my valet was doing nothing to raise my spirits either. 'Do you snore?' I asked him, absently. I hadn't shared a room with him before, though we had been next door to each other at the hotel the previous evening.

'No, Monsieur. Unlike you, I sleep very soundly.' He pulled my wash bag from the suitcase and positioned it on the ledge above the sink.

I glared at him. 'What the devil do you mean by that?'

'Nothing, Monsieur.' He did not meet my eye but he unfastened the wash bag and pulled out the sleeping draught Lazenby had given me that morning. I would certainly need that if I was going to get any sleep on this trip. The bottle, however, was not what Maurice had been referring to.

'I've warned you before about your attitude, Morris.'

'Yes, Monsieur.' He pulled out my tooth brush and my shaving mug and placed them neatly next to the glass bottle in front of the mirror.

I pulled back the door of the cabin and moved out into the corridor. I needed a cigarette. I was sure the steward had said there was a smoking room somewhere on board.

I spotted Miss Tanner heading in my direction, her eyes and her short black curls now free of the sun bonnet. She had a cabin somewhere at the far end of the corridor. There were two blocks of three rooms on the starboard side of the airship. The entrance to the lounge was in the centre of the corridor and several passengers were making their way through the doorway towards the promenade; but Miss Tanner moved past it to the cabin where her fiancé was berthed. It was the room next door to mine.

McGilton's door was open and he poked his head out as Miss Tanner arrived. 'How are you settling in, darling?' he asked.

'It's delightful,' she exclaimed. 'I'm sharing with Miss Hurst again.' That, I assumed, was one of the women who had disappeared into the lounge. Perhaps the one McGilton had spoken to yesterday afternoon. 'We're going to look out the windows and see the take off.'

'Sounds like a good idea,' said McGilton. 'I'll be with you in a jiffy.'

Miss Tanner turned to address me. 'Will you be coming, Mr Bland?'

I shook my head. 'I'm afraid I don't have much of a head for heights.'

'You've come to the wrong place!' the Irishman laughed, moving back into his cabin.

'Oh nonsense!' Miss Tanner exclaimed. She stepped forward and took my arm. 'You simply must come. I insist on it. You will regret it if you don't.'

McGilton laughed again, from inside the cabin. 'When Lucy insists on something, there's no point trying to resist. She always gets her way.' He would know, of course.

'I shall hold your hand, Mr Bland, if you really are frightened.' She was mocking me again, the damned woman. But I couldn't see any way of declining her request. 'And your valet should come too.'

There I drew the line. 'He has work to do,' I muttered. 'He's not on holiday.'

'I'm sure you can spare him for five minutes.' And with that the infuriating woman manoeuvred me towards the door of the lounge. The morning sun was filtering in through the windows as we stepped across the threshold.

The lounge room was a large, thoroughly modern space, bedecked with squat aluminium chairs and drably functional square tables. A baby grand piano sat incongruously in one corner, the only concession to history. The rest of the room was cursed with the same ghastly colour scheme as the cabins, the burnt orange of the carpet somehow failing to complement the orange of the table tops and the lightly padded chair covers. The bland cream coloured walls were relieved by random

41

illustrations of native peoples from around the world. Beyond a set of low railings was the more obvious focal point of the room, the promenade stretching along the side of the airship with its windows angled downwards in six solid blocks, four panes of glass apiece. And it was here that the other passengers had assembled.

They were a rum looking bunch, about a dozen of them, mostly men of varying nationalities, dressed as I was in jacket, tie and waistcoat of differing shades and textures.

A shrill whistle from somewhere up front signalled the beginnings of the launch and Miss Tanner led me determinedly up to the middle window, where her room mate, Miss Hurst, had already found a place. Miss Tanner made the introductions.

Annabel Hurst was a nervous, pale faced woman in her mid twenties. She wore a smart tailored dress with a pleated woollen skirt and matching beige coat. She smiled weakly at me but her eyes quickly returned to the windows. I was glad to see I was not the only one feeling apprehensive about the launch.

The airship was still only a few feet above the ground. I could see the faces of the groundsmen, gripping tightly to the mooring lines, and to my left, towards the front of the ship, hands holding the gondola with equal firmness.

'Looks like we've been detached from the mooring tower!' somebody declared.

The ship wobbled slightly beneath my feet and I felt a flutter in my stomach. There was another blow of a whistle and then, all at once, we were aloft. The ground started to recede at an alarming rate. One second, I could see the whites of the eyes of the groundsmen, the next we were so high I could barely differentiate one man's cap from another. For all the sophisticated engineering, the launch procedure was like nothing so much as a little boy letting go of a piece of string and watching his balloon shoot upwards into the sky; except I was inside the balloon, looking down. I grabbed hold of a metal strut, separating two blocks of windows, and clung onto it for dear life. I am no coward, but if God had intended us to fly He would have inflated our stomachs with helium.

Mr McGilton had joined his fiancée and was grinning broadly at the sight of the rapidly disappearing earth. We could see the whole airfield now, all the cars and horses and people milling about, all those victorious republicans looking like ants, no doubt conspiring to lop off the head of their queen. Miss Tanner was waving enthusiastically down at them and they seemed to be waving back, though we were too high now for any of us to really see each other. 'You're looking a bit green,' McGilton observed, glancing across at me.

I nodded. 'Wishing I hadn't had those eggs for breakfast. Or the whisky, come to that.' In hindsight, it had not been an ideal combination and the contents of my stomach were now threatening to reassert themselves. 'You'll have to excuse me.' I disentangled myself from the beam and lurched back towards the passenger cabins, past Maurice who had disobeyed my orders and followed us over to the promenade. A figure in a peaked cap and great coat was striding towards me through the lounge room door. I felt light headed. I was not sure of the ground beneath my feet. The whole craft seemed to be shifting in the breeze.

The man nodded a greeting as I hurtled past.

'Good morning, ladies and gentlemen,' I heard him say, his booming voice loud enough to be heard right across the ship. 'My name is Herntz Albrecht. I am the captain of the Richthofen and I would like to welcome you all on board.' His accent was slight, his manners impeccable. That the captain of the ship would introduce himself to the passengers mere seconds after lift off was a striking display of confidence. In other circumstances, I might have found that reassuring. At the moment, however, I had more important things to think about.

The cabins had no facilities of their own and the water closets were on the far side of the deck. I flung open the door of the nearest cubicle.

'We will soon level out,' the captain continued, still audible across the length of the connecting corridor, 'at an altitude of two hundred and ten metres.'

The thought of that made my stomach lurch a second time. Why did I ever agree to this?

'…and we will then make our way south towards Cadiz. The weather forecast is good and we should be over the Atlantic well before mid-day.'

I sunk to my knees. pulling up the lid of the lavatory bowl. At that moment, my breakfast made an abrupt reappearance.

'I wish you all a pleasant flight,' the captain said.

I closed my eyes and let nature take its course. I had a feeling this was going to be rather a long voyage.

Chapter Four

'The National Socialists are a spent force,' Walter Kendall declared firmly. He was a small man in his mid fifties with a chubby face, thinning hair and rounded spectacles. From his photograph, and from what Lazenby had told me, I had pictured him as a cigar chewing, Randolph Hearst figure, a brash, no nonsense New Yorker, telling it like it was and not giving a damn what you thought of him. The reality was somewhat different. This fellow was altogether quieter and more considered. He spoke with an intelligent precision, his soft hands gently emphasising each point. 'Herr Hitler made a grave error of judgement, leaving the Reichstag when he did. Now some of his allies are openly questioning his leadership. One or two have even joined the Communist party. It is difficult to see how the Nazi party can continue in its current form.' Kendall had rolled himself a small cigarette, which he took a puff of now. He had taken considerable care over it, ensuring the cigarette had a uniform length and shape. Everything about the fellow spoke of attention to detail.

I had made my way shakily down a set of metal stairs to the smoking room on the lower deck. After the undignified spectacle of my retreat from the promenade, I had badly needed a shot of tobacco to calm my nerves. I am not a heavy smoker; I get through maybe five or six cigarettes a day. Gambling and alcohol are my preferred vices and, as luck would have it, there was a bar adjacent to the smokers' cabin.

A smiling barman greeted me as I stepped through the double doors of the airlock into the pressurised outer room. The bar was small but well stocked. I ordered a Scotch with just a dash of soda. The barman was a friendly, muscular fellow. He had a big nose and the kind of moustache one would normally expect to see on an army recruitment poster. He fixed the drink with commendable alacrity and then showed me through another door into the smoking room.

The saloon was a wide, dimly lit space with padded leather seats lining the length of two walls and the usual ghastly array of metal tables. The colour scheme was blue rather than orange and the walls were plastered with images of earlier Zeppelins. The far wall was white, however, and marked a centre point to the room, with a set of window panels at floor level and two large oval maps looming above them. Needless to say, this time, I kept well away from the windows. The room was large enough to accommodate all of the passengers, but I had been relieved to discover I was the first to arrive, and could settle my nerves in peace.

There was an electric lighter attached to a cord on the far wall. I pulled out a Piccadilly – my preferred brand of cigarette – and lit it awkwardly, before finding a place on the leather sofa and taking a long slow drag.

I had barely got halfway through the cigarette before my tranquillity was shattered by the arrival of Walter Kendall and his voluble companion. This was my first opportunity to study the American up close. He had a rather sober manner, but he introduced himself with a firm handshake. He really wasn't like any kind of journalist I had ever met before. He seemed far more concerned with the minutiae of German politics than in the scandals and tittle-tattle that were the stock in trade of most of his fellow newsmen. Maybe that was why Gerhard Schulz had approached him with the stolen documents. The American would understand their true value.

'If Herr Hitler had properly engaged in the democratic process,' Kendall asserted, continuing his point, 'none of this would have happened.'

His companion, Karl Lindt, let out a snort of derision. 'Democracy is for fools!' Lindt was an oily looking fellow of about thirty-five, with slick black hair and a smug expression. He was a tin merchant, apparently. He had paid me no attention when the two of them arrived in the saloon and it had been left to Walter Kendall to conduct the introductions. After a brief, half-hearted enquiry into the state of my health – I had a feeling I would not be living that down for some time – they quickly resumed their discussion. 'Look at these Spanish peasants,' Lindt continued. 'They have no idea what is in their best interests. Why bother to consult them? Far better to impose order from above. Strong leadership is in everybody's interest.'

'Is that what your Mr Hitler intends to do?' I asked, reluctantly allowing myself to be drawn in to the debate. 'Impose order from above?'

'I cannot speak for him. But he has been underestimated before. I would not write him off just yet.'

'There is certainly some residual support for the National Socialists, away from the cities,' Kendall conceded. He was a fair minded fellow, even when it came to the Nazis. 'But most Germans are rational people. They will not be seduced by such naked opportunism. One can at least respect the sincerity of the Spanish republicans.'

Karl Lindt snorted again. 'They are just a rabble. They don't know what they believe in. And they haven't a hope of forming a coherent government.'

'It's King Alfonso I feel sorry for,' I said, tapping out the end of my cigarette on the metal ashtray. 'How on earth is he going to cope with a bunch of republicans in government?'

Walter Kendall was very clear on that point. 'He will have to abdicate. His position is untenable now.'

'Good lord! Do you think it will come to that?'

'I am afraid so.' King Alfonso had lent his support to the dictatorship and the people were not likely to forgive him.

'He will have no choice,' Lindt agreed. 'It is the honourable thing to do.' Somehow, the tin merchant managed to make the word 'honourable' sound like an insult. 'That is what comes of allowing the people their say. Alfonso was always a weak man. It is his own fault he is in this position. I will not mourn his passing.'

'All the same, you can't help feeling sorry for the fellow. I mean, all that history, abandoned over night.' It was simply not cricket.

Lindt eyed me with amusement. 'You have a sentimental streak, Mr Bland. That is admirable, but in this case it is misplaced.'

Before I could shoot back a reply, a heavy clunk announced the opening of the bar room door.

Lucy Tanner moved into the smoking room,

accompanied by a tubby, bland looking fellow of about forty-five. I recognised him vaguely from the promenade.

Walter Kendall rose to his feet. 'Miss Tanner. Herr Kaufmann. Please come and join us.' I stubbed out the end of my cigarette and stood up beside Mr Lindt.

The newcomers moved across the room towards us and Miss Tanner flashed the American a dazzling smile. She had changed out of her travel clothes into a rather more flattering two piece dress, light blue with white trimmings. She was carrying a small cigarette case in her hand, which she opened at once. It was no longer unusual for a woman to be seen smoking in public, though it was still considered a little vulgar. It did not surprise me that Miss Tanner indulged in the habit, though I was scarcely in a position to judge. Luckily, living as a man, people were less quick to judge my behaviour. Mr Kendall directed the young woman across to the lighter.

'Please, take my seat,' I said, stepping aside as she lit her cigarette and then joined us at the table. 'I think I'm going to have a bit of a lie down.' It was clear I was not going to get any peace in the smoking room and I had a horrible feeling Miss Tanner would want to join in with the men's political discussion. Mr Lindt, I suspected, would not be at all happy about that. He already looked put out by her sudden intrusion into the male environment.

Miss Tanner was more concerned with my feelings. 'You poor darling,' she cooed, breathing out a cloud of smoke. 'You're still feeling queasy? How awful! And it's all my fault. I shouldn't have dragged you over to the windows.'

'I'm all right if I keep away from the glass. Not too good with heights I'm afraid.'

'It may be easier once we move away from the land,' Walter Kendall suggested, resuming his seat. 'Many people feel a little disorientation the first time they take to the air.'

'Though not those with a strong constitution,' Karl Lindt put in. 'You have met my associate, Herr Kaufmann?'

The tubby fellow was seating himself on the couch, next to Miss Tanner. He met my eyes briefly.

'I don't believe so,' I said. Kaufmann was an

unassuming barrel of a man in his mid-forties, with a ruddy complexion and small, sad looking eyes. 'A pleasure to meet you, Mr Kaufmann. You'll have to forgive my impromptu departure.'

'I quite understand.' The German inclined his head graciously.

And with that, I made my way to the door, leaving Mr Lindt and the new arrivals to continue their debate without me.

Thomas McGilton was sitting at the bar, engaged in light conversation with the big-nosed barman, whose name, I discovered, was Max. The new arrivals had ordered their drinks before they had made their way into the smoking room and the barman was busily preparing a tray for them. I had no wish to indulge in further chit chat, but as Max was on hand I supposed one more drink would do me no harm. It might help me to brave the stairs back up onto A Deck. I greeted the steward and the Irishman and grabbed an adjacent stool. 'Are you not joining Miss Tanner in the smoking room?' I asked McGilton.

He shook his head. 'No, I don't react well to the smell of tobacco. I have a bit of a weak chest.'

'I'm sorry to hear that.' At least I wasn't the only one displaying weakness this morning. 'Mr Kendall and Miss Tanner have met before, I gather.' The two of them had seemed on very friendly terms.

'At the hotel yesterday evening. But Lucy's a great admirer of his work.'

'Oh. She reads American newspapers, does she?'

'When she's staying with her parents.'

'Yes, of course.' He had told me they lived in America.

'She dabbles a bit herself,' the Irishman added, with a hint of pride. 'Writing articles for ladies magazines.'

I smiled. That made sense, anyway. 'Cocktail parties and what to wear at them?' One only had to look at Miss Tanner to see how well informed she was in matters of fashion.

McGilton nodded wryly. His clothes were also well cut, I noticed. Savile Row. Not at all cheap. That would be Miss

Tanner's influence, I guessed.

'She wants to move into news journalism. I think she's hoping Mr Kendall might put in a word for her.'

I laughed. 'She's left it a bit late, if you're getting married in July.' Women were usually expected to stop work as soon as they got hitched.

'Oh, I won't do anything to discourage her. When Lucy gets an idea into her head, there's nothing in the world that will get in her way.'

'Yes, so I've discovered.'

Max had finished preparing the tray of drinks for the smoking room. He looked up, to see if I wanted anything else before he carried it through to the other chamber. He had a dual role as barman. He didn't just mix the drinks, he was also there to stand guard, ensuring nobody left the pressurised areas of the ship with a lighted cigarette in their hand.

'What can I get you?' I asked McGilton. The drinks, unlike the gratuities, were not included in the price of the ticket.

'Oh, nothing, thank you. I don't.'

'Don't?' I stared at him blankly.

'I don't drink.'

I blinked. 'Good lord.'

His lips curled in amusement. 'Is that really such a surprise?'

'Well, no, but…you're an Irishman.'

McGilton laughed. 'We're not all drunkards and layabouts, you know.' His eyes were twinkling. He really was a good match for Miss Tanner.

'I wasn't suggesting that for a minute. I just…I wouldn't have taken you for one of the temperance brigade.'

'Oh, I'm not, believe me. But my father…he drank rather too much. Died when I was a boy. I don't plan on letting history repeat itself.'

'Right. I see.' I rather regretted asking now.

'But don't let me stop you,' he added.

The moustachioed barman was waiting politely to take my order.

50

'Actually,' I said, 'I think I really *could* do with a bit of a lie down.'

Maurice was loitering at the top of the stairs, back on A Deck. I had no idea why he was out and about just now. 'What on earth are you doing here?' I demanded. I was still irritated with him for joining us in the lounge at lift off, against my express instructions. I really needed to curb this rebellious streak of his, before it got out of hand.

'I am waiting for Crewman Ostermann,' the valet replied calmly, as if that explained the matter. He was wearing a great coat over his suit, as if he were about to pop out for a newspaper.

At the far end of the corridor, Annabel Hurst had rounded a corner and was heading in our direction. The woman hesitated as she caught sight of us loitering by the stairs. She was a nervous creature with a pale face and a slender, washboard figure. Unlike Miss Tanner, she was wearing the same tailored dress she had worn on her arrival. She attempted a smile as she made her way along the connecting passageway.

'Are you feeling better, Mr Bland?' she enquired politely, coming to a halt in front of us. Her voice was a soft whisper. I had to strain to hear what she was saying. Some people just don't know how to make themselves heard.

'Still a little woozy, I'm afraid. Are you heading down to the bar?' We were rather obstructing her path. 'That seems to be where all the action is.'

'I...I wasn't sure. I thought I might write a couple of letters. Is...is Herr Lindt downstairs, do you know?' She spoke the name with some hesitation.

'Yes, making a prize fool of himself in the smoking salon. Likes the sound of his own voice, that one.'

'Yes...well, then perhaps I'll just settle down quietly in the reading room.'

'Good idea,' I said.

The reading room was situated on the starboard side of the deck, back the way she had come. Miss Hurst smiled nervously, turned on her heels and headed back along the corridor.

'I look forward to seeing you at lunch,' I called after her. I would make a point of finding a different table. The woman was a mouse. At least Miss Tanner had some spirit to her, I thought, even if she was every bit as impertinent as her fiancé.

Miss Hurst disappeared through the far door into the lounge.

'Did you find out about the cabins?' I asked Maurice, now that we were alone. A row of six cabins ran parallel to the dining room on the port side. One of them had to belong to Walter Kendall and if I was to find this damn film of Lazenby's I needed to know where the American was berthed. I had asked my valet to find out what he could. Perhaps that was why he was wearing that great coat. Maybe he was on his way down to the crew quarters to ask for a passenger list. If so, I would put a stop to that right now. I wanted him to keep his eyes peeled, not draw attention to himself. I had already made myself look like a prize idiot this morning and any odd behaviour on his part would only serve to thrust me back into the limelight. Thankfully, Maurice was ahead of me.

'I believe he may be in one of these cabins, Monsieur,' he said, gesturing to the back end of the corridor. 'Opposite the water closets.' I peered along the passageway. There were three identical doors on the left hand side, running towards the rear of the ship.

'Do you know which one is his?'

'No, Monsieur. But I saw Mr Kendall coming from that direction after the launch and proceeding down the stairs to B Deck.'

'That's right, to the smoking room. He's down there now, with Mr Lindt and the others. But he might just have been answering a call of nature.' Everyone would be using the facilities along here at some point on the journey.

'I do not believe so, Monsieur. He was pocketing his cigarette case.'

'Ah. Stopped by his cabin, you think, to pick it up?'

Maurice nodded. 'Perhaps the second or third door

along.'

That narrowed it down a bit. 'I wonder if he's sharing with anyone?' That ghastly German fellow, perhaps?

My valet did not venture an opinion.

A rough looking individual was clanking up the stairs from the lower deck. I could hear him on the metal steps before his head came into view. He came to a halt at the top of the stairs. 'Monsieur Sauveterre? *Êtes-vous prêt?*'

'*Oui, je suis prêt,*' Maurice responded, in his native Frog. I only knew a few words of the language, but I got the gist.

I stared at the crewman, in his cloth clap and cheap suit. A below stairs sort of fellow with rough hands and a badly shaven chin. He looked out of place on the passenger decks, though he seemed polite enough. He had removed his cap and was looking at Maurice expectantly.

'I asked the captain if I might have a tour of the aircraft,' my valet explained. 'I thought it might prove useful.'

'Did you now? You spoke to the captain?'

'Yes, Monsieur.' The Frenchman's gall knew no bounds. But that's the Frogs for you. I suppose that is where the word 'Gaul' comes from.

'You are okay to come also, if you like,' the crewman suggested, in broken English, his craggy face breaking into a gap-toothed smile.

'No, that's quite all right.' I was having enough trouble acclimatising to the passenger decks, with their huge windows. To see the mechanics of the beast laid bare would be more than my stomach could bear. And judging by the heavy coats, there was little or no central heating in the business end of the ship. 'You run along.' I would have a word or two with Maurice later, in private. He should not be making a nuisance of himself with the captain, even if he had been trying to help. I waved the two of them away and watched them disappear down the stairwell.

I closed the door after them and loitered for a moment, looking down the short corridor Maurice had indicated. Walter Kendall was in the smoking room and most of the other guests had settled for a time in whatever place suited their fancy. My stomach had just about settled and there was unlikely to be a better time than this to have a look at the man's cabin, if I could manage to get inside. The doors were lightweight sliding panels and flimsy enough that I could probably put a fist through them; but I would need to employ a little more subtlety than that. I had a couple of hair pins stashed away in my wallet to have a go at the lock.

The middle or far cabin, my valet had suggested. I stepped forward and moved halfway up the corridor. There were several water closets to my right. If anyone came by I could always slip inside one of those. I hesitated for a moment before committing myself. I have never been much good at the cloak and dagger stuff, though even I can manage a bit of breaking and entering. I had learnt a few lock-picking tricks in my younger days.

First things first, though – just to be on the safe side – I raised my hand and rapped gently on the middle door.

There was a clunk from within. '*Ja?*' It was a woman's voice. '*Liebling, bist du das?*' There was a bit of fumbling and then the door slid open a crack. A face peered out at me, a blue eyed woman in her early thirties. At the sight of me, her forehead creased into a heavy frown.

'I'm terribly sorry,' I said. 'I think I've got the wrong cabin.'

'*Ja!*' she agreed. The door thumped closed before I could say another word. '*Dummkopf!*'

I took a moment to recover my wits. Who on earth was that? I wondered. She must have been on the promenade at the launch but I had been too worried about the ground falling away beneath me to pay too much attention. This was a woman, clearly, it would be better to steer clear of. At least her presence narrowed down the options. Kendall had to be in the end cabin. But did I dare break in with the angry Fräulein squatting next door? I would have to take a chance. I might not get another opportunity.

I shifted along, glancing back down the corridor to make sure no one had arrived at the top of the stairs. I knocked gently on the cabin door and waited. There was no reply. I checked the corridor again, then pulled out my wallet and removed the hair pins, which I quickly bent into shape.

The lock, I had determined, was a standard pin and tumbler mechanism. All it needed was a lever and a pick. The hair pins would do the job nicely. I slid the lever into place, putting pressure on the barrel and, to my surprise, it swung around freely. The door wasn't locked. I retrieved the pin in irritation and grabbed the handle of the door. It was unlikely Mr Kendall would have left anything of value in the cabin if he hadn't bothered to lock it up, but I might as well look inside, now that I was here. I slid back the panel and nipped into the room, flicking on the electric light and sliding the door shut behind me. The flap of my jacket caught in the groove. I growled, twisting myself around and pulling the door open to disentangle myself. Once that was done, I closed it up again and locked it up for good measure; then I turned my attention to the interior of the room.

It had the same orange colour scheme as my own cabin. The bed was on the opposite side and the upper bunk had been removed, but in every other respect it was identical. A suit was hanging in the closet and there was a spare pair of shoes on the floor. A mug and a shaving brush had been laid out on a shelf above the wash basin. A typewriter rested on a side table above a closed wicker case and a small suitcase had been slid under the bed. Kendall was fortunate to have a cabin to himself, I thought. I wondered if he had paid extra for the privilege. I wasn't looking forward to spending the next few nights with my valet.

I pulled the suitcase out and popped it onto a small fold out chair. The case was not locked. There were a few clothes in there, underwear and such like, a notebook and some family photographs. Nothing of any consequence. I flicked through the notebook. Kendall had written out several of his most recent articles long hand, rather than using the typewriter. The hand-writing was neat if rather small. The most recent article looked to be a treatise on the Spanish Republican movement. There was nothing here about Britain, though, or any misbehaviour on the part of a British subject. I let out a sigh and closed up the suitcase. No documents or photographs and no roll of film.

I was just preparing to slide the case back underneath the bed when I heard footsteps nearby. Somebody was pacing the corridor outside. I took a deep breath and prayed to God they were just answering a call of nature. At least I had had the foresight to lock the cabin door. The footsteps reached the end of the corridor and stopped outside the cabin. There was a polite rap on the door. What if it was the steward? I wondered, in a state of alarm. He would have a set of keys. How could I possibly explain my presence in another man's cabin, if he opened up the door? My cover would be blown completely.

There was a long, heavy pause and at last the footsteps moved away. I closed my eyes and let out the breath I had been holding. I really wasn't cut out for the life of a secret agent.

Chapter Five

The Atlantic stretched out as far as the eye could see in every direction. I focused grimly on the horizon – a surprisingly crisp line of greenish blue – and took a solid lungful of air. Walter Kendall had been right. Now that we were over the water, I was not feeling quite so unsettled. Perhaps I was beginning to find my sea legs, or whatever the appropriate aeronautical expression might be. I was not alone at the window, looking out across the ocean. Josef Kaufmann, the tubby businessman from the smoking room, had joined me on the promenade in contemplative silence. He was a stout fellow of medium height, a little grey around the temples, with a rather taciturn manner. From what I had gathered in the smoking room, he was a business associate of Mr Lindt.

The other German was seated behind us, in the dining area, pontificating once again on some terribly significant political matter. I was doing my best to ignore the babble of noise, but the dining room was starting to fill now, as the midday meal drew close, and Lindt's voice was louder than any other. I looked back at the fellow with some distaste. He was sitting at the same table as Walter Kendall. I had marked out my seat next to the American before strolling over to the promenade and it was bad luck that Lindt had chosen the one opposite. I didn't want to sit anywhere near him, but I needed to stay close to the journalist. I wasn't intending to pick-pocket the fellow just yet – I wasn't that desperate – but the more I found out about him, the better placed I would be to devise a plan of attack.

Lucy Tanner and Thomas McGilton arrived in the dining hall and took the remaining two chairs. I grimaced. I had no desire to renew my acquaintance with them either. Miss Tanner smiled warmly at Mr Kendall as she settled herself down on the light aluminium chair. She was paying a lot of attention to the American, I noticed, as he replied to some idiotic point made by Mr Lindt. Perhaps her association with him went a little deeper than her fiancé was aware of. The two did not act as if they had just met and it was not beyond the bounds of possibility that they had known each other for some time. Miss Tanner's parents lived in America, after all. And of course, the young woman had visited the Torre del Oro in Seville at the same time as Gerhard Schulz. A bit of a coincidence that, now I came to think about it, given the likely connection between Mr Schulz and Walter Kendall. It seemed unlikely to me that Miss Tanner could have acted as courier for the American, but I supposed it was not inconceivable. McGilton did not seem concerned at her friendliness towards Mr Kendall – so far as I could tell, the woman flirted with everyone and the Irishman was probably used to it by now – but I would have to keep a close eye on the pair of them over the next few days.

Kendall finished the point he was making and Miss Tanner nodded her agreement; but Karl Lindt snorted derisively. She rolled her eyes and met my gaze across the floor. I smiled despite myself. It was clear she had no more liking for the German than I did.

'Are you travelling alone?' Mr Kaufmann asked me politely, interrupting my thoughts. I was wondering how long we could stand together on the promenade before common courtesy would force one of us to attempt conversation. The German had buckled first.

'Yes, just me. Oh and my valet. A bit of business in America. Thought I might as well travel in style.' I had recovered my wits enough, now, to lie with conviction. 'Are you on a business trip as well?'

Kaufmann nodded. 'To Rio. Herr Lindt and I are travelling together, to attend a business conference in Sao Paulo.'

'Sounds a bit dull,' I said.

'That is the nature of business, sadly.'

I scratched my chin. 'Have you known him long? Mr Lindt?'

'For several years. We are colleagues.' Kaufmann's voice lacked a certain warmth, I noticed, when talking of the younger man.

'But you're not friends?'

'No. We work together. He has a good business brain but he is not…the easiest of men.'

'Rather opinionated?'

'He enjoys a robust discussion.'

'That's putting it mildly.' Kaufmann was far more of a diplomat than I was. We gazed out to sea again.

'You are feeling better now?' the man asked.

'Yes. Never been much good with heights. But it doesn't seem so bad, over water. There's no way to tell how high up you are.' The clouds were few and far between at the moment, just a few light wisps against the bright blue sky and most of them well above us. 'We could almost be skimming the surface of the sea,' I observed.

'It is a beautiful view,' Kaufmann agreed. Behind us, a steward was banging a small gong. 'Ah, I think lunch is about to be served.'

I sighed. Time to head back into the throng.

The Zeppelin was under capacity and only three dining tables had been laid out. My valet had joined Annabel Hurst at one of these tables, alongside the mad woman from Cabin 2, whose name, I had learnt, was Adelina Koenig. Sir George Westlake, the noted explorer, was sitting opposite her, laughing heartily at some bland comment from another Briton, a Mr Frederick Gray. I was uncomfortable seeing my valet sat at table with these august personages – especially Sir George, who was a world renowned adventurer – but there was nothing I could do to prevent it. Even servants have to eat and the captain would not hear of a paying passenger dining with the crewmen below decks. I just hoped the other diners would not take offence. Sir George seemed to be in his element, regaling the passengers with tales of his latest Antarctic expedition, and I was content to leave them to it.

Josef Kaufmann seated himself at the second dining table, on the opposite side of the room. This table was presided over by our host, Captain Herntz Albrecht. It was generous of the captain to find the time to eat with us rather than in the mess with his fellow officers but it was unfortunate he had been lumbered with the runts of the passenger litter – a ginger haired

Englishman and a little Spanish chap whose name I had not yet caught. Kaufmann greeted them all politely. Mr Finch, the Englishman, was a stockbroker, apparently. He had a perpetually anxious look on his face. The Spaniard was bald and bespectacled with a rather fine moustache. He was tucking his napkin into the top of his shirt, in preparation for the first course.

A chef in a traditional white mushroom hat was carving meat at an adjacent table and several stewards, also decked out in white tunics, were rushing around the dining area, ladling out the tomato soup and serving the wine. The smell of beef permeated the saloon and my stomach began to rumble. I was finally starting to regain my appetite.

At my own table, as I had feared, a heated debate was in progress, drowning out Sir George at the far end. Needless to say, Karl Lindt was at the centre of it.

'It is not a question of education,' he declared firmly, as I took my seat opposite him. 'The fact is some races are genetically inferior to others.' His eyes were glowing with pleasure at the sound of his own voice. 'How else can you explain the differences in attainment between one society and another? We Germans have built great airships that fly through the sky. Yet the aboriginal peoples of Australia do not even have the capacity to grow their own food.'

'The beef looks nice,' I said, tucking my napkin into place and taking a slurp of hot soup. I was determined, this time, not to get involved in the debate. Young Heinrich was pouring out the *vino*, but I waved him away. I have never liked wine. I did briefly consider ordering a proper drink but I would wait to see how my stomach coped with the beef and tomato first.

'I doubt there's much opportunity for growing crops in the desert,' Thomas McGilton observed, in reply to Mr Lindt.

'That did not stop the Egyptians,' the German responded smugly. '*Rot, bitte.*' Heinrich poured out the wine. 'And like the Egyptians, within any racial group, there is always an elite. There are the Pharaohs and there are the slaves, even if we no longer call them slaves.'

McGilton was tiring of the debate. 'Isn't this conversation getting a little bit heavy for the dinner table?' he asked, politely. 'There are ladies present.'

'Oh nonsense,' Miss Tanner said, downing her soup spoon. 'I'm always interested to hear differing opinions. What is your view, Mr Kendall?'

The American had a glass of white wine in his hand, which Heinrich had just poured out for him. He raised the glass to his lips and considered the matter carefully for a moment. 'The differences in development between cultures is striking,' Kendall admitted. 'Genetics may well play a role in that. But there may be other factors that we are not aware of. The aboriginal people were isolated from the rest of humanity, whereas the peoples of Europe and the Middle East have had thousands of years to interact with each other. It is much easier for ideas to spread and develop if a number of cultures are operating in close proximity to each other. Each will aid the development of the other. But Herr Lindt is correct, in that every society has hierarchies and it may well be that certain groups are more naturally suited to authority than others.'

'Blood will out, is that it?' McGilton asked, sipping his tomato soup with some scepticism.

'The great families of Europe did not rise to their positions of power by simple accident,' Lindt stated firmly.

'Maybe not,' I said, reluctantly throwing my twopenn'orth in. 'But breeding isn't everything. I've known fellows from the finest families who are absolute idiots.'

'There are variations within any group,' Lindt conceded. 'But you cannot deny that your own heritage is superior to that of, for example, an African tribesman. You would not expect a coloured man living in a mud hut in Senegal to be your intellectual equal.'

'Perhaps not,' McGilton cut in. 'But he hasn't had the same advantages as we have.'

'A decent education,' I agreed. 'Hundreds of years of scientific progress. And, yes, you're right, Mr Lindt, a fair amount of breeding, too. But give the fellow a few hundred years and I'm sure he'd catch up. That's what the British

61

Empire is all about. Offering native peoples the world over a bit of a leg up. Saving them all that bother of doing it for themselves.'

'If only that were true, Mr Bland,' Lindt replied. He dabbed his lips with the edge of his napkin. He had finished his soup in record time, especially in light of all the talking he had been doing. 'But the fact is, some races are simply genetically inferior. You could not hold an intelligent discourse with our notional African.'

I shrugged. 'Well, I doubt if I could converse with him in Latin or discuss the finer points of Cartesian Dualism. But I dare say if I kidnapped a couple of his sprogs and sent them to Eton or Harrow they'd acquit themselves perfectly well.'

'I disagree, Mr Bland. They would not have the intellectual capacity to succeed in such a rarefied environment.'

I laughed. 'Intellectual capacity has never been a requirement for Eton.'

'And what of the European peoples?' Miss Tanner enquired. 'The Russians or the Spanish?'

'There is variation there, too, of course. The Western Europeans, the Aryan people, clearly demonstrate a greater capacity for innovation than many of these other groups.'

'And the Jews?' Miss Tanner asked. McGilton raised a warning hand but the girl took no notice. 'Do you believe they are intellectually inferior?' There was an edge to her question that only Lindt failed to notice.

'The Jews possess a certain low cunning,' he conceded, 'which enables them to embed themselves effectively into the underbelly of a civilised society. But I do not believe they can be regarded as our equals. In many respects...'

'Miss Tanner is Jewish,' McGilton pointed out quietly.

Lindt stopped mid flow. He stared at the woman for a moment. 'Tanner is not a Jewish name.'

'Tannenbaum, originally,' she said.

He nodded. 'Of course. I should have realised.' Lindt looked from her to McGilton. 'I meant no offence to your fiancée. As I have said, within any racial group, there is considerable variation. I am sure Miss Tanner is at the higher end of the spectrum.'

'You're too kind,' she muttered.

'And what about the Irish people?' McGilton enquired, his eyes flashing with anger. 'I suppose you think we're all congenital idiots?'

'Gentlemen, please.' Walter Kendall raised a hand. 'The debate is becoming a little heated. I think perhaps we might change the subject?'

'I think that might be wise,' the Irishman agreed. Beneath the table, his hands were trembling.

The reading room on the starboard side of the ship was an oasis of calm in the aftermath of lunch. The tinkling of the aluminium piano wafted through the flimsy panelled walls from the adjacent lounge, but the room itself was blissfully quiet. Most of the passengers had headed to the smoking room after lunch, the draw of tobacco outweighing the pleasure of an hours reading or writing. A variety of newspapers and magazines had been provided in the saloon, in several languages. There was a stack of writing paper, too, in a cupboard hanging from the wall. I was content to scan the contents of a five day old Manchester Guardian. It was not my newspaper of choice, but Sir George Westlake had grabbed the only copy of the Times. I settled back contentedly to read. The only thing missing from the scene was alcohol and, with this in mind – now that I had had my fill of beef – I separated Maurice from his Le Figaro and sent him to my cabin for a glass of whisky. I had brought a bottle with me, for emergencies, and it would be quicker to pour out a glass in my cabin than it would be to send a steward all the way down to the smoking room.

Sir George Westlake, sat at the opposite table to me, had overheard my instructions and was a little confused. When I explained to him that Maurice was my valet, he roared with laughter. 'You surely can't be serious?' I nodded, my face reddening. 'That man is your servant? But I had lunch with him!' Sir George's tone was one of bafflement rather than offence. 'And he called you "Monsieur".'

'Yes, it's a…Gallic eccentricity. He hasn't been with me long. I did ask if he might dine with the stewards but as he is a paying guest they wouldn't hear of it. I must apologise for inflicting him upon you like that. But I'm sure he can't be the worst dining companion you've ever had.'

'That's true enough.' Sir George threw his head back and roared a second time. He was a large man in his mid forties, with a tidy beard, big ears and a receding hairline. He wore his fame lightly, but every schoolboy in England knew his name. He had been on the Antarctic expedition with Ernest Shackleton in 1922 and had recently made one of the first aerial surveys of the south pole. I was worried that he might be something of a bore, but he seemed a good humoured fellow – not the sort to take offence – and his laugh was loud enough to fill the entire airship. Even the tinkling of the piano in the other room had stopped in apparent surprise.

'I'm afraid I haven't quite broken him in yet,' I admitted.

'Well, don't leave it too long,' he warned me, amiably. 'The sooner they learn their place, the better. Don't you agree, Mr Gray?'

'Indeed, Sir George.' Frederick Gray was a dull looking man with wispy brown hair and an earnest manner. Conversation was discouraged in the reading room but as there were only the three of us sitting here that did not seem to matter just now. I had Gray down as a businessman of some sort – the ship seemed to be full of them – and his nasal, high pitched voice was already starting to grate. 'Although he seemed quite well mannered to me.'

'Maurice is a decent enough fellow, I suppose,' I admitted grudgingly. 'For a Frog. What did you think of that German girl? Mrs Koenig?'

'Adelina? Marvellous woman!' Sir George declared. 'Just got back from North Africa. Flew solo from Bamako to Tangiers in a souped up Tiger Moth, can you believe? My kind of woman. Hefty, too. Lot of meat on her. Not like these skinny young things back home. The Krauts know how to breed their women, what?'

64

'They certainly do,' I agreed.

'Crashed the old kite in the Sahara. Had to walk thirty miles on foot to Timbuktu to get help. What a woman!' He laughed. 'I could have done with her in the Antarctic.'

'Your…lady wife doesn't accompany you on your expeditions?'

'Good god, no. Suzanne wouldn't know one end of a propeller from the other. Not mechanically minded. Not like us, eh, Mr Gray?'

'No, Sir George.'

My attention shifted to the other Englishman. 'You're an aviator too?' I asked, with some surprise. He looked more like a bank clerk than a pilot.

Mr Gray shook his head sadly. 'No, my skills are of a far more mundane variety.'

'Works for the post office,' Sir George explained. 'Something to do with wireless telegraphy. Useful but dull, eh?'

'I'm afraid so, Sir George. I'm due to give a demonstration in San Francisco of a new experimental facsimile machine.'

'Facsimile?' I raised an eyebrow. It seemed only civil to take an interest.

'Wireless facsimile, yes.'

'What, sending photographs through the ether?' Like the ones printed in the Times.

'No, not photographs,' Gray said. 'Our device scans plain text and transmits it wirelessly to another machine, which then prints out a copy of the same text. We can transmit over almost any distance, up to sixty typewritten pages an hour.'

Sir George and I exchanged a look. 'Fascinating,' I said. 'So tell me a little more about Antarctica, Sir George.'

'Well, I…oh, here's your chap with the whisky.'

Maurice stepped forward and placed a glass down on the table top in front of me. 'Thank you, Morris. Oh, how was your tour of the inner workings?' I hadn't thought to ask before.

'Most enlightening, Monsieur. Will there be anything else?'

'No, toddle along.' I picked up the glass and took a sip.

'Had the grand tour, did he?' Sir George asked, after the valet had departed. I hadn't offered him any whisky, as he had already brought a glass of wine with him from the dining hall. 'Well worth doing.'

'The captain showed some of us around yesterday morning,' Mr Gray added, 'before we arrived in Seville. The radio room was most interesting.'

'It was the scale of the thing that got me,' Sir George declared. 'Fascinating construction. And such a well run sh...' He stopped mid-sentence. A young officer had entered the reading room, smartly dressed in a dark blue uniform, with a flat cap held in front of his chest.

'Gentlemen, I am sorry to disturb you. Captain Albrecht wishes to address the passengers in the lounge room.'

'Come to give us another tune?' Sir George enquired. The captain had been one of those tinkling at the piano earlier on.

The officer shook his head gravely.

'Is something wrong?' I asked.

The man was reluctant to say. 'Captain Albrecht will explain.'

We rose, puzzled, from our chairs and made our way out onto the promenade. The rest of the passengers were already beginning to assemble in the lounge area. Thomas McGilton was standing by one of the windows and I came to a halt beside him, throwing him a questioning look. He shrugged his shoulders. He didn't know what was going on either.

Captain Herntz Albrecht waited for the last of the passengers to arrive. He was a tall, sturdy man in late middle age with neat, thinning hair and a blandly handsome face. The amiable half smile he usually reserved for the passenger decks was absent, replaced by the same grave expression I had seen on the face of the junior officer. 'Ladies and gentlemen, *Damen und Herren*, I apologise for summoning you all like this.' His voice was rich and lightly accented. The man had a commanding presence, even when addressing the paying guests; the sort of fellow you expected to be carrying a pipe at all times. He had that paternal air to him. 'We have just received a rather sad communication from the telegraph office in Seville. Those of you who have been with us from Friedrichshafen may remember Herr Gerhard Schulz, who travelled with us on the first leg of our journey. It is with great regret that I inform you that Herr Schulz was discovered dead in his hotel room at eleven o'clock this morning. It is believed that he took his own life.'

Chapter Six

There was a stunned silence in the lounge. For a moment, only the hum of the engines could be heard and the distant swell of the sea. It took me a moment to gather my wits. I glanced at the assembled passengers. Walter Kendall seemed calm, his expression entirely neutral. Miss Tanner was standing to the left of the captain, with her room mate Miss Hurst. They were both looking shocked. Miss Hurst brought a hand up to her mouth and let out a silent cry. Adelina Koenig, the stout German woman, appeared angry rather than upset; but perhaps that was just the natural set of her face. It was left to Sir George Westlake to speak for everyone.

'Poor chap,' he breathed quietly, breaking the silence. 'I had no idea.'

'I have communicated with the authorities in Seville,' Captain Albrecht continued, 'and asked if they would like us to return to Spain. It would not be an easy manoeuvre but, in the circumstances, we would be willing to accommodate such a request. However, the authorities have informed me that this will not be necessary.' He paused a moment to allow the news to sink in. I suspected he was pleased not to have to bother.

'They have requested, however, that any passengers who spoke to Herr Schulz in the last couple of days and, perhaps, formed an impression of his state of mind would kindly convey their thoughts to me or my first officer and we will pass them on to the Spanish police. They are particularly keen to hear from anyone who saw or spoke to Herr Schulz after he left the airship yesterday afternoon.'

Mrs Koenig nodded seriously. I wondered if she had been friends with the Austrian.

'I thank you for your cooperation and apologise for having to deliver such distressing news,' the captain concluded. 'Our thoughts, of course, are with Herr Schulz's family in Austria.'

And with that, Captain Albrecht and his first officer departed. The passengers were quick to follow suit, the ladies retiring to their cabins and most of the men returning to the smoking room on B Deck for a much needed cigarette.

Thomas McGilton idled for a moment to my left.

'Did you know the fellow?' I asked, glancing across at him.

'No, not at all. I suppose I must have seen him disembark yesterday afternoon. But no, I didn't know him.'

'I hope the women aren't too upset.' I noticed McGilton had not followed his fiancée out of the lounge.

'They'll be fine. Lucy's got a hide like a rhinoceros.'

I laughed. 'Yes, so I gathered. Has she recovered from lunch?'

'Oh, she's endured far worse than that, believe me.' He grinned. 'The Herr Lindts of this world are two-a-penny. To be honest, I think *I* find it harder to cope with than she does.'

'You're not Jewish yourself?'

'Roman Catholic. But I'm beginning to understand what she has to put up with.'

'Not all Germans are as odious as Mr Lindt. I've met one or two thoroughly decent Krauts. They're not all bigots, you know.'

'No, I suppose not. No worse than the English anyway.' He grinned again. 'But Lucy does like to put herself in the firing line. You know she interviewed that Mr Hitler last year?'

'Miss Tanner did?' I blinked. 'Good lord!'

'For one of her ladies magazines.'

I stared at the man in disbelief. 'You can't be serious.'

'Oh, it's true, I assure you.'

'She *interviewed* him?'

'Leapt at the chance. It was nothing political, mind you. A lifestyle feature.'

'She speaks German then?'

'Like a native. Studied in Vienna.'

'But...did Mr Hitler know she was *Jewish*?'

'Of course not.' McGilton laughed. 'He wouldn't have agreed to the interview if he had. And she wasn't about to tell him.'

I shook my head. Miss Tanner, it seemed, was every bit

69

as formidable as our resident female aviator, Mrs Koenig. 'So what did she make of the fellow?'

McGilton shrugged. 'Said he was charming. Intense. Didn't think much of his dress sense or his hair.'

'And she didn't ask any political questions?'

'Wasn't that kind of interview. But I've read one or two of his speeches. He's a nasty piece of work.'

'A mindless thug, like Mussolini,' I agreed. 'And, according to Mr Kendall, people are already beginning to see through him. Just like we all are with Mr Lindt.'

'I hope so.' McGilton sighed. 'I always like to see the good in people, but with someone like that it does take a fair bit of effort.'

'Better not to try, in my experience. Sometimes you just have to accept the person's a blackguard and leave it at that.'

'I suppose. But I like to think that nobody is beyond redemption. Not even a National Socialist.'

I glanced across at him. 'That sounds suspiciously like the prelude to another philosophical debate.'

The Irishman laughed. 'Oh, I'm done with debates on this trip, believe me! From now on it's just the weather and "what do you do for a living?"'

'Quite right,' I agreed.

He turned to me, that mischievous glint returning to his eye. 'So what do you do for a living?' he enquired.

I smiled back benignly. 'I ignore impertinent questions.'

I tapped my feet together on the end of the bed. 'It doesn't make any sense, Morris.' I hadn't bothered to take off my shoes. I was far too agitated. 'Why would Gerhard Schulz take his own life? He'd just earned himself a small fortune.' I kept my voice low, in deference to the walls, but the cabins either side of us were empty just now. 'He was in good health, racing up and down that damned tower. And he'd just booked a train ticket to Madrid. That doesn't speak of a man at the end of his tether.'

'No, Monsieur.' Maurice was sitting on the small

collapsible chair, darning a pair of my socks.

'We don't even know what time he died.' I growled in frustration. Captain Albrecht had said that Schulz's body had been discovered at eleven o'clock but he might well have killed himself much earlier than that, before the Richthofen had even left Seville. 'And how did he do it. Did he string himself up? Or cut himself with a knife and bleed to death in the bath?' I pulled myself forward and swung my legs off the bed. 'It's a bad business, Morris.'

'Yes, Monsieur.'

I gripped a hand on the metal ladder to my left. 'I can't help thinking that there's something else going on here. It's too much of a coincidence. He's carrying these important documents. We follow him around all afternoon. He passes them on to Gods knows who and then, a few hours later, he's found dead, having taken his own life. It just doesn't ring true, somehow.' I bit my lip. 'I wonder if there was a note. There would have to be, wouldn't there, if it was suicide?'

Maurice shrugged. 'Not always, Monsieur.'

'Lazenby would know.' I scratched my head. 'I wonder if we could get a message to him? If he's still in Seville?'

'You could send him a telegram, Monsieur.'

'I suppose so.' There was a wireless telegraph on board, which the passengers were allowed to use. 'Bit expensive mind.' Telegrams were charged by the word and on an airship it would not come cheap. I had promised to contact Lazenby when I had secured the negatives, but he would not be expecting to hear from me until we arrived in Brazil. Besides, if I contacted him now and enquired about the Austrian, the crew would be sure to notice. As yet, nobody on board suspected there was any connection between me and Gerhard Schulz; and I was happy to keep it that way. I did not wish to advertise the fact that I had spent Sunday afternoon following the poor fellow around Seville. 'If it has to go through the telegraph operator, it'll need to be something short and cryptic.' Unfortunately, I had left my code book back in Gibraltar. 'Shame Mr Gray didn't bring that facsimile machine of his on board,' I muttered idly. 'Then I could have written out a dozen questions and fed the paper through myself, without anyone else seeing it.'

'That would only work if Monsieur Lazenby had a receiving device.'

'I wasn't being serious, Morris. You're no help at all. No, it'll have to be a telegram. To dear old Uncle Charles or something of that order. But I'll have to go down to the radio room myself. The fewer people who know about this, the better.'

The gap toothed crewman led me through a metal doorway into the bowels of the ship. Up until now, even passing by the kitchens and the officers' mess on B Deck, there had been the rudiments of civilisation. Stepping through the door, however, onto a narrow metal walkway, with the entirety of the airship laid out before me, there was no escape. The crewman pointed upwards with a grin at the huge bags suspended above our heads. They were enclosed in a lattice work of wires and bloated with deadly hydrogen gas. The circular frame of the airship was visible beyond them, interwoven with supports and counter supports, the fragile exterior cloth shrouding the network of wires in a merciful gloom. The scale of the craft was breathtaking and terrifying in equal measure. I scrambled around for something to grab onto, whilst at the same time trying not to lose my footing. The plimsolls I had been given did not help matters. The light, rubber soled shoes were mandatory in this part of the ship, but they were proving far too big for me. I stopped, clutching a support strut, and closed my eyes for a moment, gathering my nerves. Despite the chilly air and the presence of Maurice's great coat – which I had insisted on borrowing – I was sweating profusely. It had been a mistake to come down here in person. I should have just posted the telegram like everyone else – there was a box in the reading room that was emptied at regular intervals – or perhaps just handed it to one of the stewards. But no, I had insisted on coming myself, and now I was paying the price.

The crewman was ahead of me, waiting patiently for me

to catch up, and with great reluctance I moved after him, not for a moment taking my eyes off the keel walkway. This was barely three feet across, supported by a series of diagonal struts. It ran the length of the ship, turning into the more manageable corridor behind me for a few yards and then disappearing into the bowels of the aircraft. Large rounded water tanks loomed either side of me – a more practical ballast than the traditional sand bags – and beyond that, to my right, was the entrance to the radio room. The crewman stood back to gesture me inside.

The room was much larger than I had anticipated, with a row of windows on the starboard side providing substantial light. Desks lined every wall, piled high with radio equipment, all dials and switches. A typewriter sat in one corner and there were fans in the wall to cool the equipment. A door at the far end gave access to a metal ladder which descended through a hole in the floor to God knows where.

The chief radio operator was sitting with his back to me, in a small chair on the near side of the cabin, a pair of metal headphones clamped to his short cropped hair. As I stepped into the room, he turned, removed the headphones and rose to his feet.

We shook hands formally and he introduced himself as Adolph Schäuble, a name I was unlikely to be able to remember. He was a sober looking fellow with a youthful complexion but a confident manner. The pleasantries over, I reached into my jacket pocket and pulled out the slip of paper, which I had spent some minutes composing in the reading room. I had wanted something short and sharp, but brevity has never been my strong point. I just hoped I would be able to claim the money back when I reached America. 'I'd like to send this to my Uncle Charles in Seville,' I said, handing the note across. 'I thought I'd come down here and deliver it in person. Have a bit of a look round.' I attempted a smile but my heart wasn't in it. The officer looked down at the paper and read it through briefly.

"SO SORRY TO HEAR ABOUT AUNT SOFIA STOP HOPE NOTHING UNTOWARD HAS HAPPENED STOP

QUIET FLIGHT SO FAR STOP SPECTACULAR VIEWS OF THE ATLANTIC STOP HAVE NOT YET TAKEN ANY PHOTOGRAPHS"

The meaning would be clear to Lazenby – "Sofia" was the name of the hotel where Schulz had spent the night, and the lack of photographs would speak for itself – but there was nothing to draw the attention of the radio operator or anyone at the telegraph office in Seville.

'Your aunt is not well?' Adolph asked, looking up.

'I think she may have had a bit of a fall,' I lied.

'I am sorry to hear that, Mr Bland.'

'My uncle will be able to tell me. I didn't really catch the details. Bit of a hurry to get on board this morning.'

'Well, I hope it is good news,' the officer said, returning to his chair. 'I will transmit this for you right away.' He reached for a clipboard on the desk beside him.

'Do I...have to pay anything?'

'It will be added to your account.' He looked down at the message again. 'If you are interested in photography, the views from the window here are very good.'

'Yes, I...I'm sure. I'll have to bring my camera along. Well, thank you for your help.'

'A pleasure, Mr Bland. Perhaps you would like to see the rest of the ship? Herr Ostermann will be delighted to show you.' He indicated the gangway and the smiling crewman, who had waited politely outside during the exchange.

I gritted my teeth. 'I...wouldn't want to put you to any trouble.'

'It is no trouble,' the gap-toothed crewman insisted, stepping aside to give me access to the corridor. There was another cabin on the opposite side of the gangway. It looked like some sort of post room. A short fellow with a lazy eye was busily franking envelopes inside. 'We see tail of ship,' Ostermann suggested. 'Or you like to see control car first?'

'Er...well...'

'It is right here.' He gestured to the far end of the radio room. 'There is *eine leiter*...a ladder. A good view of the sky

74

from there.'

'A ladder?' I caught sight of the hole in the floor, through the open doorway. 'Good grief! No, I don't think...'

'It is very short. Come. I help you.' The young man squeezed into the radio room and directed me towards the hole. It was clear the damned fellow was not going to give me any choice in the matter.

'Very well,' I muttered, clenching my fists tightly. 'Just a quick look.'

I stepped through the door and grabbed hold of the metal ladder, tentatively placing an oversized plimsoll on one of the higher rungs. Thankfully, the crewman had not lied. The ladder was a short affair. I descended with great care into a small utility room at the rear of the control car. The windows here, below the level of the balloon, were even larger than in the radio room.

The gap-toothed crewman descended in quick order and moved across to the empty door frame in front of us. '*Herr Kapitän*! Mr Reginald Bland,' he called through, by way of introduction. He added a few extra words in Kraut which I didn't understand. I was trying hard to ignore the enormous windows. There seemed to be more glass than metal down here.

Captain Albrecht strode through from the navigation room. The man had a quiet smile that radiated confidence. 'Welcome to the heart of the Richthofen,' he said, proffering a hand. 'Please, come through.' He gestured me into the second room – full of charts and measuring equipment – and towards the bridge.

A harsh female voice ricocheted across the length of the gondola. Mrs Koenig was standing at the far end of the control room, talking to a grim faced man in a peak cap, who I recognised as the first officer. Evidently, I was not the only one having a guided tour of the facilities this afternoon. Adelina Koenig took a moment to glare at me as I arrived on the bridge before resuming her conversation with the officer.

'We have made good progress so far,' the captain told me, as we moved into the busy control room. 'We have travelled seven hundred kilometres from Seville.' Five officers were at work on the bridge, monitoring various instruments. One was at the rudder wheel at the front of the gondola and a second stood by another wheel to the side. There were dials and switches everywhere, bits of machinery bolted together like a Meccano set. A second telegraph machine, adjacent to the rudder wheel, apparently enabled communication with the poor blighters stuck out in the engine cars on the side of the airship.

Captain Albrecht took me over to a window, to take a peek at one of the engines in action, but I focused instead on the machinery above the elevator wheel. The roast beef from lunch time was threatening to reassert itself and I was trying hard to keep my eyes on the interior of the gondola. I did not wish to embarrass myself a second time in one day, but there were so many windows in the control cabin that we might as well have been outside, flying with the birds.

The officers, in their peak caps and great coats, were a friendly bunch. Unlike the crewman, their English was flawless, their accents a strange mix of German and American English, but serviceable all the same.

Mrs Koenig was only speaking in German, however, at least within earshot of me. I had seen her conversing with the other passengers at lunch, though, so I suspected she did speak a little English, but it was clearly beneath her dignity to do so here. She was only interested in the first officer and his detailed explanations of the workings of the various devices. It was probably a professional interest, if the woman really was the reckless aviator Sir George had painted her. Mrs Koenig was younger than I had first taken her to be – perhaps late twenties rather than early thirties – and despite a rather stocky gait was quite attractive in the brisk light of the afternoon. She might almost have been described as pretty, if only she had taken the trouble to stop frowning. She had wavy dark brown hair slicked from right to left across the top of her forehead and piercing blue eyes. The hefty woollen coat she wore was a sensible precaution in such a remorselessly chilly environment. There was plenty here to interest a female engineer, but she kept throwing angry glances at me, as if I were interrupting an illicit assignation.

The first officer volunteered to escort her back to the passenger deck. They moved together through to the rear of the gondola. He scurried up the connecting ladder first, to protect her modesty, and Mrs Koenig followed on in her long skirt. The two were still engaged in conversation and, though I couldn't possibly catch any of the details as they disappeared back up into the radio room, I did manage to pick out three words: 'Dankeschön' from the first officer, meaning thank you. And then: 'Gerhard Schulz.'

Sir George Westlake lit the end of a fat cigar and moved back to the padded chair. I was already halfway through my second Piccadilly. I rarely smoked more than one cigarette at a time but after my hair-raising trip into the control gondola I felt I deserved a treat. Half a dozen people had settled in the smoking room, in two small groups of three. The atmosphere was subdued, despite the tobacco and the regular appearance of Max the barman with our drinks. The death of a fellow passenger, even away from the airship, had put a bit of a dampener on the afternoon. 'He was an odd cove, that Mr Schulz,' Sir George reflected. 'Wouldn't have put him down as the suicidal type. Far too interested in life.' The veteran explorer had been with the airship since Friedrichshafen so he was well placed to judge.

'He was an interesting man,' Josef Kaufmann agreed, taking a puff of his own cigarette. The tubby German seemed more affected by the Austrian's death than Sir George. Kaufmann was drinking black coffee rather than wine or beer. Perhaps he was tee-total, like Mr McGilton. But he was at least smoking, and he tapped the end of his cigarette on the ashtray between us. 'He had a zest for life. He was forever asking questions of the stewards. How high are we flying? How does the airship manoeuvre in the wind?'

'Did he have a look at the control room?' I asked.

'Yes, more than once,' Kaufmann replied. 'With us and also during the landing yesterday afternoon.'

That was probably why he had been the last of the

77

passengers to disembark. 'I...gather he was a journalist of some kind?' I saw no reason not to probe a little deeper, since we were already discussing the fellow. I was curious to know what the other passengers thought of him.

'Yes, that is right,' Kaufmann confirmed.

'I suppose it pays to have an enquiring mind in that line of work. Did he mix much with you all?' I was particularly interested to discover how well he had known Adelina Koenig.

'Yes, he was very sociable.'

'Jolly good pianist, too,' Sir George put in. 'And rather a fine card player. Could have bankrupted the lot of us, if we'd been playing for serious money.' He chuckled. 'Upset Herr Lindt, he did. That one doesn't like to lose.'

'I can imagine.' I glanced across the smoking room floor. Karl Lindt had been sat at the other table, with Walter Kendall and Frederick Gray, but had disappeared off to answer a call of nature. I got the impression his companions were happy to see the back of him.

'It was not simply the cards,' Kaufmann reflected. 'Herr Schulz and Herr Lindt did not get on. They had differing political opinions.'

'I'll say!' Sir George laughed. 'Bit of a Red, our Mr Schulz.'

'A socialist rather than a communist,' Kaufmann corrected. 'He wrote articles for a left wing newspaper in Vienna.'

'Good lord,' I said.

'But the distinction was lost on Herr Lindt.' The German took a last drag of his cigarette and stubbed out the end of it in the ashtray.

'Thought they were going to come to blows at one point,' Sir George chuckled. 'But Schulz wasn't one for a punch up. He just got up and walked away. Which just made the other chap even madder.'

'I can imagine.' I lifted my glass and took a quick slurp. 'It looks like you had an eventful journey, that first leg.'

'Oh, it was just the one incident, old boy,' Sir George said. He tapped out the end of his cigar. 'We didn't board the

78

ship in Friedrichshafen until nine o'clock on Saturday evening, but a few of us stayed up to watch the launch and play a few hands before bed time. To tell you the truth, we all rather liked the chap. Miss Hurst had a bit of a soft spot for him, as I recall.'

'I think he found her a kindred spirit,' Kaufmann agreed.

I had not seen Miss Hurst since lunch and there was no sign of her in the smoking room. I gathered from McGilton that she had been quite distressed at the news of Mr Schulz's death so perhaps she was drowning her sorrows in her cabin.

'I was not sure to what extent his feelings were reciprocated,' Kaufmann observed. 'Herr Schulz was some years older than the Fräulein.'

The door to the smoking room opened and Captain Albrecht popped his head inside. He was making his regular round of the passenger decks. He smiled and came across to our table. 'Gentlemen, how are you enjoying the flight?' He had pulled a pipe from his breast pocket and removed a pouch of tobacco from his jacket.

'Absolutely marvellous!' Sir George exclaimed. 'Better food than I get at home and first class brandy.' He raised his glass to the captain.

It was left to Mr Kaufmann to lower the mood. 'We were just discussing Herr Schulz,' he said.

The captain's face fell.

'Were you able to pass on much to the authorities?' I asked, unable to hide my curiosity. 'Mrs Koenig was helpful?'

'Yes, indeed. She is a remarkable woman.' Captain Albrecht filled the end of his pipe and moved across to the cigarette lighter on the wall, which was not far from our table.

'And you've spoken to Miss Hurst? I gather she was quite close to Mr Schulz.'

'Yes, I have spoken to her as well,' the captain confirmed, bringing the lit pipe up to his mouth and taking a quick puff. 'And Miss Tanner.' All the women, it seemed. Perhaps Schulz had been a bit of a lady killer, as well as a socialist. 'And Herr Kaufmann here was kind enough to provide some additional thoughts. These have been passed on to the authorities in Seville. Sadly, I do not think it is an urgent matter for them today.'

'I suppose not,' I agreed. They would be too busy coping with the aftermath of the election.

'We must try not to allow it to spoil the voyage,' the captain added, taking another puff from his pipe and exhaling a large cloud of smoke. He was obviously in a hurry to draw a line under the matter.

A steward had slipped into the smoking room, with a silver platter. It was that young fellow, Heinrich. The boy headed straight for our table. 'A telegram has arrived for Mr Bland,' he informed the captain.

'Ah!' Albrecht waved him forward. 'Gentlemen, if you will excuse me.' He moved across to say hello to the other guests.

Heinrich proffered me the note, which I grabbed from the platter and read.

'It doesn't tell us anything,' I muttered, some minutes later, back in the cabin. I handed the message across to Maurice. 'The man's being deliberately obtuse.'

The valet scanned the contents briefly.

"DO NOT CONCERN YOURSELF WITH AUNT SOFIA STOP NOTHING UNTOWARD HAS HAPPENED TO HER STOP ANXIOUS TO SEE PHOTOGRAPHS SOONEST STOP HOPE YOU GET A GOOD NIGHTS SLEEP STOP UNCLE CHARLIE"

'Nothing untoward, indeed! The poor fellow's dead!'

'Yes, Monsieur. But it seems there was nothing suspicious about his death.'

'Yes, I gathered that, Morris. I'm not a complete imbecile. But it still doesn't tell us anything. Other than how anxious Mr Lazenby is for me to get hold of those damned negatives. A good nights sleep indeed!' I couldn't believe he had wasted seven words on the state of my health. I stopped for a moment, a sudden thought striking me. 'Wait a minute...'

'Monsieur?'

'Where's my wash bag?'

'It is here, Monsieur. Above the sink.'

Maurice stepped away and I moved across to the bag, which I rifled inside. I quickly found what I was looking for: the small glass bottle Lazenby had given me that morning. 'He lent me this before I left. Said it might help me sleep.'

'I remember, Monsieur.'

I pulled the bottle up in front of my face. It was a perfectly ordinary sleeping draught. The dosage was written on the side in Spanish. Half a teaspoon dissolved in water before bedtime. 'You don't think...?'

I placed the bottle back down on the sink and retrieved the telegram from Maurice. Before I had left Seville that morning, Lazenby had jokingly suggested I might use the sleeping draught on Mr Kendall, if all else failed.

"HOPE YOU GET A GOOD NIGHTS SLEEP STOP"

I let out a sigh. I was beginning to think he wasn't joking.

Chapter Seven

It was the best hand I'd had in several years. The seven, nine and jack of clubs were face up on the gaming table; and in my hand I had the eight and the ten. A straight flush. If I had been dealt a hand like that in Monte Carlo I could have broken the bank. If I'd had the same cards a week ago, in Gibraltar, I wouldn't now be in hock to an irate Italian to the sum of thirty pounds. And now, with a pot of forty-five American dollars on the table and every prospect of another twenty being laid out before betting was concluded, I should have been dancing a quiet jig on the table. But Lady Luck can be a cruel mistress and circumstances were already conspiring against me.

Karl Lindt had not taken his eyes from my face when I'd added the last two dollars to the pot. By common agreement we were playing with American currency rather than pounds or reichsmarks. Sir George Westlake had been kind enough to convert some cash for me at the start of the evening. He was still in the game, as was Jacob Finch, the red-haired stockbroker, but Josef Kaufmann and Thomas McGilton had already folded. I was glad the Irishman had joined us at the table, despite the hefty stake. He needed at least one vice to his name and the fellow was proving to be rather a good player. His most recent hand might not have been the best but he was up a good five dollars overall, which was better than I was doing. I needed to win this round if I was to recoup my earlier losses.

Strictly speaking, the six of us should not have been gambling at all. The games room on the Richthofen was reserved for non-competitive sport, though the stewards were prepared to turn a blind eye, so long as the sums involved were not ridiculously high. A friendly bridge contest was taking place at one of the square tables on the near side of the games room, between us and the promenade, and with that as camouflage nobody official was asking any awkward questions.

The money was piling up in front of us and I could see from the smug expression on his face that Mr Lindt had every intention of bleeding the rest of us dry. But there was no hand the belligerent German could possess that would beat the one in front of me. I had the little sod exactly where I wanted him.

And then the bridge match reached its conclusion and the four players rose up to leave their table; Walter Kendall among them. The American had joined the game after dinner, partnering Annabel Hurst against Frederick Gray and Lucy Tanner. I got the feeling Kendall was not a regular player and was only taking part out of politeness, but the game had been a surprisingly animated affair. Miss Tanner was in her element, teasing the men, and the usually dull Mr Gray, under the influence of one too many glasses of wine at supper, had started to come into his own. But now, with the English team victorious over the Anglo-Americans, the foursome had decided to call it a night.

And so, despite being in possession of one of the best hands I had ever been dealt, it looked like I would have no choice but to abandon the game and follow them out.

Maurice had been sceptical of my scheme from the outset. 'You intend to drug the American?' he had asked, before supper, his usual pained expression ratcheting up from twisted-ankle to finger-in-the-door.

'Not me, Morris. *You.* A small sprinkling of powder in his whisky before he goes to bed and he'll be out like a light.'

My valet's expression jumped from finger-in-the-door to electro-shock therapy. 'I do not think that would be a good idea, Monsieur.'

'I don't pay you to think, Morris!' I snapped. 'You'll do as you're damned well told.' I kept my voice at a low hiss, in deference to the walls, but I was no less vehement for that. 'It's me that's going to have to break into his room in the dead of night. It's me that'll suffer the consequences if I'm caught doing it. All you have to do is serve a couple of glasses of whisky.'

'A *couple* of glasses?'

'Well, yes, of course. Pay attention!' It was a simple enough strategy. 'I'll offer him a night cap after supper. Then you can slip the powder into one of the glasses. Don't look at me like that. It won't do him any harm. The dosage is written very clearly on the side of the bottle.'

Maurice raised an eyebrow but he did not challenge my assertion. 'And you think Monsieur Kendall will accept the invitation?'

'For a drink? Of course he will. He's far too polite to refuse. Especially if it's one of my own bottles.' I had not brought much luggage with me from Gibraltar, but I never travelled anywhere without a decent supply of whisky.

'If you say so, Monsieur.'

I could see Maurice was not happy, so I adopted a more conciliatory tone. 'Look, I know this isn't strictly within your job description. But you know how important this is to me. I have to prove my mettle to the people in London. Show that I'm up to the job. And they wouldn't have paid a small fortune for both of us to travel on this airship if it wasn't *very* important.'

Maurice acknowledged the truth of that with a dip of his head.

'I need to get hold of those negatives and I can't see any other way to do it. Kendall hasn't left the damned things lying around anywhere. He has to be carrying them with him, in one of his pockets. And the only way I can search his clothes is when he's not wearing them; when he's undressed and fast asleep. If you slip him the sleeping draught, he'll toddle off quietly to bed and when he's out for the count I can break into his cabin and do the necessary.'

'But are you sure you will be *able* to break in?' Maurice enquired.

'Well, of course I'll be able to break in!' I did not appreciate the man casting aspersions on my lock-picking capabilities. 'There won't be anyone around to disturb me, not in the early hours of the morning. I'll have plenty of time to do it.' And I still had the hair pins from earlier in the day.

'If you say so, Monsieur.'

'I *do* say so, Morris. I want to get this over with tonight. Throw the damned photos out to sea and have done with it.'

'Very well, Monsieur.' The valet bowed his head. He

84

was still not happy but he had accepted the necessity.

All that remained to do was the deed itself. It would be a simple matter to approach Kendall after supper and he would be bound to accept my invitation. Better to do it tonight, I thought, while there was still plenty of time. My resolution had not wavered over dinner, when the American had sat at a far table, talking animatedly to Miss Tanner. I had even held back on my alcohol intake, to make sure I kept a clear head. But now, as the man rose up from the card table and prepared to head off to his cabin, my resolve was beginning to falter.

The eight and ten of clubs were burning a hole in my hand and I was having second thoughts about the whole idea.

We would be on board the airship for at least another night before we reached Rio. I could leave it until tomorrow. That would still give me plenty of time and I would be able to play out my hand in peace. It wasn't just the prospect of winning a tidy sum that made me hesitate, however. I also wanted to see the expression on Mr Lindt's face when I laid down my cards in front of him. That was part of the attraction of a game like this. Delaying the attack on Walter Kendall would be something of a gamble, though. There would be no second chance if I got it wrong tomorrow night. What if he chose to retire early? What if he refused the drink? The whole scheme would be in ruins. We would be in Rio shortly after that and then anything might happen. He could get the prints developed and wire the results to New York. No, if I was serious about doing this, it had to be done tonight. And that meant abandoning the pot right now and following Kendall out of the games room.

I gripped the cards tightly in my hands, unwilling to let go of them, despite myself.

'I'm off to bed, darling,' Miss Tanner called across to her fiancé. 'Good night, gentlemen!'

'Sleep well,' McGilton called back, amid general murmurings from the other players.

Miss Tanner and Miss Hurst stepped out onto the promenade, with Mr Gray following behind. The Englishman was a little unsteady on his feet and Miss Tanner gave him her arm, to prevent him from losing his footing. Walter Kendall was close behind them and stopped for a moment at the windows, gazing out at the darkness of the ocean.

Lindt was still intent on the game. Mr Finch had folded but the German had matched my two dollars and raised another three. Sir George was still in the game, however, which meant the betting might well go on for another five minutes. I gave out a heavy sigh, shook my head and placed my cards face down on the table. 'That's me out, I'm afraid. Time to retire.'

The German's eyes lit up in triumph.

'Can't take the heat, eh?' Sir George laughed good-naturedly as I rose to my feet. Out of the corner of my eye, moving away from the table, I saw him throw down a five dollar bill. 'I'll see you, old chap.'

Lindt crowed with pleasure as he spread out his cards on the table. 'Two pairs. Sevens and nines.' It was a good hand, though nowhere near as good as the one I had just abandoned.

Sir George roared with delight. 'Three jacks,' he countered, throwing them down on the table.

Karl Lindt let out an anguished cry.

'Bad luck, old boy!'

I had reached the promenade by now but I couldn't help glancing back to catch sight of Mr Lindt scraping his chair away from the table in disgust. 'I think I will also call it a night!'

'Now, now!' Sir George chided him. 'No need to be a sore loser.'

'I am not a sore loser. I am going to bed.' The German stormed angrily past me.

I exchanged a look with Walter Kendall, who had also witnessed the tantrum. 'Some people,' I muttered.

Kendall nodded. 'In my experience, it's never a good idea to play for money on social occasions. It spoils your enjoyment of the evening.'

'What rot! The money is half the fun.' I had just lost twenty-five dollars – about five pounds in real money – but it had been worth it to see the look on Lindt's face. 'Do you fancy a night cap, Mr Kendall? I have a bottle of whisky in my cabin.' I managed to make the invitation sound casual, as if it had just occurred to me.

The American masked his surprise well. 'That's very kind of you, Mr Bland.'

'Not at all! Always pays to be hospitable. Morris!' I had ordered my valet to linger in the lounge area. 'Fetch the whisky will you, and a couple of glasses?'

Maurice closed the book he was reading, removed his glasses and rose to his feet. 'Yes, Monsieur.'

Kendall frowned slightly at our exchange.

'You've met my valet, Morris?'

'Yes, I was speaking to him over dinner. He is a very well educated man.'

I blinked. 'Is he?' It was the first I had heard of it.

'Indeed. Self-educated, like myself.' There was an implied criticism there but I let it go. 'Perhaps we should move to the reading room?' the American suggested. Sir George's booming laugh was still a little too close for comfort. It sounded like the game was going to continue, with the four remaining passengers.

I followed Walter Kendall into the far saloon.

'So what brought you to Europe?' I enquired amiably, as we settled ourselves down. I was itching to find out anything I could about him but I didn't want to push my luck. There was no point putting the fellow on his guard. 'Business or pleasure?'

'A little of both,' the American replied, removing his glasses and wiping them meticulously with the handkerchief in his jacket pocket. 'I wanted to see how Europe was coping with the economic downturn. I proposed a series of articles to my editor in New York and he was happy to fund the enterprise.'

I did not believe that for a minute. 'And how *is* Europe coping?'

'On the whole, better than the United States. Germany is the exception, of course. They are having it very badly just now. And the war reparations demanded by the allies have created a lot of ill feeling. France is still in the doldrums, of course. I was in Paris last week. England is better placed than most to cope, but they are not through the worst of it yet, I fear.'

'Budget cuts all over,' I agreed.

'And of course the discontent in Spain we have seen for ourselves. It was economics that brought down the dictatorship. Industrial strife and unemployment. Those are the principal factors which led to these elections.' The American was in his element, lecturing me on political affairs, and given that I had invited him here, I had no choice but to let him burble on; at least until Maurice arrived with the whisky.

'I'm surprised you didn't hang around in Spain to cover the results of the elections.'

'I was sorely tempted,' Kendall admitted, replacing his glasses. 'I was in Madrid on Wednesday. The strength of feeling in the streets was remarkable. But I was convinced the monarchists would win and, as my editor wanted me back in New York, I booked my passage on the Richthofen. By the time I had realised my mistake, it was too late for me to change my plans.'

That tied in with what Lazenby had told me. 'So it's a happy accident you're on board with us?'

'Indeed,' Kendall agreed. 'Though I confess I did have a certain curiosity to see an airship from the inside.' I tried hard to mask my scepticism. The Richthofen was a convenient choice, not the fulfilment of a dream. Kendall had needed to get out of the country as quickly as possible, after he had acquired those photographs from Gerhard Schulz. 'The Germans are very proud of their innovation,' he added, 'and rightly so, in my opinion.'

'Yes, I had a good look round the place this afternoon. It was a bit overwhelming.'

Kendall showed polite concern as he folded his handkerchief and returned it to his breast pocket. 'You're feeling better now?'

'Much, yes. Miss Tanner was right. It didn't take me long to find my feet.' I left it a moment before following up the reference to the Englishwoman. 'Have you known her long?'

'Miss Tanner?' His eyes flickered for a moment, though

whether in irritation or surprise I could not be certain.

'I...gathered you'd met before.' Kendall was looking wary, but it was a valid question and I was curious to know the truth. Miss Tanner had chosen to sit next to him at supper, well away from her fiancé. And I hadn't forgotten bumping into the girl halfway up the Torre del Oro at the same time that Gerhard Schulz had been wandering about.

'We have...corresponded,' Kendall admitted reluctantly. 'She has an interest in newspaper journalism and has sought my advice. I understand she is hoping to pursue a career as a news journalist.' That was what McGilton had told me too. The American was being very careful with his words.

'But you didn't know she would be on this flight?'

'No. It was a complete coincidence, albeit a happy one.'

Maurice arrived with the whisky and the glasses, saving Kendall from any further embarrassment. 'You took your time,' I muttered to the valet.

'I am sorry, Monsieur.'

He opened the bottle and set the glasses down on the table. I watched him closely as he poured out the two measures. He did it well, keeping the glasses away from us so that Kendall could not see the powder already present in the bottom of one of the tumblers. We had practised the procedure in the cabin to make sure that the draught dissolved properly in whisky. It had been a terrible waste of a fine spirit, but it was as well to be sure. As it turned out, the powder just needed a bit of a stir. Maurice masked the process with his body as he mixed the glass, then turned back to us and handed the tumbler to Mr Kendall.

'It'll have to be just the one,' the man said. 'I want to get a bit of writing done before I retire.'

'The life of a journalist is never finished, eh?' I said, taking the second glass. I hoped to goodness Maurice hadn't got the tumblers mixed up. It would be just like him. I couldn't afford to get myself knocked out; not when I'd lost almost five pounds to put myself in this masterful position. I wondered briefly if I would be able to claim the money back on expenses. 'Well, bottoms up!' I said, raising my glass to the American.

We clinked the tumblers together.

Kendall took a slow sip of the doped concoction. If he tasted anything untoward in the mix, he was too polite to mention it. 'A very fine malt,' he declared, smacking his lips together gently.

Maurice folded up my trousers and hung them on the hanger. Even in the confines of the cabin he had found space to properly hang and store my clothes, the few of them that I had managed to bring with me. He was an efficient fellow when it came to that sort of thing. My shoes had been left outside the door, to be taken care of by the steward and, in a spirit of generosity, I had allowed the valet to place his own shoes outside as well. I was feeling particularly well disposed towards him this evening. He had done a good job with that sleeping draught.

He took my shirt now, helping me off with it and folding it neatly, before tucking it away in the closet.

I stared across at the mirror above the wash basin. I was looking rather haggard. There were a couple of errant hairs growing on my upper lip – the shaving mug wasn't entirely for show – and there were wrinkles forming around my eyes. I squinted at them in the artificial light. My eyesight was not what it was, especially during the night. A sign of age, I supposed. My cheeks were a little ruddier than they had been in the past and I suspected my waistline was a little wider than it had been the year before. Too much Yorkshire pudding and not enough exercise. But I had a few years left in me yet, I thought. At least my hair hadn't started going grey.

I gave out a weary sigh. I ought to go through the motions of going to bed, I supposed. It would be a couple of hours yet before I could creep out and attend to Walter Kendall. The American had been getting a little drowsy as we left the reading room, but he had toddled off to his cabin without too much trouble.

The ship was now filled with the sounds of people settling down for the night, above the omnipresent hum of the engines. I wondered briefly if the men in the engine cars had to stay out all night. It must be freezing out there. There was probably some sort of rota. Once everyone was asleep and the passenger decks were quiet, I would creep out and attend to the business at hand. It was not a prospect I relished, but it was as well to get it over with. I had been right to abandon the poker game.

'Do you wish me to remove your bandages, Monsieur?' Maurice asked, looking down at my heavily swathed torso.

I shook my head. I have never been particularly well endowed but I liked to spend a few hours free of restrictions whenever it was safe to do so. 'Not tonight, Morris,' I replied. I didn't trust the lock on our cabin door. It didn't seem to click properly, like the others. I would have to have a word with Heinrich about that. 'Don't want to frighten the horses when I'm out and about.' I hated sleeping with the bandages in place – it made for a very uncomfortable night – but it was always a wise precaution when I was away from home.

'Very good, Monsieur.' He lifted my night shirt and I bobbed down as he pulled the cotton garment over the top of me. I wriggled my arms into the sleeves and allowed the shirt to drop down to my ankles. Maurice buttoned up the neck with his usual efficiency.

I moved closer to the mirror and grabbed hold of my toothbrush. *Away from home.* The realisation was just beginning to set in: I didn't really have a home any more. I wouldn't be returning to Gibraltar and I couldn't return to England. Nobody back there even knew I was alive, apart from the Colonel. As far as the world was concerned, Sir Hilary Manningham-Butler was dead and buried. And now I was heading for a new life in a new country; a country I had never even heard of, in a region bedevilled by earthquakes. Lazenby had got me in such a lather about Kendall and the Austrian fellow that I hadn't had proper time to consider the job I had been offered at the other end. What would happen when we got to New York? What would the people at the British Legation be like, when I finally arrived? What would I do if they were a bunch of idiots and I hated every single one of them?

'Is everything all right. Monsieur?' Maurice had looked up and seen me staring quietly at myself in the mirror. He was starting to undress, now that he had taken care of me. It was not a pretty sight. His craggy face was the only presentable part of him.

I waved a hand dismissively. 'Oh, fine. I was just thinking about home. Gibraltar. England. I wonder if I'll ever see it again.'

'Probably not, Monsieur,' he answered, with unnecessary candour.

I glared at him angrily, my gratitude to the man evaporating in an instant. 'Fat lot of good you are, Morris.' I stabbed some toothpaste onto my brush and set to work on my teeth.

It is not easy sitting up in bed for two and a half hours in the dark with nothing to occupy yourself. I had thought it better to leave the bedroom light off, so as not to draw attention, but now I felt my head beginning to droop. I had set an alarm clock, buried deep beneath my pillow, just to be on the safe side. If I should nod off, I would at least feel the vibration. I had set the clock for three am but my intention was to creep out of the cabin at half past two.

I jerked myself awake and pulled myself off the bed. Maurice was lying on his back on the upper bunk. I could just about make him out from the residual light creeping under the cabin door. The corridor lights were dimmed during the night, to save on power, but they were not switched off completely. The valet was breathing quietly though I could not tell if he was asleep. It had to be half past two by now, I thought.

I moved across to the light switch but banged my knee on my suitcase as I stepped forward. I cursed silently but then found the switch and flicked it on. Maurice blinked on the top bed and stared across at me. I put a finger to my lips and grabbed my fob watch. It was five minutes to two. To hell with it, I thought, that's close enough.

I moved back over to my bed and switched off the

alarm. Then I returned to the cabin door. I glanced back at Maurice. He had closed his eyes once again. His nerves were better than mine. But then, he wasn't about to break into another man's bedroom. I checked my breast pocket, to make sure I still had the improvised lever and pick, then switched out the light and slid open the bedroom door.

The starboard corridor was gloomy and quiet. I could hear the sounds of gentle snoring from the cabin next door. That would be Mr McGilton or perhaps his Spanish room mate, who had retired early. I glanced down at the carpet outside. My shoes had been removed by the steward along with Maurice's and all the others along the corridor. At least there was nothing here for me to trip over. I slid the door closed behind me and tip-toed bare foot along the passageway towards the central aisle.

Walter Kendall's cabin was on the far side of the passenger deck, opposite the water closets. I moved cautiously along the connecting corridor towards the port side. At the far end, I peered right, towards the stewards' cabin at the front of the passageway. A light was visible beneath the door. Someone would be on duty all night – I wondered if it was Heinrich – but, whoever it was, they would not pay any attention to a few shuffling footsteps. It was hardly unusual for a guest to pay a visit to the bathroom during the small hours.

The room I wanted was in the opposite direction, one of the three cabins set out along the rear section. I had no idea who was berthed in the room on the corner, but the German woman, Mrs Koenig, was in the middle. Hopefully, she would be fast asleep by now. I moved furtively along the corridor but, as I shuffled past her room, I heard a muffled groan coming from inside the cabin. More than one in fact. I stopped in my tracks.

Please tell me she isn't awake, I thought.

I leaned in as close as I dared, trying not to let my shadow fall across the base of the door. No, I had not imagined it. There were whispered voices coming from inside – two people, not one – and the distinctive sound of bed sheets ruffling. Good God, I thought, Mrs Koenig has a man in her cabin. It had to be a man, I reasoned. There were only three women on board ship, apart from myself, and Miss Hurst and Miss Tanner shared a cabin on the starboard side. It took an effort of will to stop myself from laughing. It did not take a scholar to work out what was happening in that room. I was not the only one creeping about after dark, doing things that they oughtn't to be doing.

I strained to hear more. The voices were speaking softly, in German, and both of them sounded rather excited. But try as I might I couldn't identify the second voice. It certainly wasn't *Mister* Koenig, anyway. He was not on board, so far as I was aware. I wondered for an instant if it might be Sir George Westlake. He had made no bones about his admiration for Adelina Koenig and he spoke a little German too. The mental image of him and her together tickled me for a moment and it was all I could do not to laugh out loud. But the German woman had also been rather friendly towards that first officer on the control deck. What was his name? Rüdiger. Perhaps he was Mrs Koenig's night time companion. Whoever it was, though, I had to admire her nerve. The shameless hussy. It was clear the two of them were not playing chess.

The unexpected distraction had soothed my nerves momentarily, but I forced myself to return to the task at hand. It would have been better for me if Mrs Koenig had been fast asleep, but it need not interfere with my plans. She and her companion would not be paying attention to anything but each other just now.

I shuffled along the corridor to the far door and stopped outside Walter Kendall's cabin. I reached into my breast pocket to retrieve the hair pin I had brought with me. This was the trickiest part of the operation. The last time I had tried to pick a lock, in Gibraltar, the pin had snapped off in my hand. But the principal was simple enough.

I grasped the handle of the door and pulled it gently, to make sure the cabin was actually locked; then I slid the lever into position and applied the necessary pressure. That done, I inserted the pick into the lock and felt for the first of the pins holding the barrel in place. It put up no resistance – the pin moved up and down freely – so I moved on to the next one. It wasn't until I hit the third pin that I felt any downward pressure. I manoeuvred this one gently upwards and heard a satisfying click. The last two pins proved a little more tricky but, after a bit of fiddling, I managed to get both of them out of the way and, to my astonishment, felt the small barrel rotate under the pressure of the lever. I closed my eyes and let out the breath I had been holding. For all my bravado with Maurice, I hadn't been entirely sure I would be able to do it. Quickly, I retrieved the hair pins from the lock.

So far, so good. And not a sound to disturb anybody.

My luck could not last, however. At that moment, I heard a cabin door slide open on the opposite side of the deck, the starboard side. I tensed at the sound of footsteps, which began moving briskly along the central corridor, in my direction. I had no time to ponder my options. I slid open the door to Kendall's cabin and dashed inside, closing it quietly behind me.

I listened for a moment, my eyes acclimatising to the darkness, and heard someone step into one of the water closets on the opposite side. It was a man – I heard the tell tale tinkling sound in the lavatory bowl – and after a quick flush he made his way out and away. He had spent perhaps thirty seconds in there. And then, save for the quiet groans in the adjacent cabin, all was as it should be.

I breathed out and turned my attention to the inside of the room. I didn't dare risk turning on the light – that might wake Kendall, even with the sleeping draught in his system – so I would have to fumble around in the dark. If I had known I would be doing this when I had left Gibraltar I would have brought a torch with me. As it was, I would have to rely on touch and the vague outlines visible from the dim light coming under the door.

My eyes had already made the most of the gloom and I could see Kendall's jacket hanging up in front of the closet. He had managed to get partially undressed before going to bed. The man himself, as far as I could make out, was lying on top of the bed, in his shirt sleeves and trousers. Kendall had the room to himself, the lucky beggar, so there was only the one bed.

I wondered what the man would think, if he knew I was in here. Would he put two and two together when he woke up and found the documents missing? He might round on me over the breakfast table. He was a hefty fellow, for all his diminutive stature, and he had spent a small fortune acquiring those papers. But I would cross that bridge when I came to it. First I had to find the damn things.

I still didn't know if I was looking for a roll of film, a booklet of negatives or a pouch of printed photographs. Charles Lazenby had been worryingly vague on the details.

I ran my hands through the jacket pockets. There was nothing on the inside or outside. I fumbled along the lining to make sure nothing had been secreted inside, but there were no irregularities in the cloth. I pulled back the curtain and had a rumble through the closet for good measure. There was nothing in any of his clothes, but it was as well to be thorough. Perhaps the photos had been left lying around the room somewhere. Once the door was locked there would be no need to keep them close to hand and I didn't want to start groping the man himself if there was a chance they were resting on a bedside table.

I crouched down and shuffled across the floor. The wash basin was lowered and there was a stool at the far end of the cabin. A small desk had also been lowered and the portable typewriter placed on top of it. There was a sheet of paper in there and a wad of notes to the left hand side; but that was just Kendall's notebook. Perhaps he had managed to scribble a few short words as he had intended, before realising how sleepy he was and giving up.

I moved over to the bed and ran a quick hand underneath the mattress, trying not to disturb the serene but rather heavy figure lying on top of the bed. Carefully, I extended a hand towards his head and my fingers traced the edges of his pillow. Walter Kendall was a surprisingly quiet sleeper, though in truth the noise of Mrs Koenig next door would probably have masked all but the most persistent of snorers. Her nocturnal endeavours seemed to be reaching some kind of climax. I slid a hand tentatively underneath the near edge of the pillow, but there was nothing lodged there for me to find. I leaned across carefully to check the far side of the mattress, but there was nothing there either. I wrinkled my nose. Kendall had an unpleasant odour close up; but I suppose few of us are at our most fragrant in the early hours of the morning. I pulled back and regarded the sleeping man irritably. I was left with no choice now. I would have to search the American himself. And that meant slipping a hand inside his trouser pockets. I grimaced. It was not a prospect I relished but there was nowhere else left to look. The things I did for England. Why couldn't the damned fellow have undressed himself properly?

Cautiously, I felt for the edge of his trousers and slid my hand gently into the nearside pocket. Luckily, Kendall did not seem to feel the touch. It was fortunate for me that he was sleeping on his back, meaning both the pockets were easy to access. I rummaged around inside as best I could. There was a wallet and a set of keys; some loose change as well. I would have to pull it all out, as gently as I could. While I was working, I kept my eyes on Kendall's sleeping face, what I could make out of it in the gloom, anxious not to disturb the dormant figure.

He hadn't even removed his glasses, I noticed now. And he really was a *very* quiet sleeper.

It was as I was manoeuvring the leather wallet out of his pocket that my arm gently brushed against Kendall's right hand. I jolted in surprise. The hand seemed oddly cold. I abandoned the wallet halfway out of the pocket and laid my own hand gently on his. It wasn't just cold, the skin was freezing, as chill as ice.

I grabbed hold of his wrist, pulling back the cuff of his shirt sleeve. His arm was rigid. With rising panic, I raised up to place a hand on his forehead, banging my knee on the side of the bed as I did so but dismissing the pain. Good God. His forehead was also cold. I searched for a pulse but there was nothing to find.

Walter Kendall was dead.

Chapter Eight

I crouched for some moments beside the bed, my mind numb, staring across at the prone figure lying on top of the bed sheets. It was not possible, I thought. How could Walter Kendall be dead? He had been the picture of health in the reading room a few hours earlier. And it wasn't as if he was an old man; in his mid-fifties perhaps. He couldn't just have popped his clogs randomly. Could he have had a heart attack? I wondered. Perhaps he had a dicky ticker and it just happened to peg out tonight. Or maybe he had banged his head somehow when he was getting into bed and had died from internal bleeding. He would have been drowsy from the sleeping draught and might easily have...

The sleeping draught.

My God. I brought a hand up to my mouth in horror. Could that have been the cause of his death? I sat back on the floor and my hands started to shake. Surely not. How could it have been? It was a completely harmless concoction; about as dangerous as a couple of aspirins. And for all his faults, Maurice would not have misjudged the dosage. It was written clearly on the side of the bottle. No, it must have been a heart condition, I thought. It couldn't be anything to do with the sleeping draught. Not unless it was some kind of allergic reaction. That was a possibility, I supposed. People could be allergic to all kinds of things. I remembered reading of one poor fellow who had died from eating a peanut. But gazing across at the darkened silhouette resting on the bunk, the why didn't really matter. Walter Kendall was dead and it looked like I had killed him. A healthy, intelligent individual who might have lived for another twenty or thirty years. Maurice may have administered the powder, but I had been the one who had told him to do it. This was a disaster. Panic was beginning to bubble up in my gut. I was responsible for his death and I would be held to account for it. What the devil was I going to do?

I gritted my teeth and brought my trembling hands under control. I couldn't afford to lose my wits just now. Difficult as it was, I had to consider the matter rationally.

Walter Kendall's body would not be disturbed until the stewards made their rounds first thing in the morning. When he didn't turn up to breakfast, they would knock and open up the cabin. His body would be discovered and everyone would know I had been the last person to see him alive. We had been seen together, going off for a night cap.

But would anyone know *how* he had died? That was the crux of the matter. The natural thing would be to assume he had died in his sleep, of a heart attack or a stroke. Such things happened. That had been my first thought, after all. So no one would have any reason to blame me.

Was there a doctor on board ship? I hadn't heard anybody mention one. I try to avoid doctors as a rule, but they seem to get everywhere. Even if there was a medical man on board, however, it was unlikely he would have the facilities to perform a full blown autopsy. A proper diagnosis would have to wait until our next port of call. That would give me a little breathing space, perhaps allowing me time to muddy the waters and divert suspicion. It may sound callous, considering all this when the man was lying dead on the bed next to me, but there was nothing I could do for him now and I had my own neck to think of. Some kind of enquiry was inevitable, when we arrived in Rio de Janeiro. The drug in his bloodstream would be discovered and my fingerprints found all over the inside of the cabin. So one way or another, the blame would eventually settle on me. I closed my eyes. The Good Lord really did have it in for me on this trip. Retribution for sins past, perhaps; I had not exactly led a blameless life. But there was no point worrying about that now. The important thing was to get away from Kendall's cabin without being seen.

Things had quietened down somewhat next door, though I could still make out a bit of post-coital activity. Fortunately, it sounded like Mrs Koenig's guest was preparing to leave, presumably to slip back to his own cabin. I would have to wait until the damned fellow was well away.

A sudden thought struck me. I hadn't looked inside Kendall's wallet yet. Those damned negatives. I wondered if they were here at all. Not that it would be much consolation to me now if I did find them; but I supposed I might as well finish the job.

I slid forward and grabbed the wallet, which was still sticking halfway out of Kendall's trouser pocket. There was nothing of any consequence inside; some bank notes and a few coins. A small photograph. Probably a portrait of his wife. He had a wedding ring, so there must be a Mrs Kendall. Poor bloody woman, I thought. She would be sound asleep now, somewhere in America, doubtless dreaming of her dear husband, unaware that he had already gasped his last. There had been family photographs on the inside of his suitcase, I recalled. I wondered if this picture was the same, but it was too dark to make out the image.

The door to the next cabin slid open quietly on its tracks and I heard footsteps creeping off down the passage. I couldn't tell where they were headed, but there were no clangs on the stairs down to B deck, so it couldn't be one of the crew. Sir George, then, or perhaps one of the Germans.

I returned the photograph to the wallet and placed it back where I had found it. Briefly, I searched Kendall's other pockets. A calmness had descended upon me now. Fate had thrown everything it could at me and there was nothing more that could go wrong.

There was no sign of the negatives, on Kendall or anywhere else. The whole exercise had been a fools errand from the start.

I moved to the door and listened carefully. Everything seemed quiet now, but I didn't want to take any chances. I slid the door open a crack and gazed through it at the poorly lit corridor. The passageway was deserted. I pulled the door open a little further and adjusted the latch. If I was careful, I could manoeuvre it so that the door would lock itself as soon as I slid it shut behind me. That would save me any further bother with the lock pick.

I slipped out sideways through the gap and pulled the door closed behind me, but as I tried to move away I felt a hard tug from behind. I stifled a curse. Part of my nightshirt had caught in the frame of the door. So much for nothing else going wrong.

I slipped a hand down behind me and tried to free the cloth, but the catch was right in the centre of my back and the fabric was jammed firmly into the lock. I grasped for the handle, which was digging into my rear, but I couldn't budge it; and I wouldn't be able to pull away without tearing my nightshirt.

Dammit, what the hell was I going to do? I couldn't leave a piece of my shirt hanging from the door of a dead man.

There was only one option. Somehow, I had to pull myself out of it; then I would be able to turn around and set to work on reopening the cabin. At least my hands were both free. I unbuttoned the front of the nightshirt at the top and awkwardly raised my arms. Pulling my left sleeve forward, I retracted my elbow inside and followed on with the rest of the arm. I did the same with my other arm and then pulled my head inside the shirt and slid down to the floor and out of the garment. It dropped and hung limp behind me in the doorway. I stood up for a moment, my body shaking, but not from the cold. I glanced nervously along the length of the port corridor. I hoped to god nobody saw me like this. Without the nightshirt I was virtually naked, except for the bandages around my chest and a pair of silk drawers. I crouched down in front of the lock to see if I could retrieve the nightshirt. It was jammed fast. With shaking fingers, I retrieved the hair pins from the breast pocket, then crouched down and set to work on the lock. This time, the lever did the trick on its own. With a little pressure applied to the cloth, the nightshirt sprang free, without even unlocking the door. I grabbed the garment and rose to my feet, hurriedly setting off towards my cabin.

I arced right into the connecting corridor and collided with Miss Annabel Hurst, who was heading in the opposite direction.

I don't know who was more surprised. Miss Hurst looked momentarily terrified, as we recoiled from the impact and my nightshirt dropped to the floor between us. 'Miss Hurst!' I exclaimed, as shocked to see her as she was to see me.

I hadn't heard any footsteps.

'Mr Bland!' she replied, in equal horror. 'I...I do apologise.' She must have been as quiet as a mouse, creeping out of her bedroom. Her eyes flicked nervously to the bandages around my chest, then to my drawers, then back up to my chest before finally settling on my face.

'It...it was my fault entirely,' I breathed, trying not to let my eyes wander in a similar fashion. Miss Hurst was barefoot in an ankle length cotton nightdress, her hair loose around her shoulders, her face even paler than usual in the dim electric light. 'I shouldn't have been in such a hurry,' I said. 'I...haven't hurt you?'

'No, not all,' she insisted, her voice a girlish whisper. Having had a moment to reflect, she was now averting her eyes, shock gradually giving way to a profound sense of embarrassment.

I bobbed down quickly to pick up my nightshirt, which I gathered together as best I could in front of myself. 'I...I got my shirt caught...in the door,' I muttered lamely. 'Of the water closet,' I added, for clarification. 'Couldn't get it out.'

She nodded absently, her eyes now focused determinedly on the nearest wall. I wasn't sure if she had heard what I had said, less still if she had understood it. But then, I was babbling rather.

'I'm so sorry,' she ventured, as if I had just confided a family tragedy. 'I was just going...' Her voice trailed away. She was off to the little girls' room. Why wouldn't she be? I only wished she had thumped around and made a bit of noise, like everyone else. Then I might have been able to keep out of her way.

'Well,' I said, anxious to move on, 'I'd better....'

She nodded vaguely and the conversation stuttered to a halt.

We moved silently past each other and continued on our separate paths. I reached the end of the central passageway, my heart thudding so hard beneath the bandages that I thought it would explode, and rushed finally towards the sanctuary of my own cabin. I slipped inside, closed the door behind me, dropped my nightshirt to the floor and let out a silent wail.

I might just as well have woken the whole bloody ship. Nobody would be in any doubt come morning that I had been skulking about, even if they hadn't overheard my conversation with Miss Hurst. And I had stood there in my underclothes, all but naked, in front of the little English woman. She had to have seen the truth. She had to have realised that it wasn't a man she was looking at. She would expose me as a fraud and then the stewards would label me a murderer. I clamped my hands to my face in despair and slid down the inside of the door. I was supposed to be heading to a new life in the Americas but it looked as if my life was already over.

It was all Lazenby's fault. Why did he have to go putting ideas into my head? That damned sleeping draught. I rose to my feet and fumbled over to the bed. Maurice was still resting on the upper bunk. I jabbed him in the shoulder and clamped a hand over his mouth, to prevent him crying out as he woke up suddenly. I pulled back, once I was sure he was awake, and gestured as broadly as I could towards the door. I wasn't sure if he could see me, but I moved back and a moment later he was swinging his legs over the edge of the bed and descending the metal steps. I opened the door a crack to let in some light and, as I slipped back into my nightshirt, he pulled on a dressing gown. I gestured for him to wait a moment. I wanted to make sure Miss Hurst had returned to her room after her nocturnal voyage. When I was sure she was safely back inside her cabin, I slid the door fully open and indicated for Maurice to follow me out into the corridor.

The lights were off in the passenger lounge. I closed the main door behind me, once the valet had stepped through it, and navigated cautiously through the tables and chairs towards the promenade and its multiplicity of windows. It was a clear, dark night – no moon reflected off the water that I could see – but the stars were out in force. I found a padded sofa just off to the left, out of view of the door, and gestured for Maurice to take the seat next to me. Here at least we could talk in peace.

My valet had not spoken a word since I had woken him. I hoped he was being tactful – it must have been obvious how distressed I was – but it was difficult to tell with Maurice. I leaned in close to him. 'Something's gone horribly wrong,' I said.

He did not blink. 'Monsieur?'

'Walter Kendall is dead. I found him lying in his shirt sleeves on the bed, stone cold.'

There was a long pause. 'That is...most regrettable.'

'Regrettable! It's disastrous! It must have been the sleeping draught we gave him.'

'That is a possibility,' the valet conceded, after a moment's consideration.

'It's hardly a possibility. It's a cast iron certainty. We killed him, Morris, you and I. And when the police investigate we'll both be hanged for murder.'

Maurice frowned. 'That does not seem likely, Monsieur.'

'What do you mean, not likely?' I exclaimed. I was having trouble keeping control of my voice.

'In America,' he said, 'they prefer the electric chair.'

I stifled a cry of horror. 'You're not helping, Morris!'

'No, Monsieur.'

'I was seen outside the room. That mouse of a woman, Miss Hurst. I bumped straight into her. Half naked, I might add.'

Maurice raised an eyebrow.

'Me, not her. But that's not important. The point is, I was seen leaving the scene of the crime. And my fingerprints are all over that cabin. Listen, that sleeping draught. Are you sure you had the right dosage?'

'Yes, Monsieur. I followed the instructions precisely.'

I exhaled angrily. 'Then how in heavens name did Kendall end up dead?'

The valet did not have an answer.

'We're going to be blamed for this, Morris. *I'm* going to be blamed. When they find that drug in his system, they'll trace it back to me. As soon as....' I stopped, retracing my thoughts.

'Is there a doctor on board?'

'I do not believe so, Monsieur.'

'Well, that's something anyway. They won't know for sure what killed him until we get to port.' I bit my upper lip, thinking furiously.

'And did you find the negatives?' the valet asked.

'What? No, I didn't. What does that matter?'

Maurice rubbed the side of his face. 'They were not in the room?'

'No. Not a sign of them. I searched everywhere.'

'That is rather curious.'

'I don't give a damn about the negatives! A man's just died, for heaven's sake. What are we going to do? They'll find the sleeping draught in our cabin and we'll be hung out to dry.'

'Not necessarily, Monsieur.'

'What do you mean, not necessarily? We can't just throw the bottle out of the window.' I stopped. Why couldn't we throw it out of the window? Come to think of it, that was exactly what we should do. The windows could be opened and at this time of night it was unlikely the men in the engine cars would see us doing it. But, no. 'That wouldn't do any good in the long run. My fingerprints would still be all over the cabin.'

'Yes, Monsieur.' Maurice had a better idea, however. 'But what if the sleeping draught were also discovered in the cabin?'

'I don't follow.'

'If the bottle was placed next to the bed then it would be natural to conclude that Monsieur Kendall had accidentally overdosed himself.'

I thought for a moment. 'I suppose so.'

'The authorities would be unlikely to enquire further.'

'Well...perhaps not,' I conceded. 'If we wiped the fingerprints from the bottle at least. But...I can't just break into his room a third time and pop the bottle on the sideboard.'

'Why not, Monsieur? It would avert suspicion.'

'Yes, but....' I took a deep breath. 'Look, Morris. I can't go back in there. I simply can't. My nerves wouldn't stand it.' It had been bad enough with the body; but then bumping into

Miss Hurst. It was as if my whole life had suddenly unravelled before me.

'But I can do it, Monsieur,' Maurice suggested.

I stared at him for a moment. '*You*?' I was hard pushed not to start laughing. Maurice was not the type to volunteer for anything. It had taken all my hectoring just to get him to drive me out to the airfield on Sunday afternoon. And he was hardly secret agent material. 'Look, Morris, I appreciate the offer. But you don't have the necessary skills. You don't know the first thing about lock picking.'

'I do have some experience, Monsieur. If you are prepared to lend me your pick.'

I stared at him, dumbfounded. The man was full of surprises. 'You know how to unlock a door? With a hairpin?'

'Yes, Monsieur.'

I waited for him to provide an explanation, but none was forthcoming. 'How on earth would you pick up a skill like that? You worked in a draper's shop, didn't you?' It struck me then just how little I knew about the man, even after all this time.

'Yes, Monsieur. But my father was a locksmith. I worked with him as a boy. I am familiar with every type of lock.'

I blinked. Then I scowled. 'Why the devil didn't you tell me this before?' I thought back to all the occasions when I could have used a decent pick lock, in the pursuit of my work.

'It has never come up, Monsieur.'

'Never come up! For goodness sake, Morris, you must have realised how useful this could be to me, in my line of work. I could have sent you off to do all kinds of dirty work.' Instead of putting my own head in the noose.

'Yes, Monsieur. But it is you who works for the Security Service,' he told me firmly. 'I do not.'

That was typical of him, I thought. Always digging in his heels at the most inconvenient of times. 'But you're willing to slip into Kendall's apartment now?'

'Yes, Monsieur.'

'And stash the sleeping draught?'

'Yes, Monsieur.'

'But why now, if not before? Why would you take the risk this time?'

'I am paid to look after you, Monsieur. If you are executed for murder, I would have to find a new employer.'

I threw up my hands. 'Good God. Morris, I am speechless.' I had no idea what to make of the fellow. He seemed to exist on an entirely different plane from me. We had just had the longest conversation the two of us had ever had and I still had no idea what was going on inside his head. What other skills was he keeping from me? I wondered.

'I will attend to the matter now, Monsieur,' he said, before I had the chance to enquire further. He rose up and headed for the passenger quarters without another word.

I remained where I was for some moments, in a state of complete bewilderment.

The knife scraped the butter from the block and Maurice spread it gently across the toast. The dining hall was full now, with white-coated stewards flitting around, attending to the passengers. Thomas McGilton was sitting opposite me, his mouth full of scrambled egg. My valet was perched to his right, pouring himself a cup of coffee. I had not raised any objection, when Maurice had joined us at the table. The man deserved a hearty breakfast, after what he had accomplished a few hours earlier. I could scarcely believe he had managed to do it. He had crept into Walter Kendall's cabin, secreted the glass bottle and then returned to our own room and promptly fallen asleep. I, by contrast, had barely slept a wink. I felt like the condemned man, awaiting sentence. Or the condemned woman. That would come out too, if I was brought to trial. The walk to breakfast might as well have been a stroll to the gallows. It could only be a matter of minutes before the American's body was discovered. With all of us at breakfast, the stewards would be unlocking the cabins and changing the bed linen. I had sat myself opposite the main door, so that I could see what was going on. The entrance was wide open at the moment. A serving hatch was positioned just to the left of the door on the far side. I could see the stewards – those who were not waiting tables – moving back and forth with the bed linen beyond the door. Even with the powder skilfully planted – and fingerprints dutifully removed, according to Maurice – it would only be a matter of time after the body was found before suspicion fell upon me.

The rest of the diners were in damnably good spirits. A news sheet had been posted up by the crew and Karl Lindt was holding forth on the fate of King Alfonso, who was had apparently fled from Spain the previous evening. Mr Gray, the post office fellow, was more interested in the weather report, with Sir George Westlake relishing the prospect of a little turbulence ahead. He was sitting with Mrs Koenig, I noticed. I wondered if anyone had noticed her extra-curricular activities last night. The walls were thin enough for that kind of sound to travel, but doubtless most of the passengers would have been fast asleep.

Miss Hurst was sitting at another table, nursing a cup of milky tea with Josef Kaufmann and that Spanish fellow, whose name I still hadn't caught. I had glanced over at her several times during the course of breakfast, but she had never looked back. What had she made of our nocturnal encounter? I wondered. My panicked reaction to it all seemed rather absurd now. Miss Hurst had only glanced at me for the briefest of moments. She couldn't have learnt the truth in that one instant, even if she had looked directly at my drawers. People invariably see what they want to see and she had no reason to expect anything other than a man in his underpants. Funnily enough, it was Lucy Tanner who was looking at me oddly this morning, across the floor of the dining room. She was sitting away from her fiancé again – they were not the clingy couple that some love birds are, forever in each other's pockets – and the Irishman seemed in good spirits.

'You missed out last night,' he informed me cheerfully. 'The game was just getting interesting when you left.' The poker game. I had all but forgotten about that.

'It was a slaughterhouse,' Jacob Finch lamented, clutching his hands together in distress. The red-haired fellow

108

never seemed to have a calm reaction to anything. You would have thought a stockbroker would be used to the occasional bad luck.

'Sir George didn't take any prisoners,' McGilton agreed. 'You were probably wise to leave when you did.'

'I wasn't prepared to lose another twenty five dollars,' I grumbled.

'You got off lightly,' Finch observed. 'He took me to the cleaners. It was a disaster! I'm lucky I've still got the shirt on my back.'

'All good fun, though.' McGilton smiled. He had obviously not lost quite as much as the Englishman.

'If you say so,' I muttered. I was not in the mood for gentle badinage this morning. I bit into my toast and stared past the Irishman at the door.

All through the early hours, lying in bed, I had been running back through the sequence of events that had led me to this point. I couldn't understand any of it. Gerhard Schulz committing suicide and now Walter Kendall dying in bed. The more I thought about it, the less plausible any of it seemed. Two men who had been in possession of documents vital to the security of Great Britain had died within half a day of each other. Could that really just be a coincidence or was something more sinister going on? And then I remembered that it was Charles Lazenby who had given me the sleeping draught and at that point my blood had run cold. It was Lazenby who had suggested drugging the American – albeit jokingly – and had then reinforced the idea with a telegram. What if the bottle he had given me did not contain a sleeping draught at all? What if it was a poison of some kind, something he had slipped me in order to deliberately murder Walter Kendall? There was no way of checking the powder, now that Maurice had planted the bottle in the American's cabin, but could Lazenby really have set me up? He had certainly organised the tickets for the Richthofen well in advance. If he had arranged Kendall's death, might he also have bumped off Gerhard Schulz and made it look like a suicide? After all, Lazenby had still been in Seville on Monday afternoon when I had sent him that telegram. On a

109

day like that, with the king about to flee Spain, he should have been on the first train back to Madrid. The possibilities swam around in my head like a set of hungry piranhas. Could it really be true? Charles Lazenby, one of His Majesty's finest, in truth a cold-blooded murderer? It didn't seem possible. What motive could he have had for arranging a double killing? He had nothing to gain, so far as I could see, and everything to lose. No, I told myself firmly, Lazenby could not be responsible for any of this. I was letting my imagination run away with me. As like as not, it was just a tragic accident. Gerhard Schulz had taken his own life and either Kendall had a heart condition or we had misjudged the dose of the powder. And then he had died. It was as simple as that.

But whatever the truth, one thing was certain: it was I who was going to be held to account.

'Mind you, it's Herr Lindt I feel sorry for,' Mr Finch proclaimed, interrupting my reverie. 'Three nights in a row he's lost out.'

I had no idea what the ginger fellow was talking about. 'Three nights?'

'Three games of poker,' McGilton explained, as Finch pushed back his chair and rose to his feet. 'Couldn't have happened to a nicer fellow. And I don't begrudge Sir George his winnings.' He glanced across the room at the veteran explorer. 'He needs every penny he can get, so I've heard.'

'Sir George does?'

The Irishman nodded. 'His last Antarctic expedition practically bankrupted him, so I hear. I was talking to Mr Gray about it. Lost a small fortune.'

'He can't be that badly off,' I said, looking round, 'if he can afford a ticket on the Richthofen.'

'Oh, he's not paying for it. He had it written into his contract. He's doing another lecture tour, in America this time. Bit of a come down for the great explorer,' McGilton thought.

'He doesn't seem to have let it get him down,' I said, taking a last sip of tea from my cup. The man himself was hooting with laughter at another table. I wished he would quieten down. I was starting to get a headache.

Breakfast was beginning to wind up. Mr Finch had made his excuses and some of the other diners were preparing to vacate the hall. The stewards were collecting up their plates and, out in the passengers quarters, the dirty bed linen was being gathered together and carted away. That was dashed peculiar, I thought. No one at breakfast had commented on Mr Kendall's absence. No one had cried out in alarm at the discovery of a corpse. And none of the stewards seemed to be panicking. I checked my pocket watch. It was half past nine, the cabins had all been cleaned, and no one had discovered the body of Walter Kendall.

Chapter Nine

'You haven't seen Mr Kendall, have you?' I asked the steward, out in the corridor, as the guests were departing the dining room. 'He wasn't at breakfast.' I tried to make the question sound as casual as possible. It was a reasonable thing to ask, though I knew it was something of a risk, drawing attention to myself in this manner. But I couldn't think of any other way to find out what was going on. How could the crew not have found the corpse of Walter Kendall?

Heinrich shook his head, in answer to my question. The steward was on his way back to the dining hall, to lend a hand with the cleaning up. I had buttoned-holed him midway along the connecting passage. He had thought for a moment before answering. 'I am afraid not, sir. I haven't seen him since last night. Is something the matter?'

'No, not at all,' I insisted, a little too firmly. 'I just wanted to check he was all right. We had a bit of an extended night cap last night. Probably had a bit too much of the old sauce.'

The steward did not understand. 'Sauce?'

'Lemonade. Alcohol.'

'Oh, I see.' He smiled.

'Must have a splitting headache this morning. Probably still in his cabin sleeping it off. Did you...clean the rooms yourself?'

'Yes, sir. Myself and two other cabin stewards. We change the sheets every day, for your comfort.' The young man was doing his best to be helpful but he wasn't making any sense.

'So...Mr Kendall was in there when you cleaned it?'

The steward considered for a moment. 'No, sir. He couldn't have been. We don't clean the cabins if they are occupied.'

'Ah. So he must be up and about then?'

'I suppose so, sir,' Heinrich said. 'I believe he may have been intending to send a telegram this morning. Perhaps he has gone to the radio room?'

'Yes, of course. That must be it. Journalists, eh? Always keeping busy. Can't trust them as far as you can throw them.'

'No, sir.' The steward hesitated. 'Is there anything else I can help you with?' I was hovering, rather, and he did have duties to attend to.

'No, nothing else.' My brain was racing, trying to make sense of the situation. How could the stewards not have found Walter Kendall's body? The American was stone cold dead. There was no way they could have missed him. What on earth was going on? 'And you're certain his cabin was cleaned?' I asked again. I had no reason to doubt Heinrich's word – he certainly had an honest face – but the body couldn't just have gone walkabouts. Kendall had been as dead as the proverbial dodo.

'Yes, sir. All the rooms have been cleaned. Those that are occupied.'

I scratched my chin distractedly. 'Occupied? Why, are there empty cabins?'

'Yes, sir. We are not fully booked.' He gestured to the port corridor. 'This one on the corner is empty. And one of the rooms next door to your own cabin.' On the other side from Thomas McGilton.

A sudden, mad thought struck me. Could someone have *moved* the body, before the room was cleaned? No, that was ridiculous. No one could have broken into Kendall's cabin after Maurice and I had both been in there and dragged a hefty corpse across the deck. And even if they had, they could not have got far. The passenger decks may have been quiet, in the small hours, but the rest of the ship, even in the dead of night, would have been swarming with crewmen. Unless they had dumped the body somewhere nearby, I thought. Perhaps in one of these empty rooms.

Heinrich was attempting, very politely, to make sense of my rambling questions. 'Do you wish to change cabins, sir?'

'No, I...' I considered for a moment. I didn't want to provoke his suspicion any further than I already had. 'Well, yes, actually. Not me, my manservant. Maurice. Can't get a wink of sleep with him in the room,' I said. 'He snores abominably. Thought I might shuffle him off somewhere else.'

'I understand, sir. It was quite a noise.'

'I'm sorry?' I stared at the lad blankly.

He grinned again and his whole face lit up. 'I heard quite a noise when I was returning the boots to your door this morning.'

What on earth was he babbling about? Maurice didn't really snore. He was quieter in bed than Walter Kendall and Kendall was dead. 'I'm not sure I understand.'

The steward's smile vanished as he realised he had overstepped the mark. 'Nothing, sir.' Perhaps he had heard McGilton next door. 'If your valet wishes to move, I can arrange it for you.' He gestured again to the cabin on the corner. 'Would you like me to open it up so that you can have a look?'

'No!' I exclaimed. That was the last thing I wanted. If I was right and Kendall's body *had* been moved, then like as not it would have been dumped somewhere close by, where no one was likely to look. And that cabin was the best bet available. It was next door to Mrs Koenig, two doors down from Kendall himself. If the body was in there, the last thing I wanted was Heinrich stumbling across it at my behest. 'No, I think the one next door to mine will do. Keep my man close at hand, for emergencies.'

'I understand, sir. I will arrange it for you.'

'Thank you, Heinrich. I appreciate it. Oh, you might have a look at the lock on my door, while you're at it.' I was saying anything now, just to distract his attention. 'I can't get the damn thing to close properly.'

'I will attend to it this morning,' he assured me.

'Good man.' My hand went automatically to my pocket, to grab a few coins, but I stopped myself, knowing the young lad would not accept them. I was trying my best not to appear flustered, but I was not making a good job of it. Thankfully, the steward was already heading off about his duties.

I lingered in the corridor for a moment, sweating profusely. What in god's name was going on? Could the body really have been shifted, without anyone noticing? What other explanation could there be for him not being found? Unless of course they *had* found the body but were just keeping quiet. That, surely, was a more plausible hypothesis. Perhaps they didn't want to alarm anyone, so soon after Gerhard Schulz's death. But I had been watching the corridor like a hawk over breakfast. None of the officers had been summoned. Even if the stewards had dealt with the discovery in a calm and professional manner, rather than running around like headless chickens as I probably would have done, the captain or the first officer would have been summoned, to inspect the scene. And neither of them had been anywhere near the cabin. So, logically, someone must have moved the body before the stewards arrived to clean it. But that was just mad. Nobody else had known he was dead, apart from Maurice and myself. I let out a sigh. There was no making sense of it.

'A penny for them, Mr Bland.' Lucy Tanner beamed. The woman had crept up on me, while I had been wool-gathering.

'I...was just contemplating a trip down to the bar,' I lied, quickly regaining my composure.

'It's far too early for that,' she informed me mischievously. Her large brown eyes shone at me from the depths of her narrow, painted face. 'Come and join me on the promenade.' She grabbed my arm and manoeuvred me towards the lounge before I had any opportunity to object. 'You haven't seen Walter, have you? I mean, Mr Kendall. He wasn't at breakfast.'

'No, I haven't.' It was no surprise that Lucy Tanner was the first to comment on his absence and it wouldn't be long before everyone noticed. In the circumstances, it seemed wise to stick with the line I had fed the steward. 'Probably recovering from last night. We did have a bit of an extended night cap.'

'The poor dear!' Miss Tanner lamented. 'He never could hold his drink. Probably best to let him sleep it off.' We moved through into the lounge. 'How was your first night in the bunk beds?'

'Er...passable, I suppose. Didn't get much sleep. I'm not

115

used to sharing. And the cabins are far too cramped.'

'Yes, aren't they? Annabel and I have to take it in turns to get dressed! There isn't the room for two of us.' She beamed, waving a hand at a couple of passengers as we passed them by. 'You frightened the life out of her last night, you know.'

'Did I?' I coughed. 'Yes, I...she told you about that, did she?' That was all I needed, Miss Hurst spreading the word about my nocturnal activities.

'Oh, yes. All the sordid details. Do you always walk about the corridors in your under things?'

'I...well, no, I...'

She laughed merrily, enjoying my discomfort. 'Mr Bland! I do believe you're embarrassed.'

'Not at all. It was just an unfortunate accident.'

'I'm only teasing.' She beamed again. 'I once caught the hem of my skirt in the door of a taxi cab. Ripped the thing to shreds. It took me years to live it down.' Her eyes twinkled at the memory. We had reached the promenade now and found a padded sofa at the far end, well away from the lounge. I wasn't quite as comfortable sitting here next to the windows, in broad daylight, as I had been in the early hours, but it didn't look like I would be given any choice in the matter. 'It's a super day, isn't it?' Miss Tanner exclaimed, settling herself next to me. 'You can see the sunlight glittering right across the clouds.'

'There's a storm brewing later, according to the weather report.'

'Is there? What fun! I wonder if there'll be thunder and lightning.'

'Lord, I hope not.' With everything else that was going on, that would just about kill me off.

'Don't tell me you didn't bring a rain coat?' Miss Tanner asked, her eyes sparkling with mischief.

'Oddly enough no. I didn't bring much clothing with me at all, as a matter of fact.'

'Yes, I noticed that. Your suit is very nicely cut,' she observed, gazing down at my jacket, 'but you really ought to have brought more than one with you.' I was wearing the same linen suit as I had upon my arrival. Miss Tanner was on her

116

fourth or fifth outfit, a black rayon dress with a colourful floral design. She must have paid a fortune in excess baggage fees.

'I do have a dinner jacket as well,' I responded stiffly. I would never travel anywhere without appropriate evening wear.

Miss Tanner was not to be put off. 'Yes, I saw that last night at supper. You looked very dashing. You mustn't mind me asking.' She leaned in confidentially. 'But Annabel told me that when she saw you last night, you were all...well, bandaged up.'

'I...yes, that's right.' So that was why Miss Tanner had manhandled me out here. She wanted to know what the bandages were for. I supposed it made sense that Miss Hurst would notice those rather than the flaccid line of my drawers.

'Have you hurt yourself in some way?'

'Burns,' I said, the first word that came into my head. 'I was in a...a fire.'

'You poor dear!' Miss Tanner exclaimed, her voice full of concern.

'Quite badly burnt, as a matter of fact. Around the...' I indicated my chest vaguely.

'That's awful! Does it hurt terribly?' She wasn't being ghoulish, she was just showing concern for my welfare.

'Not too much now, thankfully. I'm through the worst of it. It's healing, according to my doctor, but it's as well to keep it covered up. Prevents infection, or some such rot.' I was really getting into the flow of the lie now and Miss Tanner was lapping it up.

She placed a casual hand on my thigh. The woman seemed incapable of communicating without touching people, but I was getting used to it by now. 'Well, you must look after yourself. Walter once had...' She stopped herself mid sentence, probably wondering if she was about to be indiscreet; but after a moment's consideration she decided to continue with the train of thought. 'Mr Kendall was a war correspondent, for a time, in France. He was injured – a bullet in the leg – but he's a typical man. He was up and about before it was fully healed, which caused all sorts of problems later on. So you must look after yourself, Mr Bland. Don't do anything energetic. Wait until you're properly healed.'

117

'Have no fear, Miss Tanner. I have no intention of doing anything energetic on this flight.' It was my turn to change the subject. 'I hope you don't mind me saying so, but you seem to know Mr Kendall quite well.' She had called him Walter twice now. 'I understood that you had only just met.'

She looked out the window and gave a half smile. 'Ah, you've caught me out. Yes, I've known Walter – Mr Kendall – for quite some years. Since I was a little girl, in fact. He is a friend of my father's. We used to see him every summer when we went out to America for the holidays. I suppose I shouldn't really admit this, but I had a terrible crush on him. He was so handsome and wise. He still is.' She smiled again. 'When I was older, I'm afraid I made rather a fool of myself.'

'A fool?'

'It was just a silly girlish infatuation. Walter was very kind about it. But he's a married man. And it's all in the past now. I haven't told Thomas about it. I don't want to upset him. He has enough to worry about at the moment, the poor dear. He's trying not to show it, but he's rather anxious about meeting my parents in Chicago.'

'That's understandable,' I thought. Mixed marriages were always a complicated affair. 'How do they feel about you marrying a Roman Catholic?'

'Daddy's keeping an open mind. He just wants me to be happy. He's terribly sweet like that. But my mother can be a bit of an ogre, sometimes.'

'I'm sure she'll come round,' I said, though in truth I was sure of no such thing. 'But it seems a bit rum, keeping your friendship with Mr Kendall a secret from your fiancé. What will you do when he meets your parents and they happen to mention their old friend?'

'I don't think that's very likely. They're not as close as they once were. But I will tell Thomas all about it when we reach New York. You're right, I shouldn't deceive him. It's terribly cruel, especially as we are to be married so soon. There should be no secrets between newly weds.'

I laughed. 'I wouldn't go that far. I'm sure Mr McGilton must have one or two skeletons in his closet.'

Miss Tanner shook her head in mock outrage. 'He is an angel, perfect in every regard. He's always been very honest with me,' she added, more seriously.

'And Mr Kendall, was he pleased to see you, when he realised you were on this flight?'

She nodded happily. 'He was very charming. He hasn't changed a bit. He's such a dear, dear man. He's offered to help me find work in New York.'

Lord, I thought. Another opportunity ruined. Kendall wasn't going to be helping anybody from now on, least of all Miss Tanner.

The brief pause gave the woman a moment to reflect. 'Goodness!' she exclaimed, pulling back. 'I don't know why I'm telling you all this. I'm such a terrible gossip. My brothers always say to me, if you want to keep a secret you shouldn't tell anybody at all, but I can't help myself!' She grinned. 'It all comes babbling out. But I'm sure I can trust you, Mr Bland. You have such a kind face!'

I laughed. 'I don't know about that.....'

She raised a hand and tutted disapprovingly. 'You should always accept a compliment gracefully. How will you ever find a wife if you keep contradicting people?'

'I'm not exactly...'

'You're not getting any younger, Mr Bland. It's not right, a man of your age being without a wife. Mrs Koenig is a widow. Perhaps she might be interested in you, if you paid her some attention.'

I grimaced. 'You're teasing me again, Miss Tanner.'

'Only a little, Mr Bland.' She laughed gently. 'Only a little.'

Adelina Koenig was hunched over a large map, which was spread across the central table of the reading area. I had strode towards the room at some speed, in search of a telegraph slip, pleased at last to be free of Miss Tanner's relentless flirting. It had been an instructive conversation, for all its apparent frivolity. I was now convinced that Miss Tanner had acted as courier for Walter Kendall in Seville. If they were such good friends, what could be more natural than her running an errand for him? I doubted she would have known any of the specifics, but the thought of helping her dear pal in acquiring a "scoop" would doubtless appeal to the woman's innate sense of mischief. I could just picture her swapping envelopes with the late Gerhard Schulz halfway up the Torre del Oro, while I was grunting my way to the top.

Another thought occurred to me. I wondered, perhaps, if she had held on to the negatives for safe keeping, at Kendall's request. That might explain why I could not find them in the American's cabin. I hoped I was wrong. I had no desire to indulge in any more breaking and entering on this trip.

Miss Tanner had gone off in search of her fiancé. I could see why McGilton was enamoured with the girl. A lot of people might have been offended by her frivolity, but there was a charm underlying her impertinence and I confess I was starting to warm to her.

The same could not be said of Mrs Koenig. The stocky German was attacking her map with a ruler and pencil, her cold, pretty face screwed up in concentration. I had not known she was a widow. I wondered what her husband had died of. On second thoughts, I didn't want to know.

Annabel Hurst was sitting in the far corner of the room writing a letter. Mr Gray – the dull post office man – was over to the left, absorbed in a heavy textbook. At sight of the three of them, I almost turned around and ran. But it was too late. I had crossed the threshold. 'Don't mind me,' I said, striding across the room to the notice board. 'Just want to pick up a telegraph slip.'

Miss Hurst flinched at the sound of my voice and then buried herself in her writing. Frederick Gray gave a quiet nod of greeting but Mrs Koenig barely grunted.

There was a pile of blank slips on a table just below the notice board. I had decided to give Charles Lazenby the benefit of the doubt and fire off another telegram. I couldn't tell him that Kendall was dead – at least not yet – but I could let him know that I hadn't managed to find the negatives. There might yet be a need to have somebody on standby in Rio. I stared down at the empty slips and sighed. Admitting one's failure is never easy. But it was his damned fault for sending me out here in the first place.

I glanced up at the morning news sheet, which had been pinned to the middle of the board. It had a brief selection of headlines. There was nothing of any great interest. I had already heard about King Alfonso. The Graf Zeppelin – our sister ship – had returned to Friedrichshafen from North Africa, apparently, and there was more political violence in Germany. Apart from that and one line about King George's illness – which had been going on for some time – there was nothing of any value. There wasn't even any sports news. I liked to keep up with the cricket when I could, and the racing at Newmarket was about to begin, but there was nothing on that at all. 'Shame they can't telegraph out a copy of the Times,' I muttered to myself.

'I was thinking the same thing myself, Mr Bland,' Frederick Gray volunteered, in his whining, nasal voice. 'But it will only be a matter of time. The technology to transmit newspaper print already exists.' He would know, I suppose. A GPO man.

'There is no talking!' Mrs Koenig snapped at the two of us. 'I am trying to concentrate.'

I glared across at the woman. It was bad enough being interrupted by Mr Gray but to be told off by the German woman was too much to bear. 'Oh, you do speak English,' I observed, acidly.

'Ja,' she agreed, her head still bent over the map. She was drawing a line across the middle of it. I moved over to get a better view. It was a world map and it looked as if she was charting our progress across the Atlantic.

'How far have we come?' I asked her, with genuine interest. The further we had travelled, the closer we were to the Brazilian police and my inevitable arrest.

'We are three thousand kilometres from Seville and four thousand seven hundred kilometres from Friedrichshafen.' Her accent was the thickest I had encountered since boarding the

121

Richthofen but, with a little concentration, I could just about follow her words.

'What's that in miles?' I asked. Kilometres meant nothing to me.

'One thousand eight hundred and seventy five, from Seville,' Mr Gray threw in helpfully. 'You divide by eight and then multiply by five.'

'I'll try to remember that.' I looked down at the line Mrs Koenig had drawn. 'So we're about halfway.'

'No, that is not correct,' she disagreed. 'We are four thousand seven hundred and fifty kilometres from Rio de Janeiro. We will arrive late tomorrow evening.'

'Weather permitting,' I said. There had been a brief note about the upcoming storm on the news sheet. If it was a bad one, the Richthofen would have to change course and move around it, which would doubtless add a few hours to the journey time. 'Are you getting off at Rio?' I asked Mrs Koenig. I crossed my fingers, hoping she would say yes.

'No.' She shook her head emphatically. 'I go all the way.'

I stifled a laugh, remembering the activity in her cabin from a few hours before. 'Yes, I'm sure you do. Do you have business in New York?'

'In Los Angeles, *ja*. I fly there myself from New York. They want to speak to me, the movie people.'

'Movie people?'

'*Ja*. They make a film of my life. The woman aviator.'

'Good lord.' I wasn't quite sure whether she was having me on, but I didn't feel inclined to challenge her. 'That will make an interesting film. So who will they get to play you? Greta Garbo?'

She grunted with disdain. 'I will play me!' she declared, looking up from the map.

The clouds were getting darker outside and only the thought of a cigarette and Max the barman fixing me the necessary was keeping me on an even keel. I got as far as the passenger cabins

122

and halfway along the connecting corridor before my progress was interrupted. An officer was barrelling up the stairs from B Deck. He was a tall, stern faced man in the usual heavy coat and peaked cap. This was the officer who had been speaking to Mrs Koenig in the control cabin yesterday afternoon. 'Good morning, Mr Bland,' he said. He was a grim looking fellow in his late forties.

'Good morning, Mr....Rüdiger, was it?'

'Captain Rüdiger,' he confirmed, extending a hand.

'Captain,' I agreed. Most of the officers sported that title, though it was Herntz Albrecht who had overall charge of the ship. Rüdiger was second in command. 'Making your morning rounds?' I asked. If Captain Albrecht was busy, he would send an underling to cosy up to the passengers. There was nothing cosy about this fellow, however. Rüdiger had an abrupt, unfriendly bearing that complimented his granite-like face.

'No, it is you I wish to speak to,' he replied.

I stared at him blankly. 'Me?' Why would he want to speak to me? I didn't like the sound of that at all.

'Perhaps you would accompany me to the steward's cabin?' He gestured along the port corridor, leading towards the front of the ship. 'We can talk privately there.' I had a horrible feeling it was not a request.

'By all means,' I said, trying not to sound concerned. But my brain had already turned to ice. Did Rüdiger know something about my activities the previous evening? Perhaps he had been talking to Mrs Koenig. At the very least, the German woman would have overheard my unfortunate conversation with Annabel Hurst out in the corridor. I tried to keep my expression neutral as we shuffled along the forward passage.

The first officer knocked on the stewards' door and entered before the man inside had any opportunity to respond. 'Stefan, I wish to talk privately with Mr Bland.' Out of courtesy to me, Rüdiger spoke to the chief steward in English. Stefan, a bald middle-aged man with heavy eyebrows, was happy to absent himself. I followed Rüdiger into the narrow, L-shaped room. His expression was grave as he addressed himself to me. 'I understand from one of our stewards that you were enquiring about Mr Kendall?'

I gulped. 'Er...yes, that's right. He wasn't at breakfast. We had a bit of drinking session last night. Just wanted to check he was all right.'

'I see.' There was a pregnant pause.

'Is he? All right, I mean?'

The first officer shook his head sadly. 'No, I am afraid he is not. Mr Kendall died in his cabin last night.'

'Good lord!' I tried to show the appropriate level of surprise. 'Died?'

'Yes, I am afraid so.'

I allowed myself a moment to let the news sink in. 'Poor fellow,' I breathed. I have never been a virtuoso when it comes to play-acting, but when my neck is on the line I pride myself I can lie with the best of them. 'He can't have been more than...what, fifty five?' I shook my head. 'Did one of the stewards find him?' Heinrich had sworn blind that he had not seen Kendall since last night.

'That is correct. He was discovered in his cabin at a quarter to seven this morning.'

'In his cabin?' So the young lad *had* been lying. But that didn't make any sense. Why would one of the stewards enter Kendall's cabin a good hour and a half before breakfast? Rüdiger saw my confusion and was quick to explain.

'Mr Kendall asked for an early morning call. I understand he wanted to send a telegram before breakfast. It was a matter of some urgency, he said. The steward knocked and when he did not answer, the door was opened and the man was discovered lying on top of his bed.'

'Lord,' I breathed. 'How awful.' That at least explained why there had been no fuss at breakfast time. The corpse had already been discovered, long before any of the passengers had surfaced. 'So how did he die?' I asked.

'That we are trying to determine.'

'You've had a doctor in there to take a look, I imagine.' I knew very well that they hadn't, but I couldn't resist baiting the fellow. It doesn't do, in these situations, to always be on the back foot.

'Unfortunately not. We do not have a medical officer on board.'

'No doctor?' My eyes boggled in apparent surprise. 'Seems a bit lax, if you don't mind me saying so.'

Irritation flashed across the first officer's face. 'It is something that has been discussed but it has never been thought necessary until now. We will have to wait until Rio for a full examination; but it seems likely that Mr Kendall died in his sleep. There was a sleeping draught by his bed which he may have used. The instructions were in Spanish, so perhaps he misread the dosage. A doctor will be able to determine that. In the meantime, we will leave the body in the cabin.' At last, something that did make sense. So Kendall had not been moved after all. Heinrich must have known he was dead when I had spoken to him, even if he had not been the one to discover the body. The lad was a surprisingly good liar. Not that I blamed him. He had clearly been under orders to keep quiet. 'We are only a day and a half from our next port,' Rüdiger added.

'So why wasn't there an announcement at breakfast?' I asked.

'Captain Albrecht felt it would be better to wait until lunchtime. We do not wish to cause any undue distress, especially after the unfortunate news concerning Herr Schulz yesterday afternoon. Better to wait until we are through the storm and the matter can be attended to properly. Captain Albrecht does not have the time to visit the passenger decks this morning. But when we heard from the steward that you had enquired about Mr Kendall, the captain thought it best I had a quiet word with you.'

'I understand.' So I wasn't under suspicion. I was just being a bit of a nuisance. That was the first good news I had had all day. 'Well you can rely on my discretion,' I told him. 'Lord, two passengers dead in less than two days. Not a good run.'

The first officer nodded gravely. 'Captain Albrecht is very upset. He has never lost a passenger before. It is most

125

regrettable.'

'Not his fault, Captain Rüdiger. These things happen. It's Miss Tanner I feel sorry for. She'll be mortified.'

'The Fräulein was close to Mr Kendall?'

'No, but she admired him. He was a singular fellow.'

'A journalist, I understand. Captain Albrecht said he was highly respected in his field.'

'I'll say.' Another pause descended. 'Was there anything else, captain?'

'No.' The first officer pulled himself up. 'You will excuse me. I must return to the control room now. The storm will be upon us shortly.' He reached for the door and stepped out into the corridor.

'It's not going to be a bad one, is it?'

'There is nothing to fear, Mr Bland.' He smiled tightly. He was aiming for reassurance but the expression did not suit him at all. 'We are already moving around the edges of the storm. And the Richthofen is designed to cope with anything that nature can throw at it.'

I grimaced. 'Forgive me if I'm not reassured.'

'You are welcome to join us in the control room, if you wish to have...what is the phrase...a grandstand view?'

Now the man was being facetious. 'I think I'll pass on that,' I muttered.

'As you wish. Ah, good morning, Mr Finch.'

The first officer tipped his hat as Jacob Finch, the stockbroker, made his way purposefully along the passage towards us. I tried very hard not to scowl at him. It seemed like I couldn't walk anywhere on the ship this morning without bumping into some idiot or other. Unfortunately, Finch's cabin appeared to be directly opposite the steward's. Finch was clutching two pieces of paper in his hands, one of which looked to be a telegram. He nodded perfunctorily to the first officer, who moved smoothly past him and continued on his way. Finch grimaced at the sight of me, which was a bit rich considering he was the one obstructing the corridor.

'I wish it *was* a good morning,' he exclaimed, waving the telegram in front of me. 'It's an absolute disaster.'

126

'Stocks taken a dive?' I enquired. The last thing I wanted to do was engage him in conversation – I had too much else to think about just now – but the damned fellow was standing between me and the rest of the deck.

'If only it was that simple!' he declared. 'Everything's going horribly wrong. One hand doesn't know what the other hand is doing. I wish I *were* a stockbroker, then we might not be in this mess.'

I didn't understand. 'What do you mean, not a stockbroker?'

'You really don't know, do you?' He shook his head sadly. 'You poor sap. You're up to your neck in it and you haven't got a clue what it's all about.'

I no longer had the patience to be polite. 'Mr Finch, I really have no idea what you're talking about.'

'No. How could you? I've just been in touch with London. You're not going to like this one little bit.' He fumbled in his jacket and produced a leather wallet with a small metal star. 'Jacob Finch. Special Branch. There's been the most god-awful cock-up. You shouldn't be here at all.'

Chapter Ten

The outer edges of the storm were beginning to make their mark on the hull of the Richthofen. I was well away from any of the windows, in a tiny cabin towards the front of the passenger deck, but the sound of the rain battering the canvas exterior of the Zeppelin was becoming audible even in the depths of the ship. The wind was whistling around us and, in the distance, I could hear the first grumble of thunder. That should have been enough to give me palpitations but at the moment, in the cramped confines of a passenger bedroom, my attention was focused wholly on Mr Jacob Finch.

He was a strange looking fellow, a little under six feet tall, with bright ginger hair and an anxious, square jawed face. He might have been considered handsome, if only he had managed to stay still long enough to be photographed. But his eyes and hands were constantly on the move and there was a shifty air to him, born – I suspected – more of anxiety than any attempt at duplicity.

'Does the captain know you're on board?' I asked him, incredulously. I had followed the man into his cabin in something of a daze. The last thing I had expected to find on a German airship was a British policeman.

'Yes, he knows,' Finch confirmed. 'He's not at all happy about it. Why would he be? It's an appalling situation. I have no jurisdiction. We're in international waters. I can't arrest anybody. I can't do anything. But the captain's allowing me to pursue a few enquiries, so long as I'm discreet. Not that he really knows what I'm looking for. I could hardly go into details. But he's given me access to the telegraph, so I've been able to keep in touch with London.' He gestured to the notes in his lap. He had left breakfast early, I recalled. Perhaps he had been summoned to the radio room. 'Not that they're much help either. We're on our own out here. It's been a shambles from start to finish.'

'And you're really a member of Special Branch?' I asked, not bothering to hide my incredulity. He did not seem like a policeman to me. I glanced down at his shoes. He didn't even have flat feet.

'I'm afraid so,' Finch replied, fidgeting in his chair. I was sitting on the bed, on a freshly tidied orange blanket. He had propped himself up on a stool, with his back pressed against the folded up wash basin. 'I flew out from Croydon to Friedrichshafen on Saturday afternoon and joined the Richthofen at the eleventh hour.'

'That sounds familiar,' I observed.

'You can imagine the shock when I found out you were on board as well. You're not meant to be here at all.' He lifted the notes from his lap and rustled them absently. The damned fellow seemed incapable of keeping still. One of the papers was a telegram slip. The other was a white sheet with pencil marks scribbled across it, presumably a decryption of the message he had been sent from London. I wondered briefly what book code he was using; then I noticed a copy of *Alice in Wonderland* projecting out of his jacket pocket. MI5 were not the only ones with a sense of humour, it appeared. 'It's a total nightmare. Things should never have been allowed to get this far. I've checked your credentials with London.' He waved the telegram towards me, for emphasis. 'They've given you the all clear. So I'm afraid it's up to the two of us to sort out this sorry mess. But you really shouldn't have been on board in the first place.'

'Yes, you said that before. Look, can we start at the beginning?' I was not altogether sure I trusted this strange, anxious looking man. He had checked my credentials but I had not had the opportunity to check his. The identification he had given me looked genuine, but I was not about to take it at face value. And even if it were true, my opinion of Special Branch had never been that high. 'Why don't you tell me what this is all about?'

He nodded, folding up the papers in his hand and cramming them into the inside pocket of his jacket, next to the book. 'You won't believe a word of it. The level of incompetence involved.'

'I'll believe anything when it comes to your lot,' I said, only half jokingly. The boys from Special Branch were a laughing stock among the Intelligence community. When MI5 identified a spy ring, it was Scotland Yard who were called in to make the arrests and it was they who received the credit. But behind the scenes the organisation was an unmitigated disaster. They had been infiltrated by Soviet agents at the tail end of the twenties and had leaked all kinds of state secrets to the Russians, something that would never happen with MI5 or the SIS. Staring across the cabin at the policeman, I was curious to know what had gone wrong this time.

Finch gripped his hands on his thighs, took a deep breath and began his story.

'We have a file in the depths of Scotland Yard which isn't supposed to exist. Only a handful of people know about it. It can't be removed from the archive and only seven people have direct access to it. The security is supposed to be watertight.' Finch grimaced. 'I only wish it had been. One of these seven people accessed the file on Saturday morning, in order to update it. And, when he did, he discovered the documents had been tampered with. God knows how, but someone had got hold of the file and made a complete photographic copy.'

'You mean someone just waltzed into Scotland Yard with a miniature camera in their pocket?'

The policeman laughed bitterly. 'You know, I wouldn't be at all surprised. Security is an absolute joke. But no, this time, it was an internal job. Which only makes it worse. One of our own people! It's absolutely shameful.' His fingernails, I saw, were digging into the fabric of his trousers. This was not a man who viewed his work dispassionately. 'You think you can trust someone and then...'

A rumble of thunder served to underscore the point and for an instant the room seemed to shift sideways. I clutched onto the edge of the bed to support myself. The effect of the wind was starting to be felt even here. But I had more important things to concern myself with than a bit of turbulence.

'But if the file was still there, how did you know it had been photographed?'

Finch rolled his eyes. 'Because the papers were all over the place. Staples removed. Everything out of order. It must have been put back in a rush.'

'Do you have any idea who accessed the file?'

'Yes. It's practically the only thing we do know. We know who accessed it and we know what she did with the photographs.'

'She?'

'One of our female clerks.' Finch shuddered. 'Came on shift in the early hours of Saturday morning. We always have somebody there to keep an eye on things. And this was a woman of impeccable character. Been with us for years. From a good family. The highest level of clearance for her pay grade. It makes me despair, Mr Bland, if you can't trust a woman like that.'

I shrugged. 'There are rotten apples in every organisation.'

'But we do seem to have more of them in the Metropolitan Police than anywhere else.' Finch let out a heavy sigh.

'Perhaps you just notice them more.' But we were straying from the point. 'You say this "lady clerk" of yours made off with a copy of the file?'

Finch clamped his lips together and nodded. 'Yes. She was the only one who could have done it. We arrested her at Croydon aerodrome a couple of hours later. She admitted everything, but by then it was too late. The films were already on a plane to Friedrichshafen. We had to browbeat a local pilot into flying me out there in a two seater a couple of hours later. I didn't even have time to pack a suitcase.' He gestured apologetically to his clothes. His suit was a bit frayed, I noticed, though his shirt looked new.

'But if you knew a copy of this file was on one particular flight, why didn't you ask for the passengers to be detained when they arrived in Germany?'

'There wasn't time. And this is far too sensitive to involve the German authorities.' Finch leaned in close to me then, the stool he was sitting on tilting slightly in my direction as he shifted his weight. 'It's a question of national security. The fewer people who know about this, the better.'

That was the line Charles Lazenby had fed me. 'You know, Mr Finch, I think it's about time I was told exactly what was in this file.' I was fed up with all the secrecy. 'What's so horrendous about it that you've had to go to all this trouble?' Why had I been press ganged into travelling on this airship?

'You mean you haven't been told?' Finch boggled at me. Another gust of wind rocked the ship and he shot out a hand to steady himself as the stool threatened to topple from under him. 'How on earth could you be expected to help if they didn't tell you what it was all about?' he exclaimed.

I pursed my lips irritably. 'I've been asking myself that very question. I gathered from Charles Lazenby that it was something pretty scandalous, but nothing military.' That at least was what I had read between the lines. 'So I assume it's not just a few photographs of the Prince of Wales with his pants around his ankles.'

The electric light fluttered slightly and there was a boom of thunder. At least the pelting rain would serve to mask our conversation, if anyone happened to be passing by. The man from Special Branch looked away in embarrassment.

I blinked. Finch had gone red at the mention of the heir to the throne. I regarded him dubiously. 'It isn't Prince Edward is it?' A sex scandal seemed far too trivial to be worth all this fuss. And nobody would bat an eyelid at a bit of royal bed hopping. 'Everyone already knows what a libertine he is.'

Finch gripped his hands together again. 'People don't know the half of it, I'm afraid. Look, Mr Bland, this is absolutely top secret. It cannot leave these four walls.' Another rumble of thunder served to underscore the drama of the moment.

So it *was* something to do with Prince Edward. 'Go on.'

'We've been keeping a detailed file on the comings and goings of the Prince of Wales for some years now.'

I frowned. 'But that's your job isn't it, at Special Branch? To look after the prince and make sure he comes to no harm?'

'I only wish it were that simple. Yes, we provide protection, but this file goes far beyond anything like that. It contains details of every movement Prince Edward has made in the last ten years. Every illicit liaison. Even copies of his private correspondence. That was why one of our people was looking at it on Saturday morning. It was being updated, now the prince is on his way home from Brazil. But Special Branch is only charged with protecting him. It's not part of our remit to spy on the heir to the throne.'

I sat back on the mattress. 'Well, that may be a breach of protocol,' I admitted, 'but it's hardly a hanging offence.'

'You don't understand. It goes far beyond ordinary record keeping. This file makes shocking reading. It shows...well, I hate to even say it.' His hands were trembling with embarrassment. 'But it shows that the heir to the throne is...' He closed his eyes and spoke the words in a hoarse whisper, '...faithless, dishonourable and utterly unreliable. That's not my opinion, you understand,' he added anxiously, 'but the opinion of the British government. They have no faith whatever in Prince Edward as a future King of England. And this file makes that abundantly clear.' He opened his eyes. 'Have you ever heard of a woman called Maggie Meller?'

I shrugged. 'Can't say I have.'

'She was a French...well, a tart, for want of a better word.' He gripped his hands together again. 'A courtesan. Marguerite Alibert, to give her her real name. Absolutely dreadful woman. She made a fortune praying on the aristocracy during the war. A viper, she was, completely without scruples. The prince should never have got involved with a woman like that; but he only has himself to blame. He got his fingers burnt and since then we've been keeping tabs on all his amorous encounters. Most of them with married women.'

'That's hardly a surprise, though.' I chuckled quietly. 'The Prince of Wales associating with women of dubious character. It's practically in the job description.' I laughed again. 'Old Bertie, the late king, had a string of mistresses. Nobody ever batted an eyelid.' I could see why the American press might be interested, however. A scandal involving British royalty would shift an awful lot of newspapers. But it wouldn't do the prince any harm in the long run. 'If that's all that's in this file then publish and be damned, I say. It might make shocking reading for an elderly dowager or a maiden aunt but it's hardly likely to bring down the Empire.'

'You don't know the half of it.' Finch shivered. 'This Maggie Meller was hooked up with the prince at the tail end of the war. Then, shortly afterwards, she took up with another man, a young Egyptian millionaire named Ali Fahmy. She married him, in fact. And in 1923 she was brought to trial at the Old Bailey for his murder.'

I blinked. 'Murder?'

'Shot him from behind with a Browning .32 pistol. Appalling women, utterly callous, guilty as hell but certain that she would get away with it, because of her connections with the establishment.'

'Actually, I think I remember that trial,' I said. It had been quite a celebrated court case at the time.

'Just imagine the situation. This dreadful woman had in her possession a set of letters, written to her by the prince during the war. Letters of a severely compromising nature. Prince Edward spent most of the Great War in Paris, debauching himself with prostitutes, I'm sorry to say, while our brave lads were dying on the front line. He wrote a whole raft of letters to this Maggie Meller, many of which contained sensitive military information that would have had a lesser man shot for treason. These letters could not be allowed to enter the public domain; but after murdering her husband, the frightful woman had no reason to hold them back.'

'But she was acquitted, wasn't she? Of murder?' I remembered that much of the trial.

'Oh, yes, she got away with it. That's the crux of the matter. That's why everything's such an unmitigated disaster!' Finch threw up his hands in despair. 'The establishment intervened. The royal family cut a deal. They would make sure she was acquitted of the crime, if she promised to return the letters and not to mention her affair with the prince in open court. She agreed to keep quiet and walked from the courtroom

134

a free woman.'

'Lord.' I sucked in a mouthful of air.

'You see what this means?' He shuddered. 'This file proves beyond a shadow of a doubt that the royal family, in collusion with the British government, allowed a murderess to go free, to protect the reputation of the heir to the throne. The course of justice was deliberately perverted. If this gets out,' Finch concluded, in a whisper, 'the monarchy will be finished.'

There was a long pause. 'Does Prince Edward know about the file?' I asked, at length.

'No!' Finch was horrified at the very idea. 'He couldn't be *allowed* to know. The British government has no faith in him whatsoever. The man's an idiot, an adolescent boy not fit to run a sweet shop. That's not my opinion,' he added, hastily. 'That's the opinion of the prime minister. And this file proves it in no uncertain terms. But, god help us, Edward is going to be king and we cannot allow any of this to get out. Especially not now, when the king's health is in such a poor state.'

'You mean, because Prince Edward might become king any day?'

'Exactly, it's a time bomb ticking away.' Finch sat back on his stool. 'That's why we need to secure these negatives. We cannot allow them to enter the public domain. You understand now why London considered this so important?'

I nodded. Lazenby had been right. If this got out, there would be a constitutional crisis. It was difficult to see how the monarchy could survive. Prince Edward would be forced to flee the country, even before he had got home from Brazil. Just like King Alfonso in Spain. It did not bear thinking about.

'We've narrowed the suspects down to four people,' Finch told me, returning to practical matters. 'Those who disembarked from the plane in Friedrichshafen. And all four of them are travelling with us on board the Richthofen.'

'*Four* people?' I didn't understand. 'But surely Gerhard Schulz had the file originally? And he handed it on to Walter Kendall.'

Finch looked blank. 'Gerhard Schulz? What's he got to do with it?' The policeman regarded me with some surprise.

'Well...he was a journalist, like Walter Kendall. And it was Kendall who was going to publish the story. And now they're both dead. Er...you do know Mr Kendall died last night?'

Finch bit his lip. 'Yes, the captain told me. The poor man. But that can't have anything to do with our file. How could it? Mr Kendall didn't board the Richthofen until Seville.'

'Yes, but he was going to buy the file from Gerhard Schulz, during the stopover in Spain. Kendall's newspaper was going to publish it.' That was what Charles Lazenby had told me.

Finch shook his head. 'This is the first I've heard of it.'

I stared at the fellow in confusion. 'But Lazenby spent Sunday afternoon following him around Seville. He was convinced they were going to complete the deal in Spain. And I followed Gerhard Schulz all over town, on the understanding that he already had possession of the documents. And since Schulz ended the day with quite a bit of cash in his pocket we assumed he must have passed the file on, without us seeing him.'

'Cash?' Finch's eyes widened. 'Gerhard Schulz?'

'Yes. Well at any rate, the concierge at his hotel said he paid for his room in American dollars. Not conclusive proof, I admit, now I come to think of it. But that's what Charles Lazenby told me. And I assumed, from what you said, that your lady clerk must have given the file to the Austrian in the first place.'

The policeman shook his head. 'But Schulz wasn't on the plane from Croydon,' he said, sounding even more confused than I was. 'We saw his name on the passenger list for the Richthofen, of course, and as a journalist we assumed he might have an interest – particularly given his left wing sympathies. But he had nothing to do with the acquisition of the file. He couldn't have. He's never been anywhere near London.' Finch frowned heavily. 'But perhaps the SIS had information we didn't. Your people never tell us anything. It's absurd. We're forced to work with both hands tied behind our backs.' He had a point there, I had to concede. 'But we contacted the SIS as soon as we knew a copy of the file had left the country. For all the good it might do. That was why Mr Lazenby was brought in. Four of the passengers on the Croydon flight had booked tickets on the Richthofen. We knew the Zeppelin was stopping over in Seville and we needed someone to keep tabs on the suspects away from the airship. I presume you were drafted in to help out with that. Lazenby must have got hold of a passenger list in Seville and realised Mr Kendall was a potential buyer. But the first I heard of the American was when I arrived in Seville.' Finch took a gulp of air. The fellow had a tendency to gabble somewhat, I noticed. 'But as to Gerhard Schulz, he was never really a suspect. And having met the chap, I would have ruled him out as a criminal in any case.'

'Ruled him out? Why?'

'Intuition, more than anything. Not that I have much of a flare for that kind of thing. I only wish I did. But I sat up playing cards with him on Saturday evening – getting to know everyone on the quiet – and he didn't strike me as a man on a mission. More a man in love, I should say, the poor deluded chap.'

'Love?'

Finch nodded sadly. 'Had a bit of a thing for Miss Hurst.'

'Yes, I'd heard about that. But if you didn't think he had the documents, what was the point of me following him around Seville on Sunday afternoon? Or Lazenby following Kendall?'

'I haven't the faintest idea,' Finch admitted. 'We just needed a couple of extra boots on the ground. I couldn't keep tabs on everyone away from the airship. Your job was to keep an eye on anyone who left the hotel. But as it turned out, the only people who went sight-seeing were Mr Kendall, Miss Tanner and Herr Schulz. We certainly weren't expecting the documents to be passed on in Seville. The thief wouldn't have had time to develop the negatives.' That was a point. No potential buyer would pay out for photographs without having seen them first. 'And as for you being put on board the Richthofen when we left Spain, that certainly wasn't part of the plan. That was my job, not yours.' There was no bitterness in his voice, just bewilderment. 'It's been one enormous cock up right from the word go.'

'But why would Lazenby put me on board, if you were already here?'

'Heaven knows. We were both in communication with London, but perhaps the wires got crossed somewhere. Typical Special Branch bungling.'

Or perhaps, I thought quietly, my own people wanted me to keep an eye on this dubious policeman. He seemed rather highly strung, for a man who was meant to be one of Scotland Yard's finest. But if the SIS had any suspicion of him, why the devil hadn't Lazenby told me about it?

'And it wasn't until this morning,' Finch continued, 'that I had final confirmation of your identity.' He gestured to the telegram in his pocket.

I sat back on the bed. In the distance, there was another rumble of thunder. 'But if Gerhard Schulz never had the file then who on Earth did? Who carried it over from London?'

Finch threw up his hands. 'Well, that's the question. I wish I knew! It must have been one of these four people coming out of Croydon. But I'm no closer to finding out now than I was when I arrived in Germany. It's been an absolute nightmare from the word go.'

'Can't this clerk woman tell you who she passed the documents on to? She must have been questioned by now.'

Finch brought a hand up to his face. 'She doesn't know. She handed the films on to a baggage handler at the aerodrome. A Mick Durrant. Former Merchant Navy chap. She had some kind of romantic association with him, apparently. Lost her head, the foolish girl. The two of them were going to run away together once they collected their fee. Purely mercenary on their part. They must have photographed the file to order and passed the negatives on to a contact on that plane. Absolutely appalling behaviour. Unfortunately, we haven't been able to trace Mr Durrant.'

'But this woman, she must have known she couldn't get away with it. Photographing the file. Someone was bound to notice it had been tampered with.'

'Eventually, yes. But she wouldn't have expected it to happen so soon. The Prince of Wales has been in South America for the last few months. There wouldn't have been any reason to access the file before his return. But the embassy in Rio has a secure line and our man there sent us an update before heading off home on the *Arlanza*.' That was the ship that was now en route for Britain, with the prince on board. 'The woman only had time to get out to Croydon and hand on the documents to her boyfriend before we picked her up. But she doesn't know who he passed them on to. There's an alert out for Durrant, but until we find him, we just have the passengers on the plane; the ones who flew out to Friedrichshafen from Croydon aerodrome.' He leaned in closely. 'There were eight people on board that flight. A wealthy family from Düsseldorf, two adults and two children, returning home from an Easter holiday. And four passengers heading for the Richthofen on Saturday evening.'

'So who were they, if not Gerhard Schulz?'

'Annabel Hurst, Josef Kaufmann, Adelina Koenig and Frederick Gray.'

I laughed. 'Well, I think we can discount Miss Hurst. She's nothing more than a mouse. And Adelina Koenig is as mad as a fruitcake.' I considered for a moment. 'Kaufmann seems a decent enough fellow, if a little maudlin. No, if those are the suspects, then my money is on Frederick Gray. He's altogether too clever for a GPO man.' Converting kilometres into miles without prompting, I ask you. 'But I still don't understand why it was I spent Sunday afternoon following Gerhard Schulz around Seville if you'd already ruled him out.'

'Perhaps Charles Lazenby had information from his bosses that wasn't available to us.'

That was always a possibility. Given the organisation's propensity to leak information, the SIS was always loathe to pass anything on to Special Branch that it didn't have to. 'Or perhaps he thought the sale had already been made. Schulz bought the file from one of your four and was about to sell it on to Walter Kendall. But if that was the case, why would the original seller stay with the Zeppelin all the way to New York? It makes no sense at all.'

'It doesn't, does it?' Finch agreed.

I grimaced as another peal of thunder rocked the ship. It seemed to be getting louder with every burst.

'And the poor fellow committing suicide shortly after we left. It's an unmitigated disaster. All we know for certain is that the negatives are somewhere on board this ship. I've searched Kaufmann's cabin, and Frederick Gray's, and haven't found anything. I'm going to have to look at the women's rooms at some point. I'm not looking forward to that. All those frilly clothes...' He shuddered. 'But it has to be done. The captain...'

Before he could finish the thought, there was a firm knock at the door. I hadn't heard footsteps approaching the cabin, but then there was little chance of hearing much just at the moment. I did hear one sound, however: my valet's voice. 'Monsieur?' he called and knocked again.

Finch shot me a perplexed look. I rose up unsteadily, making sure to keep my hands on the side of the bed at all times, lest another gust of wind should rock the boat and send me flying. Maurice was standing out in the port corridor as I pulled back the door, his battered face it's usual pained self.

'Morris?' I said.

'Will you come with me, Monsieur?'

'How on earth did you know I was here?'

'I heard you talking. Our cabin is on the opposite side.' He gestured to the far wall. So much for the rain masking our conversation. But then Maurice had always had particularly good hearing.

'You overheard us?' the policeman gasped, his eyes widening in horror.

'Only the voices, Monsieur.'

'It's all right,' I reassured Finch. 'Morris is with me. He's been fully vetted.'

Finch was growing agitated once again. 'Even so, everything we've discussed is absolutely confidential!'

'Of course. He won't breathe a word. What do you want,

140

Morris? Can't you see I'm in the middle of an important conversation?'

'Yes, Monsieur. But there is something you need to see.'

I growled at him in irritation. 'Can't it wait?'

'No, Monsieur.'

I sighed and glanced apologetically at Finch. For all his faults, Maurice would not interrupt me like this without good reason.

'You go on,' the policeman suggested, pressing his back against the wash basin. 'We can talk more later, once we're through the storm. Are there many people out and about?' This question was aimed at my valet.

'Most of them are in the starboard lounge, Monsieur, watching the storm.'

'Well, that's something, anyway.' Finch waved a finger and drew me in close. 'The captain's asked me to take a look at Mr Kendall's cabin.' He produced a key from his breast pocket. 'I can't believe his death has anything to do with our business, but Captain Albrecht wants me to cast a professional eye over the scene, just to be on the safe side.'

'You really don't think it's connected?' I said. 'His death, I mean. The second journalist in two days?'

'Heaven knows. But I don't see how it can be. I'll make a thorough check of the crime scene in any case. If it is a crime scene. Not that it will do much good. I don't have any forensic equipment with me.' No fingerprint powder. That was a relief. 'Everything was done in such a rush. I didn't even have time to pack a change of clothes. I had to buy a couple of clean shirts in Friedrichshafen.'

Maurice was looking impatient at the door.

'I'll leave you to it, then,' I said. 'This had better be important, Morris.'

'It is, Monsieur,' the valet replied firmly, as I moved out into the corridor. 'I would not have summoned you if it was not.' We made our way towards the connecting corridor. 'Monsieur Finch is a policeman?' he asked.

'Special Branch. It's their file that's gone missing, apparently. Or a copy of it.' Even with Maurice, I couldn't say anything more than that.

'I see.'

We turned left and moved along the central passageway. Up ahead, the door to the lounge room was open and I could see several passengers standing at the far window, looking out at the storm. A flash of lightning electrified the saloon but it was some moments before the rumble of thunder caught up with the light show. I turned gratefully left towards my own cabin.

'The steward informed me that you wished me to move rooms,' Maurice said, as we arrived at the door.

I had forgotten about that. 'Yes, I was asking about empty cabins. Needed an excuse and that was the first thing I could think of. You haven't dragged me back here just to complain?'

'No, Monsieur. I was with the steward when he opened up the room next door to us.' The valet took a key and opened the far cabin. 'He invited me to have a look, while he was checking that the linen was fresh.' Maurice moved inside the new room.

'And? Get to the point, Morris.'

The valet switched on the light. The cabin was identical to my own except that there were no clothes hanging in the closet. Maurice had not had time to move in as yet. All I could see of any note was a small metal tin on the desk at the far end of the room. 'The cabin was empty except for this one small object,' Maurice said, moving forward, 'which the steward found in a drawer at the bottom of the closet.' He picked up the tin and handed it across to me. It was circular with a solid screw top lid. A brightly coloured label on the front of it had a single word written in elaborate German script: "*Rattengift*".

I frowned. 'Something to do with rats?'

Maurice nodded gravely. 'It is rat poison,' he said. There was a small skull and crossbones printed underneath.

'Good lord.' I revolved the tin in my hand. 'Do they have rats on the Richthofen?'

'No, Monsieur.' The valet seemed very sure of that. He must have asked the steward.

142

I unscrewed the metal lid and examined the contents. My eyes boggled. The powder inside was white and crystalline. It was not unlike... 'Morris, this looks just like the sleeping draught.'

'Yes, Monsieur.'

He stood next to me and together we stared down at the powder. All kinds of mad ideas were sparking in my mind. 'You don't think...?'

'It's a possibility, Monsieur.' Had this rat poison somehow been introduced into our glass bottle?

'But what...I mean, how did it get on board?' Who would bring a tin of rat poison onto an airship?

'I do not know, Monsieur. But, according to the steward, this was the cabin that belonged to Gerhard Schulz.'

Chapter Eleven

Rain was battering hard against the slanted windows of the Richthofen. The storm was getting closer and visibility had been reduced to virtually nothing. The lightning could be seen only as a sudden illumination of the clouds. A heavy flash was followed twelve seconds later by the diabolical rumble of thunder. I was at the edge of one of the windows on the starboard side, holding on to a support strut for dear life. It was not a dignified position, but the whole ship was being buffeted by the wind. The engine cars were struggling to maintain an even course. In ordinary circumstances, I would have had no fear of a heavy storm like this; but to be inside a balloon with that much electricity crackling around was a distressing proposition.

Most of the passengers were gathered along the length of the starboard promenade, gazing out at the maelstrom on the other side of the glass with varying degrees of awe and apprehension.

'I thought we were meant to be going *around* it,' I muttered anxiously.

'I'm sure the captain's doing his best,' Thomas McGilton replied, his voice a soothing Irish lilt. 'It's difficult to know exactly where the outer edges are going to be. If the storm's directly ahead of us he only has so much room to manoeuvre.'

'You're being terribly brave!' Miss Tanner observed, placing a hand on my shoulder to reassure me. 'I do admire your spirit, coming out here to look.'

It had not been a matter of choice. I had emerged from the empty starboard cabin a few minutes earlier, my thoughts full of murder and dark deeds. The discovery of the rat poison had shocked me far more than the presence on board of an officer from Scotland Yard. Any chance I might have had to reflect upon its significance had been dashed, however, by the sight of Miss Tanner striding determinedly out of the passenger lounge ahead of me, intent on summoning her American friend from his cabin, in order that he might enjoy the full glory of the storm. Luckily, I had managed to intercept her before she got anywhere near the port side and had convinced her to leave Walter Kendall be, on the unarguable grounds that a man with a hangover shouldn't be walking around on a ship that was rolling every which way beneath our feet. The unfortunate upshot of this intervention was that I had been forced to accompany Miss Tanner back to the promenade, to take the American's place at the window.

My stomach was protesting violently with every shudder of the ship. I was kneeling on a padded chair, my arms around the support strut between two large sets of glass. I was surprised so many of the other passengers were gathered here. Why anyone would want to stand and stare at such appalling weather, I had no idea. But I supposed, if we were all going to die, we might as well look fate directly in the face.

Sir George Westlake was not among the crowd and neither was Adelina Koenig. I had a sneaking suspicion the mad pair had taken up an open invitation to view the storm from the control car. Good luck to them, I thought. I would not have survived the journey along the central walkway, let alone climbing down that narrow metal ladder into the gondola.

Another flash of lightning was followed by the inevitable boom. Ten seconds this time. 'It's getting closer.' I could not keep the anxiety from my voice. 'What happens if the lightning hits us?' We weren't even allowed to light a cigarette on board, except in a pressurised saloon. What would a lightning bolt do to us?

'There's nothing to worry about,' McGilton assured me, dismissing the several million cubic feet of hydrogen hanging above us with the wave of his hand. 'The surface of the ship is designed to defuse electrical currents. The storm can't hurt us.' Another gust of wind had the man rocking momentarily to maintain his balance.

'I bow to your expertise,' I mumbled, without conviction. The Irishman seemed to know what he was talking about, but I would have preferred to hear it from the captain. Albrecht had been happy enough to stroll around the passenger decks during take-off, but he wasn't confident enough to go walkabouts during *this*, I noticed.

Lucy Tanner had let go of my shoulder and was gazing out of the window in a state of rapture. 'It's so exciting,' she gushed. 'I'll have so much to write about when I reach New York. Mr Kendall really should come out and see this.'

McGilton shook his head. 'Best to leave him be. You heard what Mr Bland said. He's in no fit state this morning.'

Karl Lindt had his feet firmly wedged against the base of the outer wall a few feet further along the observation deck. 'It is a magnificent spectacle,' he declared. The German had been staring ramrod-like out of the viewing panel for some minutes without saying a word. I was not sure if he was stiff with fear or simply lost in thought. 'The full force of nature in action laid out before us. The sound, the light and colour, elemental and fierce. And here we stand, in the centre of it, unafraid, holding our heads high, like the ancient gods on Mount Olympus, defiant of the very elements themselves.'

'Goodness,' Miss Tanner exclaimed. 'How poetic! I didn't realise you had a romantic streak, Herr Lindt.' She was being surprisingly civil to the man, all things considered, though I noticed she maintained a respectable distance from him, which she never did with me.

'Would you like me to put a bit of Wagner on the gramophone for you?' McGilton enquired dryly.

The German drew his gaze from the window for a brief moment, his eyes blazing. 'Your attempts at humour are not appreciated, Mr McGilton.'

The Irishman grinned sourly. 'Just trying to be helpful.'

'Now, now, boys, please don't spoil the moment,' Miss Tanner said. 'We can all enjoy the storm without rancour. It's too thrilling to do anything else.' She frowned. 'It's not right, Walter staying locked up in bed and missing all this. Sore head or no sore head, he simply *has* to see it. He'll be so upset when he realises he's missed it all.'

'If he'd wanted to come out, darling, he'd have come out already,' McGilton suggested. 'Better to leave him be.'

Miss Tanner shook her head. 'Nonsense. It's almost

eleven o'clock. He shouldn't be in bed at this hour. I shall go and wake him.' Before I could move to intercede, she had stepped across the promenade towards the lounge.

McGilton shrugged. He shot me a comradely look, his when-she-gets-an-idea-into-her-head-what-can-you-do look. Unfortunately, I was not in a position to treat the matter so lightly.

'I really wouldn't disturb him just now,' I called after her, my voice loud and firm above the hiss of the storm.

Miss Tanner glanced back. 'He'll thank me in the long run.'

'No. Miss Tanner, you really ought to leave him alone.' I stepped away from the window and staggered as the floor shifted suddenly beneath me. I put out a hand to steady myself on the reading room door.

'But surely...'

'You must leave him in his cabin,' I insisted, speaking more stridently than I had intended. The other passengers turned away from the windows and stared at me in surprise.

Miss Tanner had stopped in her tracks, her brow furrowed. 'Nothing's wrong, is there?' Her eyes were illuminated by the lightning and I could see the concern there. I hesitated, not knowing how to reply. 'He's not ill, is he?' she asked, her voice suddenly uncertain. 'I mean, seriously ill?'

'No,' I shook my head sadly, as the thunder roared. 'He's not ill.' But I had come too far now to withhold the truth. Everyone on the promenade was staring at me. 'I'm terribly sorry, Miss Tanner. Ladies, Gentlemen. Mr Kendall died in his sleep last night.'

Lucy Tanner let out a gasp and her hand went to her mouth.

'I'm sorry to break it like this. The captain wanted to wait until after the storm before making the announcement.'

'And he's really dead?' Miss Tanner whispered. 'Dear Walter?'

'I'm afraid so.'

McGilton rushed across and placed a supportive arm around his fiancée.

Mr Lindt was staring at me angrily. 'And why did the captain tell you this and not the rest of us?'

'I...noticed he was missing at breakfast.' Better to stick to the well-worn account, I thought, quickly trotting out the details of my conversation with the first officer. 'He asked me to keep quiet for a couple of hours. He didn't want to alarm anyone with all this going on.' I gestured vaguely towards the windows.

Miss Tanner was shaking now. She was having some difficulty keeping her hands under control. 'How did he die?' she asked softly.

'I don't know. In his sleep, I think. The first officer said something about a sleeping draught.' Perhaps it wasn't wise to mention the poison just yet. Better to talk to Finch about that first. 'He may have misjudged the dose.'

The Englishwoman shook her head. 'Walter simply wouldn't...he didn't...'

'Let's get you back to your cabin,' McGilton suggested. He tightened his grip around her waist.

'No. No, I want to watch the storm,' she muttered vaguely.

'I don't think...'

'I want to watch the storm,' the woman repeated, with greater conviction.

McGilton just nodded. 'All right,' he said. 'Come and sit over here.' He manoeuvred her gently across to the sofa at the far end of the promenade. I watched her sit and gaze numbly out of the windows. Her fiancé settled next to her, his hands holding hers gently on top of her lap, his eyes not moving from her face.

Max the barman had remained at his post, his big nose and walrus-like moustache the most reassuring sight I had seen since I had woken that morning. A cigarette and a drink were the only things that could calm my nerves. Josef Kaufmann, the tubby German, had arrived at the bar ahead of me. I had been unavoidably diverted on my way down, though I doubt many people had been aware of my unfortunate repeat performance in the little girls' room. It was the stairs afterwards that had proved my Achilles heel, however. A brief lull in the turbulence had convinced me to risk the descent – the prospect of a Piccadilly and a glass of Scotch were more than enough encouragement – but a sudden gust had sent the Richthofen reeling sideways and I had lost my footing. It was only the handrail that had saved me from flying head first down to B Deck. My legs had swung through the air but I had grabbed on to the rail with both arms and had managed to recover my footing. Now, more than ever, I needed a drink. How long was this damned storm going to last?

Kaufmann had already ordered his drink and the barman was looking at me expectantly. 'Whisky,' I said, reaching inside my jacket pocket for my cigarette case. 'No soda.'

Max seemed completely unconcerned by the buffeting of the ship as he prepared the drinks. The bottles behind him were rattling on their shelves, but they were all well restrained, protected from the effects of gravity by the wire stretched out in front of them. 'I will bring the drinks through to you,' he said, with an easy smile.

Kaufmann lowered himself from the stool and made for the intersecting door. 'You are looking very pale,' he observed, with concern, as I lurched after him. I careered right, before I had the opportunity to reply, and grabbed the near edge of the padded sofa. I shuffled along the wall as best I could until I reached one of the tables and was able to wedge myself in. The German had remained on his feet all the while and, to my consternation, proved able to navigate the length of the room. He lit a cigarette from the lighter on the far wall and returned to the table, only a little unsteadily. He offered me the end of his cigarette and I used it to light my own.

I took a long, slow drag. 'Thank you. That was very thoughtful, Mr Kaufmann.'

The tubby German sat himself down opposite me. He was a funny looking fellow, I thought, older then Mr Lindt, with a chubby, reddish face. 'It has been a difficult morning,' he observed, with typical understatement. 'I can scarcely believe Mr Kendall is dead.' There weren't many things that would take people's minds off a storm like this, but the American's death had proved to be one of them.

I breathed out a lungful of smoke and nodded. 'Terrible. I was only drinking with him last night.'

A lightning flash illuminated Max the barman as he came through the door with our drinks. I had forgotten about the underfloor windows on the far side of the saloon. Even here, in the bowels of the ship, I could not escape the untamed fury of the Atlantic. The inevitable roar of thunder followed, barely four seconds later. We could not be far now from the eye of the storm. I stowed my cigarette nervously on the edge of the ashtray and grabbed the glass which Max was preparing to set down. I downed the drink in one.

'Another, sir?' the barman asked, placing a small glass of sherry in front of his larger countryman. I handed the glass back to him and did my best to smile.

'You read my mind.'

I retrieved my cigarette and took another drag. I would have to make the most of this. I only had three Piccadillys left and I had a feeling I would be smoking all of them in the next few minutes.

'Do not worry, sir,' Max reassured me, his small eyes twinkling either side of that enormous hooter. 'We are perfectly safe. Another half an hour and we will be through the storm.'

I nodded as agreeably as I could. If anything, the rain sounded heavier now than it had done when I had first sat down.

Kaufmann puffed at his own cigarette, while the barman retreated to the rattling drinks cabinet in the outer room. Even he was watching his feet, however, as he made his way towards the door, though as a matter of pride he was still balancing his tray with one hand as the lightning flashed again. 'I could have done with a man like him in Gibraltar,' I said.

Kaufmann sipped his sherry as the sound of thunder ricocheted across the saloon. 'Was Mr Kendall in good spirits when you said good night to him last night?' he enquired.

'Yes, I believe so. Why do you ask?'

'It seems strange to me. Two passengers dying like this, one after the other. Both of them journalists, both of them showing a marked affection for an English woman.'

I frowned for a moment. 'Yes, that is rather odd. Though I think Miss Tanner and Mr Kendall were just good friends. The Austrian was...?'

'He was very fond of Miss Hurst, I believe.'

'Oh yes. I remember someone saying. Do you think that's why he....?'

The German took another ship of sherry. 'It is a possibility. I understand he had been pursuing the Fräulein for some time. Unfortunately, his feelings were not reciprocated. She liked him, I think. She enjoyed his company. But she did not wish to take things further.'

'Often the way. Do you think that was why he killed himself?'

'I am convinced of it,' Kaufmann said. 'I believe he took his own life, as we have been told. Affairs of the heart, they are very complicated.' He sighed wistfully and put down his sherry glass. He had no wedding ring, I noticed. Probably a confirmed bachelor. 'And yet...this second death.' He picked up his cigarette.

'You think there may be a connection between the two?' I did my best to sound sceptical.

'It does not seem possible. But, even so, it is strange. Karl had an argument with Gerhard Schulz late on Saturday evening at the poker table. He accused him of cheating. I was involved in the game and I saw no evidence of it. But Karl was convinced.'

'Your friend doesn't like to lose,' I said. 'He'll blame anyone if he gets a bad hand. I saw that myself last night, when Sir George beat him.'

'Perhaps. But it was an unpleasant scene. And shortly after that, Herr Schulz died. Then, last night, he had another disagreement, this time with Mr Kendall, just before supper.'

'A disagreement?'

'I am not sure what it was about,' Kaufmann confessed. 'His behaviour at lunch yesterday, perhaps. In relation to the

Fräulein. He is not the most tactful of men.'

'Oh, the Jewish thing, you mean? Yes, that was a bit off.'

Kaufmann had not been at our table but the whole saloon must have overheard the conversation.

'He also has a tendency to be a little...over familiar with women.'

I grimaced. 'Wandering hands, you mean?' That didn't surprise me. He had that look about him. Miss Hurst, I noticed, had always kept well clear of the fellow.

Kaufmann nodded unhappily. 'I'm afraid so. It may be that he behaved inappropriately in a...physical manner.' The German was trying to phrase his concerns as delicately as he could.

'And you think Mr Kendall may have leapt to her defence?' That did make sense. Ever the gentleman. No wonder Miss Tanner had kept her distance from Mr Lindt up on the promenade. I hoped to God McGilton didn't get to hear of it or there would soon be another death on board ship. 'But you're not suggesting that Mr Lindt had something to do with Kendall's death? Or Mr Schulz's? I mean, he couldn't have, could he? They both died of natural causes.'

'Apparently so,' Kaufmann agreed. 'I am certain at least that Gerhard Schulz took his own life. But perhaps Karl may have driven him to it, in part. He has something of a temper.'

'That's an understatement. But as to Mr Kendall, you need have no fear. He died in his sleep. That's what the first officer told me. There was nothing odd about it, so far as I am aware.'

'You are probably right,' Kaufmann agreed, downing the last of his sherry. 'But I do feel partly responsible. Karl is my colleague, after all.'

'You're not his mother, Mr Kaufmann. It's not your job to keep him on a leash.' I stubbed out the end of my Piccadilly and an awkward silence descended; or at least, as much of a silence as there could be with that rain battering away against the canvas.

It seemed I was not the only one to have my suspicions

about these two deaths. I had done my best to put the German off – there was no point alarming anyone any further – but after the discovery of the rat poison in Gerhard Schulz's cabin I was finding it difficult to reach any other conclusion. Kaufmann was right, it was too much of a coincidence, both men dying like that within twenty four hours of each other. And I was certain now, having considered the matter carefully, that the sleeping draught Maurice had used to drug Walter Kendall had been tampered with. When I had first arrived on board ship, on Monday morning, I had taken the bottle out of my wash bag and placed it on the shelf above the sink. But when I had come back to grab it that afternoon it was not on the shelf but back inside the bag. I hadn't noticed at the time but now, on reflection, I was certain it had been moved. Maurice had not shifted it; he had assured me he had not been anywhere near it. So someone must have slipped into my cabin and substituted the sleeping draught for rat poison. It wouldn't have been difficult, what with that damned lock of mine. And if someone had done that, it meant Walter Kendall had been murdered. Maurice may have unwittingly carried out the deed, but someone else had been behind it. I struggled for some time to make sense of the notion. No one on board could have known we were planning to dope the American. The idea had come from Charles Lazenby, who was thousands of miles away in Spain. He could not have broken into my cabin and doctored the contents of that bottle. There was, however, one slightly more chilling option, which Maurice had cheerfully suggested to me before I had left the cabin. It could be that the poison had been intended for me. I pulled out a second cigarette from my case. That was one idea I did not wish to dwell on.

Once again, Josef Kaufmann was kind enough to provide a light. Even at close quarters, however, I was having difficulty igniting the cigarette. The airship was shuddering now to such an extent that I had some difficulty maintaining a steady hand. Part of me just wanted to grab hold of the sofa from the bottom and hang on for dear life. We were stuck down here, I realised, for the duration of the storm. I doubted I could even stand up now, less still walk over to the door. And I wasn't even within stumbling distance of a water closet.

'This weather,' the German sighed, taking a puff from his own cigarette. The thunder and lightning were firing more or less in tandem now. 'I hope it does not delay us. Karl and I have an important meeting in Sao Paulo on Friday afternoon.'

'I don't care about being *delayed*,' I said, raising my voice involuntarily as the lightning crackled again. 'I just want to get out of here alive. I don't think my nerves will suffer much more of this.' With a trembling hand, I took a quick drag of the cigarette. 'I think I'm going to get off at Rio. If we get that far. Where's that man with my Scotch?'

'Here he comes,' Kaufmann said.

The door to the bar crashed backwards and the barman staggered with his tray. There was an almighty roar and I cried out as the room tilted upwards. Max went flying through the air towards us, the whisky glass shattering on the floor, and I heard a heavy ripping sound. There were screams from the passenger deck above us. Crewmen were calling out urgently to each other in indecipherable German.

And, at that moment, my stomach lurched and I felt the Zeppelin plummet from the sky.

Chapter Twelve

Sea water slapped hard against the shell of the dinghy. There were eight of us in the boat, six passengers and two crew. The grizzled young crewmen were pulling at the oars but the rest of us were staring up at the airship, hanging morbidly above us, its lower tail fin ripped apart. A second dinghy had positioned itself as best it could below the damaged fin and men on wires were already crawling around it, doing their best to effect repairs. A patch of cloth had been torn off the roof of the ship towards the front and another group of crewmen were braving the slippery surface on top of the Richthofen to patch it up. It was lucky that they had enough material on board to replace it. Captain Albrecht was in the second dinghy, overseeing the repairs in person. He would doubtless say it was not luck, but preparation.

One of the crewmen in our boat – the gap-toothed fellow who had given me the guided tour – confided to us in his broken English that this was not the first time something like this had happened to a Zeppelin airship.

'There was nothing about that in the guide book,' I muttered.

When the fin had ripped, chaos had broken out on board ship. Screams from the passenger deck had mixed with urgent exchanges from the engineers and crewmen across the length of the Richthofen. It had seemed obvious to me that we were going to die. The craft had plummeted some distance through the air, though in truth we had fallen for no more than a couple of seconds. The captain had struggled to regain control of the ship, but with a damaged rudder the only way to do that was by moving into a less turbulent air stream. In this case, that meant lowering the craft, since the worst of the storm was playing out at a higher altitude. And so we had dropped down and gradually the crew had managed to regain some semblance of control.

I only learnt the details of this afterwards. At the time, having been flung the length of the smoking room and scared half to death, all I was aware of was that the attitude of the cabin was gradually re-established. Josef Kaufmann had faired better than I – he had grabbed onto the edge of the sofa – and was back on his feet within half a minute. A couple of chairs had overturned and our ashtray had skidded across the peach wood floor, but otherwise little damage had been done to our small corner of the world. It was Max, the barman, who had suffered the worst of it. He had smacked into the bar room door and blood was streaming out of that enormous nose of his. Kaufmann rushed over to the dazed crewman, who was slumped by the far wall. I struggled across to join them as soon as I had recovered my wits.

'How is he?' I asked.

Kaufmann had grabbed the top of Max's head and was examining his reactions. 'He has concussion, I think.'

I pulled my handkerchief from my breast pocket and knelt down in front of him, wiping the blood from the man's nose and his heavy moustache. It was already starting to congeal. The poor fellow was shaking his head, trying to bring himself round.

'You're going to be all right,' I reassured him. There was no other wound that I could see. 'Just a bit of a bump.'

He nodded and tried to grin.

I looked across at Kaufmann. 'What the hell happened?' The airship was still juddering, even at the lower altitude, and there was an unpleasant whacking sound coming from behind us.

Kaufmann did not know. 'We must have sustained some damage.'

I grunted. 'You have a knack for understatement.'

'But we are still alive and in one piece,' he added, thankfully.

'Just about. My God, I thought we were done for.'

The German nodded. 'And the storm is not yet over.' Lightning was continuing to flash at us through the underfloor windows.

A crewman arrived a moment later to check up on the passengers in the smoking room. He summoned a second steward and they quickly saw to Max.

I stumbled over to the viewing windows, to see if anything more was heading our way but the angle was too low to see anything and – as it transpired – we were already through the worst of it. The airship was now cruising at about sixty feet, having suffered only minor damage. But for the quick thinking of the captain, the situation might have been an awful lot worse.

'Captain Albrecht is a fine airman,' Kaufmann concluded, rising to his feet, and – despite the sheer terror of the experience – I was inclined to agree. More than anything, I was just glad to be alive.

When the storm had died down, the stewards politely directed us back up onto A Deck and into the dining area. The crew wanted to make sure all the passengers were accounted for. I had to make another quick diversion on the way and this time I was not the only one. Thankfully, none of the guests had suffered serious injuries, although nerves were understandably frayed.

Sir George Westlake had a small plaster on his forehead. He had nipped out from the control gondola at the height of the storm and had been making use of the facilities when the rear fin had torn. 'Crashed my head on the wash basin,' he explained, with a chuckle. He was taking it in surprisingly good spirits. 'I spent three months in Antarctica without a scratch but thirty seconds in a German water closet...' He roared with laughter.

Not everyone was coping with the situation as well as the explorer. Karl Lindt had a face like a bruised kipper. He had been so proud of his country's aeronautical prowess and was upset to discover the airship was not quite as invincible as he had supposed. Josef Kaufmann leant in and whispered to me that, in fact, Lindt was rather more worried about the possibility of arriving late in Brazil.

The stewards were doing their best to normalise the situation and, to their credit, they quickly managed to organise a spot of lunch for us all. Goodness knows what carnage the storm had caused in the kitchens, but somehow the chef and his acolytes had knocked together a light meal and it was served on the dot of twelve o'clock, as scheduled. With that and the storm receding, spirits gradually began to revive. Captain Albrecht was already outside inspecting the damage – the aircraft had come to a halt now and was hovering gently a few feet above the ocean – so it was left to Captain Rüdiger, the first officer, to visit the passenger decks and soothe our nerves. It was not a job he was well suited to.

'Repairs will be effected over the next two or three hours,' he told us, his stern, granite face not quite communicating the reassurance the situation required; but at least his brisk manner prevented any dissembling. 'We hope to resume our journey sometime in the late afternoon, but we may have to continue at a slower speed. This may set back our arrival time by some hours.'

Karl Lindt grimaced at that but made no comment.

Captain Rüdiger confirmed the sad news about Walter Kendall and apologised for not passing on the information sooner. 'We will radio the appropriate authorities shortly and make sure the news is passed on to his relatives in New York,' he said.

Sir George was more interested in the repairs. He had seen Captain Albrecht head out in one of the dinghies and, true to form, was keen to venture outside himself and inspect the damage. 'You've got a couple of those things, haven't you?'

'There is a second dinghy, yes,' Rüdiger admitted, reluctantly.

'There you go then!' The Englishman beamed.

The other man shook his head. 'I am afraid the sea is far too rough to allow...'

'Nonsense!' Sir George declared. 'I've been trapped in Antarctic pack ice. This will be a picnic in comparison.'

'The storm *is* dying off,' Mrs Koenig volunteered, in her harsh German growl. As an aviator, I guessed, she would know about such things. And doubtless she would be just as happy to head off into danger.

'Take it from a veteran, old boy,' Sir George added, 'that sea will be as calm as a bath tub in an hour's time.'

The first officer was not about to be bullied into

anything. 'I am sorry, Sir George, I do not think it will be possible...'

'You can at least ask Captain Albrecht,' Mr Lindt suggested testily. Why on earth he was voicing support for the scheme I could not begin to fathom. Perhaps he wanted to see for himself how bad the damage was.

Rüdiger pursed his lips together. 'Very well.' It was clear he was under orders not to upset any of the guests. 'I will speak to the captain, when he returns to the ship. But I do not think he will allow it. Passenger safety is paramount.'

I snorted. 'Yes, we noticed that.'

'If you will excuse me,' he said, ignoring the barb, 'there is much work to be done.'

Sir George was not willing to let the idea go, however, and once the rains had evaporated he took the matter into his own hands, button-holing Captain Albrecht when the officer returned briefly to the Richthofen and securing his agreement to let a few of the passengers go outside. I was surprised the captain agreed to it, but it was probably more hassle than it was worth for him to refuse.

My mind was elsewhere, in any case. I was already in deep conversation with Jacob Finch. The ginger-haired policeman had been searching Walter Kendall's cabin when the ship had dropped and he had banged his hip on the metal ladder. The pain did not stop his leg from wobbling, however, as we settled ourselves at the far end of the port promenade. The damned fellow could not keep still to save his life; but he was anxious to pass on his findings.

'I'm not a pathologist, you understand,' Finch told me, his left foot tapping self-consciously on the carpet. 'I don't know one end of a body from the other. And it's a horrible thing, having to examine a corpse.' His eyes screwed shut with distaste. 'I try to avoid it where I can. Just the stench of it. It's appalling. No bowel control, the dead.'

I nodded sympathetically. I had noticed a bit of a smell last night and clearly it had worsened with time.

'But I have seen a few dead bodies in my time and I'm fairly sure Mr Kendall didn't die of a heart attack.'

'How did he die then?'

Finch clutched his fists together. 'I can't be certain, but I think the poor chap was poisoned.'

'Good grief!' I did my best to sound surprised.

'It was the lips that were the giveaway.' Finch shuddered. 'And the tongue. I've seen pictures of that sort of thing. Horrible way to die. Of course, I could be completely wrong. Without a proper medical examination, there's no way of knowing for certain. But I did find a sleeping draught next to his bed and I have a horrible feeling it may contain arsenic.'

'Good lord,' I said.

'He may even have administered it himself, unwittingly.' Finch clamped a hand to his leg, to keep it under control. 'It wouldn't have been at all pleasant, if it was arsenic. I remember reading up on the subject.' He shuddered at the memory. 'There'd be dizziness and confusion to start with, then stomach cramps and a splitting headache. He must have got himself half undressed before the worst of it kicked in, then collapsed onto the mattress.' Finch shook his head. 'The poor chap, in his shirt sleeves, breathing his last and no one to know.'

'Good God,' I whispered. 'So there really is a murderer on board.' I'd had some time to get used to the idea, but speaking the words out loud served to underline the horror of the situation.

'It looks like it,' Finch agreed, closing his eyes in despair. 'In cold blood, in the dead of the night. It's appalling! Utterly depraved.' He took a moment to gather himself together. 'Unfortunately, I'm working in the dark here. We can't know for certain if he was poisoned until the powder is properly analysed. But the way he was lying there...' He shuddered again. 'I have a terrible feeling, this time, my intuition is spot on. I'll have to tell the captain. The poor chap. He'll be absolutely mortified. A murderer on board the Richthofen. And most likely it'll be one of the other passengers.' Finch released the grip on his leg. 'What I don't understand is why would anyone want to kill Walter Kendall. It doesn't make sense. He had nothing to do with our missing file. Even if he *was* a potential buyer, there would be no reason for anyone to want to murder him.' He gazed across at me, completely baffled. 'I don't know what to make of it all, Mr Bland. What on earth am I going to tell the authorities, when we arrive in Brazil?'

'Lord knows,' I said. We would have to cross that bridge when we came to it. 'Did you find anything else in the cabin? Anything suspicious?' Perhaps the telegram he had been intending to send, if he had ever got around to writing it? Or, more to the point, anything that might incriminate *me* in his death. After all, I had no reason to suppose the murderer had even been in Walter Kendall's cabin. The poison must have been added to that sleeping draught well in advance of my valet planting the bottle there.

'I did find one curious thing,' the policeman admitted. He glanced across at the dining hall. A couple of stewards were clearing away the lunch things but the passengers had vacated the room. Finch reached into his jacket and pulled out a pale blue pad. 'This is Mr Kendall's notebook,' he said. 'It was lying on the table on top of a portable typewriter.' He opened the book up for me to see. I remembered flicking through it, on Monday morning. 'Look, two pages have been torn out.'

My eyes widened as I took hold of the pad. The leaves had been torn very neatly. At first glance, I would not even have noticed they were missing. But flipping to the back of the book, the two corresponding pages could be seen hanging loose. The pad had definitely been tampered with. 'It wasn't like that yesterday morning,' I said. 'When I was in there.'

Finch peered at me in confusion. 'You were in his room?'

I had not yet had the chance to tell him about my visits to Walter Kendall's cabin. The subject hadn't cropped up the last time we had spoken. And since I didn't want to implicate myself in Kendall's murder, I had no intention of telling him about the second of those visits now. But there was no harm in mentioning the first. Finch regarded me with bewilderment as I explained to him how I had crept into the American's cabin the previous morning. 'I had a look at this book when I was searching for the negatives,' I said. 'But I'm sure there was

161

nothing missing from it then.' I handed the pad back to the detective. 'Still, it doesn't tell us much.' Had someone crept into the room after me, last night, to tear the pages out? It seemed unlikely. Maurice had been in there, of course, to plant the draught, but he would have no reason to rip anything out of a notebook.

'That's not the worst of it,' Finch said. He lifted up the leaf just below the tear. 'One trick I did learn from the forensic chaps. There's a bit of an impression left on the page underneath. You can make out a few of the words if you hold it up to the light.' He handed the pad back to me and I held it up against the window. One of the stewards was polishing a nearby table and he glanced across at us with curiosity.

I screwed my eyes, gazing at the impression that Kendall's pencil must have made on the under sheet. Two words I recognised instantly: *Adelina Koenig*. I frowned at the rest of the passage. I could only pick out a smattering of it. '*...had a* (something) *knowledge of* (something) *engineering...*' Aeronautical engineering? '*...and a less than* (something something) *of geography.*' I dropped the pad and regarded Finch quietly for a few moments. 'Sounds like character assassination,' I concluded. 'You don't think *Mrs Koenig* had something to do with Kendall's death?'

Finch shrugged. 'I've no idea. I wish I did.'

It made me smile just to think of it, it seemed so improbable. 'She was one of the people on the Croydon flight, wasn't she?'

'Yes, she was.'

'So she might have had something to do with the original theft of your documents.'

Finch did not think that likely. 'How could a German woman know anything about a file from Special Branch?'

I had no answer to that. 'But you think she might have had something to do with Kendall's death?' Adelina Koenig was as mad as a box of frogs, but she seemed completely harmless to me. Besides, she had been too busy debauching herself last night to creep anywhere and tear out pages from a notebook.

'She may have had some grievance that we know nothing about,' Finch suggested. 'That notepad is the only real evidence we have. And it's pretty incriminating. Tearing the pages out like that.'

'But you can't be sure it has anything to do with Kendall's death.'

'I can't be sure of anything!' Finch declared mournfully. 'That's the trouble. At the very least, I think I'm going to have to search her cabin. I should have done it already, her and Miss Hurst's. It's a dreadful business, having to rifle through a lady's luggage, but I can't see any alternative.'

'She's going out on the dinghy. You could nip in there while she's outside.'

He gripped his legs again. 'I suppose so.' I could see the idea did not appeal to him.

'It'll be the best time to do it,' I said. 'There are quite a few people going out, by the sounds of it. They're all stark staring mad.'

'I suppose so. But we'll need to keep an eye on Frau Koenig in the meantime. If she *is* mixed up in this, we daren't let her out of our sight.'

I shrugged. 'She can't do much harm in a dinghy.'

'I wouldn't be so sure. If she did kill Walter Randall, she might be capable of anything. She might try to dispose of the evidence, if she hasn't already. Who knows, you might be able to catch her in the act.'

'Wait a minute. You're not suggesting...?'

'I think you should go out with her, in the dinghy. Just to be on the safe side.'

'Don't be ridiculous,' I scoffed. 'I'm not getting on a boat.' I had only just survived one catastrophe. I wasn't about to risk another.

'Well, I can't go, if I'm searching her room. You don't get sea sick do you?' he asked.

'Well, no, but...'

'Thank goodness for that. One of us needs to keep an eye on her. She might try to toss the poison over the side while everyone's looking the other way.'

Finch was assuming Mrs Koenig had brought her own poison with her. He did not know about the tin Maurice and I had found in Gerhard Schulz's old room. I could put him straight on that easily enough, but I wasn't entirely sure how far I trusted this strange policeman. Adelina Koenig might not have known anything about the Special Branch file, but Finch certainly did and I could not be certain he was not involved in this affair himself. I only had his word, after all, that he was acting in any kind of official capacity.

'But if there *was* a poison,' I said, 'it would have been in the sleeping draught they found in Kendall's cabin.'

'Yes, but he must have bought that himself in Seville. It's got Spanish scribbled all over it. If Frau Koenig did interfere with it, she had to have done it later on. Look, I know it's asking a lot. Heaven knows, *I* wouldn't want to step on a boat with Adelina Koenig on it, but we really do need to keep a watch on her now, especially away from the ship. If she *is* involved in all this, there's no telling what she might do.'

I scowled at the fellow. Why was it, I wondered, that people kept expecting me to put my neck on the line? I had half a mind to refuse the request. If I had stood up to Charles Lazenby I would not be in this mess in the first place. Perhaps I should get Maurice to do it, I thought; but then I remembered his abject fear of boats. I would have to take care of this myself. 'Very well. I just hope you find what you're looking for in her cabin.'

'So do I,' Finch said. 'So do I. Then we might be able to make some sense of this god-awful mess.'

I left him to his search and followed the other passengers down to B Deck. A group of crewmen were noisily manoeuvring a large dinghy towards an exit ramp out of view of us on the far side of the deck, but another ramp had also been lowered at the near end of the port corridor, to allow the passengers access to the boat once it had been successfully dropped into the water.

Miss Tanner was waiting in line. I was surprised to see her here, given her reaction to the news of Walter Kendall's death a few hours earlier. She had left her coat in her cabin but was sporting the same black rayon dress, with its elegant floral design, that she had worn at the breakfast table that morning. Either she was running out of clothes, or her thoughts were elsewhere.

'How are you doing?' I asked her, as sympathetically as I could.

She frowned for a moment, reflecting on her own state of mind. 'I don't know,' she admitted, taking her place in line. 'I just feel numb. Thomas doesn't want me to go outside, but I need a distraction.'

McGilton was standing a little way ahead of us, in his shirt sleeves and a light yellow waistcoat. The stewards were handing out life jackets and the Irishman was being strapped into one of them. He had a camera with him, which he had placed on the floor while the crewman helped him into the cumbersome brown jacket.

'It's certainly that,' I said. A distraction. I suspected that was why Captain Albrecht was allowing the expedition to go ahead; to distract us all, so that we didn't dwell too much on all that had gone wrong. That, and the fact that the sea was now as calm as a fish pond, as Sir George had predicted.

The dinghy dropped to the sea with a muffled thud as Miss Tanner and I took hold of our life jackets. The gap toothed crewman showed us how to strap ourselves in and then we waited as the first two people were guided down the gangway onto the gently rocking dinghy.

Miss Tanner leaned her head in to me. 'There's something not right about Walter's death,' she whispered, confidentially. I could see the matter had been playing on her mind for some time. 'He always slept like a log. He used to joke about being asleep before his head hit the pillow He wouldn't need a sleeping draught.' I cursed my own stupidity, for mentioning the powder in the first place.

'How long is it since you last saw him?' I asked. 'I mean, before this trip?'

She shrugged, pulling the cord tight around her waist. 'Three years, I suppose.'

'A lot can happen in that time.'

165

'But he would have mentioned it,' Miss Tanner insisted. 'The poor dear.' Her eyes were beginning to moisten, but she stiffened herself. Now was not the time for tears and Lucy Tanner was an Englishwoman through and through.

'One of the stewards told me he was planning to send a cable this morning. Was he writing an article?' I asked. Perhaps she might have some idea what he had been scribbling in that notebook.

She nodded. 'I believe so. A colour piece, for his newspaper.'

The terminology was unfamiliar too me. 'A *colour* piece?'

'Life on board ship. What it's like to travel on an airship. A sort of general feature, rather than a news article. Not really Walter's forte, but his editor sent him a telegram shortly after we left Seville, insisting that he write one.'

A telegram. That would have been around the time I was searching his room on Monday morning. Someone had knocked on the door and frightened the life out of me. It must have been one of the stewards, trying to deliver the message. When there was no reply, he had gone looking elsewhere. 'And would he have written about *us*? The passengers?'

'Oh, absolutely. But he's always scrupulously fair. Was fair,' she added, her face falling.

The gap-toothed crewman was gesturing the next two passengers forward. McGilton was at the head now and Miss Tanner moved across to join him, so that the couple could descend together. I watched them disappear and my stomach tightened as I was gestured forward in their wake.

Even with the comfort of a life jacket the metal steps down to the sea were an alarming sight. Miss Tanner gazed up at me with reassuring eyes from the gently bobbing dinghy as I descended. I could scarcely believe I was joining Sir George's mad expedition, but I supposed a dinghy adrift in the middle of the Atlantic was no less safe just now than a German airship.

Adelina Koenig was in her element, examining the damage to the exterior of the craft as we floated gracefully away from the ship. The English knight was sitting next to her

166

on the boat, pointing out aspects of the damage. I was gripping tightly on to the rope running along the edge of the dinghy, my life vest firmly secured, looking back at the Richthofen. I had not wanted to be on this boat, but I had to confess, now I was out here, it was a relief to be away from the airship. I was no sailor, but the breeze on my face and the gentle lap of the ocean provided far more reassurance to me than the constant buzz of the Zeppelin's five engines.

Thomas McGilton was busy taking photographs with his Leica camera, at Miss Tanner's insistence. In other circumstances, I suspected he would rather have enjoyed the experience, but it had not been his idea to allow his fiancée out onto the water. Even in her grief, the woman was as stubborn as a mule.

Sir George had a pair of binoculars and was examining the damage in fine detail. Captain Albrecht was in a second dinghy, positioned once again underneath the lower fin, directing the repairs in person. Half of the rudder had been torn away. Sir George handed his binoculars across to Mrs Koenig. 'A fine ship, the Richthofen,' he declared. 'Battered but not unbowed, eh, what?'

'Battered, certainly,' I observed.

A handful of brave fellows were scampering about on top of the craft, at the opposite end. Mrs Koenig was paying particular attention to them, I noticed. There was a relatively minor tear in the outer fabric and the crewmen were clinging on to various guide ropes in order to patch it up.

Karl Lindt was more concerned with the damaged fin. 'I hope the repairs will not take long.'

At the passenger windows, I could make out one or two familiar figures staring back at us; that Spanish fellow McGilton shared with standing next to Miss Annabel Hurst. There was no sign of Jacob Finch, however. He would be in Mrs Koenig's room by now, searching for any incriminating evidence. I had lent him my home made lock pick so he could get through the door. I doubted the captain would be willing to provide him with a key.

I looked back at Adelina Koenig, sat on the edge of the

167

dinghy. She was a fearsome dragon of a woman, for all her comparative youth, but I could not picture her as a murderess. A couple of sheets torn out of a notebook were not enough to incriminate her, even assuming it was she who had torn them out. That did not seem likely, given all the other activity in her cabin last night. And even though she had been on that flight out of Croydon, Finch was right, she could not know anything about the Special Branch file. But what had prompted Walter Kendall to write about her? A 'colour' piece surely wasn't the place to stick in the proverbial knife. From the few words I had made out on the under sheet, it sounded like he had doubted some of the details of her heroic exploits. Was she really an expert aviator or was she a clever fraud? It seemed rather tenuous. And would the prospect of a few harsh scribblings in the American press be enough to provoke murder? In any case, how would she have managed to get hold of both the rat poison and the bottle of sleeping draught? She might have slipped into my cabin without being seen, but she would have had to break into Gerhard Schulz's first, and his cabin had been properly locked up. And, come to that, how would she have known I had a sleeping draught with me in the first place or that I was planning to use it on Walter Kendall? The American's death, I was convinced, must have had something to do with those documents from Scotland Yard, and if the German woman had any involvement with that then she had to have an English accomplice.

Only two individuals, that I was aware of, had any prior knowledge of the Maggie Meller affair: Jacob Finch and Charles Lazenby. Could she be in collusion with one of them? I wondered. Jacob Finch was on board, but if he had been working with Mrs Koenig, he would not have drawn attention to her like this. That just left Charles Lazenby. His instructions to me had been completely at odds with the reality of the situation. Why had he not told me Finch was on board? Could he really not have known? Or did he have a more sinister motive? He provided the sleeping draught, after all, and perhaps he had met up with Mrs Koenig in Seville and told her all about it. It was a possibility, I had to admit, though it did not seem particularly likely. Perhaps the murder of Walter Kendall had nothing to do with the Special Branch file. Or perhaps Mrs Koenig's accomplice was somebody else, who I hadn't considered yet. I couldn't really believe Charles Lazenby would sell out his country for a few pounds and Finch didn't have the wit to do it.

Sir George Westlake was chuckling away heartily to my left. He and Mrs Koenig were becoming very close, I observed. Could he be involved in it somehow? He was certainly in need of the funds, according to McGilton. Mrs Koenig might not have the clout to purloin secret files, but Sir George was a pillar of the establishment. He would have access to all kinds of sensitive information and there was no guarantee he would be any more discreet than the Prince of Wales. Ordinarily, I would have dismissed the notion of such a grand person being involved in something quite this grubby, but I supposed, on reflection, that his elevated status was no bar to criminality. He had not been on the flight from Croydon, of course – he was already in Germany as part of his lecture tour – but Mrs Koenig had been on the flight and the two of them had certainly spent quite a bit of time together in the control gondola this morning. Sir George might even have been the gentleman caller in her bedroom last night.

There were several other contenders, however. The remaining passengers on board that London flight.

Annabel Hurst was a frail, insipid creature but she did have a strong connection to Gerhard Schulz. It was possible she had acted as a courier, if nothing else.

Frederick Gray was another possibility. He still seemed to me the most likely suspect, if Adelina Koenig was discounted. I could see him up on the passenger deck now, chatting to the Spanish fellow. Gray was clearly not a workaday postman. The pinched looking GPO man was involved in research and development. It was not beyond the bounds of possibility that he had connections with Special Branch or MI5. I knew from experience that the GPO had regular contact with the security services. If MI5 wanted a letter intercepted, it was the post office that opened it and photographed it for them. I had had lunch with a couple of GPO Censors during my time in Gibraltar and they always seemed to be in the know about everything. Perhaps Mr Gray had heard tell of Prince Edward's file and marked it out as a decent retirement fund. It was always the middle men you had to watch, after all. But he had shown no interest whatever in Adelina Koenig.

A sudden cry interrupted my reverie. '*Mein Gott!*' Mrs Koenig pointed a stubby finger towards the top of the Richthofen. One of the crewmen had slipped and was dangling by a piece of cord from the upper edge. The poor fellow only had one hand gripping the rope, which had come away from the side of the ship. He was struggling to find a footing while his other arm tried to grab hold of the line.

Lucy Tanner brought her hand up to her mouth. 'Oh, my goodness!'

All at once, the man lost his grip and skidded across the upper curve of the airship. The relentless pull of gravity had him in its clutches and there was no way for him to recover himself. 'Ludwig!' Mrs Koenig cried out in horror. The drop to the ocean had to be a hundred feet or more. I heard the man scream as he plummeted to his doom but the splash of water was barely audible as he hit the sea.

Could he survive a drop of that distance? I wondered.

The oarsmen were already manoeuvring our dinghy in his direction. We were closer than the captain, whose boat in any case had been secured to the rear fin.

Sir George had his binoculars trained on the water. 'He's surfaced!' he announced to the rest of us. The man was splashing and calling out. He was alive. I could see the stricken face bobbing up and down in the water. It wasn't clear whether he was able to swim. He might be too dazed in any case. And he certainly wasn't wearing a life jacket.

The boat was rocking violently as we moved towards him. Adelina Koenig was disentangling herself from her own life vest. Before any of us had any idea what she was doing, the German woman had thrown her jacket to one side and dived head first into the sea.

Chapter Thirteen

'Good god,' I exclaimed, as Mrs Koenig churned across the water towards the stricken crewman. The woman moved with a grace I would not have credited. She seemed as at home in the water as she was in the air. In less than a minute, she had reached the blindly thrashing crewman and grabbed him from behind, sliding her arms underneath his armpits and – making sure to keep his head above the water – dragging him back towards the boat.

The men at the oars were too astonished at the sight even to stop paddling. Sir George Westlake and Thomas McGilton reached over the edge of the dinghy and manhandled the crewman on board. There was blood smeared on the side of his face but the fellow was at least conscious. We laid him out in the centre of the dinghy and Lucy Tanner bent over to examine him.

'He seems to be all right,' she observed, crouching down as the crewman blinked the water from his eyes. He had a bit of a squint, I noticed, and a badly shaven chin.

'He is a fool,' Karl Lindt declared. 'He should have secured himself properly.'

The boat rocked again as McGilton and Sir George hefted Adelina Koenig awkwardly back into the dinghy. Her hair was slicked back against her scalp, her dress indecently wet, but her eyes were flashing with excitement.

'That was a very brave thing to do,' McGilton said.

'It was first class, my dear!' Sir George agreed, enthusiastically. 'You've put the rest of us to shame.'

Mrs Koenig waved a hand dismissively. 'It was nothing. Ludwig. How is he?'

'He looks just fine,' Miss Tanner reassured her, looking up. 'Ludwig?'

'*Ja,*' the German woman admitted. 'He is *mein Neffe.* My nephew.' She sat herself on the edge of the boat and gazed down at the crewman with what I can only describe as a look of motherly contempt. '*Dummkopf!*' she muttered, as much to herself as to the man in question.

'It was extraordinary,' I told Maurice, some time later. 'She just dived straight in there, without compunction.'

'She has a taste for excitement, Monsieur,' the valet agreed, pulling the bandages tight around my chest.

'I'll say.' I had my arms up in the air. Maurice had been winding the fresh bandage in place and now he secured the back of it with a safety pin. The lock on the door had been fixed and I'd had no choice but to disrobe. My clothes were soaked through. I had got absolutely drenched helping young Ludwig back on board the Richthofen.

We had had a devil of a job manoeuvring the fellow off that dinghy. The gap-toothed man had kept the boat steady at the bottom of the stairs but it was McGilton and I who had lifted the fellow up between us. Sir George stood below, in the centre of the dinghy, ready to help out if either of us should slip. The boggle eyed crewman was still somewhat dazed, so I kept my arm firmly around his waist. A couple of stewards were waiting at the top of the steps and I was grateful to pass the semi-conscious lump into their rough hands. The group exchanged good natured jibes in quiet German as they carried the man off to his quarters. A couple of others remained behind to help us off with our life jackets.

Adelina Koenig clomped up the stairs behind us, gripping the hand rail tightly. She was followed by Lucy Tanner. The Irishman stepped forward to help his fiancée into the safety of the lower corridor.

'Gosh, I'm wet through,' she lamented, looking down at her damp rayon dress, 'and I didn't even go in the water.' She shuffled along the corridor so one of the crewmen could retract the steps and secure them properly behind us.

Mrs Koenig's frock was also clinging to her in a rather unseemly fashion – she was quite a well-endowed woman – but one of the stewards found a towel to wrap around her top half. '*Danke*,' she said.

I scarcely knew what to make of her extraordinary

rescue mission. If Walter Kendall had doubted her navigational expertise, he could not have doubted her pluck. Her nephew might well have survived in any case – it would only have taken a minute longer for us to arrive with the dinghy – but those few seconds might equally have made all the difference. Mrs Koenig was a woman, clearly, who was not afraid to put her life on the line for those that she loved. Even Karl Lindt was expressing his admiration, in strident German, though he was lucky to get a word in between the jolly acclamations of Sir George Westlake.

'Never seen anything like it,' the explorer confessed, from the far end of the corridor. 'What a woman!'

Mrs Koenig headed upstairs to change her clothes, while the dinghy was brought back on board ship via the second gangway. I doubted the German woman's wardrobe was as extensive as that of Miss Tanner, but she probably had more to change into than I did.

Maurice had laid out a fresh shirt on top of the bed, which he helped me into. I only had the two shirts with me but somehow my valet had managed to get the other one laundered in between times. 'Are you going to be able to dry it before tomorrow?' I asked him, eyeing the discarded garment, which was sopping wet.

'I think so, Monsieur. But it will take a few hours.' He was more interested now in the details of the rescue. He had not been at the window when Mrs Koenig had dived into the sea. 'And you say it was her nephew who fell?'

I nodded. 'Apparently so. I've seen him before somewhere, in the bowels of the ship. Young fellow. Jack of all trades. He's been with the Zeppelin company for a couple of years, so people are saying.' Young Ludwig had been the subject of much gossip on the way back up to the passenger cabins.

Maurice had finished buttoning my shirt. He turned to the closet and pulled out a neck tie, which was dangling from the same hanger as my jacket. I had at least had the foresight not to wear that outside; otherwise I would have been forced to spend the rest of the voyage in my dinner jacket. 'A curious coincidence, in light of Monsieur Finch's hypothesis,' the valet suggested, looping the tie around my neck and fastening it with expert hands.

'I'll say.' Mrs Koenig travelling on an airship her nephew was employed on. More fuel to add to Jacob Finch's suspicions. 'I could do with a bath,' I muttered, gazing across at myself in the mirror. Despite Maurice's careful ministrations, I was still looking somewhat dishevelled; and I had missed my usual Monday night scrub. There was a shower on the Richthofen but I didn't hold with such things and by all accounts it was a piddling affair. Give me a good metal tub any day. Besides, I could hardly walk around the passenger decks in a towel. I had done my best to clean myself up, however, using the cabin's wash basin. 'And, of course,' I said, remembering the final indignity, 'as soon as I got back on board, dripping wet, with my shirt clinging to my chest, who is the first person I bump into?'

Maurice could guess that easily enough. 'Mademoiselle Hurst?'

'Bang on the nose. You should have seen her expression, when she looked at me. Those bandages were visible, clear as day, through my shirt. Dripping wet. If this carries on, she's going to cotton on to the truth. She's bound to.'

'I would not worry about it, Monsieur,' he said, helping me into my light grey waistcoat. 'I am sure her thoughts are elsewhere at the moment.'

'Oh, the late Mr Schulz, you mean? Yes, I suppose so.'

My stomach lurched abruptly as a ragged cheer sounded from the crew decks.

'Good lord,' I said, 'it looks like we're on the move again.'

Maurice turned back to the closet and whipped out a large paper bag, but I waved it away. There were no windows in the cabin and, after the terrors of the storm, a gentle ascent into the heavens was not going to get my stomach excited.

There was a knock on the door.

'Mr Bland?' It was one of the stewards. 'The passengers are assembling in the lounge, if you would care to join us?'

174

Maurice helped me into my jacket and then nodded. 'I'll be with you in a minute.'

Captain Albrecht confirmed the good news in person. The Richthofen was under way once more, with no harm done. Albrecht had a more relaxed manner with the passengers than his first officer. Even after all the troubles of the day, he greeted the assembled guests with an easy smile. 'Thanks to the hard work of the crew, we are now continuing our voyage. We have received the latest weather report and are told to expect fair skies from now until we reach our destination. However, as a precaution, we will be travelling at a lower altitude for the remainder of the journey and at a maximum speed of eighty kilometres per hour.'

'So we will be arriving late!' Karl Lindt concluded, barely masking his irritation. He was sitting on a metal chair, staring up at the captain.

Thomas McGilton was standing to his left. He had changed out of his wet clothes and looked in better shape than I did. But then, he was some years younger than me. 'Better late than dead,' he commented dryly.

'The repairs we have made are temporary in nature and it is better to proceed with caution,' Albrecht said. Perhaps there had been some structural damage, I thought. But I kept the notion to myself.

Adelina Koenig was standing next to the baby piano. She had also changed out of her wet clothes. She had emerged from the reading room a few moments earlier carrying her map of the world, which she had quickly folded up. Now she fired a question at the captain in incomprehensible German. From her gesticulations, I gathered she had noticed some abnormality in our bearing.

The captain replied in English, showing the rest of us the courtesy Mrs Koenig had not. 'Yes, that is correct. Ladies and gentlemen, *Damen und Herren,* I am afraid we have been forced to change our course. We are now approximately four and a half thousand kilometres from Rio De Janeiro and a similar distance from New York.' He glanced down momentarily at the cuffs of his overcoat. 'In consultation with my fellow officers, I have therefore taken the decision to proceed directly to Lakehurst for repairs.' A storm of protest erupted from the passengers, but the captain raised a hand. 'There is no choice in this matter, I am afraid. There are not the facilities in Brazil to effect full repairs of the Richthofen. We will therefore proceed to New York, where we can attend to the matter properly.'

'I have a ticket to Rio de Janeiro,' Lindt protested, rising to his feet angrily. 'You cannot change course! Herr Kaufmann and I have paid to go to Brazil.'

'And so you will,' the captain replied firmly. 'Once we have made our repairs at the facility in Lakehurst, we will proceed to Rio and drop off our three passengers.' The two Germans and the Spaniard. 'From there we will make the return journey across the Atlantic. I apologise to you for the inconvenience, but the safety of the ship is paramount.'

'That is not acceptable!' Lindt exclaimed. 'We have a conference to attend in Sao Paulo on Friday afternoon. If I am not there our business will suffer. I will lose thousands of dollars!' In his frustration, he lapsed into German and his voice rose to a harsh roar. From the reaction of the stewards at the door, I gathered his language was becoming rather colourful. Captain Albrecht replied sternly and Lindt's voice became even harsher. But the captain maintained his cool and at length it was Lindt who backed down.

Albrecht took a moment to collect himself. 'If there are no further questions?' He glanced around the room. A few heads shook. Lindt was seething, but he said nothing more, resuming his seat with ill grace and glaring at Josef Kaufmann, who had not said a word in his support. 'Good. Then I will leave you to enjoy the rest of the afternoon. Once again, I apologise for the inconvenience. There is one piece of good news, however.' His face expanded into a broad smile. 'I am told the bar has just reopened.' The barman, Max, was obviously back on his feet. 'So, for the rest of the day, if any of you are thirsty, the drinks are on the house.'

Jacob Finch button-holed me before I could join the stampede. The ginger haired policeman had important news and the refreshments would have to wait. 'It's all my fault,' he admitted, on the quiet. 'This change in course. We didn't have a choice. I spoke to the captain, as soon as he came back on board, and told him Mr Kendall had been murdered.' He grimaced, clutching his hands to his head. 'It's an absolute nightmare. He knows there will have to be a full investigation when we reach our next port. Captain Albrecht agreed with me that the Americans would be a better bet to handle things than the Brazilians. That's the real reason we're heading for New York.'

'But that means...' I grimaced at the thought of American policemen. 'The Yanks will be all over the ship when we arrive at Lakehurst.'

'I'm afraid so. But there was no other choice. London will clear the way before we arrive. We might even be able to get a warrant for the arrest of Mrs Koenig. See if we can't get her extradited to the UK.'

My eyes widened. 'You're that convinced she's guilty?' I was starting to have serious doubts about the German woman's involvement in this affair. What evidence did we really have against her? 'Just on the basis of a torn notepad?'

'There's more to it than that. I did as you suggested and searched her room.' He fumbled inside his jacket. 'And, I hate to say it, but I found what I was looking for.' He pulled out two rolls of used film. 'In one of her coat pockets, hanging up in the closet.' He handed me the small canisters. 'I believe these are the photos which were taken back at the Yard.'

I examined the two rolls. 'So you think Kendall's death *was* connected to the theft of your file?' The films in my hand had been used but not developed.

'I'm starting to believe so. A conspiracy.' He shivered. 'I'm going to search the other rooms, just to be on the safe side. And then the luggage in the hold. Captain Albrecht's given me free rein now, thank heavens. But those films and the note pad together. It's very suggestive.'

I was not so sure. 'They might just be holiday snaps,' I suggested. 'Pictures of Seville from the air.' I remembered the Richthofen hovering for some time above the cathedral. 'Does Mrs Koenig have a camera?'

'There was one in her case.'

'There you are then.'

Finch shook his head. 'Look at the edge of the film.'

I examined the rolls in my hand, peering closely at the manufacturer's label. KG Corfield Ltd. A British company.

'I don't think they would sell those in Germany. I can check, of course. But it was a British woman who photographed our file.'

'Still not conclusive,' I replied, looking up. There could be half a dozen perfectly valid reasons as to how Mrs Koenig had got hold of British-made film. She had been in England, after all, giving a series of interviews about her recent African adventure. She could have bought the films while she was there. 'Can we develop the photographs? Have a proper look at them?'

Finch frowned at the suggestion. 'What, on board ship?'

'Why not? Knock up a dark room or something?'

The policeman was sceptical. 'I don't know anything about photography.' He shook his head. 'We'd need developing fluid. Special photographic paper.'

'I could always ask around. There's bound to be someone on board who...'

'No, no, no!' Finch exclaimed in alarm. 'That's out of the question. We can't involve anyone else in this.' The man was adamant. 'If there's even a chance these are the films we're looking for, we can't breathe a word about them to anybody. As it is, we'll have to destroy them before we reach America.'

I nodded. He was right about that, I supposed. We couldn't allow the American police to get hold of the photographs. The US was a friendly nation, but it wasn't *that* friendly. If these documents were to enter the public domain, even accidentally, the damage would be incalculable. 'But if we *destroy* the films, then we won't have any evidence against Mrs

Koenig. All you'll have is that notebook.'

'Yes. And the fact that she was on the Croydon flight.'

'Her and three others.' I scratched my head. It was frustrating, not being able to examine the films properly. But Finch was right; better to assume the worst and get shot of the damned things. 'You really think Mrs Koenig is at the bottom of all this?'

'Yes, I really do.' He shivered. 'A woman like that, a national hero. It doesn't bear thinking about. But nobody else would have torn those pages out of Mr Kendall's notebook. And why would anyone keep used film in their jacket pockets? A normal person would put them in their suitcase.' Finch closed his eyes. 'She's guilty. I'm convinced of it.'

'Will you be able to prove it, though?'

'Heaven knows. It won't stand up in a court of law. But there might be some fingerprints in Mr Kendall's cabin. The Americans will be able to check when we arrive. That might be enough to convict her. That and the notebook. If we keep everyone else out of there.'

'Possibly,' I said. 'But hers are not the only fingerprints in that cabin. I searched the room as well. And the stewards will have been in and out every day. And goodness knows who else.'

'Didn't you wear gloves?' Finch looked at me in astonishment.

'I'm afraid not. Look, Mr Finch, there's something I haven't told you.'

He regarded me with some concern. 'What is it?' he asked.

I had discussed the matter with Maurice and he had agreed with me: it was time to make a clean breast of things. The more time I spent with Jacob Finch, the more certain I was that he was acting in good faith. No master criminal could blunder about in the dark as much as he had been doing. And if I was to help him get to the bottom of things, he needed to know all the facts, even if quite a few of them did not reflect well on me. 'The poison that was used to kill Walter Kendall, I think it was rat poison. There's a tin of it in Gerhard Schulz's

179

cabin. Of German manufacture.' I took a deep breath. 'And I think I know how it got into Walter Kendall's room. It was nothing to do with Adelina Koenig.' I gripped my hands together and slowly took the policeman through the story.

Finch's eyes widened in horror as I outlined my doomed scheme to dope Walter Kendall and my disastrous second journey to the American's cabin in the middle of the night. I left out nothing, except the unfortunate business with the night shirt.

'So the sleeping draught didn't belong to Walter Kendall at all?' he breathed at last, when I had finished my story.

'I'm afraid not.'

Finch was aghast. 'But I assumed that Mrs Koenig had crept in and doctored the bottle, sometime during the day.'

I shook my head. 'No. That was Maurice. He placed the bottle in Kendall's cabin, after the American had been killed.'

'With the rat poison?'

'Yes. But I now believe someone got hold of the sleeping draught and introduced the poison to the bottle while it was still in my cabin.'

Finch lifted his hands to his face. 'But that's appalling!' he exclaimed. 'And you have no idea who did it?'

'No. But I don't think it was Adelina Koenig. And I'm certain she didn't break into Walter Kendall's cabin last night. She had other things on her mind.' I had already mentioned the noises I had heard coming from her room. 'If someone did spike that sleeping draught, they must have slipped into my cabin earlier in the day.' I explained about the faulty lock. 'And broke into Gerhard Schulz's room before that. But how they knew I had the sleeping draught in the first place, I have no idea. And they couldn't have known what I was intending to do with Kendall. Only Charles Lazenby, myself and Maurice knew about that. And Lazenby's not on board.'

I could almost see the smoke coming out of the policeman's ears as his brain struggled to cope with all the possibilities. 'So you think *you* might have been the intended victim, rather than Mr Kendall?'

'It's a possibility, I suppose.' I didn't want to dwell on

that idea. 'But I don't think so. To be honest, I don't know what to think. I still haven't worked out how they managed to get into Schulz's cabin in broad daylight. Maurice said the room was locked up. So whoever we're looking for, they must be a pretty good lock pick.'

'It might be a member of the crew,' Finch suggested. 'They would have access to the keys.'

I blinked. I had not considered that possibility. 'It could be, I suppose.'

'What about Mrs Koenig's nephew?' Even now, despite everything I had told him, Finch was not willing to let go of the idea that the German woman was involved.

'Possibly. But he's a crewman, not a steward. Members of the crew aren't usually allowed on the passenger decks. And anyone who saw him creeping about would be sure to remember it.' The poor fellow's lazy eye did rather draw attention. 'No, in my opinion, it's far more likely to be one of the passengers.'

Jacob Finch slumped back into his seat. 'This is an unmitigated disaster.' The information I had given him had completely undermined every one of his theories. And it didn't exactly paint a rosy picture of my own behaviour on board.

'Special Branch isn't the only one who makes mistakes,' I admitted ruefully.

He closed his eyes for a moment, his hands gripping tightly onto the padded sofa. 'Why didn't you tell me any of this before?'

'Maurice only discovered the rat poison this morning, after I'd first spoken to you.'

'In Gerhard Schultz's room?'

'Yes. Maurice thinks the Austrian may have been intending to use it to kill himself.'

Finch bunched his hands into a ball. 'I assumed Herr Schulz had taken the poison with him when he left the ship.'

It was my turn to be surprised. 'You *knew* about the rat poison?'

The other man nodded. 'But only second hand. That tin belonged to Herr Kaufmann.'

'Kaufmann? Josef Kaufmann?' The tubby German.

'Yes. He told the captain about it when he heard Herr Schulz had committed suicide. He had the tin in his cabin, but it went missing during the time they were in Seville. He didn't notice it until yesterday afternoon. And he told the captain straight away, so that they could pass the information on to the police in Seville.'

No wonder Kaufmann had been so certain Gerhard Schulz had committed suicide.

'But why would Kaufmann be carrying rat poison to South America?'

Finch shrugged. 'Don't ask me to explain it. It was a gift of some kind, apparently. Herr Lindt is tendering for a business contract in Sao Paulo. There's some kind of conference taking place, with lots of deals being negotiated.'

'Yes, I heard about that. That's why he's so upset about the change of course.'

'Apparently, he heard that one of the factories over there had a problem with rats. He asked Herr Kaufmann to bring along some rat poison. I understand it was intended as a joke. A means of establishing a rapport with the chairman of the company.'

'It all sounds a bit dubious to me.'

'I know, I didn't give it much credence. But the poison was there and it went missing. I thought it was possible that Herr Schulz had taken it. Affairs of the heart and all that.'

'But how would he have got into Kaufmann's room? To steal it?'

'He was given the key. He'd run out of film for his camera, shortly before we arrived in Seville, and Kaufmann told him to take a couple of rolls from his case. Schulz must have gone in there and stolen the powder at the same time. That's what we thought, anyway. But if you say you've found the tin in the Austrian's cabin...?'

'Yes. Well, Maurice did anyway. Do you know if Schulz used poison to kill himself?'

Finch shook his head. 'I didn't think to check. I can cable London to find out. I'll get onto it later today.'

'This gets more and more confusing by the minute.'

'It's dreadful,' the policeman agreed. 'I thought I had Mrs Koenig banged to rights. She crept out of her room, doctored Mr Kendall's sleeping draught and then killed him. But if she had a man in her cabin last night and you administered the poison, then there's no evidence against her at all. Apart from a few impressions on a notepad. Well, and these rolls of film. And, as you say, they could just be holiday snaps. This is a disaster. Do you...do you know who Mrs Koenig was entertaining?'

'No, I don't. My first thought was Captain Rüdiger. She was very chatty with him yesterday afternoon. And I heard them talking about Gerhard Schulz, down in the control cabin.'

Finch nodded. 'Yes, she was telling him about Miss Hurst and Herr Schulz. She'd noticed how friendly the two of them were. It was information for the police in Seville. I saw the telegrams they sent out. But you say she was particularly friendly with the first officer?'

'I thought so at the time. But she's a lot more friendly with Sir George. If I had to put money on it, I'd say he was more likely to be her gentleman caller.'

'Perhaps they're in cahoots.'

'Maybe,' I said, thinking the matter over carefully. 'Sir George wasn't on the Croydon flight, but he certainly needs the money, from what I hear. But it's the getting in and out of Schulz's room that bothers me. How could anyone get away with that without being seen?' I had made a pigs ear of it *and* bumped into Miss Hurst into the bargain; and I was supposed to know what I was doing. 'It's difficult enough in the dead of night, but during the day...'

'That brings us back to the staff,' the policeman thought. 'And Mrs Koenig's nephew.'

I shook my head. 'One of the stewards, more likely. Slipped a fiver to look the other way, or to lend them their keys. You can never rule out the servants.' I had learnt that from bitter experience.

As if on cue, a white coated steward appeared with a metal tray. 'There you are, Mr Finch. I have been looking for you.' At the sound of his voice, the policeman sprang away from me, as if the two of us had been caught in an illicit embrace. How the damned fellow had ever reached the rank of detective was beyond me. The steward didn't bat an eyelid, of course. 'Another telegram for you, sir.'

'Thank you,' Finch said, pulling the message off the tray. He waited until Stefan had gone before opening the folded paper. 'More bad news, I expect. I wonder what they want this time.' He looked down at the message and frowned.

'Encrypted?' I asked.

Finch nodded and sighed. The usual unreadable gibberish. 'It takes forever to decode. I'll have to pop back to my cabin. I really don't have time for this.'

'It might be important.'

'It's *always* important,' he agreed anxiously. 'That's what I'm worried about. Look, can you take care of the negatives?' He gestured to the rolls of film in my hands.

'Certainly. What do you want me to do with them?'

Finch was unequivocal. 'Destroy them, any way you can.'

I grimaced. 'You're sure?' This was the only real evidence we had.

He nodded firmly. 'As soon as possible. Get rid of the dreadful things before they do any more harm.'

'All right,' I agreed, lifting up one of the films and gently easing out the tab with my fingernail. 'If these *are* just holiday snaps, Mrs Koenig is not going to be at all happy.' I grabbed the tab with my fingers and kept pulling until the entire film had been exposed to the light. Then I did the same with the other roll. I glanced across the promenade, to make sure there were no stewards about, then bundled up the jumble of exposed celluloid and lifted the window.

'I'm not sure if that's a good idea,' Finch said. 'The engine cars...'

'It'll be fine,' I assured him. The engines were higher up than the windows on either side of the Zeppelin. I had just had a good look at them from the outside. I tossed the bundle of film into the air. It shot backwards but down and was soon lost to sight. I closed the window firmly behind them. 'Good riddance,' I said, flashing a grin at Jacob Finch. 'Well, that's the monarchy taken care of. Now we just need to find our murderer.'

Chapter Fourteen

Thomas McGilton was hunched over a telegraph slip, pencil in hand, his brownish green eyes half closed. He was considering his words carefully before he transcribed them. It was the first time I had seen him writing anything.

'You not coming for a drink?' I called out, through the reading room window. Everyone with an ounce of sense was already down in the bar. 'Oh no, you don't, do you?'

He looked up from the central table. 'No, but I'll be down in a minute. Just want to finish off this telegram.'

I stepped into the room. 'Don't tell me,' I said, observing the slip of paper in front of him. ' *"Having a lovely time on the airship. Haven't died yet. Love Thomas."* '

McGilton laughed. 'You're not far wrong.' He glanced down at his stubby pencil and grabbed a sharpener from the table. 'I'm going to write to Lucy's parents. Let them know we'll be arriving in New York a few day's early. I want to get it sent off this afternoon. The press are going to have a field day when they hear we've been diverted.'

'Lord, yes.' I hadn't thought of that. A damaged Zeppelin would be headline news. 'I had hoped to slip away quietly at the end of this trip.'

'No chance of that,' the Irishman asserted. 'Two people dead and a damaged tail fin. The newspapers will lap it up. Was that our Mr Finch I saw heading off downstairs?'

Finch and I had been sat at the far end of the promenade. McGilton must have seen him heading for the lounge room door. 'Er...yes, that's right.' I perched myself on a chair.

'He's an odd fellow, that one.' McGilton finished sharpening his pencil and placed the sharpener back down on the table top. 'What do you make of him?'

'Finch?' I shrugged, not quite sure why I was being asked. 'He's amiable enough, I suppose. A bit highly strung.'

'Yes, I've noticed that.' McGilton frowned. He had not written anything on the telegraph slip as yet, beyond the address. 'Never stops fidgeting. But, you know, it's an odd

186

thing. I heard somebody say a little while ago that he was a policeman.'

'A *policeman*?' I did my best to sound surprised. It was no great stretch for me just now. 'I thought he was a stockbroker.'

'So did I. But apparently he's from *Scotland Yard*.' McGilton emphasised these last two words, as if he were talking about a man from Mars.

'Good lord. First I've heard of it. Who told you that?' I was curious to know who had rumbled him.

'Oh, one of the Germans, after we got off the dinghy. Just something I overheard. Probably got the wrong end of the stick. German's not my strong point. I can barely string a sentence together.'

'That's more than I can manage.'

'Lucy's better at it than I am. She speaks it like a native.'

'I remember you saying. Where is she now? Down at the bar?'

'No, she's in her room. Writing an obituary.'

'An obituary?' I blinked in bemusement. 'Oh, for Mr Kendall, you mean?'

'Yes. Always has to keep busy. She thinks it's the least she can do. It's hit her really hard, him dying like that.'

'It was quite a shock for all of us.'

'That it was,' McGilton agreed. 'But she knew him better than anyone.'

'Knew him? But I...I thought they'd only just met.' It was probably best to play dumb on that point. I didn't know how much the Irishman had been told.

'That's what she said to me. But apparently he was a friend of her fathers. I didn't have a clue until this afternoon. She swore blind she'd never met him before.' McGilton grimaced. 'Said she just admired his work'

'That's a bit off,' I suggested.

'It's not like her to lie to me like that. But she's known him since she was a girl. She says the relationship was platonic – she thought of him as an uncle figure – but I think there may have been more to it than that.'

'Perhaps she was worried you might be jealous. With him being on board ship.'

'I suppose so. As if I would be.' McGilton had certainly turned a blind eye to some outrageous flirting since we had left Seville.

'Did Miss Tanner book the tickets?' I enquired, now the subject had been broached. 'On the Richthofen, I mean?' Had it really been a coincidence that she was on the same flight as Walter Kendall?

'No, that was me. Lucy was visiting an old school friend in Andalucía. We were going to catch a boat to America when she got back. But when I heard the Richthofen was stopping in Seville at around the same time, I couldn't resist it. I've always wanted to go on an airship.'

I remembered the schoolboy gleam in his eye the first time I had met him. 'You must be regretting it now.'

He chuckled. 'Not a bit of it. She's a fine ship. Herr Lindt is right about that, if nothing else. You couldn't ask for a better way to travel.'

'There I think we may have to disagree. So her meeting Mr Kendall really was just a matter of chance?'

'That it was. All of us heading to the States. Lucy should have told me about it, though. What he'd meant to her. I wouldn't have minded.' He shrugged. 'Even if they *were* old flames. We've all got our histories. I never expected to marry a saint.'

'That's very broad minded of you. Most men expect their brides to come to the marriage bed ignorant of everything.'

McGilton laughed. 'Now where would be the fun in that? But I have to be honest, Mr Bland, I am worried about her. She was feeling guilty enough about Herr Schulz. This business with Mr Kendall might finish her off.'

'Why would she feel guilty about Schulz?'

'She feels responsible for what happened to him.'

I didn't understand. 'How can *she* be responsible? She never met him, did she?'

'Only the once.' The Irishman put down his pencil. 'You know Herr Schulz had a bit of a thing for Miss Hurst?'

'Yes, I'd heard that.'

'Well, apparently, he booked a ticket on the Richthofen just to be with her. He wanted to persuade her not to go and live in America. But he could only afford to come as far as Seville. And on Sunday morning, after breakfast, he proposed to her. He asked her to marry him.'

'Good lord.' That I had not heard. 'And she turned him down?'

'Not straight away. She agreed to have a think about it. I only know all this because of Lucy, by the way. She has a way of worming information out from people.'

'Yes, I've noticed that.'

'Well, anyway, they arrived in Seville and Herr Schulz suggested they meet up later that afternoon. She was going to tell him no, of course, but she wanted to do it in person.'

'Quite right too.'

'But when she got to the hotel, the Alfonso, she couldn't go through with it. Lucy has a way of picking up on things, even with people she's only just met. Miss Hurst burst into tears as soon as she walked into the room and Lucy got the whole story out of her. And when she said she couldn't bear to give Herr Schulz the bad news, Lucy volunteered to go in her place. She met up with him in town and told him Miss Hurst didn't want to see him again.'

'At the Torre del Oro?'

'I think so, yes. How did you know that?'

'I...bumped into her there. On the stairs.' So that was why she had been rushing around. It had nothing to do with Walter Kendall.

'Did you now? Well, anyway, she delivered the news and the next thing we know the fellow's topped himself. Lucy can't help holding herself responsible.'

'Hardly her fault. She was just the messenger.'

'She knows that. But it's human nature to blame yourself. And Miss Hurst feels even more responsible; with some reason, I suppose. Lucy was too busy comforting her yesterday to dwell too much on her own part in it, but now with Mr Kendall as well...it's all been too much for her.'

'Yes, poor woman. Two deaths in two days and one of them an old friend. And Miss Hurst too. No wonder that woman walks around the place looking like a ghost.' I glanced down at the telegram in McGilton's hand. 'And your fiancée's writing an obituary, you say?'

'Helps take her mind off things. She likes to keep busy. It wouldn't surprise me if she wrote something about the storm, as well. She's always looking for stories. Even had me going out taking photographs of the damage, to illustrate what she's going to write.'

'An enterprising woman.'

'It's just her way of coping. Two deaths and a storm, it's enough to rattle anyone. But they say bad luck comes in threes, so hopefully we've had our ration for this trip.'

I raised an eyebrow. 'There's nothing like tempting fate, Mr McGilton.'

It was the last cigarette in the case and I didn't know how long it would be before I could get hold of another. There is nothing quite like a Piccadilly to soothe the nerves at the end of a stressful day but the atmosphere was marred somewhat by a smoking room packed with loud voiced passengers. I needed time to think and it was clear I was not going to get it.

Adelina Koenig was gnashing away in her harsh German voice on the opposite side of the room, cutting through the fog of tobacco like a knife through charred flesh. I had the impression the woman was upset about something, but as she was speaking fluent Kraut I had no idea what had annoyed her. It couldn't be Karl Lindt. He was sitting to her right, having just returned from the bar, and I doubted even he would have the nerve to get fresh with the likes of Adelina Koenig. Besides, Sir George Westlake was sitting at the table with them, a glass of brandy in one hand and a fat cigar in the other, and he would make sure there was no impropriety.

Josef Kaufmann was keeping well away from his odious

colleague. The tubby German was over in the corner, talking to that Spanish fellow McGilton shared with, a rather small man with an egg-shaped head and a rakish moustache. I was sure somebody had mentioned his name to me but for the life of me I couldn't recall it.

Frederick Gray arrived back at the table with my whisky and soda. I grunted my thanks as the GPO man placed the tumbler down in front of me and resumed his seat. Not that he had paid for it – the drinks were on the house this evening – but he had at least made the effort to deliver the glass.

I took a final sad gasp of the Piccadilly and stubbed it out in the ashtray. 'What's Mrs Koenig so upset about?' I enquired, before Gray had the chance to say anything. He had been droning on about his facsimile machine for some minutes before he had headed off to the bar – it was being shipped out to New York, apparently, and then put on a train for San Francisco, in readiness for some demonstration or other – and I was determined not to allow him to resume his dreary monologue.

The man glanced back at the Germans and then leaned across the table towards me. He lowered his voice, as if imparting some great secret. 'Frau Koenig believes someone has broken into her cabin, at least according to Herr Lindt.' Gray must have had a brief chat with the businessman while he was getting the drinks. 'Somebody's been rifling through her clothes,' he added, salaciously.

'Was anything stolen?' I reached for my glass. Had anyone put two and two together, now that Finch's identity was in the public domain? Did they realise it was the policeman who had been snooping about?

'Not that she's aware of,' Gray replied, his irritating voice reverting to its usual nasal tone as he leant back in his seat. 'Herr Lindt thinks it must be one of the staff. He says the whole trip has been a shambles from the start.'

I took a large gulp of whisky. 'He's not wrong there.' Mind you, Lindt was probably still fuming about the change of course. I wondered briefly whether it had upset anybody else's plans. Lindt seemed to be on rather good terms with Mrs

Koenig, anyway. Was there some prior connection between the two of them that I wasn't aware of? I growled, dismissing the idea. I was starting to think like Jacob Finch.

Sir George Westlake guffawed loudly from the other table and I saw the Spanish fellow look across in surprise. Josef Kaufmann met my eye and raised his glass. He had been due to leave the Richthofen in Rio, as had his companion. What did the Dago make of all this? I wondered. Actually, I didn't much care. 'Sir George seems to be enjoying the trip anyway,' I commented dryly.

Frederick Gray's eyes lit up at the mention of the explorer. 'He's promised to show me the sights in New York. I'm not due in San Francisco until next week. I'll have a bit of free time now, since we're going straight there.' He picked up his glass and took a small sip of water. 'This trip has been a lot livelier than any of us anticipated.'

'I'll say. I'm not looking forward to America, though. All that publicity.' I shuddered at the thought. McGilton was right. The Richthofen would be headline news. I finished off the whisky and soda in another quick gulp. 'You not drinking?' I asked, as the GPO man set down his glass of water.

Gray shook his head sadly. 'I think I ought to wait until after supper. Otherwise it'll go straight to my head.'

The dinner gong sounded from across the deck and Maurice adjusted my tie with some satisfaction. It seemed absurd, given the events of the day, that everyone should retire from the bar half an hour before dinner to change their clothes, but there was something reassuring in the upholdance of this tradition. My valet had not been able to get my other shirt dried in time, much to his annoyance, but I had at least been able to put on my dinner jacket and a fresh tie. Maurice had moved his clothes out of the cabin into the room next door, but was spending far more time in my own cabin than was probably required. He did fuss rather. Luckily, the man had had the foresight to change his own clothes before I had returned from the bar. For all his faults, Maurice knew the correct order of these things. I was still smarting at the thought of him joining us for dinner, but I was not holding it against him personally. 'Better make tracks,' I said, glancing at my pocket watch as the sound of the gong faded away. I had moderated my intake of alcohol in the run up to supper, but once I had a bit of food inside me I could allow my thirst full rein.

Maurice pulled opened the cabin door and stepped into the corridor. McGilton was just emerging from his own room next door. He waved a hand at me as I came out and then greeted his fiancée and Miss Hurst, who were already on their way to the dining hall. They had emerged from the stairs running down to B Deck, at the far end of the central passageway. Miss Tanner must have dressed for supper while the rest of us were down at the bar.

Maurice was hovering in the starboard corridor, waiting for me to follow the Irishman, but I waved him forward. 'You go on. I want to have a quick word with Mr Finch, before I sit down to dinner.' I had not heard back from the detective yet about that telegram he had received.

'Very good, Monsieur,' the valet replied.

Finch was probably still in his bedroom on the port side but I nipped left first, into the lounge area, on the off-chance that he might be out and about. As I entered the saloon, I spotted Josef Kaufmann making his way out from the reading room.

'Feeling hungry?' I asked.

'Indeed,' the man replied, passing me by with a genial smile. He had a surprisingly modest appetite, given his size, but the rotund German was always very complimentary about the quality of the food.

There was no sign of Finch on this side of the ship, so I followed Kaufmann back through the door. Karl Lindt had just appeared from his cabin on the corner of the starboard passage and the two men greeted each other politely. I hung back for a moment, not wishing to get into a conversation with either of them. The two Germans headed off down the central passage while I dawdled behind them. I glanced left, idly, and noticed Lindt had left a crack open in the door to his cabin. No, hang on, that wasn't his room. It was the second door along. The ladies' room. That's odd, I thought. I had already seen Miss Hurst and Miss Tanner heading for the dining hall.

There was a flicker of movement from inside the cabin. A shadow. So that was where Finch was. I grinned. He had said he wanted to look through the women's cabin at some point, but the idea had been lost in all the furore over Mrs Koenig. Perhaps he had seen his chance and nipped in now.

The two Germans had disappeared through the far door into the dining room, leaving me free to shuffle unobserved along the length of the starboard corridor. There was the usual row of three rooms here, clumped together at the rear of the deck. Mr Lindt, the two girls and Mr Kaufmann at the far end. I smiled to myself and grabbed the handle of the middle door. Finch would have the fright of his life when I opened it.

I tugged at the handle but the panel would not budge. An aroma of perfume assaulted my nostrils – the typical smells of a woman's boudoir – but there was something obstructing the door. I used a little more force and the panel slid back another couple of inches, giving me a brief glimpse of the interior of the cabin. As I had suspected, clothes were hanging everywhere. There were probably a couple of dresses on the back of the door getting in the way of the tracks. I pulled harder and the panel finally trundled to one side. There was a ledge above the wash basin piled high with make up and other beauty products. But my attention shifted abruptly as a pair of feet thudded out into the corridor at ground level. Jacob Finch was lying face down across the length of the cabin, in a swamp of his own blood. His body was twitching and there was a gaping wound in the middle of his back.

'Good God!' I exclaimed, from the doorway.

At the sound of my voice, Finch let out a low moan. He was still alive. I moved quickly into the room, stepping awkwardly across his legs, which had been obstructing the door. That must have been the movement I had seen; him kicking against it. I lowered myself to my knees and rolled the poor fellow onto his side. 'Finch, what happened?'

The man was shuddering uncontrollably. His jacket was

caked in blood, as was quite a large section of the carpet beneath him. Most of it had congealed, suggesting he had been here for some time. Perhaps he had been unconscious. But he was awake now, barely. He gestured as best he could to the bunk bed. Underneath it I could make out a large, bloodied knife with a serrated edge. A steak knife, perhaps.

'Somebody stabbed you?' I exclaimed. My God, in broad daylight. Well, the lighting was electric, but in full view of anyone who might happen by.

He nodded his head, though with some difficulty. An unpleasant liquid bubbled up from his mouth.

'I should summon a doctor,' I said, then cursed as I remembered there was no medical man on board. And even at a glance I could see the poor fellow was not long for this world.

Finch shook his head emphatically. 'No...no...you...' He was having difficulty talking. There was too much fluid in his mouth and I could see the effort he was expending trying to communicate with me. 'You must...you must tell...'

'Who did this to you?'

'...tell the captain...it's...it's...' His left hand grabbed my shoulder. With an enormous effort of will, he shook his head, gathered together the last of his wits, and managed to form one final coherent sentence. 'I just knew something like this was going to happen,' he said.

And then he died.

Chapter Fifteen

I stood for some moments staring down at the lifeless body. My mind was struggling to make sense of what had happened. I had only known Jacob Finch for a few hours and now here he was, lying dead in a pool of blood. I could scarcely believe it. Anger welled up inside me. Who had done this horrible thing? What kind of callous brute would stab a man in the back and then leave him for dead on the bedroom floor? Finch may have been a policeman, and as such a potential threat to somebody on board, but he was only doing his job. He did not deserve to die like this.

I reached down and closed his eyes. In life, Jacob Finch had never stopped moving, but now the poor fellow would never move again. He looked strangely peaceful lying there, childlike almost. His features had relaxed, the wrinkles on his brow smoothing themselves out in death. It was only the blood splattered across his shirt and jacket that gave testament to the pain he had endured in his final moments.

At least no one could blame me for this murder, I thought. It is strange how quickly one's attention returns to one's own predicament in these circumstances. It was typical of my luck, however, that I should be the one to stumble across the body. Now I would have to call the alarm and deal with all the fuss. The fates really did have it in for me; though not, perhaps, as much as they did for Jacob Finch.

How had he been knifed without anybody noticing? I wondered. The run up to dinner was one of the busiest times of day on the passenger decks. And, come to that, why hadn't Miss Hurst and Miss Tanner been in their cabin, changing for supper, like everybody else? Why had they been down on B Deck? It was very odd. I couldn't tell how long the policeman had been lying here before I had found him. Ten minutes? Fifteen at most. And what had drawn him to search this particular room at a time when all sorts of people might have been flitting about? It could surely have waited until tomorrow.

Whatever his reasons, Finch must have discovered

something important. Why else would anybody have bothered to stab him like this? He must have been getting close to the truth. If only he had managed to hold on for a few more moments and told me something useful. I growled. But there was no point getting upset about that now.

I lifted myself up and pulled the arm of my jacket over my hands. Gingerly, I reached under the bed and retrieved the bloodied knife. I held it by the hilt, with my fingers under the cuff of the jacket. I wasn't about to put my fingerprints on it, but I wanted to get a good look. It was definitely a steak knife. We had used them at dinner the day before and any one of the passengers might have stolen it. But who would have the nerve to creep in here and stab Finch from behind?

The telegram. It had to be something to do with that. Some new information from London. I looked down at the corpse. If Finch had decrypted the message, perhaps he had the English translation with him in one of his pockets. I could see his copy of *Alice In Wonderland* poking out of the inside of his jacket.

No. I wasn't going to start rifling through those blood soaked clothes. Not yet, anyway. For once, I was going to play this by the book. I would summon Captain Albrecht, tell him all I knew and let him sort it out. I had come on board the Richthofen to retrieve a roll of film and – so far as I knew – that task had been completed. I wasn't going to offer myself up as the next sacrificial victim, if someone on board had it in for policemen.

I rose to my feet, placed the knife carefully back where I had found it and slid out the doorway. I would summon a steward and get him to call the captain. I moved out into the starboard corridor. The stewards would be hovering around the serving hatch about now, on the port side, conveying food into the dining hall. I rounded the corner into the connecting passage and walked slap bang into Miss Annabel Hurst, who was returning to her cabin.

This time, I think she was more surprised than I was. She recoiled from the brief impact but then recovered herself and shot past me with a barely audible 'excuse me' before I could even begin to apologise. She had already slipped around the corner and was at the door of her room before I could call a word of warning. 'Miss Hurst, I wouldn't...'

It was too late. I had left the cabin door wide open and in an instant the girl had caught sight of Jacob Finch in all his deathly glory. Her hand went to her mouth and she let out a piercing scream. She tottered backwards for a moment and then looked at me in horror. I glanced down at my shirt and it was then I noticed the blood stains. Finch must have dribbled a bit over me when he had grabbed my shoulder. Miss Hurst shrank away in terror.

I was standing at the intersection of the corridors, with the door to the lounge just behind me. At the far end of the central passageway, a steward had been lifting a platter of cold meats from the serving hatch. On hearing the scream he had nearly dropped it. He looked across at me in alarm and I gestured for him to come. He returned the platter to the ledge and raced over to find out what was going on.

'Miss Hurst has had a terrible shock,' I said. 'Get her into the lounge. I'll fetch some whisky.'

I didn't give the young fellow any time to enquire further. I rushed back to my own cabin to grab the bottle and a glass. I poured out a measure for myself and downed it in one before heading back out into the corridor. Miss Hurst was not the only one in a state of shock. Then I quickly crossed into the lounge room.

The young woman was sitting in a chair halfway across the saloon. She tensed at the sight of me.

'Don't be afraid,' I said, holding up the glass and bottle in my hands and gesturing to the steward. His presence would serve to reassure her of my good intentions. 'I saw the door of your room open. I went to investigate and discovered Mr Finch. He'd been stabbed in the back. Not by me,' I added.

The steward poured out the whisky and handed the glass to Miss Hurst. 'Mr Finch is dead?' he enquired, screwing the lid back onto the bottle top.

'I'm afraid so. He was searching Miss Hurst's room.'

'Someone...someone said he was a policeman,' the

young woman muttered absently. So she too had heard the rumour.

'Yes, him and me both.' It was a white lie but I was aiming for reassurance. 'We've been investigating a theft. Look, do you know *why* he was searching your room?'

She nodded numbly. Her hands were trembling, gripping tightly to the glass. 'I think so, yes. You've found out, haven't you?'

'What's going on?' a voice called from the doorway behind us. It was the chief steward, Stefan. 'Sir, is Miss Hurst all right?'

'No, she's not.' I turned back to look at the new arrival. 'She's had a hell of a shock.' We both have, I thought. 'Keep an eye on her.' This instruction I shot at the junior steward as I moved across to talk to Stefan. 'You need to fetch the captain at once. There's been a terrible incident. Another one.'

'An incident, sir?'

I nodded. Before I could say another word, a third voice echoed from outside the lounge. Thomas McGilton was making his way along the central aisle from the dining hall. Stefan stepped back into the corridor and I followed him out.

'We heard a scream,' McGilton said. 'Is everything all right?' The Irishman had been delegated by the other diners to find out what was going on.

'I'm afraid not,' I replied. 'Mr Finch is dead. He's been stabbed in the back. In Miss Tanner's cabin.'

That shut the fellow up.

'I'll fetch the captain,' Stefan muttered, moving past us.

'Dead?' McGilton repeated numbly. His mouth opened and closed a couple of times but no sound came out.

'Miss Hurst just found the body. Well, we both did.'

At the serving hatch, the head steward started issuing instructions to some of his underlings. One of them ran off towards the stairs.

'Poor woman,' McGilton said, at last. His eyes flicked down to the blood on my shirt and he frowned momentarily.

'There was a lot of blood in there,' I explained, somewhat hastily, as his gaze returned to my face. 'I had

199

to...make sure he was really dead.'

The Irishman nodded, accepting my explanation. 'But what was Mr Finch doing in the girls' bedroom?'

'That I don't know. Look, can you keep everyone quiet in the dining room until the captain gets here? We don't want people clomping about all over the place.'

'Consider it done. Oh. Should I send Lucy out, to look after Miss Hurst?'

I nodded. 'Good idea.' I would have enough on my plate, explaining things to the captain, without having to take charge of a distressed female.

'This is going to put a bit of a downer on supper,' McGilton commented dryly. 'Is there anything else I can do?'

'Not just now. Oh, wait a minute. You've got a camera, haven't you?'

He hesitated. 'In my cabin, yes.'

'I might need to borrow that.'

'Help yourself. It's on the top bunk. The door's not locked. Help yourself to a roll of film.'

'Thank you,' I said. The crime scene would have to be thoroughly documented. I was not a member of the Metropolitan Police, but I knew that much at least.

'A dreadful business,' McGilton breathed.

'The worst,' I said, taking a moment at last to close my eyes. 'The very worst.'

Captain Albrecht peered through the door of the cabin, his face understandably grim. He had removed his cap, and his gently thinning hair, combined with an unusually sombre expression, added some years to the senior officer as he regarded the distressing scene.

Everything in the cabin was just how I had found it. 'He was still alive when I got here. I tried to help him but...it was too late.' I was standing back from the door, a little way along the corridor. The head steward was hovering between us. He would be able to provide at least some corroboration of my story.

Albrecht noticed the knife almost at once. I had replaced it carefully where I had found it. 'He was stabbed in the back?'

'It looks that way. He may not have seen his assailant.' The knife had been abandoned when the murderer had fled the scene. Better that, I presumed, than carrying a blood stained weapon out into the corridors for everyone to see.

The captain pulled away from the door. 'This is a bad business,' he muttered. 'I should never have let that man on board.' He adjusted his cap. 'But what's done is done. There'll be time for recriminations later.'

'I suppose there'll have to be an enquiry,' I said. Finch had mentioned the possibility, before he had died, but that had been in relation to Walter Kendall. Now there would be two deaths to investigate. Or three, if it turned out Gerhard Schulz had been murdered as well. 'You won't be able to cover this up. It's all gone too far.' And Captain Albrecht, as the man in charge, would carry the can for everything. His career would be lucky to survive.

I lifted up McGilton's camera and opened the back of it. 'I've taken a few photographs of the crime scene. I thought it might be helpful for the American police when they come on board. Your head steward supervised me doing it.' I didn't want the captain to think I had tampered with anything before he had arrived. I handed over the roll of Kodak.

'You photographed everything?' Albrecht asked, turning the film over in his hand.

'Yes. Not a pleasant task.' I moved in and took another look around the room. 'I got a couple of photos of the murder weapon, under the bed. I'm not sure how well they'll come out.' Conditions in the cabin were hardly ideal.

'That looks like a steak knife,' Captain Albrecht observed. He moved back into the corridor and gestured Stefan into the doorway.

'That's one of ours,' the head steward confirmed. 'We were a knife short after supper last night.'

I blinked in surprise. Not that they were a knife short but that Stefan was aware of the fact. 'Didn't you try to find it?'

The steward smiled apologetically. 'Small items often

go missing from the passenger decks. Cutlery. Salt cellars. Hand towels.'

'What, you mean people steal them?'

'It is not unusual,' the steward confirmed, moving away from the door. 'So long as it is nothing expensive, we "turn a blind eye". I believe that is the expression?'

I nodded. It wasn't really such a surprise. Anyone who could afford a ticket on the Richthofen could not be short of a bob or two, but the temptation to pocket a few souvenirs was something even the wealthiest of people found hard to resist. I had been guilty of that kind of petty pilfering myself. 'It might equally well have been a member of staff, though.'

'I can assure you, Mr Bland,' Captain Albrecht responded firmly, 'all our staff are scrupulously honest. Any theft among the crew would be dealt with most severely. Thank you, Stefan. That will be all.' The steward bowed half-heartedly and left us be. 'Some of the crew are saying this trip is cursed. I am beginning to believe they may have a point. And it is only our third flight. This is a dreadful business, Mr Bland.'

'Dreadful,' I agreed.

'Do you know why Mr Finch was searching Miss Tanner's cabin?'

'I think so. Miss Hurst was one of the people on the flight out from Croydon. I presume Mr Finch told you about that?'

Albrecht inclined his head.

'He wanted to have a look at their rooms. But I haven't the foggiest idea why he chose to search this particular cabin just before dinner. Although he did say you'd given him permission to search the luggage.'

'In the hold, yes. But that was not due to begin until tomorrow morning.'

'Couldn't wait, I suppose. He...received a telegram late this afternoon which might shed some light on the matter. I have a feeling it may be in his jacket pocket. Now we've documented everything, I wonder if I might take a look?'

The captain considered long and hard. He glanced down at my blood-spattered shirt. I could tell what he was thinking and I could hardly blame him. I had discovered the body. Who was to say I was not responsible for the death itself? 'Mr Finch said that you were working with him and that you were a man to be trusted,' he replied cautiously. 'But I think I may need to have official confirmation of that.'

'That's fair enough,' I agreed. I could hardly blame him for questioning my credentials. I would have done the same thing, in his position. I racked my brains quickly, thinking of who I could get in contact with. I didn't have my code book with me, so I couldn't get in touch with the Colonel or anyone at SIS. And Charles Lazenby was too far down the food chain to impress the likes of Captain Albrecht. 'I'll telegraph the people at Special Branch. They need to know about Finch anyway.' Always assuming the captain would let me take possession of the code book.

He nodded curtly. 'Very well.'

'In the meantime...?'

'In the meantime, you are welcome to take a look. It may be helpful to see this telegram.'

I moved forward, with the captain's eyes burning a hole in the back of my dinner jacket, and squatted in front of the prone figure. I reached forward and extracted the code book from the inside of his coat. I flicked through the pages, making sure Albrecht could see everything I was doing, but the telegram was not inside. I slid a hand into his waist pocket instead. 'Bingo!' I exclaimed, pulling out two small slips of paper. One was the telegram, the other was Finch's hastily scribbled translation.

Captain Albrecht coughed politely and extended a hand.

I hesitated for a moment. 'This may contain confidential information,' I said.

'I am the legal authority on the Richthofen,' he told me calmly. 'A man has been murdered. If you please...?'

Reluctantly, I handed the papers across. Albrecht unfurled the two sheets and scanned them briefly. His expression was unreadable. The fellow might have been reading a course correction. Even in such dire circumstances as these, he had an air of unflappability that was immensely

203

reassuring. 'This first line...?' He handed the translation back to me.

I looked at the decrypted message.

"NO PASSPORT ISSUED MATCHING AGE AND DESCRIPTION ANNABEL HURST STOP"

Hurst? 'Good lord. That must be why he was searching her room.' I scanned the line again. 'He must have asked for passport checks on all the passengers. Those out of Croydon, anyway. And someone must have picked up an anomaly.' I considered this for a moment. 'Bit odd. No Annabel Hursts. It must be a common enough name.'

'I allowed Mr Finch access to the passport details of all the passengers on board, as a courtesy. He would have known her date of birth and country of origin.'

'But, according to this, no British passport has ever been issued to her. If it turns out she's travelling on a fake passport, he would be bound to search her room.' I shook my head in disbelief. 'But why on earth would Miss Hurst be travelling incognito?'

'A fugitive?' Captain Albrecht guessed.

I laughed. 'Miss Hurst!? Have you met the woman?'

'It does seem unlikely,' he conceded.

'Perhaps she acted as a courier. Carried the stolen documents from Croydon to hand on to somebody. If she *is* involved in all this, I don't think she can be at the centre of it.'

'Nevertheless, she will need to be questioned,' Albrecht said. 'The second part of the telegram?'

I looked down again at Finch's half-formed scribble.

"MICK DURRANT ARRESTED HOLYHEAD STOP WILL MOVE TO LONDON FOR INTERROGATION," it read.

The captain looked to me for an explanation. 'Mick Durrant. That was the name of the baggage handler.' I remembered Finch telling me about him. 'A former merchant navy man. He was the one who organised the theft in the first place. Under orders. It looks like they've got him under lock and key.' In Holyhead. 'He must have been trying to catch a ferry to Ireland. Perhaps he was going home.'

The other man regarded me blankly.

'A name like "Mick", he's bound to be Irish. Perhaps he's a Fenian.' Irish republicans, I thought. They would certainly relish the prospect of damaging the British establishment, and the money from the American newspapers would keep them in dynamite for years. 'Maybe that's what all this is about. A republican plot.' A sudden thought struck me. 'McGilton's an Irishman. And a Roman Catholic.' I shook my head. I was reading far too much into just one name. 'Ignore me,' I said. 'I'm clutching at straws.' I glanced down at the paper again.

"WILL MOVE TO LONDON FOR INTERROGATION."

'At least they have the fellow under lock and key. He won't last long when Special Branch get hold of him.'

The captain was perplexed. '"*Last long*"? They will hurt him?'

'Good lord, no. We don't torture people. We're British.' I chuckled at the very idea. 'But he'll crack soon enough under interrogation. They all do. With any luck, this time tomorrow we'll know precisely who's behind all this.' I stared down at the sad, dead body of Jacob Finch. 'And who exactly is responsible for that.'

Captain Albrecht shook his head wistfully. 'Tomorrow may not be soon enough.' There was a brief pause. 'I will have to inform the other passengers.'

'Yes. It will spoil their supper rather. But better to get it over with.' To my surprise, I was beginning to feel somewhat blasé about the whole affair. But then, I had not really known Finch. 'And with your permission, I'd like to question Miss Hurst?' I didn't really fancy myself assuming the policeman's role, but if anyone had an inkling of what might be going on it

205

would be Miss Annabel Hurst.

The captain was in two minds whether to permit it. He had not yet decided if he could trust me. 'Under close supervision,' he agreed, after a moment's reflection. He met my eye with a half smile. 'But first you must send your telegram to Scotland Yard.'

Maurice was an unexpected source of help. 'You understand the principle?' I asked him, in surprise, as he flicked through Finch's copy of *Alice In Wonderland*. I had already written out a brief note to send to Special Branch but encrypting the message would take some time and Captain Albrecht had agreed with me on the urgency of questioning Miss Hurst. The valet flipped to the correct page of the book at once. Pin pricks beneath the letters of the third paragraph signalled the start of the relevant passage.

'I understand, Monsieur,' Maurice confirmed. 'It is a simple poly-alphabetic substitution cypher.'

'Good lord.' I blinked. 'How on earth...? No, don't tell me.' I waved my hands at him before he could offer an explanation. 'Your father, as well as being a locksmith, was also a member of the French Secret Service.' Nothing would surprise me now, when it came to Maurice.

The valet shook his head. 'No, Monsieur. I read an article on the subject in a magazine last month.'

'Oh. Right. Fair enough.'

I left him with the message and went through to the lounge area, where Lucy Tanner had been comforting Annabel Hurst. The latter looked up like a frightened rabbit as I appeared. Miss Tanner caught my eye and I moved away with her for a moment.

A steward hovered in the doorway, observing the two of us. Captain Albrecht had ordered one of the crew to stand watch at every junction of A Deck so there could be no repetition of the cabin incident. It was a sensible precaution. The captain himself was now in the dining hall, addressing the remaining passengers in a calm and concise manner. I could hear his voice droning in the background, as steady and reliable as the hum of the engines.

'It's so beastly,' Miss Tanner breathed, echoing the cries of horror and alarm beginning to emerge from the other side of the deck, in response to the dreadful news. 'That poor man. I was only speaking to him an hour ago. And one of us must have...' She looked past me at the steward. I grimaced and she placed a hand on my shoulder by way of an apology. 'Oh, I don't believe you had anything to do with it. I know you're on the side of the angels, Mr Bland.' She smiled prettily. 'You were helping Mr Finch with his enquiries.'

'In a manner of speaking. So you knew he was a policeman?'

'Yes. Thomas told me earlier this evening. I would never have believed it. Well, I didn't believe it,' she admitted, 'so I asked him myself. I bumped into him outside his cabin while Annabel was changing for supper. I was on my way to see the head steward with a telegram.'

'Your obituary for Mr Kendall?'

Her face fell. 'Yes. I *knew* there was something not quite right about his death. When I saw Mr Finch, I thought, well, if he *is* a policeman, I should talk to him about it.' I could just picture her grabbing him by the elbow and carting him off to some distant corner of the ship to interrogate the poor man, as she had done with me on more than one occasion. 'As it turned out, he wanted to speak to me too. About Miss Hurst.' She glanced over to the other woman, who was sitting numbly out of earshot, staring into the middle distance. Her pale face had become even paler in the aftermath of such a terrible shock. 'He'd received information that she was travelling under a false passport and wanted to search her room.'

'Yes, that's what I've just found out.'

'I'd already changed for dinner, while Annabel was having a wash, and he asked if I could draw her away from the cabin for a few minutes before supper so he could have a quick look around.'

'And you agreed to it?'

'He told me he had the full authority of the captain and I

could see that there was something not quite right. But I can't believe Annabel has anything to do with Walter's death. And we were both downstairs at the bar when Mr Finch...well, when Mr Finch was searching our room.'

'At the bar?'

'It was all I could think of. We had a quick drink. It was just the two of us down there, and that sweetie pie, Max. Everyone else had returned to their cabins to change for supper.'

'And you went straight from there to the dining hall when you heard the gong? Yes, of course you did,' I answered for her. 'I saw you in the corridor, coming up the stairs.'

'And now Mr Finch is dead. It's such a ghastly thing to happen. That poor man.' She gulped. For all her bravado, she was not accustomed to this kind of horror. 'I suppose you see this sort of thing a lot in your line of work?'

'Not as often as you'd think,' I said. 'Thank the Lord. I'm not really a policeman. I'm...with the foreign office.'

'Goodness!' Her eyes lit up in excitement. 'You're not a spy, are you?'

'No. Absolutely not.' I allowed myself a gentle smirk. 'Though if I were, I wouldn't be able to tell you.'

'Of course.' She winked conspiratorially. 'But you are going to interrogate Miss Hurst?'

I nodded. Circumstances had conspired to leave me with little alternative. 'I'll try to be as gentle as I can.' I glanced across at the frightened woman, who was still clutching my whisky glass, though there was nothing in it now. 'What do you make of the girl?' I asked. 'You've shared a room with her for a couple of days.'

Miss Tanner frowned. 'She's a very private person. Extraordinarily shy. I think she's led quite a sheltered life. She hasn't seen much of the world, the poor dear.' Miss Tanner smiled sadly. 'But she really did love Gerhard Schulz. It broke her heart, turning down his proposal. And since he died, she's become even more withdrawn. You must be very gentle with her, Mr Bland.'

I pursed my lips together. 'I will do my very best.'

The role of policeman was one to which I was particularly ill-suited. I have never been much of a one for detective work, particularly when it comes to the interrogation of suspects. I like to keep my own affairs private and where possible I am happy to extend the same courtesy to other people. Nor do I have a particularly analytical brain. I can stare and stare and stare and still not see a pattern in that damned wallpaper. And, with the death of Finch, I had to throw up my hands and confess: I didn't have the foggiest idea what was going on. People were dying left, right and centre and – if I was honest – my principal concern now was getting off the damned ship with my own skin intact. The truth could go hang, as far as I was concerned. I just wanted to lock myself in my cabin and stay there until we all arrived safely in Lakehurst. But I knew that the murderer on board the Richthofen was unlikely to allow that to happen. He or she had already demonstrated an uncanny ability to get through closed doors; and as a now publicly acknowledged ally of a Scotland Yard detective I was next in line for the steak knife. Perhaps Maurice had been right, and the poisoned sleeping draught had been intended for me all along. No, if I was to get through this, it was far better for me to throw myself about, play the policeman, and make damned sure I wasn't left alone with anyone even for a second.

I moved across to the chair where Miss Hurst was sitting. The steward had thoughtfully laid out a tray of sandwiches for her, as consolation for the interruption of her supper, and the young woman was nibbling disconsolately at the edges of a cucumber sandwich. She looked up at me as I loomed over her. There was no fear in her eyes this time, just an acceptance of the inevitable, like a rabbit that knew it could not escape the pot and had given up trying. 'Miss Hurst? Shall we go somewhere private?'

She nodded numbly but did not move.

'The games room?' I gestured across to the far end of the promenade.

She nodded again and rose stiffly to her feet. A prisoner

being led to the gallows.

I gesticulated to the steward at the door and he followed us across the promenade, stationing himself politely by the far window. I did not have any fear of Miss Hurst, but there was no harm in being careful. He would be able to see us through the games room window and his presence might serve to reassure the Englishwoman that she was in no danger from me. I would shut the door, however, so that he could not overhear our conversation.

I ushered Miss Hurst inside the small, square room and we found ourselves a couple of chairs at the larger of the three gaming tables. The steward had sat himself down at the exterior window on the far side of the promenade.

'Do you know what this is about?' I asked her gently as we settled ourselves in the ugly metal chairs.

'Mr Finch found out the truth about me,' she mumbled, numbly. 'And you know it too.'

'Yes, I do,' I informed her sombrely. 'But don't worry. I know you didn't kill Mr Finch. You were with Miss Tanner down in the smoking room when the murder took place.' I would have to check up on that at some point, I thought. I only had Miss Tanner's word for it, though I had seen her arriving at the top of the stairs. But I doubted both ladies would lie about something that would be so easy to check. 'But there is this matter of your...' I tried to think how to phrase it delicately. 'Your double life.'

Miss Hurst swallowed hard. 'You've known about it for a while, haven't you?' she said, meeting my eyes firmly for the first time.

I wasn't quite sure what she meant but I nodded sagely. It's as well, in these situations, to pretend you know everything. Then the other person inevitably fills in any blanks for you, without you having to ask.

'I knew you would work it out,' she breathed. 'Every time we bumped into each other, I could see it in your eyes.' She shuddered. Her hands were shaking on the table top. 'You saw straight through me. He knows, I thought. He knows the truth.' She closed her eyes briefly and swallowed again. 'Have you...have you told Miss Tanner?'

'Not me. Mr Finch informed her, before he....'

The girl started to sniffle. I reached into my breast pocket and produced a handkerchief, which I handed across.

'She must despise me. The damage I've done to her.' Miss Hurst rubbed her nose with the handkerchief.

'Damage?' Again, I wasn't quite sure what she was getting at.

'To her reputation. What will people think, knowing she's been sharing a cabin with a man?'

'Well, I can't imagine.' I blinked. 'I beg your pardon?'

'And what will Mr McGilton think?'

The girl was making no sense. What on Earth was she babbling on about? 'Sorry, you've lost me. What man? She's been sharing her cabin with a man?'

Miss Hurst regarded me uncertainly. 'Yes, all this time.'

I stared at her for a moment. I still hadn't a clue what she was talking about. 'I don't follow. I thought *you* were sharing the cabin with her.'

She brought the handkerchief back up to her mouth. 'You mean, you *didn't* know?'

'Know what? What man? What are you talking about...?' And then the penny dropped. I stared at Miss Hurst in disbelief. For a moment, there was silence. 'You don't mean...*you*?' The woman swallowed hard and nodded. 'You mean...you're a *man*?'

She nodded again. Or rather, *he* nodded.

I could not think of an appropriate response.

'Good grief,' I said.

Chapter Sixteen

There was a long, embarrassed silence. I don't know who was more disconcerted, Miss Hurst or myself. Her eyes were rooted to my face, waiting for a reaction. I had seen that same look in my own eyes many times, staring back at me from the bathroom mirror. I gazed across the table at her in an understandable state of confusion. She couldn't be a man, I thought. It wasn't possible. Her face was rounded and feminine, her lips a soft pink set against that ghastly pallid complexion. Even allowing for the make up, there was nothing remotely masculine in her appearance. That slender neck, the slim figure. And as for her voice... I shook my head. I had spent my life masquerading as a member of the opposite sex and I felt sure I would have known if anybody else was trying to pull off the same trick, even if it was the other way round. But I had not had a moment's suspicion of Miss Annabel Hurst. 'You can't be a man,' I said at last. 'I don't believe it.'

'It's true,' she mumbled, without a hint of duplicity. 'I thought you *knew*. I thought that was why you wanted to talk to me. Because you'd found out the truth.'

'We found out you were travelling under a false passport,' I blustered, 'but I had no idea about...about this.' I gestured vaguely towards her lap. Her skirt was brushed neatly over the edge of her knees. Even her legs looked feminine, I thought. 'You *can't* be a man,' I muttered again.

'I'm afraid I am. I was so sure that you had guessed.'

'But you were...I mean, it's not possible...' If anything, when we kept bumping into each other all over the ship, I had thought she had guessed *my* secret. This was absurd. It couldn't be true. I had half a mind to shove a hand up her skirt and prove her wrong; but the steward was still watching us carefully through the window and even I could not contemplate such a drastic and ungentlemanly course of action. Miss Hurst saw the idea flash across my face, however, and to my surprise, she placed her hands on her lap and gently pulled up the hem of her skirt. I regarded her dubiously. We were both sitting upright with the circular table between us, our lower halves out of sight through the promenade window. She hitched the skirt as high as it would go, but I couldn't exactly get a good view of it from this angle and I wasn't sure that I wanted to. It didn't feel right, staring at the woman when her under things were exposed like that. Could it be true? I wondered. Was Miss Hurst really a man? I could see a small section of her undergarments – the plain cotton drawers above the brown stocking tops – but the view was not good enough to draw any conclusion regarding their contents. I shook my head irritably. From this distance, I couldn't tell one way or the other. If she had been a woman pretending to be a man then she could have just unbuttoned her blouse and that would have been that. But a man pretending to be a woman...there was only one way that could ever be proved.

An embarrassing memory flashed up in my mind. When I had searched Walter Kendall's cabin, I had been so desperate to find that Special Branch file that I had slid a hand into his trouser pockets. It had not been a pleasant thing to do – less still the second time around, when I had known he was dead – but I had done it anyway. And now another, equally unpleasant course of action opened itself up to me. Perhaps if I were to slip off one of my shoes...

Miss Hurst was watching me carefully, her skirt still hitched up at the front. She knew her fate depended on whatever I decided in the next few moments. As far as she was concerned, I was the representative of law and order on board this ship.

I placed my right foot on the back heel of my left shoe and slipped my foot out of it. Extending my leg underneath the table, I aimed the foot vaguely towards the opposite chair and flicked my eyes down at it. Miss Hurst followed my gaze and saw the leg underneath the table. She swallowed hard and gave her consent with a barely perceptible nod. It was an unchivalrous and down-right depraved thing to suggest but what choice did I have? There was no other way to determine the truth of the matter.

With a profound sense of embarrassment, I slipped my

toes under the hem of her skirt, which had slid back down a little from her waist. At this point, edging forward in my seat, my leg was somewhat over extended. At the last moment, I misjudged the distance involved and my foot leapt forward several inches, my sock smacking solidly against the woman's crotch. Or rather, against the *man's* crotch.

Miss Hurst flinched and I pulled my foot away in alarm, almost falling off my chair.

'Good God!' I exclaimed, dropping my leg and pulling myself back up in the chair. 'You *are* a man!' I put my hand to my mouth, worried for a moment about the volume of my voice. The steward, however, was looking out of the far window. I took a moment to collect myself. There was absolutely no doubt about it. Annabel Hurst was a man. Good heavens, I thought. I bent down and slid my foot back into the shoe, to cover my embarrassment. Miss Hurst quickly smoothed down her skirt. Her hands were shaking too. *His* hands were shaking. I stared at the fellow in astonishment. 'I would never have believed it.'

'I thought you knew,' she mumbled again, her face even paler now than before. 'I would never have said anything if...' She took a deep breath and lifted her hand, which she held out across the table tentatively. 'My name's Andrew,' he said. 'Andrew Hurst.' Numbly, I leaned forward and grabbed the hand. His palms were unpleasantly sweaty but, then again, so were mine just now. I do not know who was more discomforted, Miss Hurst or I.

Even with the evidence of my own foot, I still could not believe I was looking at a man. I regarded him quietly for some moments. His face was gently made up, his hair shoulder length. If he was a man he couldn't be much older than twenty-one or twenty-two. There was nothing approaching a stubble that I could see. He had less hair on his chin than I did.

'But you've been sharing with Miss Tanner.'

'I know. I didn't intend to. I had hoped to have a cabin to myself all the way to New York. When I got to Seville and found we were sharing a room, I didn't know what to do. But there's been no impropriety. We take it in turns to get changed.

She thinks I'm a dreadful prude. I won't undress when she's in the room and she gets changed while I'm in the bathroom.'

At least the cramped cabins were benefiting someone, I thought. 'And how long have you been living as a woman?'

She sighed, folding up the handkerchief gently. 'Not long. A year or so.'

'But...what's wrong with being a man?' I asked her. 'Why would you want to pretend otherwise?'

'You wouldn't understand.'

I was probably better placed than anyone else on the planet to understand, but I wasn't about to tell her that. Perhaps her father had been as deranged as mine.

'It's not a matter of pretence,' she insisted. 'It's who I am.'

'Did Mr Schulz know?'

She shook her head sadly. 'He had no idea. We fell in love. I met him in Berlin last summer. I'd heard there were places in Germany that were...more accepting of people who were different.'

I narrowed my eyes. 'You're attracted to other men?'

A flash of fear shot across her face. That was an even bigger admission to make. But she nodded sadly. 'It's disgusting, I know, but I can't help myself. I've always...I've always preferred men.' She shuddered again, looking down at her lap. 'You must think me absolutely vile.'

'You are as God made you.' I shrugged. I was hardly in a position to cast stones. 'I can't pretend to understand, but if it brings you some pleasure, then where's the harm?' I have never really understood why people take so vehemently against queers. They are a fairly harmless bunch, as a rule, and what people do in the privacy of their own homes is their own affair. There are far greater depravities in the world and some of them are actually worthy of a little scorn. Andrew Hurst was doing no harm to anyone.

'That's what I told myself. It wasn't just that I was attracted to men. I never felt like a man myself. It was as if I had always been a woman, at least on the inside.'

That, I had to confess, I couldn't quite grasp. My father

215

had beaten me into accepting my own situation but I had never felt like anything other than a woman pretending to be a man. I nodded sympathetically in any case.

'So I went to Berlin,' she continued, 'where no one would know me, and I set myself up as Miss Annabel Hurst. I thought I'd see how it went.' Her face lit up suddenly. 'I didn't expect to fall in love. We spent the summer together.' She flushed happily at the memory. 'Gerhard was the perfect gentleman. So kind and courteous. But I felt so guilty. I tried to break it off with him when I returned to England. But he wouldn't take no for an answer. I couldn't bear being back in England, with my parents, living a lie. So I decided to go and live in the United States. I had some savings. Enough to start anew. I wrote to Gerhard, telling him of my intentions. He begged me not to go, asked me to see him one last time. I met up with him in Germany. The silly fool had bought a ticket on the Richthofen. He could only afford to go as far as Seville. But he proposed to me on the flight. What could I say?' She sniffled. 'I had to turn him down. He would never have accepted me if he'd found out the truth. He fell in love with a dream, but it wasn't really me. I feel so awful. He took his life because of me. It's all my fault.'

'You're not to blame,' I told her firmly. 'If it wasn't you, he'd have lost his head over somebody else. These romantic types always do.'

'But if I hadn't been...if I hadn't been this way...' She glanced down again at her skirt in despair. 'I'm a pervert, Mr Bland. A depraved sinner.'

'Nonsense. You're nothing of the kind. Believe me, I've committed far worse crimes.'

She looked up in surprise. 'That can't be true. You're a *policeman.*'

'After a fashion. But in my line of work, things have a habit of getting a little grey.'

Miss Hurst shook her head. 'I'm sure that isn't the case. But if you didn't know about any of this, then...why was Mr Finch investigating me? Why was he searching my room?'

Back to the business in hand. 'He and I were

investigating the theft of some important documents from London. We discovered that you were using a false passport and naturally suspicion fell on you.'

'Documents? I don't know anything about any documents.'

I could see at a glance that she was telling the truth. *He* was telling the truth. Even now, I was finding it difficult to think of Miss Hurst as a man. Dammit, why did people have to make life so complicated? 'But your passport *is* false?'

'Yes,' she admitted. 'I paid a man forty pounds to arrange it. He didn't know anything about me. I just told him I wanted to start life afresh. I provided a photograph – as Miss Annabel Hurst – and that was that.'

'But this fellow. He didn't ask you for a favour in return?'

'A favour?'

'Like acting as a courier on that flight you took on Saturday morning. Maybe carrying a small parcel for him from Croydon to Friedrichshafen?'

'No. I got hold of the passport last year. I've never been a courier. I don't know anything about that.'

'Right.' So despite everything I had learned in the last ten minutes, it looked like I was no further forward with my investigations.

'You're not going to expose my secret, are you?'

I shook my head. Why would I? The popular press would tear her to pieces, on both sides of the Atlantic. I couldn't put the woman through that. Not when it might just as easily have been me in her place. 'There's no reason why I should, my dear. So long as you're telling me the truth. But the thing of it is, we know that these documents were on that flight. And one of the passengers must have been carrying them. If it wasn't you, then it must have been either Josef Kaufmann, Adelina Koenig or Frederick Gray.'

'Or Captain Rüdiger,' Miss Hurst added.

I regarded her blankly. 'I'm sorry?'

'Captain Rüdiger. He was the pilot.'

'I...sorry, what?

217

'Captain Rüdiger was the pilot of the plane.'

I snorted. 'Don't be ridiculous!'

The girl was insistent. 'He flew the plane out from Croydon aerodrome. I remember him welcoming us on board. He knew we were going to be travelling on the Richthofen so he came back to say hello, before we took off.'

'Captain Rüdiger?' That couldn't be true. The first officer of a German airship wouldn't be piloting a passenger plane from London. 'Was it a Zeppelin flight?' I asked. 'I didn't know they ran their own flights.'

Miss Hurst was a bit vague on the details. 'It was a Lufthansa flight, I think. It was all part of the package. I believe they're some sort of affiliate company.'

'You mean, they run connecting flights for the Zeppelin company?'

'I think so. That was what Herr Kaufmann told me, anyway. I gather one of their pilots was off sick. They had all the airmail from England to collect and they didn't want their passengers arriving late, so Captain Rüdiger stepped in.'

'Good lord.' I sat back in my chair and took a moment to digest the news. So the grim looking first officer had been in England on Saturday morning as well. How come nobody had mentioned that to me? Could Rüdiger have been involved in the theft somehow? Was he a friend of Mick Durrant? 'You didn't see him speaking to anyone else before you boarded the plane?' I asked. 'Like a baggage handler or someone like that?'

Miss Hurst hesitated. 'I'm afraid I don't recall.'

I scratched my chin. I was probably grasping at straws. 'If the first officer was moonlighting, then Captain Albrecht must surely have known about it.'

'I imagine so,' Miss Hurst agreed.

'So why didn't he mention it to Jacob Finch?' I frowned. The captain knew the importance the policeman placed on that particular flight. He would surely have passed on any pertinent information; and you could hardly get more pertinent than the name of the pilot. But if he *had* told Finch, that information had not been passed on to me. Perhaps the Englishman had ruled Rüdiger out as a suspect early on; then there would have been no reason for him to mention it. But there was another, more sinister possibility. What if Captain Albrecht had known his first officer was on the flight but had kept it a secret? What if he was in on the whole thing, in cahoots with Captain Rüdiger? I shook myself. No, that was absurd. The captain of a Zeppelin airship would not involve himself in criminal activity. It was unthinkable.

'What did you make of the other passengers?' I asked. 'Frederick Gray, Adelina Koenig and Josef Kaufmann?'

'I didn't speak to Mr Gray. Herr Kaufmann was very kind. A very warm hearted man.'

'He didn't seem nervous at all on the flight?'

'Not that I noticed. But my mind was on the journey – and meeting up with Gerhard – so I wasn't really paying attention to anything else. But Frau Koenig was very friendly with the captain. I do remember that.'

'Captain Rüdiger?'

'Yes.'

I nodded. Those two had been as thick as thieves since day one. I would have to ask Captain Albrecht a few hard questions about his first officer, the next time I spoke to him. I wasn't going to rule the fellow out as a suspect just yet. I growled. This case was becoming ever more complicated. Why couldn't a criminal just wear a mask and carry a swag bag, like they did in the pictures?

I pushed back my chair. There was nothing more Miss Hurst could tell me, though she had given me plenty to think about. *He* had given me, I thought. I stared at the fellow again, unable to quite believe what she had told me. But there was no doubting the physical evidence. 'I have to be honest, my dear,' I said. 'You make a damned fine woman.'

She beamed then. It was the first time I had seen her smile and her face lit up. 'I do my best. Although heaven knows where I'll sleep tonight.'

That was a thought. 'Yes, bit unfortunate, Finch being knifed to death in your cabin.' She flinched at the unpleasant image. 'You won't have to go back in there,' I reassured her hastily. 'The stewards will sort something out for you. There's a spare room on the far corner. I imagine they'll put you both in there. You and Miss Tanner. All girls together.'

Miss Hurst looked at her lap in embarrassment. 'Will you tell her? I suppose she ought to know. It's not right, me sharing a room with her. What will she think when she finds out the truth?'

'It's only for another couple of days,' I said. 'No harm done so far. Best just to leave well alone.'

'You...you're not going to tell her either?'

'No reason why I should. What she doesn't know can't hurt her. Although you will have to concoct some explanation for that passport of yours.'

'I...I'm sure I'll think of something.'

I smiled. 'It's not easy leading a double life, Miss Hurst. I know that as well as anyone. But I believe you've got what it takes. You fooled me, after all, and more importantly you fooled Miss Tanner. Good grief, in the same cabin!' I chuckled. 'That's got to count for something.' I stood up and shook the woman by the hand. 'And as to the passport....well, I don't see that there's any need for anyone to follow up on that.'

'You're very kind, Mr Bland. I'm not sure I deserve it.'

'No, I'm not sure of that either,' I joked. 'But to be honest, Miss Hurst, I have far more important things to worry about right now.'

My valet was hovering in the corridor outside the lounge room. A couple of stewards were ransacking Mr Lindt's room, immediately to our left. The sliding door was wide open and I could see one of the stewards rifling through the clothes hanging in his closet. 'What's going on?' I asked Maurice.

'The captain has ordered all the cabins searched. They are starting with Monsieur Lindt.'

I grimaced. 'Lord, he won't be happy about that. Have you sent off that telegram?'

'Yes, Monsieur. Some time ago. The head steward took it down to the radio room.'

'Well, let's hope we get a reply this evening.' I crossed

220

my fingers. It was getting a bit late for that sort of thing. I gestured Maurice along the connecting corridor towards the dining room. Loud voices could be heard coming from the other side of the doorway. As usual, Karl Lindt was the loudest of them. As I had predicted, the man was not at all happy. Captain Albrecht's briefing of the passengers had not gone well.

'This is not acceptable,' Lindt was saying, as I slipped through the entrance into the dining hall. 'You have no right to treat us like criminals.' The businessman was sitting at a table to the left of the door. Captain Albrecht, whom he was addressing, was standing opposite it, with his back to the far windows. 'All our luggage was checked before we came on board. You have no right to ransack our cabins.'

'I do not have a choice in this matter,' Albrecht insisted. 'A man has just been murdered. Someone on board this ship is responsible for his death.'

'Jacob Finch should never have been allowed on board,' Lindt snarled, as I padded quietly over to a far table and found myself a seat. I didn't want to get involved in a slanging match but it might be fun to observe from the sidelines. 'This is a German airship. It is no place for a British policeman.'

I raised a hand to Josef Kaufmann as I sat myself down next to him. The tubby fellow was sensibly keeping well away from his business partner. The tables were covered with the remnants of a light supper, which the stewards had not yet started to clear. I was feeling famished, so I grabbed a sandwich from one of the plates, while the argument continued on the other side of the room.

'I was not aware that he *was* a policeman until after we left Friedrichshafen,' the captain explained. 'It was then that he approached me and told me of his investigation.'

'You should have thrown him off the ship in Seville,' Lindt declared. 'Then none of this would have happened.'

'I had no reason to do so, Herr Lindt. Mr Finch behaved impeccably. Of course, had I known that people might be endangered by his investigation then I might have behaved differently.'

221

'You should have foreseen it!' Lindt glared at the captain.

'He seems rather put out,' I observed, leaning across to speak to Josef Kaufmann.

'It is the searching of the luggage that he objects to,' the German responded quietly.

'You have no right to search our rooms!' Lindt repeated to the room as a whole.

'Why,' I asked Kaufmann, keeping my voice low, 'has he got something to hide?'

The other man had no idea. 'Not that I am aware of, Mr Bland.'

Adelina Koenig took this moment to add her weight to the argument, in rapid-fire German. Luckily, Kaufmann was on hand to provide me with a translation. 'She also has some objection,' he whispered. 'Her room was searched earlier today and some items have apparently gone missing.'

'Yes. That was Mr Finch, this afternoon.' So Lindt was concerned that the same thing might happen to him. Or perhaps there was something incriminating in his luggage that had not been noted at customs in Germany.

'Two rolls of film were removed from her cabin,' Kaufmann continued. 'She is not happy to lose them. I have offered to replace them for her, but of course the photographs themselves cannot be replaced.'

The captain responded in English, addressing Mrs Koenig and Karl Lindt. 'Nothing will be confiscated from any of the rooms without my permission. And, I assure you, a record will be kept of everything that is taken.'

I was more interested in Kaufmann's photographic supplies. 'You have a lot of film, do you?' I asked, ignoring the raised voices for a moment.

The German smiled. 'Yes, I brought far too much with me. Travelling to Rio, I thought there would be plenty of opportunity for photography. But there are only so many photographs you can take of the ocean. Gerhard Schulz borrowed a couple of rolls of film from me before we arrived in Seville and I also lent a couple to Frau Koenig. I believe those were the ones that disappeared from her room.'

'Damn,' I said. 'Are you sure?'

'Yes, I am certain. Why, is something the matter?'

'No. Nothing important. Do you happen to know what brand the films were?'

'Brand?'

'The manufacturer?'

'I am sorry. I do not recall. I can look, if you wish.'

'It wasn't KG Corfield Ltd was it?'

'Ah yes, that is correct. I bought them in England, just before I flew out.'

I nodded. So the films Finch had confiscated – the ones I had carefully destroyed – could not have been the ones containing images of the Special Branch file. It was back to square one, as the radio people say. 'What did she want the film for anyway?' I wondered. 'I've never seen her using a camera.'

'I am afraid I do not know.'

Another question occurred to me, this time about Kaufmann. 'What were you doing in England, if you don't mind me asking?'

The man smiled again. 'You are interrogating me,' he observed, without rancour.

'Just trying to make sense of a few things.'

'Captain Albrecht said you were assisting Mr Finch with his enquiries.'

'In a manner of speaking.'

'It was a sales trip,' he explained. 'Karl sent me to London. There was a potential buyer there but it did not work out. Not many people are buying at the moment, with the state of our economies.'

'No. Things are still a little delicate,' I agreed. I remembered Walter Kendall's gloomy prognosis for European businesses.

The argument between Lindt and Albrecht was still going strong on the opposite side of the dining room. The businessman was now pointing a bony finger in my direction. 'Why are you not searching *his* room? Look at him, he is covered in blood.'

I glanced down at my shirt. Kaufmann had been too polite to mention the blood stains.

'That's not exactly surprising, Herr Lindt.' Thomas McGilton leapt to my defence. He was seated at the middle table, with his fiancée. 'It was Mr Bland who found the body.'

'We only have his word for that,' the German responded tartly.

'The poor man died in my arms,' I said, exaggerating slightly and raising my voice to carry across the room. 'I couldn't avoid getting blood on me. And I'm afraid I haven't got a change of shirt. The other one's wet through from this afternoon.' Why was he getting at me all of a sudden? I wondered. 'And as I recall, Mr Lindt, you were coming from the direction of Mr Finch's room just before I arrived there. So if you're going to hurl accusations around...'

'I am not making an accusation!' Lindt snapped back at me.

'Gentlemen,' Captain Albrecht interceded, his hands raised. 'Will you please calm yourselves? All of the passenger rooms will be searched, including that of Mr Bland. The truth will be uncovered, one way or another.'

At that moment, the head steward appeared in the doorway and coughed to attract the captain's attention. He was carrying a small green briefcase. '*Herr Kapitän?*'

'Yes, what is it Stefan?'

'We have finished searching Herr Lindt's cabin. Everything seems to be in order, but this case has a lock on it.'

Karl Lindt leapt to his feet. 'That briefcase contains private papers of no relevance whatsoever to this investigation. The contents have already been inspected.'

Captain Albrecht was striding across the room to take hold of the briefcase. He had to circumnavigate Lindt's table to do so and almost collided with the owner of the case. The other man glared at him but Albrecht remained calm, forcing the fellow to step aside with a firm look. McGilton pulled back his chair and cleared a bit of space at the middle table so the steward could place the briefcase down on top of it.

'Nevertheless, you will open the case for us, Herr Lindt,'

Captain Albrecht insisted.

'What is the point? It was already searched in Friedrichshafen.'

'Then you will not object to us looking again.'

Lindt scowled and came forward with a key. 'Very well.' He unlocked the case and pulled back the lid. As he had claimed, the inside was stuffed full of paperwork; business documents and such like. Stefan, the head steward, rifled through them quickly. 'You see? A complete waste of time. If you've quite finished?' The man seemed in rather a hurry to close the case up again.

Stefan had removed all the documents and was pressing down on the bottom of the case. '*Herr Kapitän?*' Albrecht nodded his consent and Stefan produced a small penknife from his pocket. He slid the blade between the bottom of the case and the lining. It caught underneath. The steward muttered something in German and the captain peered over his shoulder as he pulled back the base and revealed a sudden extra layer.

We all leaned forward to see what was inside.

The briefcase was stuffed with American Dollars.

Chapter Seventeen

Josef Kaufmann rose to his feet and let out a gasp of surprise.

The steward grabbed a bundle of notes and flipped through them in awe. 'There must be ten thousand dollars there,' Thomas McGilton exclaimed, from the opposite side of the table. 'That's a fair old nest egg.' There were murmurs of agreement from the other passengers.

Captain Albrecht looked up. 'Well, Herr Lindt?'

'Fifteen thousand dollars,' the man corrected. About three thousand pounds. 'What of it? Every cent of it belongs to me.'

The captain pursed his lips. 'You are aware, Herr Lindt, of the restrictions on the movement of currency?'

'I am aware of the bureaucracy. But it is hardly a serious offence. I am entitled to do what I wish with my own money.'

Josef Kaufmann was still boggling, from the other side of the room. 'But Karl. That money....'

'You were not aware that Herr Lindt was in possession of such a sum?' Albrecht asked.

'No, I...I do not know where he could have got it. Such a large amount. Karl, what is going on...?'

For once, Karl Lindt had nothing to say. The captain waved a finger at me. I rose from my chair and allowed myself to be drawn away into a quiet corner. 'Mr Bland. This money. Could it have some bearing on the matter Mr Finch was investigating?' He spoke softly, so that only I could hear him. 'The theft of your government's file?'

'What, some kind of payment you mean?' I grimaced. 'Lord, I hope not.' If the money had been paid out for the sale of the documents, then that meant the negatives had already been passed on. 'But yes, I suppose it could.' And the false bottom in the briefcase suggested Lindt had come prepared for that very eventuality.

'Very well.' Captain Albrecht turned back to the rest of the room. 'The money will be confiscated until its true ownership is determined.'

'You can't...' Lindt exclaimed.

'And Herr Lindt will be confined to his cabin for the rest of the trip.'

The businessman's mouth fell open in astonishment. 'You cannot be serious,' he breathed.

'I am deadly serious. My first duty is to the safety of my passengers and crew. I have reason to believe you may be a threat to that safety.'

Sir George Westlake, who had been sitting at the same table as Mr Lindt, thought that was a bit extreme. 'Now, hang on, old boy,' he protested.

'I am sorry. A man has been murdered. I have no choice in this matter.'

Lindt launched a tirade of furious German at the captain. Adelina Koenig, who had remained surprisingly quiet up until this point, joined in with the defence.

'This is not a discussion!' Albrecht declared. I had never seen the man so close to losing his temper. 'Stefan. You will escort Herr Lindt to his cabin and lock him in.'

'You cannot do this!' Lindt exclaimed.

'I can and I will. You will stay in your room for the rest of the trip. If you have need of anything you can ring for a steward. Stefan, escort Herr Lindt to his cabin.'

The head steward moved forward with two of his underlings. To my surprise, Mr Lindt did not put up any resistance. He could not resist a parting shot, however. 'When we arrive in New York, I will contact your superiors,' he hissed. 'You will never captain an airship again. I will see you are stripped of your rank and thrown out onto the street.'

Captain Albrecht did not rise to the bait. He stood immobile as Lindt was escorted past him and out into the passageway.

I was still standing close to the captain. 'If he *is* behind all this,' I whispered, 'a locked door won't keep him in his cabin.'

'I will have a man posted in the corridor. All night if necessary.'

'What about Mr Kaufmann?' I eyed the tubby German,

227

who had resumed his seat at the far end of the dining hall. He was frowning heavily, staring at the case full of money, which another steward was locking up and preparing to remove.

'You think he may be involved?'

'I don't know. But Lindt never went to England. He must have had an accomplice. And Kaufmann was on that flight.'

'We will keep an eye on him,' the captain agreed. 'But I do not think it is necessary to confine him to his cabin at this time.'

'No. He seems harmless enough.' I had the feeling Lindt had only been incarcerated to shut the damn fellow up. And if we locked Kaufmann up as well we would probably have to do the same with Mrs Koenig. I didn't fancy being the one to make that suggestion.

'*Herr Kapitän*?' An officer had approached us from behind. I recognised the fellow vaguely. It was the telegraph operator. He spoke to the captain and handed across a slip of paper.

'*Danke, Herr Schäuble.*' The captain quickly scanned the note. 'A communication from your Special Branch,' he said, looking up.

I smiled in surprise. 'Lord, that was quick. I thought they might have all gone home for the night.'

'Apparently not, Mr Bland.' There would always be someone on hand to deal with emergencies. The news of Jacob Finch's demise must have sent alarm bells ringing across London. 'They confirm your identity and ask that I afford you every assistance.'

I breathed a sigh of relief. 'Thank goodness.'

Albrecht turned back to the telegraph operator and exchanged a few words in German. Then he addressed the passengers. 'Ladies and gentlemen, *Damen und Herren,* it has been a distressing evening. However, I urge you all to remain calm. Stewards will be on duty all night to ensure your safety. There is food available for those who have not yet had the opportunity to dine. However, once you have eaten, I would urge everyone to retire to their cabins. For the rest of the evening and until these matters are sorted out, I must ask that you do not leave the deck. If you require any assistance, as always, the stewards will be on hand to help you.'

'No chance of a quick cigarette before bedtime?' I enquired, half-heartedly. I was out of Piccadillys now but Max kept a stock of German tobacco behind the bar.

'I am afraid that will not be possible. B Deck is now off limits, for the security of the passengers. The smoking room will be closed until morning.'

That was fair enough, I supposed.

'Now if you will all excuse me, I have some urgent telegrams to send. And of course the small matter of running a ship.' The last comment was made with a wry smile. I rather admired the way Albrecht had managed to keep his cool, in very trying circumstances. He nodded his head and went off. I hadn't had a chance to ask him about Captain Rüdiger. It could wait until tomorrow.

Young Heinrich stood watch in the doorway after the rest of the crew had departed. The passengers remained seated and for a moment there was silence.

Frederick Gray was sitting at the near side table, with Sir George and Adelina Koenig. 'What an awful day,' he sighed, in that irritating nasal voice of his. 'Poor Mr Finch.'

'Someone had it in for him, that's for sure,' Thomas McGilton agreed, from the centre table.

Mrs Koenig muttered something to herself in incomprehensible German and leapt to her feet.

'He's just doing his job, my dear,' Sir George assured her. Mrs Koenig shot the explorer a look of pure venom and then clomped angrily towards the door. Heinrich had to jump to get out of the way. Sir George chuckled to himself. 'What a woman!'

Miss Tanner was sitting at the middle table, with her fiancé and Miss Hurst. She pushed back her chair. 'I suppose we ought to sort out our sleeping accommodation,' she said, rising up and addressing the other woman. Miss Hurst shuddered but inclined her head. The stewards would be on hand to assist them but it would still take some time to arrange.

I pitied the poor blighter who had to gather up their night attire. Finch's body would still be lying on the carpet in the far cabin.

Thomas McGilton was just finishing off a ham roll. 'I'll be with you in a minute,' he called, as the two girls made their way past Heinrich and out into the corridor.

I moved across to Sir George's table and grabbed a chicken sandwich. Mr Gray gazed up at me, his eyes wide in wonder. 'So you're a policeman too,' he said.

'Well, after a fashion.'

Sir George laughed. 'I had you down as a gentleman of leisure.'

'I try to be. But life keeps getting in the way.' I took a quick bite of the sandwich.

'Do you think Herr Lindt was responsible for Mr Finch's death?' the GPO man asked.

'I really don't know.' I was not comfortable being regarded as the voice of authority on the matter, and I was acutely aware that Josef Kaufmann was sitting at the far table, well within earshot. 'He's an odious fellow, but that doesn't make him a murderer.'

'Probably a thief, though,' McGilton declared, coming across to mop up the last of the sandwiches. 'The captain said Mr Finch was investigating some kind of theft.' He grabbed a sad-looking specimen and took a quick mouthful. 'What was it? Anything valuable?'

I shifted awkwardly from one leg to the other. 'You could say that. Some...documents of a confidential nature.'

Sir George's ears pricked up. 'Sounds intriguing, old boy!'

'I'm afraid I can't go into details. It's all a bit complicated.'

He smiled. 'Don't tell me, national security.'

'But you believe Herr Lindt is involved?' Mr Gray asked again.

'It's possible,' I conceded. 'But if he is behind all this, he must have had help. We'll know the truth tomorrow, anyway. Or the day after, at the latest. Whoever the murderer was, they had an accomplice back in Blighty. A baggage handler called Mick Durrant. The police picked him up this afternoon in Holyhead. He'll confirm if Mr Lindt is the guilty party. And *if* he is then we can have a nice police car waiting to greet him in New Jersey.'

McGilton wiped his mouth with a napkin. 'Couldn't happen to a nicer fellow.'

'There's going to be an awful lot of publicity about all this,' Mr Gray reflected. 'I wonder if they'll want to interview us all.'

'Lord, I hope not.' I had wanted to slip away quietly at the end of the trip.

'I shouldn't worry, old boy,' said Sir George, sympathetically. 'They'll be too busy castigating Herr Lindt to pay you any attention.'

'I suppose so.'

'And we'll have a good few stories to dine out on at the end of it all!'

'It will certainly add a bit of spice to your lecture tour, Sir George,' Mr Gray simpered. The man really was a crawler.

'It's Captain Albrecht I feel sorry for,' McGilton said. 'He's going to get a lot of flack over this and it's hardly his fault. He's done his best to look after us all.'

'It won't just be him,' I thought. 'After this, everyone's going to think twice about airship travel. The R101 was bad enough. This may well kill off the industry all together.'

'You could be right,' the Irishman agreed, sadly. 'No one's going to want to book a ticket if they think they're going to be murdered in their beds.'

Sir George was a little more optimistic. 'You never know, a bit of notoriety might do them the power of good.'

'Perhaps,' I said. It would certainly be a mistake to underestimate the ghoulishness of the American public.

'Gives a whole new meaning to the phrase "Red Zeppelin",' the explorer chuckled.

'People certainly won't be associating it with the reds any more,' McGilton agreed.

'No.' I looked down at the blood on my chest. 'Well, not communists, anyway. I don't suppose any of you has a spare shirt I might borrow?'

'You don't have another?' Mr Gray sounded surprised.

'Yes, but it's still damp from the dinghy.'

'You got soaked as well, did you?' Sir George chuckled. 'Best part of the day, that was. Seeing Adelina churning to the rescue of that crewman. Worth the price of the ticket alone.' He smiled and pushed back his chair. 'Anyone fancy a game of cards?'

The games room on the far side of the airship was shaded in semi-darkness. The stewards had cleared up the remnants of supper from the dining hall and most of the guests had retired to bed. Mrs Koenig had been spitting venom out in the corridors, furious about Mr Lindt's incarceration. But the rest of the ship was gradually settling down for the night. Thomas McGilton had helped his fiancée and Miss Hurst to move into their new cabin on the port side and had then joined the rest of us at the card table.

I was surprised I had agreed to join the party; but after the horrors of the last few hours a few hands of cards would prove a welcome distraction. It may sound callous but sometimes a bit of enforced normality can do a lot of good, calming everybody's nerves in the aftermath of such dreadful events.

'Frau Koenig quietened down a bit when she realised the two women were going to be sleeping next door to her,' McGilton told us.

'A bit of female solidarity.' Sir George nodded cheerfully. 'That's the spirit!' He had grabbed a bottle of wine from the dining room before the stewards had managed to tidy it away. He poured out a large glass for himself and a smaller one for Frederick Gray. 'Just pennies tonight, I think,' he suggested, shuffling the pack with an expert hand.

'Quite right,' Mr Gray fawned. 'We wouldn't want to be disrespectful.'

Sir George handed the pack to the Irishman to deal and raised his glass. 'To Mr Finch and Mr Kendall,' he declared.

'And Mr Schulz,' I added, draining the dregs of a whisky and soda I had brought with me from the other side of the ship.

'Mr Schulz,' the others agreed.

McGilton dealt out the cards and we all threw in a ha'penny to start with. We were using English currency this time, rather than American. 'What did you use when you played with Mr Schulz?' I asked, out of curiosity. 'Was it dollars?'

Frederick Gray nodded. 'I think we did, yes.'

'He was a rather good player,' Sir George recalled. 'Why do you ask?'

'Oh, no particular reason. It's just...the man had a quantity of dollars with him when he arrived in Seville. He was one of Mr Finch's early suspects. But if he won it from the games table...?'

McGilton understood what I was getting at. 'You mean, from Herr Lindt?'

'Yes, that would all add up. If Mr Lindt dipped into that briefcase of his. I did think for a while that Mr Schulz had been murdered. But it looks like it was suicide after all.' The balance of his mind had certainly been disturbed.

We played out the hand in virtual silence. Without the lure of financial gain, the atmosphere was lacklustre, but Mr Gray was right, it would have been disrespectful to gamble more. And my wallet probably needed a break in any case.

After half an hour, McGilton rose to his feet and decided to call it a night.

'Time for beddy-byes,' Sir George agreed, pushing back his chair.

The GPO man had a sudden thought. 'I'll dig out that shirt for you, Mr Bland.'

'That would be very kind,' I said, rising up from the table.

The four of us moved out of the games room onto the promenade. Sir George stretched his arms above his head. He was quite a tall man with an impressively muscular bearing. The simpering Mr Gray barely reached up to his shoulder. 'I

233

could really do with a night cap. Help me nod off. Shame the bar's off limits.' We moved across to the lounge.

'I've got some whisky left, if you fancy it,' I said, pulling back the door to the main landing. Maurice had retrieved my bottle from Miss Hurst and returned it to the cabin.

A steward was standing watch in the corridor, just to the right of Karl Lindt's cabin. He stepped aside to allow us through the door.

'Capital idea!' Sir George declared, following me through into the passageway. 'Will you join us, McGilton?'

'No, I don't, I'm afraid.'

'Oh, of course, tee-total. Well, good night then, old boy.'

The Irishman made his farewells and slipped quietly into his berth, trying not to disturb the Spanish fellow he shared with.

I nipped into my own cabin, which was the next one along, and grabbed the whisky. There was no sign of Maurice. He had completed his move into the far cabin and had already retired for the night.

Sir George and Frederick Gray were out of sight when I emerged. They were chatting quietly half way along the connecting corridor. Mr Gray's cabin was on the port side. He had already collected the spare shirt and he handed it over to me now. It was a cheaply made affair, very much off-the-peg and perhaps a trifle small, but it would probably do the job come morning.

'Well, I shall bid you both good night,' Mr Gray said. He was grinning at us rather enthusiastically. That one glass of wine had gone straight to his head.

'We can't tempt you to a nightcap?' I asked.

Gray swayed unsteadily. 'I think I may have had too much already.'

'Half a glass,' Sir George declared, good naturedly, as the GPO man disappeared. 'Absolutely pitiful.'

I tossed the shirt through the door onto my bed and followed the other man back into the games room, where we quickly poured out the whisky. The steward remained out in the corridor, keeping careful watch on Mr Lindt's cabin.

'It's been a hell of a day,' I said, downing the whisky in one quick gulp. I resumed my seat at the main table and closed my eyes for a moment. 'I have to confess, I'll be glad when this is all over.'

Sir George nodded sympathetically. 'Getting a bit too much for you?'

I placed my glass back down on the table. 'I was meant to be pursuing a thief. Nobody was meant to get killed.'

'It's been a difficult couple of days,' he conceded, knocking back his own glass in one fluid movement. He smacked his lips together contentedly. 'Nice drop of whisky that. But don't fret, old boy. We're through the worst of it now. You've caught your man, haven't you?'

'Yes, I suppose so.' I looked down again at the empty tumbler. 'But it all seems too easy somehow.'

Sir George chuckled. 'Never does to overcomplicate things. All that cash hidden in his briefcase. Lindt was clearly up to no good.'

'Yes, it does look like it. But I won't sleep easily until my feet are back on terra firma. I never wanted to go up in an airship in the first place.'

'No spirit of adventure, that's your trouble,' Sir George chided me. 'I wouldn't have missed it for the world!'

I sat back in my chair and gazed at him across the table. He was an amiable fellow, I thought. It was nice to have a bit of civilized company at the end of such a horrible day.

We chatted for some minutes about the events of the last few hours and the likely repercussions we would face upon our arrival in America.

'You said you had a new job there, didn't you?' he asked, stepping over to the side table to refill the glasses. 'Or was that all part of your cover story?'

'No, it's true. I'm joining the diplomatic corps, if you can believe it. Some tinpot republic down south.'

'By Jove! Rather you than me, old boy. I couldn't bear to be stuck behind a desk.'

'Yes, but you're an adventurer. I'm just looking for a

quiet life. I've had enough excitement already to last me a lifetime.' I coughed quietly. 'What about you? Are you looking forward to your lecture tour?'

His face fell momentarily. 'Yes, I suppose so. Always good fun. People never seem to tire of the stories. But I'm not much of a one for reflection.' He returned to the table and handed me my glass.

'Bit of a come down, after all your expeditions.'

'Yes, a little. But needs must, old boy. And it's good money. They even paid for my flight on the Richthofen.'

'Will you have enough to finance another expedition?'

Sir George shook his head. 'Nowhere near enough, sadly. But I'll find the cash, one way or another.' He raised his glass. 'Well, bottom's up!'

'Here's mud in your eye,' I agreed. I raised the tumbler to my lips and knocked back the whisky in one quick mouthful. It hit the back of my throat and all at once I started to choke. 'Good God!' I exclaimed, almost dropping the glass. 'That tastes absolutely vile!'

'Yes, it would,' Sir George agreed, with a casual smile. 'That would be the rat poison.'

Chapter Eighteen

I clutched my throat in horror. I could taste the vile liquid burning at the sides of my mouth. My eyes were virtually popping out of their sockets. 'You devil!' I exclaimed, my breath a hoarse whisper. My arms were shaking and I was starting to feel dizzy. The glass fell from my hand and I grasped the sides of my chair, trying to focus on Sir George. He was smiling at me, content to watch my death throws without making any attempt to flee the scene of the crime.

'The poison is entering your gut now,' he told me, his voice calm and low. 'That was a much stronger dose than you gave Walter Kendall.' A small glass bottle, I observed abstractly, was resting next to the whisky on the side table. It had not been there a moment ago. Inside was the familiar crystalline powder. 'If I've judged it right, old boy, you have perhaps ten to fifteen minutes before it really starts to hit you. You'll feel it in the stomach first. Cramps. Nausea. Double vision. If you're lucky, after a few minutes of agony, you may pass out. Or not. Either way, you'll be dead in twenty minutes. Half an hour at the outside. It won't be at all pleasant, I'm afraid.'

'You monster!' I breathed, struggling desperately to make sense of what was happening. I put a hand to my mouth, thinking to make myself retch. But it was already too late for that.

Sir George smiled coldly. 'You look surprised. You didn't suspect me at all?'

'I...no...I...' I really hadn't. Sir George was a national hero, a world renowned explorer. Why would he get involved in anything as grubby as murder? 'You're...you're responsible for all this? For everything that's happened on board the Richthofen?' It was unbelievable. Every schoolboy in England knew his name. His exploits were reported in the Times. 'Why...why would you...?'

'Why did I do it?' He chuckled quietly. 'For the money, old boy. What else? I'm not ready to be put out to grass just yet.' He took another sip of whisky. 'There are places in this world that have never been seen by a white man. And I want to see them. But expeditions cost money. And after that last debacle in Antarctica, no one was willing to invest. So, I needed to make alternative arrangements. It wasn't *just* the money, though.' His eyes lit up. 'It was the thrill of it. Playing the odds. Taking the chance. There's nothing to beat it. The rush of adrenalin.' He downed the dregs of his glass. 'This whisky really is excellent. I might have another, if you don't mind.'

I watched the fellow in disbelief as he poured out another glassful. I couldn't believe he was standing there so calmly, rationalising his actions, after what he had just done to me. 'You're not going to get away with this,' I stammered, clutching my throat. 'I'll see you hang.' I would scream the place down, summon the steward, cry blue murder so everyone could hear.

'You're probably right,' Sir George conceded. 'I've had something of a run of bad luck these last few days. By all means summon one of the stewards. Have me restrained. Give me up to the law. But that won't save you, old boy. And if you do cause a fuss, then I'm afraid I won't be able to help you.'

'*Help* me?' I snorted. 'How can you help me?' What on earth was he talking about?

'I'm not a cruel man. You *are* going to die, but there's no need for you to suffer.' He downed the whisky in one. 'I can make it quick for you, old boy. Put you out of your misery.'

I laughed bitterly. 'What are you going to do? Slit my throat?'

'Nothing so crude.' He glanced through the door across the promenade 'It's a lovely evening. I thought you might go for a swim.'

I tried to laugh a second time, but barely a sound came out. The taste of the poison was burning the inside of my mouth. My heart was thumping ever faster and my hands were gripping tightly to the chair. 'You're mad,' I said again. 'That's your idea of help, is it? Throwing me out the window. Then you can blame me for everything that's happened.'

He nodded sagely. 'It would be convenient to have you out the way.'

'You're dreaming.' The glass panels were barely large enough to fit a man through in any case. 'I'm not going to help you. I'd rather suffer and see you exposed for the scoundrel you are.'

'It's your choice of course.' Sir George placed his glass back on the table. 'You're thinking of calling out for the steward in the corridor. A good idea. Why don't we bring him in here? Then the two of us can sit and watch you die.'

I rose unsteadily to my feet. I couldn't fathom what he was playing at. How could he be so calm? He couldn't possibly believe he would get away with any of this.

'No, don't trouble yourself,' he said, raising his hands to ward me off. 'I'll summon him myself.'

He disappeared out the door and round the corner into the lounge hall. A few seconds elapsed and then I heard a dull thud. Seconds later, there was a light scraping sound and Sir George reappeared, dragging the unconscious figure of the steward into the games room.

I regarded him with astonishment. 'You really are mad,' I breathed. 'You can't expect to get away with this.'

'Probably not,' he agreed. 'But I'm a gambling man. This is my last throw of the dice.'

'But...but...' I looked down at the prone form. Sir George appeared to have to hit him pretty hard. 'There are other people about.' There were a nearly a dozen passengers within shouting distance. 'He's not the only one who'll hear me.'

'No, you're right, Mr Bland. You can wake the whole ship if you want to. Scream and shout as much as you like.' He moved forward around the table and, before I had any idea what he was doing, he leapt at me. I felt hard metal pressed against my throat. A sweaty hand clamped my mouth shut. I couldn't see what Sir George was pressing against my neck, but I could feel the serrated edges. Another bloody steak knife. He was consistent, I had to give him credit for that. 'We're going for a little walk,' he whispered. 'Just down the stairs. It shouldn't take a minute. I would appreciate it if you kept quiet.' He started to manhandle me towards the door. 'If you struggle or make a noise, I will slit your throat without a second thought. It won't be a pleasant way to die.'

I allowed him to direct me out into the lounge towards the corridor. He was taking one hell of a risk. We had to get the length of the connecting passageway without being seen. There was at least one other fellow on duty, probably in the stewards' cabin on the port side, keeping an eye on the bell pushes. Given all that had gone on, the crewman would be bound to investigate any loud footsteps.

At this point, I could easily have made a noise, kicked my feet, drawn attention. I was dead anyway, what did a couple of minutes matter? But a knife to the throat is a powerful disincentive. I did not doubt that Sir George would carry out his threat.

We made it to the stairs and headed down to B Deck. My brain was fuzzing. I could barely breathe, but still I found a moment to wonder just what his intentions were. Was he really expecting me to jump out of the airship of my own volition? And from where? The windows of the starboard promenade were already far behind us.

The lights were dimmed in the lower corridor. Max the barman would probably be in his cot by now, on the other side of the airlock at the far end of the passageway. He would be unlikely to hear anything from this distance. The crew sections would be busy, of course, even at this hour, but none of the crewmen were likely to venture into this part of the ship. There was a set of narrow windows at floor level on the right hand side, running the length of the corridor, but these could not be opened. There was a second set of stairs behind us, parallel to the ones we had just descended. This was the exit ramp, the retractable stairs that led out of the Richthofen once the airship had landed safely. And it was this set that Sir George now directed me towards. The steps were laid out horizontally on the lower curve of the ship. A couple of bolts and a handle kept them in place during the flight but they could be lowered at will.

Sir George released my neck from his grip and thrust me towards the steps. I tripped over the uneven surface and smacked to the ground, just avoiding the aluminium handrail. While I was struggling to get myself up, the man unbolted the locks; then he grabbed the handle and gripped onto it firmly, his face beaming with triumph.

I was having difficulty finding my balance. The rat poison was slowly beginning to have its effect. I was feeling nauseous and was having trouble concentrating. Part of me wanted to vomit but nothing was coming up. I had barely eaten more than a sandwich at dinner. I dropped backwards onto the horizontal stairs, unable to lift myself up except onto the back of an elbow.

'Not feeling too well, old boy?' Sir George asked, with mock sympathy. 'It'll really start to hit you in a few minutes. This will be much quicker.' He gestured to the handle. 'Kinder in the long run, don't you think?' A quick flick of his wrist and I would plummet into the icy depths.

I clasped a hand to my face and regarded my nemesis with despair. 'People looked up to you,' I breathed. 'All those schoolchildren who learn about you. The great explorer. What would they think? You're just a common murderer!'

Sir George did not flinch. 'Hardly common, old boy. And it was never my intention to kill anybody.'

'Don't make excuses.' Anger was bubbling up inside me. 'You...you killed Jacob Finch in cold blood. And you killed Walter Kendall.'

'You can't blame me for *his* death,' Sir George countered sourly. '*You* killed the American. I wouldn't have harmed a hair on his head. Why would I? I needed him alive. *You* were the one causing all the trouble. It was you I wanted to dispose of.'

I coughed in surprise. So Maurice had been right. The rat poison had been intended for me all along. 'Well, it looks like you've got your way,' I admitted, coughing again. 'Tell me one thing though. That...that damned file. How did you get it out of England? You must have had an accomplice.' Sir George had not been on the plane out of Croydon.

He smiled, content it seemed, in my final minutes, to satisfy my curiosity. Sir George always had liked the sound of his own voice. 'I *did* have an accomplice. Chap by the name of Mick Durrant. We sailed together on my last expedition. A veteran seaman. Bit of a Lothario too. He was the one who got your file out of the country.'

I shook my head. 'But...but he fled the airfield. He was picked up in Holyhead. He wasn't on the flight to Friedrichshafen.' I flinched momentarily as a stab of pain hit my stomach, but I steeled myself against it. 'Somebody...somebody else must have acted as courier for you. Someone on board this ship.'

Sir George shook his head. 'There was no courier. I didn't need one, old chap.'

'But...'

'What do you think pays for all this?' He gestured vaguely to the ship. I looked up at the dull ceiling above us, not quite sure what he was getting at. 'How do you think they cover their running costs, the Zeppelin company? For a huge craft like this? It isn't from paying passengers.' He smirked. 'It's the mail. That's where the money is, old boy. They carry the post between Europe and the Americas. It's piled up in bags and franked during the flight. Post from France, Spain, Germany. And post from the United Kingdom.'

Suddenly I understood. 'And the post was carried on the flight from Croydon?'

'That's right.'

That was why Captain Rüdiger had been happy to deputize as pilot, when the original fellow had called in sick. The company couldn't afford to lose revenue from the mail.

'My man Durrant slipped the rolls of film into an envelope and slapped an address on it for Rio de Janeiro. The envelope wouldn't have been franked until the Zeppelin left Friedrichshafen. And if anyone searched the cabins, they wouldn't find anything.' As Finch had discovered, much to his chagrin. 'But I wasn't expecting anyone else to be on board, least of all a policeman. That was when the whole thing started to unravel.'

242

'Special Branch. They checked the original file on Saturday morning. So they were onto you from the start.'

'Durrant got away but they had a chap following the negatives. Your Mr Finch. He managed to get a ticket on board the Richthofen. And by Jove, what a fool that man was. I don't mean to speak ill of the dead, but I could tell at a glance that he was no threat to me. But then Special Branch got in touch with your people, the SIS. And they got in contact with Charles Lazenby.'

And that, of course, was how I had become involved.

'But how...how did you know about the prince's file in the first place? You've never been a member of Special Branch.' I coughed. 'And...and you're nothing to do with the security services.'

'No, I'm just an opportunist and a gambler,' Sir George admitted cheerfully. 'And so, I have to say, is Charles Lazenby.'

My mouth fell open. 'He was in it with you?'

'It was his idea. He used to work for Special Branch, until he got a transfer to the SIS.'

I did remember hearing that, come to think of it.

'He'd toyed with the idea of walking out with that file for years. A nice little nest egg for his old age. But he's clever. He knew he'd never get away with it while he was still an insider. So he bided his time. Waited a few years. And then he struck.'

'But how do *you* know him?'

'We're old friends. Gamblers. Drinking acquaintances. We've played a lot of cards together. I did a lecture in Madrid a few months ago and we met up for a game.'

'He's a card sharp like you?'

'I'm not a card sharp, old boy. I don't *need* to cheat.' The man spoke with the quiet authority of a professional gambler. 'It's easy enough to keep track of the cards, if you pay proper attention. The important thing is not to win every match, otherwise no one will play with you. You just have to make sure you're up over all.' He chuckled quietly. 'Lazenby and I were of like minds. He knew I was up for a bit of adventure.

And he knew all about the clerks in the records office back in London. That little spinster in particular. He said she was ripe for the plucking.' Sir George laughed again. 'I suggested Durrant for the job. He knows how to handle the ladies. He got a position as a baggage handler, contrived a meeting and then set about seducing the poor creature. Had her eating out of his hand. She thought they were going to run away together. The sad, deluded girl.'

'And you and...and Lazenby would split the cash when you sold the files to the American press?'

'That's the ticket. Except the damned woman made a complete hash of the documents when she pulled out the file. Too many small bits of paper, I suppose. She put everything back wrongly and it was discovered before our copy had even left the country. Of course, if things had gone to plan, I would have been in America before anyone realised anything was awry. And there would have been nothing to connect me to any of it.'

'But when it did go wrong, Charles Lazenby was called in to investigate?'

'Yes, that was the only bit of good luck we had. He's the head honcho in Spain and the airship was stopping in Seville. Your lot didn't trust Special Branch to handle the recovery. I can't say I blame them. And they weren't entirely convinced your man Finch wasn't involved in the theft himself. He had organised a second plane out of London pretty sharpish. So they wanted their own man on board. Lazenby tried to put them off, but they insisted on it. He had no choice, he had to stick somebody on the flight. He'd met you a few times, of course, and – to be blunt, old boy – he didn't rate you at all. He put your name forward, London agreed and on board you came.'

So I had been destined for the Richthofen from the moment I had received that first telegram on Saturday evening.

'And you met up with Lazenby when you arrived in Seville?'

'Yes, of course. By Jove, that was a bit of a surprise, having him turn up at the hotel. I wasn't expecting to see him for months. Not if things had gone to plan. But I knew something had gone wrong as soon as we left Germany. That chap Finch was an obvious plant. And Lazenby confirmed my suspicions. I could have coped with one damned fool on this flight, but having two of you on board, that was a bit tricky. Lazenby did his best to put you off the scent, focusing all your attention on Walter Kendall, but I was concerned that you might still stumble across the truth.'

'So you decided to bump me off?'

'It was the only way, old chap. Nothing personal. To be honest, I was all for killing Finch as well, but Lazenby had a much better idea. He suggested we kill you and frame Finch for the murder. London already suspected him. If I could confirm their suspicions, they'd have a chap from the embassy meet him in Rio and that would be that. I'd get clean away, without a whiff of scandal.'

'But you botched it, didn't you? You killed the wrong man.'

Sir George regarded me sourly. 'That was your fault. How was I to know you were carrying a sleeping draught in your cabin that you weren't intending to use?'

'Lazenby didn't tell you about that?'

'Why would he? He'd left it up to me as to how I was going to kill you. I was planning to dope your drink. That bottle of whisky. How are you feeling by the way?'

'Like hell,' I said. My stomach was churning and I was having difficulty focusing my eyes. But I wasn't gasping my last just yet. Fifteen to twenty minutes, he had said, before I passed out. That meant I still had a little time left. And if I could keep Sir George talking, there was just the chance somebody might stumble across us. Or perhaps the steward he had clobbered would wake up and raise the alarm. If Sir George was caught in the act, my death would not be completely in vain. But the damned fellow was keeping his voice low. He liked to boast but even he was not so foolish as to boast loudly just now. And I could not make a noise without him immediately pulling that handle. His left hand was still grasping the lever firmly.

'Won't be long now, old boy,' he said.

'So how...?' I coughed. 'How did you get hold of the rat poison?'

'Simplicity itself. I liberated it from Josef Kaufmann. Lindt had been crowing about that damned tin since we left Germany. His great joke. The chap really has no sense of humour. And Kaufmann rarely locked his door so I was able to nip in and out of his cabin shortly before we left Seville. As I say, I was going to slip the powder into your whisky. But then I saw the sleeping draught among your things and that seemed the ideal solution.'

'But Lazenby gave me that powder to drug Walter Kendall. He sent me a telegram, instructing me to use it on the American.'

'Did he now?' Sir George raised an eyebrow. 'That I didn't know. Oh, he's clever, you have to give him that. Covering himself with London. But I'll bet he didn't mention Kendall by name.'

'No, of course not.' I blinked. My eyes were starting to swim, but I was damned if I was going to lose my concentration just yet.

Sir George nodded knowingly. 'He'll have told his bosses he was encouraging you to dope Mr Finch, so you could search his room. That's what they would be expecting you to do. To keep an eye on the man from Special Branch.'

'But Lazenby told me nothing of the kind. I didn't...I didn't even know Finch was on board.'

'No. And with you dead, nobody would know you'd been given duff instructions from our man in Madrid.'

'You must have been horrified this morning,' I thought, 'when I turned up at breakfast and Walter Kendall didn't.'

'Yes, it was rather a shock. But I have an excellent poker face. I didn't let it rile me, old boy, even though it was a major inconvenience.'

'So did Kendall have anything to do with this at all?' Had he just been an innocent victim? I flinched as a sudden spasm of pain shot up from my stomach.

The other man shrugged, heedless of my discomfort. 'He was a possible buyer. I broached the matter with him in the broadest terms, before supper yesterday. I didn't tell him the source of the documents, but I hinted at their contents. He was going to contact his editor this morning, to get a provisional go ahead.' That had been the urgent telegram Kendall was going to send. It had been nothing to do with the "colour" piece. The American had probably intended to draft it just before he went to bed, but the sleeping draught had put a stop to that. 'He wouldn't have given them the specifics, of course, not in a public communication; just an indication of the story's importance. And, naturally, he wanted to see the file himself, to check its worth, before the paper paid out any money. I was going to get the films developed in Rio.' One fact at least that I had guessed correctly. 'Then the money could have been ready and waiting by the time we got to New York.'

'So the course change must have upset you as much as it did Mr Lindt.'

'Not at all. If anything, it speeded things up. But, thanks to you, old boy, Kendall was out of the picture. I would have to start again from scratch. Thankfully, I'd already rerouted the envelope to New York. I nipped out of the control room during the storm to change the label. I already knew where the bag was and the crew were too busy to keep track of one errant passenger.' His hand went to the small plaster on his forehead. 'That was when I banged my head. But if anything, with Kendall dead, the change of course worked to my advantage. I'd be in New York a few days early with plenty of time to develop the pictures and sound out other buyers.'

'But that's not going to happen now,' I said, trying hard to concentrate. 'Your accomplice, Mick Durrant, is under lock and key. It's only a matter of time before he spills the beans. You won't get away with any of this.'

'Durrant's a good man. He'll hold his tongue, at least long enough for me to disappear from view. But my reputation will be in tatters. And that's your fault, old boy.' There was a hint of anger in his eyes now. He had a wife back home he would never be able to see again, once the scandal broke.

'So why kill Finch? Why now, if not before?'

'I hate to admit it, but he was getting too close. The

captain had refused to allow him to conduct a thorough search of the ship. The baggage hold was off limits as was the post room. But when Finch confirmed that Kendall had been murdered, Captain Albrecht changed his mind. He gave him permission to search the entire ship. Finch would have started with the passenger luggage and then moved on to the mail. He wasn't a complete idiot. There's an awful lot of post to search, if you don't know what you're looking for, but even he would be able to feel for a couple of rolls of film. And the envelope is quite a visible one, as was the bag it was in. That's how I was able to keep track of it.'

'And if Finch had found it, that would mean everything had been for nothing.'

'Well quite.'

'But how did *you* know the captain had granted him permission to search the hold? None...none of the passengers even knew Finch was a policeman until this afternoon.'

Sir George smiled. 'I kept close to the seat of power. Adelina Koenig knows everything that happens on board the Richthofen. Her nephew gives her all the below stairs tittle-tattle – he even did a bit of franking in the post room, when we left Seville – and Captain Rüdiger filled in the rest. He is an old friend of hers. Fellow aviators, you understand. So I was ahead of the game at every stage.'

'And were you...sleeping with her too?'

Sir George regarded me oddly. 'No. Never laid a finger on her. Marvellous woman, but far too prickly for my taste. Not the type to share a sack with.' So he had not been the man in her room on Monday night. 'But I kept close to her all the same.'

'And you stabbed Finch in the back? With a steak knife?'

'Of course. I liberated the knife on Monday evening. I had a feeling it might come in useful. I heard Finch leave his cabin half an hour or so before dinner.' The two men were in adjacent rooms, just across from the stewards' cabin. 'I followed him out, there was no one about, so I took my chance. And now I can blame it all on you.' He grinned maliciously.

'I'll tell the captain you were behind it all. He'll have no reason to doubt my word and he won't find out the truth until after we've disembarked. I can say...'

A clomp sounded from the deck above. We both looked up but the noise could have come from anywhere.

'Ah. That sounds like company,' Sir George said. He sighed. 'It looks like we've run out of time, old chap.'

'No, wait a minute...' I croaked.

The explorer shook his head firmly. 'It's been nice knowing you, old boy,' he said. 'Give my regards to the fishes.'

And, with that, he pulled the lever and the stairs fell out from under me.

Chapter Nineteen

I had been lying across the steps, propped up on my elbows, with my legs aimed towards Sir George. My head was at the far end, at what was intended to be the lowest point of the stairwell. When the ramp fell away on a pivot it was my upper torso that dropped first. My elbows disappeared from under me, my head smashed against one of the lower steps and a sudden cross wind caused my legs to flip over my head as I tumbled out of the vehicle. My arms lashed out desperately and my left shoulder banged hard against the metal banister, which was bolted to the side of the stairs. My right arm hooked onto the base of it and my hand grasped the cold metal, clinging on for dear life. I was now hanging beneath the stairs, with just one arm looped around the hand rail and my legs dangling freely beneath me. The steps descended on metal wires and there was only the one banister, on the right hand side. I managed to raise my other hand to grab hold of it, alongside the existing arm, but the top of my head was barely level with the lowest rung of the steps and such was the power of the wind that my body was flailing about underneath, like a feather in a hurricane. I could feel my hands beginning to freeze in the chill air and I knew I would not be able to hold on for long.

Sir George Westlake was staring down at me from the top of the steps. I could see the irritation on his face. He had expected me to be dead already. 'Let go!' he mouthed. 'For God's sake jump.'

My heart was thumping in my chest and my fingers were barely hanging on to the metal rail. I was dead anyway, I thought. What was the point? The poison was raging in my gut, I could scarcely concentrate as it was. And there was no way I could pull myself back onto the airship. Sir George was right. Better to end it quickly. Damn the fellow. He would get away scot-free. I took a heavy lungful of air and looked down into the inky blackness. I'd had a good innings. I would probably be dead before I hit the water. To hell with that, I thought suddenly. I want to *live*.

With an effort of will I did not know I possessed, I hooked my left arm up around the banister, alongside the right one, and yanked myself several inches higher. I got my head above the bottom step – barely – and tried to drag my chest up as well. If I could get a bit of purchase on the stairs with my stomach, I might be able to slip a knee onto the lowest rung and then I was in with a chance.

Sir George observed my progress with mounting exasperation. He was glancing anxiously off to the right. The open stairwell was creating a drag effect. It was not the kind of thing a passenger would notice, but some of the crew were bound to feel the anomaly. It was like the pea under the princess's mattress. No matter how slight the effect, the airmen would notice and someone would be sent to investigate. Sir George grimaced, looking down at me. I had now managed to get a knee up onto the lower step. From his point of view, it appeared as if I might be able to inch my way back up or at least hang on where I was for several minutes. That was nonsense, of course, but I met his gaze briefly and saw the decision on his face. He could not afford to take the chance. He turned his back to me and began descending the stairs. He would finish me off in person.

The first few steps down from the corridor were partially protected from the wind by the walls of the airship and Sir George could descend this section with no real danger to himself. It was only the lower steps that were exposed to the elements. I had just got my left leg into a position of safety when I felt the boot kicking me in the face. My knee lost its purchase and only the arms clasped around the banister kept me from losing my grip altogether. Sir George kicked at me again. He was in an awkward position, above me but facing forward into the steps, with a severely restricted view. The second kick missed me entirely but the third I was prepared for. With my right arm clamped firmly around the hand rail, I thrust out my left hand and grabbed hold of his ankle. I gave it a sharp tug and this time it was Sir George who lost his purchase. His face smashed hard against the light metal rungs beneath him and his whole body began to judder down the steps. He groped desperately for something to hold onto but his body had twisted away from the banister and his momentum carried him on. He thumped into my shoulder, knocking me sideways and again I was hanging in thin air, which just one arm clamped to the hand rail. But it was worse for Sir George. He had flown straight past me and had only just managed to grab hold of the metal struts at the bottom of the steps. Gravity was now taking its toll. Sir George was laughing maniacally. He was trying to pull himself up, as I had done, but his hands were in an awkward position, just over the lip of the bottom rung.

Oh no you don't, I thought to myself. I was not about to let him scramble back on board. I had made up my mind. If I was going to die then he was going to die with me, the murdering bastard. I swung my legs through the air.

Sir George let out a hoof as my feet struck him hard in the stomach. One of his hands lost its purchase and for a moment he was suspended in mid air. His other hand remained in place, grasping the lower strut, but his grip was fragile. His eyes met mine and I was surprised to see his features abruptly relax. There was no anger there, just a sudden calm acceptance. He had played his hand and he had lost. At the last, I have to concede, he accepted his fate with good grace. His fingers uncurled and all at once the darkness swallowed him.

Good riddance, I thought, not daring to look down.

I took another breath and closed my eyes. Now I would follow him and let the sea swallow me up. There was no point drawing things out any longer. I was dead already. Davy Jones could have me. I relaxed my grip on the banister.

'Monsieur!' A voice called out from the top of the stairs. Maurice was crouching where Sir George had been standing a few moments before. He took in the scene at once, with barely a flicker of his eyebrows. Another head appeared to his left. It was the steward, Heinrich.

'*Mein Gott!*' the young lad exclaimed, momentarily forgetting himself.

I have never been so glad to see two people in my entire life.

'Do not let go!' Maurice instructed me, his cry barely

audible through the roar of the wind.

'I wasn't likely to,' I yelled back dishonestly, clutching the hand rail with renewed vigour.

'Is there a rope?' my man asked the steward. The young crewman thought for a moment and nodded.

'I don't think I can hold on forever,' I called up at them, as Heinrich disappeared to fetch it. I was not entirely sure if there was any point trying.

A flicker of concern rippled across Maurice's battered face. He looked off to the left, to see how long it would take the young lad to find what he was looking for. Evidently too long, as the valet took hold of the banister and began slowly to descend the steps.

'Don't be a fool, Morris!' I yelled. 'You'll get yourself killed!'

The valet descended carefully, his front facing inwards to the stairs, in the same manner as Sir George. 'Hold my foot, Monsieur!' he instructed, pressing himself against the steps and grabbing on to the far end of the banister. His body spanned more or less the whole of the stairway.

I took a deep breath and released one hand, swinging across as best I could. Maurice's shoe was just edging over the lip of the lowest step. I grabbed hold of it but the damn thing came off in my hand and fell away into the dark. At the second attempt, I managed to grab hold of his ankle. I pulled hard and the valet tensed, holding firmly to the top of the hand rail. Slowly, I manoeuvred a knee up onto the lower rung and then pulled myself on top of him, keeping one hand all the while on the banister to my right. For a moment, I rested there, one arm clutched awkwardly around my man's waist, the other still on the hand rail above me. 'Now what?' I muttered. We were neither of us in a dignified position.

Maurice attempted to turn his head back. 'You could try standing up, Monsieur.'

He was right. Now that my feet were back on the lower steps I could raise myself up, using the banister to steady myself. Then perhaps I could scramble over the top of him. I lifted my head as best I could and found myself out of the slipstream, inside the protective walls of the upper steps.

Heinrich appeared above me. He was already securing a length of rope to the other banister, the one leading up to A Deck. He threw the end down to me and I grabbed onto the rope with the last of my strength. Maurice was in the way rather, but he twisted to one side to allow me some purchase as I hauled myself up. Then he too began to raise himself to his feet.

'Be careful, Morris!' I called behind me.

'Of course, Monsieur.'

At last I found myself back in the narrow corridor of B Deck. Heinrich gave me a hand onto solid ground and I collapsed onto the floor opposite the main stairs, my back to the wall. The steward returned to help Maurice, who had been hobbled slightly with the loss of his shoe, before finally retrieving the rope. My valet rose up to his full height, took a slight breath, and then sat himself on the floor next to me. The steward, meantime, pulled the lever on the stairs and I watched as they retracted into the ship. Heinrich quickly secured the bolts to keep the steps in place.

The young German stared for a moment at the two of us. 'Are you all right, sir? What happened?'

I shuddered. 'Oh, I just thought I'd get a bit of fresh air,' I mumbled, distractedly. 'Sir George is dead. He tried to kill me.'

'You had better inform the captain,' Maurice instructed the crewman. He, at least, had his wits about him.

Heinrich nodded. 'Yes, sir. I'll fetch him at once.' The young lad hurried off down the corridor.

I looked across at Maurice. My hands were trembling and my eyes were having difficulty focusing. I had been rescued from the ocean, but I was still a dead man.

'Do not worry, Monsieur,' the valet attempted to reassure me. 'You are safe now. Nothing can harm you.'

'You don't understand. I'm dying. Sir George...' I coughed. 'He put rat poison in my drink. I've only...I've only got a few minutes left...'

Maurice swivelled his body round and placed a firm

hand on my forehead. 'Rat poison?' He took my wrist in his hand and listened to my pulse.

'You might as well have let me drown.'

'Sir George put rat poison in your drink?'

'Yes.' I shuddered, blinking the tears from my eyes.

The valet peered at my face and frowned slightly. 'Are you sure, Monsieur?'

'Of course I'm sure!' I exclaimed. 'My insides are burning up!'

Maurice frowned again. 'But you seem perfectly well to me. I can see no evidence of any poison.'

'What are you talking about? I feel awful.'

He dropped my wrist. 'Given what you have just been through, Monsieur, that is hardly surprising.' He loosened my neck tie and peered closely at my mouth. 'But I do not think you can have been poisoned. You would not have been able to hold on to that rail if your body had been weakened in such a way.'

'I'm telling you, Sir George put rat poison in my drink. I saw the powder. He brought it with him to the games room in a little glass bottle. And he put it in my whisky. I can still taste it in my mouth. It's absolutely vile.'

'What can you taste, Monsieur?' Maurice asked calmly. 'What does it taste like?'

I threw up my hands. 'I don't know. It's horrible. What does it matter? It tastes like...I don't know...salt water. Really nasty salt water.'

'And Sir George administered it?'

'I said that, didn't I? He was behind the whole thing. He murdered Finch and now he's murdered me too.'

'No, Monsieur.' The valet was firm on that point. 'Whatever he put in your drink, it was not rat poison. It could not have been. The tin Monsieur Kaufmann brought on board the Richthofen is in the possession of Captain Albrecht, as is the sleeping draught we left in Monsieur Kendall's cabin. You could not have been poisoned with that.' I stared at my valet, barely daring to hope. 'From what you describe, the powder you saw was probably nothing more than table salt. I suspect, if we enquire further, we will find a salt cellar went missing at supper time.'

'A salt cellar?' My mouth fell open. 'You mean, it was a *bluff*?'

'Yes, Monsieur.'

I slumped back against the wall and considered that for a moment. Could it really be true? Had Sir George simply siphoned off a bit of salt at supper, slipped it into an old pill bottle and then added it to my drink? 'But I *felt* it,' I protested. 'I felt the burning in my stomach, the nausea. I felt like I was going to pass out.'

'The mind can play tricks, Monsieur. If you are told you have been poisoned, the body will often react accordingly.'

'Poppycock! I know what I felt.'

'But you are not dead, Monsieur,' Maurice insisted. 'And when the late Monsieur Kendall drank *his* whisky, he did not notice any peculiarity in the taste.'

That was a point. I closed my eyes for a moment. My valet was right, damn it. It couldn't have been the rat poison. I wasn't dying. I had never *been* dying. It was all a ruse. Sir George was a gambling man and he had taken a chance, as he always did. 'He wanted to disconcert me,' I realised now. 'Throw me off kilter, so he could get me down here more easily.' The last throw of the dice, he had said. And I had fallen for it. 'He was mad. Absolutely mad. No, not mad.' I reconsidered. 'Reckless. All or nothing. And I would have jumped, too, in the end. If you hadn't come by.' I frowned for a moment. 'Why were you up and about anyway?'

'I was concerned for you, Monsieur, when I did not hear you retire to bed. Given all that had happened, I wished to make sure you had returned safely to your cabin.' That was typical of him, I thought. Always fussing. But on this occasion I was not about to complain. 'I came out into the corridor and was surprised to find there was no steward on guard outside Monsieur Lindt's cabin. I discovered the man lying unconscious in the games room.'

'Yes, that's right. Sir George belted him.'

'I alerted the other steward, who was on duty in his

cabin. Then we heard voices from the deck below and came to investigate.'

'I'm glad you did. Good lord. To think what might have happened otherwise.' I stared at him numbly for a moment, not wanting to think through the implications. 'That was a brave thing you did there, Morris, coming down for me like that.'

'A little foolish perhaps. But necessary, Monsieur.'

'I don't think I could have got back up on my own.' I shook my head, trying to dismiss the horror of the moment. 'If you wanted a pay rise that badly,' I joked, 'you only had to ask.'

'That will not be necessary, Monsieur. Though I may need to purchase a new pair of shoes.'

I laughed, relief washing through me. 'I think I might be persuaded to cover the cost of that.'

'Thank you, Monsieur,' he responded dryly. He glanced across at the steps, which were now mercifully secured. 'And Sir George?'

'With the fishes, where he deserves to be.' It had been a close run thing, but I was alive. My God, I was alive.

'And the photographs?'

'The what?'

'The photographs. Did Sir George have the negatives with him?'

'No. No, he didn't.' I brought a hand up to my mouth and stifled a yawn. 'But, as luck would have it, Morris, I do have some idea where they might be...'

The mail bags were jammed tightly together, blocking out most of the light from the post room window. It had a taken a couple of crewmen the better part of an hour to cart all the sacks over here from the hold. There was barely room to contain them all. The crewmen had dumped the bags in the cabin and left me to get on with it. By rights it should have been their job – menial tasks are for menial people – but unfortunately this was one job that was too important to delegate. I grabbed another pile of letters from the sack. Sir George had said the envelope and the bag it was in had been marked in some way, for easy identification, but he hadn't said what kind of marks they were. A pencil scratch of some kind? A coloured sticker? There was no way of telling. All I could do was grab a clump of envelopes from the nearest sack and feel each one for suspicious lumps. I sighed. It would take the better part of a day to look through them all. There were thousands of the damned things. And knowing my luck, the package I wanted would be buried at the bottom of the very last sack.

Maurice could have done the work for me but he was busy deciphering a long telegram from London. The message had been encrypted their end using Finch's Scotland Yard book code. I could have had a go at translating that, but given the choice between mindless envelope fondling and hard-headed brain work, I had plumped for the easier task. My head was in no fit state for anything else today and it was a relief just to be away from the passenger decks.

I had arrived at the breakfast table in a somewhat delicate state. I had barely slept a wink during the night and had emerged from my cabin with a shocking headache. Before I had even settled myself at a table, I was assaulted by a battery of questions from the other passengers. Their curiosity was understandable – no one could quite believe that Sir George Westlake had been a murderer – but all that attention was the very last thing I needed. Maurice did his best to field some of the more tedious questions, while I grabbed a bite to eat. But when an angry Karl Lindt stormed in, having finally been released from his cabin, I knew it was time to get away.

The post room was proving a welcome retreat. Even here, however, I was not entirely free of attention.

'Can I give you a hand?' Miss Tanner poked her head around the door. She was dressed in a heavy coat, against the cold, but her head was unbonneted and her short black curls were hanging free. 'Goodness. There's barely room to swing a cat in here,' she observed. Her escort, the gap-toothed crewman, waved a friendly greeting and moved on.

I grimaced, unwilling to indulge in idle chit chat. 'It's just as well I don't own a cat,' I muttered.

'Feeling a little tired?' she asked brightly, refusing to take offence. 'I just came down to see how you were getting on. Monsieur Sauveterre said you might need a hand. Is that a new shirt?'

'Er...yes. Mr Gray was kind enough to lend it to me.' I glanced down at the off-the-peg monstrosity. 'It's a bit tight, to be honest.'

'It looks very nice,' Miss Tanner pronounced, stepping forward into the small gap between the door and the first of the mail sacks. 'So how are you feeling?' she asked.

I put down the pile of letters. I never did know how to answer questions like that. I shrugged. 'Glad to be alive, I suppose.'

'You poor dear. Was it too awful?'

'I...really thought I was a goner.' I shuddered.

'That ghastly man. Trying to throw you out of the airship! It must have been absolutely frightful.'

'The worst of it is, I actually quite liked the fellow. Before he tried to poison me, I mean. I admired his spirit. The great adventurer. But it turns out he was just a common thief. A murderer. Goes to show, doesn't it? Even the best of people are not always what you think they are.'

'Well, I think you were very brave,' Miss Tanner concluded, giving my shoulder a gentle squeeze. She surveyed the mail room brightly. 'I really *would* like to help, if I can. I don't like to think of you all alone here, piled up with these letters.'

'Ludwig – Mrs Koenig's nephew – is coming by later, to steam open anything suspicious.' The captain had given me free access to the mail, but he didn't want me damaging any of the packages. It would be left to the professionals to actually open the envelopes and seal them up afterwards. 'But you're welcome to help,' I added.

Miss Tanner moved further into the room. It was a tight squeeze, the mail bags were piled up so highly. 'What am I looking for?'

'Anything that doesn't feel like a letter. A roll of film, maybe two, but perhaps not as big as a standard camera film.'

'Righty-ho.' She picked up a pile of letters and started rifling through them.

'The envelope might have some kind of marking on it. Anything paper thin you can discard.'

Miss Tanner nodded seriously. 'And I gather I'm not allowed to ask what's on these films.'

'I'm afraid not. National security. As soon as we've found the negatives I'm going to have destroy them.'

'Golly, how thrilling!'

The two of us set to work and, to her credit, Miss Tanner left it a good minute and a half before broaching the matter that had really brought her down here. 'Mr Kendall,' she said, putting down the letters and finally coming to the point. 'Walter. It wasn't an accident. Sir George really did kill him?'

'I'm afraid so.' It was true, after a fashion. I wasn't going to admit my own involvement in the American's death, but I did have to provide some kind of explanation to the other passengers; especially as the police in New Jersey would be interviewing everybody on arrival. I would stick to the truth as far as I could. 'Sir George tried to sell the films to Mr Kendall. But your friend was a man of some integrity. Bit odd for a journalist,' I observed. 'Bunch of blackguards, as a rule. But Kendall wouldn't buy stolen goods. He threatened to inform the authorities and so Sir George did him in.' That was the story, at least, that I wanted everyone to believe. The press would doubtless speculate endlessly on the nature of the secrets that had been stolen, but they would never know the whole truth. London would not allow that and the American authorities had no desire to upset their European allies.

'Gracious. How awful!' Miss Tanner said. 'That vile man. And he used Herr Kaufmann's rat poison? In a sleeping draught?'

'I believe so. He must have slipped it in there when Mr Kendall was out and about.'

'But how would he have got into the cabin?'

'Sir George's room was on the same part of the landing as the stewards'. He must have slipped in there to borrow the keys, when the fellow was away.' Come to think of it, that was probably how he had managed to gain access to Gerhard Schulz's cabin.

Miss Tanner frowned. 'But using a sleeping draught at all. It's so unlike Walter,' she declared. 'He never had any trouble sleeping.'

'Age comes to us all, my dear. And, in my experience, older men don't like to advertise their weaknesses, especially not to young ladies they are particularly fond of.'

She nodded sadly. 'I really was very fond of him,' she confided. 'But I should have told Thomas that we knew each other. I shouldn't have lied to him like that.'

'I'm sure you had the best of motives.' Actually, I wasn't sure of that at all, but one has to be polite about these things. 'Now, we really do need to get on.'

'Yes, of course.' Miss Tanner pulled herself together and we continued with our work. At least her curiosity had been satisfied. My own was still itching away in the background. There was still so much I did not understand. There was that daft business with Kendall's notebook, for a start.

Maurice was making his way along the corridor outside, a pair of plimsolls serving as a temporary replacement for his lost footwear. 'Monsieur,' he said, poking his head into the post room and nodding a greeting to Miss Tanner. 'I have decrypted the telegram.'

'About time. Give me a minute.' I added a handful of letters to the "checked" pile and manoeuvred myself past Miss Tanner, who smiled playfully as we pressed against each other. The damned woman never missed an opportunity for flirting.

I slipped out into the corridor and shivered. I had been getting a bit steamed up in the post room, but there was a definite chill on the walkway. Unlike Maurice, I was not wearing an overcoat. His escort had already disappeared into the radio room. I grabbed the note from my valet and scanned it quickly.

"DURRANT CONFIRMS INVOLVEMENT WESTLAKE AND LAZENBY STOP LAZENBY DETAINED LISBON STOP AGREE NO ACTION RE HURST STOP

LOCAL AUTHORITIES COOPERATING STOP DEBRIEFING ON ARRIVAL"

'Clear as mud,' I muttered. 'As usual.' But they had at least arrested Charles Lazenby. 'He must have got wind something had gone wrong,' I said to Maurice. 'If he tried to make a run for it.'

'Indeed, Monsieur.'

Lisbon was a stopping off point for all manner of transatlantic vessels. The authorities would throw the book at him when they got him back to London. And quite right too, the scoundrel. He would be lucky to escape the noose.

'Is it good news?' Miss Tanner called from inside the post room.

'For Miss Hurst,' I said, looking down again at the decrypted note. Maurice's handwriting was far better than Finch's had been.

"AGREE NO ACTION RE HURST"

'They're not going to pursue the matter of her passport.'

'That is good news,' Miss Tanner agreed. 'She'll be so pleased.'

'Monsieur Kaufmann has also received a telegram,' Maurice confided, keeping his voice low. 'He did not look happy.'

I frowned. 'Do you know what it was about?'

'No, Monsieur. But I will endeavour to find out.'

Mr Lindt had been eliminated as a murder suspect, but Captain Albrecht had refused to return his cash. Perhaps Mr Kaufmann had been making enquiries about where it had come from.

'Good man. Then you can come and give me a hand with these letters.' I poked my head back into the mail room.

Miss Tanner was hip deep in post bags. 'I said I would help you, Mr Bland,' she teased. 'I didn't say I would do it all myself.' She grabbed another handful of envelopes and began rifling through them. Her hands fingered a small package and

262

she let out a sudden 'Ooh!' The envelope had a bright red line running the length of it and a couple of small bulges in the centre. 'Gosh!' she exclaimed, excitedly. 'Mr Bland! I think I may have found your films!'

Chapter Twenty

After four days on board the Richthofen, I had just about come to terms with looking out of the windows; but this was the first time I had seen New York from the air. It was quite a novel experience, hovering serenely over the Statue of Liberty, staring down at the thorny crown on her head and that great big torch in her hand. It made one dizzy just looking at it. The Manhattan skyline had changed quite a bit in the last few years. The Chrysler building, the Empire State – it was all new to me. A couple of spotter planes were buzzing around us, taking photographs of the airship, and in the bay various boats were tooting their horns in greeting. It was the first glimmer of the carnival that would be awaiting us upon our arrival at the hangar in New Jersey. There would be no chance for any of us to slip away quietly.

'How far are we from Lakehurst?' I asked Adelina Koenig, who was standing next to me with a pair of binoculars.

'Seventy-two kilometres,' she said, in her harsh, guttural English. 'We are travelling at eighty kilometres an hour and will be in Lakehurst in fifty four minutes.'

I pulled out my fob watch. 'Right. Seventy-two kilometres. What's that in miles?'

Mrs Koenig regarded me contemptuously. 'I do not understand the imperial system. Miles, yards. Feet and inches. It makes no sense.'

'You'll have to get used to it in America.'

'It is too confusing.' She waved a hand dismissively, almost thumping me with her binoculars. 'The metric system, kilometres, metres, centimetres. It is far better.'

'If you say so.' It wasn't the first time there had been some confusion in that respect. 'Did you ever discuss any of that with Mr Kendall?' I enquired. The issue of that damned notebook was still niggling away at me.

'*Nein*. But we talk about my travels in Africa. There is little understanding between us. I tell him the kilometres I travel but he is speaking in miles.' She growled. 'That is why it is better to have one system.'

I nodded, thoughtfully. So Kendall had got the wrong end of the stick. He had thought Mrs Koenig had no idea about the distances between various cities in Africa and had begun to doubt the veracity of her heroic adventures. He had scribbled down a few notes in his book, no doubt intending to follow them up later. But in actual fact, the German woman had known exactly what she was talking about.

Mrs Koenig hesitated before she spoke again. 'You work with Herr Finch, *ja*?'

'Er...yes, I did.'

She frowned for a moment, almost as if she were embarrassed. 'When he looks in my room, he takes something. Two films, in my jacket. Where are they?' A slightly bitter tone had entered her voice.

'Ah.' There was no point dissembling. 'I think he may have destroyed them.' At least with Finch dead, I did not have to take responsibility for that myself.

Mrs Koenig muttered a few expletives in German, then raised up her hands. 'It is not important. I go now to say goodbye to Ludwig.' And off she went, in search of her nephew.

I watched her go with some amusement. 'What an extraordinary woman,' I mumbled, to no one in particular. I wondered what had been in those photographs of hers. I had never seen her using a camera on board.

I doubted it would be anything as contentious as the photographs I had recovered from Sir George Westlake. In some ways, it was a shame the man had not got around to developing them. I would have liked the opportunity to peruse that Special Branch file. But the negatives needed be disposed of before we arrived in America and I had consigned them to the bottom of the ocean on Wednesday evening. As a staunch monarchist, I could not risk any harm coming to a future sovereign, even a skirt-chasing half-wit like Prince Edward. Better to be rid of the bloody things. It was a little galling, though, having spent so long pursuing the files, not to have the opportunity to read them. I was itching to find out more about the dubious Madame Alibert and her scandalous hold over the British establishment. But, sadly, duty came before pleasure.

Karl Lindt was kicking up a fuss over in the lounge. 'The captain has no right to withhold my luggage!' he snarled, in reply to a comment I had not heard. 'It is my money. I can do with it as I like.' I glanced across and saw Thomas McGilton standing opposite the German, with Miss Tanner hovering to his right.

The Irishman could not resist baiting the fellow. 'That's not what I've heard,' he said.

Lindt glared back at him. '*What* have you heard?'

McGilton raised an eyebrow. 'That you stole the money from your company. Money that was owed to your creditors. Wages for your employees. Rent money.'

'That is ridiculous! Who told you that?'

McGilton gestured across the lounge to Josef Kaufmann, who was standing at the far end of the promenade, looking pointedly out of the window at the New York skyline. Despite the volume of the argument, the older man was pretending not to hear. I can't say I blamed him. 'Herr Kaufmann contacted your people back home,' McGilton continued. 'They confirmed everything. You sold up. Sent him off on a fools errand to England while you cashed in everything you could. You even sold the fixtures and fittings, none of which belonged to you.'

'That is nonsense. I was perfectly entitled...'

'Your business was failing, so you decided to grab all the cash and head off for a new life in Sao Paulo. Made up some cock and bull story about a conference there to cover your tracks. Even brought a gift for one of the directors you were supposedly planning to meet. But you never intended to come back. And you would have left Herr Kaufmann high and dry.'

'That is a monstrous accusation! It is not true at all.'

'Oh, it's true all right,' McGilton insisted. 'That was why you were in such a hurry to get there. You wanted to be away from the rest of us before anybody found out what you'd done. You may not be a murderer, Herr Lindt, but you are a thief and liar. All that talk of the superiority of the European

266

male. You're just a common criminal. You have no integrity at all.'

That was too much for Lindt. 'And you?' he sneered, eyeing up the Irishman. 'Who are you to criticize me?'

'Oh, nothing. Just another thick Paddy. Not genetically pure like you. No bloodline to speak of. But at least I'm honest, Herr Lindt. At least I know how to treat people with honour and respect.'

Lindt scoffed. 'You claim to be an honourable man? You are a hypocrite, Mr McGilton. You have no honour.' He gestured scornfully to Miss Tanner. 'An unmarried Irishman, travelling across the Atlantic with his Jewish whore!'

I barely saw the blur of McGilton's arm as it flashed out, but I heard the satisfying crunch as his fist collided with Mr Lindt's oily face. The man staggered backwards, clutching his nose. He crashed into a table, lost his footing and went sprawling across the floor. I laughed out loud. Blood was spurting from his battered nostrils as he gathered himself together on the carpet. 'You hit me!' he exclaimed in astonishment. 'You hit me!'

Captain Albrecht appeared at the lounge door just as Lindt was clambering back to his feet.

'Captain! Arrest this man! He has assaulted me!'

Albrecht did not move. 'I saw nothing, Herr Lindt.'

The businessman shone his eyes across the room. His gaze fixed on Miss Hurst, who was standing quite close to me, by the centre window. 'Fräulein, you saw what he did to me?'

She shook her head. 'I was looking out of the window, I'm afraid.'

'Josef? You saw?'

The tubby German had turned back from the glass. He pursed his lips and looked away sadly. 'I saw nothing, Karl.'

I couldn't resist chipping in my own twopenn'orth. 'You fell over that table, didn't you?' I chuckled. 'You should watch where you're going, Mr Lindt.'

The man glared across the room. He had no friends here and now he knew it. His hand was still on his nose, which was beginning to dribble blood onto the carpet.

The captain broke the brief silence. A steward had stepped forward to right the furniture. 'Stefan, you will assist Herr Lindt. Get him cleaned up. I do not want him bleeding in front of the cameras. The police will be waiting to talk to you, Herr Lindt, when we arrive at Lakehurst.' He stared coldly at the German. 'And when the ship has been repaired, you will not be accompanying us to Rio.'

Stefan came forward to assist Mr Lindt.

'You cannot do this to me!' the man declared. 'I have paid...'

'You have got off lightly,' Captain Albrecht snapped, his voice the harshest I had ever heard it. 'You will accept your punishment and get off my ship!'

And with that, Karl Lindt was bundled away.

There was a moment of palpable relief. Some people can suck the joy from a room; Mr Lindt had sucked the joy from the entire trip.

'Men like that give Germans a bad name,' Albrecht muttered. 'I apologise for the disturbance. Ladies and gentlemen, *Damen und Herren,* as you can see, we will shortly be arriving at Lakehurst. There is quite a crowd waiting for us, I am told, but the police have asked that you do not speak to any journalists before they have had a chance to talk to you. I am afraid news of events on board has already reached the American media.' He glanced down at his wristwatch. 'We will be landing at approximately twelve forty-five. A coach will take you straight to your hotel, where the police will want to speak to all of you. This is just a formality and nothing to worry about.' He shot us all a warm smile. I marvelled at the confidence of the man, considering the strain he must be under. 'You may take a change of clothes with you, but your luggage will have to remain on board. Once it has been inspected we will send it on to you at the hotel. I thank you all for your patience and understanding. It has been a difficult trip but I hope perhaps you will consider flying with us again. Our transatlantic journeys are not usually this eventful.'

We laughed gently at the wry comment.

'We'll tell them what an absolutely super job you've

done!' Miss Tanner declared. 'We would never have got here at all if it wasn't for you and your men.'

Albrecht inclined his head. 'You are very kind, Fräulein.'

'It's the simple truth, captain.'

'Thank you. Well, if you will forgive me, I must see to our arrival. I will see you all later at the hotel.'

Albrecht put on his cap and strode out of the lounge room.

'Poor fellow,' I said. 'I wonder if he'll ever fly again.' It did not seem likely. Not with four deaths on his watch.

'It's so unfair,' Annabel Hurst agreed. I had forgotten she was standing next to me. Even now, I was finding it difficult to believe she was really a man. Every time I looked at the woman, I had to stop myself from springing backwards in surprise. But the evidence was irrefutable.

'The world's not a fair place, Miss Hurst. Take it from me.' In a fair world, Walter Kendall would be heading home to his wife and Jacob Finch would be reporting his triumph to his superiors in London. 'Oh, I've got something for you,' I said. I reached into my inside pocket and produced a small black passport, which I handed across. 'The captain said to give it back to you. Not a bad forgery,' I admitted quietly. 'It should get you through customs. I've spoken to my people. They're not going to pursue the matter.'

Miss Hurst clasped the passport gratefully to her chest. Not that she had much of a chest. But then she wouldn't, of course.

'Too much else on their plate,' I explained. 'But if anyone else questions it, I'm afraid you're on your own.'

'I understand.' She unclipped her handbag and slotted the passport inside.

Lucy Tanner had seen me handing the booklet across and she flashed a smile in my direction as she headed off to her cabin for one last change of clothes.

'What did you tell Miss Tanner?' I asked. 'About the passport?'

Miss Hurst sighed gently. 'The truth, more or less.'

'Good lord. Not...?'

'No, not about that.' She smiled shyly. 'Just that I'm running away. From my parents more than anything. I told her I didn't want them to trace me in America, so I invented a whole new identity.'

'And she believed you?'

'It wasn't really a lie. That is what I'm doing.' She glanced nervously out of the window. 'A new country. A new life. To tell you the truth, Mr Bland, I am absolutely terrified.' Her lower lip was beginning to tremble.

'It's never easy starting a new life,' I agreed, anxious to forestall any water works. 'But I'm sure you'll cope, my dear.'

'Will *you* be going back to England?' she asked.

'No, I'm here for the duration. New job and all that. A couple of weeks in New York and then off to Central America.' I wasn't quite sure how I felt about that. 'Never easy starting afresh. No matter how many times you do it.'

'At least you have contacts here. People you know. I wish I knew what the future held. I don't know anybody in America.'

'I'm sure Miss Tanner will make a few introductions for you. And believe me, if you can fool her you can fool anyone. Lord, five days sharing a room. I don't think I could have managed that.'

'You're very kind. I wish you all the best for the future.' She held out her hand.

'No, no, no,' I said, refusing to shake it. 'Start as you mean to go on, Miss Hurst.' I clasped the hand instead and pulled it up to my face, kissing the back of it gently, as befitted a female acquaintance.

Annabel Hurst giggled shyly.

Maurice adjusted the scarf around my neck and I pulled the hat down tight on the top of my head. 'How do I look?' I asked.

The valet stepped back and examined me critically. 'We have covered most of your face,' he said.

'The glasses should finish it off.' Maurice had a pair of

spectacles in his breast pocket, which I could borrow to cover the journey from the airship to the car. I was damned if I was going to let a pack of slavering journalists photograph me and blow my cover. The passenger manifest was a matter of public record, so my name was compromised already, but I wasn't going to let them have my face as well. That was the one thing I couldn't replace. 'I'm going to need a new alias once all this is over. I won't be able to carry on as Reginald Bland. Not once my name's been in all the papers.'

'I am sure the consulate will arrange a new identity for you.'

'Oh, I'm not going to rely on them. I'll choose my own name this time, thank you very much. None of this "RJ Bland" nonsense. If I'm going to be a Passport Control Officer, I shall pick my own damned identity.' I considered for a moment. 'Something beginning with "B" I think. Perhaps I could even restore my title.' I was fed up with people addressing me as "mister".

The other passengers were making their way down the steps from A Deck towards the exit ramp. Maurice and I were standing further back along the lower corridor, between the stairs and the smoking room, whilst my valet made the final adjustments to my disguise. Stefan, the head steward, was standing at the base of the stairs with young Heinrich, waiting to see us all off. Karl Lindt had descended the lower steps first and Frederick Gray was following behind. I could already hear the clicking of cameras and the shouted questions of the journalists as the first of the passengers emerged from the base of the Richthofen. It was rather touching, having the staff see us off like this. Behind us, at the far end of the corridor, the head chef in his mushroom hat was standing next to Max the barman. Max was beaming happily, his enormous hooter in better shape now than Mr Lindt's battered conk. Not all the stewards were here to see us off, however. The corridor was too narrow and some of the others were carting our hand luggage down a second gangway. I wondered how Miss Tanner would cope with only the one change of clothes.

Josef Kaufmann waved a hand at us as he reached the

271

lower deck and turned right.

The sight of those steps still made me shudder. A day and a half had passed since my unfortunate near exit from the ship but the prospect of tripping down that stairwell again was more than enough to bring me out in a cold sweat. And this time I would have to do it in a state of virtual blindness. Reading glasses were probably not ideal in the circumstances.

Adelina Koenig had arrived at the base of the upper stairs and was babbling a farewell in German to one of the stewards. Her manner was almost friendly. As I watched, her hand shot out and grabbed young Heinrich on the backside. It was a momentary gesture – a quick pinch of flesh that might easily have gone unnoticed – but it was the young man's reaction that really drew the eye. 'Good lord!' I breathed. 'Did you see that, Morris?'

The valet nodded. 'Yes, Monsieur.'

Mrs Koenig had pinched Heinrich on the bottom and the young man had not even flinched. He had seemed to expect it. He smiled at her and winked as she passed him by. And there was no mistaking the look in his eye.

'You don't think...?'

Maurice had had the same idea as me. 'It is a possibility, Monsieur.'

I had thought it was Captain Rüdiger who had visited Mrs Koenig's bedroom on Monday night, but perhaps I had been mistaken. 'Good grief!' I whispered. 'Could it really have been young Heinrich?' There was certainly no mistaking that twinkle in his eye. 'Who would have thought it?' I chuckled quietly. But I couldn't fault Mrs Koenig for her taste. Heinrich was a handsome young fellow. It was a hell of a risk for him to take, though. A steward could lose his job, fraternising with the passengers like that.

The cameras were clacking furiously as Mrs Koenig stepped out in front of the slobbering hordes. She would be the one pictured in all the American newspapers tomorrow. Women were always the most popular subjects for photographs.

A sudden thought struck me. 'Those rolls of film,' I whispered, 'belonging to Mrs Koenig. You don't think they might have been photos of young Heinrich?' I brought a hand up to my mouth and stifled a laugh. Had Mrs Koenig got him to strip off in her cabin or at the hotel in Seville? And then photographed him? It would not surprise me in the slightest. At that moment, the steward caught my eye. He knew I was talking about him and he shot me a sly grin. He was a cocky devil, that one. 'No wonder she was so upset when those films went missing. She didn't even get a chance to develop them.' And I had thrown them out to sea. 'What a woman,' I laughed, shaking my head. Sir George had been right about that, if nothing else. The Americans didn't know what they were letting themselves in for.

Annabel Hurst had arrived at the bottom of the steps. She smiled shyly at me as she headed for the gangplank.

Maurice leaned in. 'It might also explain the matter of the notebook, Monsieur.'

I regarded him blankly. 'I don't follow.'

'If the young man discovered Monsieur Kendall's body on Tuesday morning.'

It took me a moment to understand what he was getting at. 'Oh, you mean, he might have seen the pad there on top of the typewriter and torn out the pages.'

'It is a possibility, Monsieur. He did not know that Monsieur Kendall had been murdered.'

'No. He probably thought the fellow had died in his sleep. And what, he picked up the notebook, saw a few disparaging remarks about his lover and thought, where's the harm in getting rid of those?'

'Perhaps, Monsieur. It would explain their disappearance.'

'But, if that was the case, surely he would have confessed to it when he realised Kendall had been murdered?'

'Not necessarily, Monsieur. To do so, he would have had to admit dereliction of duty. He was meant to be on call in the stewards' cabin throughout the night.'

'In case anyone rang the bell. Yes, I see what you mean. A bit off that,' I thought. 'Deserting his post. Leaving the cabin empty. What if someone had been ill?'

'Someone was, Monsieur.'

I blinked, not quite following.

'Monsieur Kendall.'

I scowled. 'You have a dark sense of humour, Morris.'

'Yes, Monsieur.'

'Now where are those reading glasses of yours?'

He pulled them out of his breast pocket and handed them across.

'I suppose we'd better head out into the fray,' I said, putting on the glasses. All at once, the world became a blur. 'Good grief. I can't see anything at all.'

A couple of passengers were moving about in front of me. 'Gosh, I would never have recognised you,' one of them exclaimed. It sounded like Miss Tanner, but I had to remove the glasses to be sure. Her black curls were barely visible beneath a large bonnet.

Thomas McGilton shook his head amiably, taking in my elaborate disguise. 'You *really* don't want to be photographed.' He grinned. Behind them, the bald headed Spaniard was heading for the exit ramp.

'I never did learn the name of your room mate,' I observed, nodding towards the departing passenger.

'Oh didn't I tell you? That's King Alfonso. He's travelling incognito.'

'I'm sorry?'

'King Alfonso,' the Irishman repeated. 'He got wind of the election results and wanted to get out of the country. So he hopped on the nearest Zeppelin.'

I stared at the man in disbelief. 'You can't be serious?'

McGilton grinned mischievously. 'No, I'm just messing with you, Mr Bland. His name's Gomez. He's not Spanish at all. He's Argentinian. He's on his way home.'

'You'll have to forgive my fiancé,' Miss Tanner apologised. 'He's feeling a bit light headed. He's always like that after he's thumped somebody.'

'I don't do it *that* often,' McGilton protested, good naturedly.

'There's no need to apologise,' I said. 'If anyone

deserved a good hiding, it was our Mr Lindt.

Miss Tanner, surprisingly, disagreed. 'There's no excuse for violence. Men can be such children sometimes. Thomas thinks he was defending my honour, but I keep telling him, I can look after myself.'

'She can at that,' the man agreed. 'Will we be seeing you at the hotel?'

'No, I'm meeting up with my own people. Trying to make some sense of all this mess.'

'Well, it was a pleasure to meet you,' McGilton said, taking my hand firmly. 'You too, Monsieur Sauveterre.'

'Monsieur.' Maurice bowed his head.

'Good luck with the in-laws,' I teased.

'You must keep in touch,' Miss Tanner insisted. She touched me gently on the arm and, before I knew what she was doing, she leaned in close and kissed me on the cheek.

'Steady on there!' McGilton declared. 'I might get jealous.'

Miss Tanner laughed. 'You might have cause to! Mr Bland is a very handsome man.' Her hand fell away from my arm. 'You really must find yourself a wife. Miss Hurst is developing rather a soft spot for you, you know.' She grinned at me and turned away.

I watched as the couple moved towards the steps, making their way out into the grim melee. They were a vexing pair, I reflected with a smile, but well suited to each other.

I put the spectacles back on and wobbled slightly as the world resumed its deep blur. 'You're going to have to help me, Morris,' I said.

'Of course, Monsieur.' He placed a light hand on the small of my back and guided me gently towards the gang plank.

'I never did thank you properly for...for the other night,' I said. The proximity of the steps had brought the horror of that moment back to me and I hesitated for an instant. 'You saved my life, Morris. I...I'm grateful.'

'It was nothing, Monsieur.'

I could hear the cameras clicking furiously once more as I placed a foot onto the first rung. 'Nonetheless, you have my thanks.' I hesitated again and glanced across at him, his battered face a reddish blur through the over-sized lenses. 'Thank you,' I said, *'Maurice.'*

His lips curled slightly as we stepped out into the light. 'You are most welcome. *Sir.'*

Acknowledgements

The LZ128 airship was never built, but plans were drawn up for its construction and it is these which form the basis of the vehicle portrayed in this book. In the real world, the design was abandoned in the aftermath of the R101 disaster and a new ship commissioned, the LZ129 Hindenburg.

I am indebted to Patrick Russell and Dennis Kromm for their detailed article *Before The Beginning*, available to read at:

http://projektlz129.blogspot.co.uk/2013/03/before-beginning.html.

More general information was obtained from *Hindenburg: An Illustrated History* by Rick Archbold and Ken Marschall (Weidenfeld & Nicolson, 1994). The Faces of the Hindenburg blogspot and Airships.net were also very helpful.

The relationship between Marguerite Alibert and Edward, Prince of Wales (later Edward VIII) is a matter of historical record. The extent to which her trial at the Old Bailey was compromised by the government and the royal family is a matter of some debate, but the case for the prosecution is argued persuasively by Andrew Rose in *The Prince, The Princess And The Perfect Murder* (Coronet, 2013).

The official histories of MI5 and MI6 (by Christopher Andrew and Keith Jeffery respectively) have once again proved useful, especially with regard to the shortcomings of Scotland Yard. *The Branch: A History Of The Metropolitan Police Special Branch* by Rupert Allason was also very helpful. For general period information, I am indebted to the Times Archive.

Many thanks to my beta readers, Steve, Kathryn and Willow; and to my family for insisting that I write this book in the first place ('Sequel? Why would I want to write a sequel?!?'). Oh, and apologies to Sara and Grace for stealing their surnames.

As to the future, well...Sir Hilary is now in New York, but she will soon be heading south to take up her position at the British Legation in Guatemala City. And that's when things will start to get really tricky...

Jack Treby

The Devil's Brew
by
Jack Treby

"Your predecessor was sitting in that chair when he shot himself. You can still see the blood stains on the wall behind you."

Central America, 1931. Hilary Manningham-Butler is settling into her new job as passport control officer at the British legation in Guatemala City. Her predecessor Giles Markham is dead, having embezzled a large sum of money from the office's visa receipts and then taken his own life. Freddie Reeves, a friend at the legation, believes there is more to his death than suicide. The weekend before he died, Markham spent some time at a remote coffee plantation in the north central highlands. Freddie knows the owner of the plantation and invites Hilary to accompany him there for the weekend, in the hope that she might be able to discover the truth. Hilary has no intention of getting involved, but when a house guest dies in suspicious circumstances it becomes clear that she will not be given the choice.

The Scandal At Bletchley
by
Jack Treby

"I've been a scoundrel, a thief, a blackmailer and a whore, but never a murderer. Until now..."

The year is 1929. As the world teeters on the brink of a global recession, Bletchley Park plays host to a rather special event. MI5 is celebrating its twentieth anniversary and a select band of former and current employees are gathering at the private estate for a weekend of music, dance and heavy drinking. Among them is Sir Hilary Manningham-Butler, a middle aged woman whose entire adult life has been spent masquerading as a man. She doesn't know why she has been invited – it is many years since she left the secret service – but it is clear she is not the only one with things to hide. And when one of the other guests threatens to expose her secret, the consequences could prove disastrous for everyone.

The Pineapple Republic
by
Jack Treby

Democracy is coming to the Central American Republic of San Doloroso. But it won't be staying long...

The year is 1990. Ace reporter Daniel Parr has been injured in a freak surfing accident, just as the provisional government of San Doloroso has announced the country's first democratic elections.

The Daily Herald needs a man on the spot and in desperation they turn to Patrick Malone, a feckless junior reporter who just happens to speak a few words of Spanish.

Despatched to Central America to get the inside story, our Man in Toronja finds himself at the mercy of a corrupt and brutal administration that is determined to win the election at any cost...

The Gunpowder Treason
by
Michael Dax

"If I had thought there was the least sin in the plot, I would not have been in it for all the world..."

Robert Catesby is a man in despair. His father is dead and his wife is burning in the fires of Hell – his punishment from God for marrying a Protestant. A new king presents a new hope but the persecution of Catholics in England continues unabated and Catesby can tolerate it no longer. King James bears responsibility but the whole government must be eradicated if anything is to really change. And Catesby has a plan...

The Gunpowder Treason is a fast-paced historical thriller. Every character is based on a real person and almost every scene is derived from eye-witness accounts. This is the story of the Gunpowder Plot, as told by the people who were there...

Murder At Flaxton Isle
by
Greg Wilson

A remote Scottish island plays host to a deadly reunion...

It should be a lot of fun, meeting up for a long weekend in a
rented lighthouse on a chunk of rock miles from anywhere.
There will be drinks and games and all sorts of other
amusements. It is ten years since the last get-together and
twenty years since Nadia and her friends graduated from
university. But not everything goes according to plan. One of
the group has a more sinister agenda and, as events begin to
spiral out of control, it becomes clear that not everyone will get
off the island alive...

Made in the USA
Columbia, SC
27 April 2019

Made in the USA
Lexington, KY
31 January 2015